CRITICS PRAISE JAN ZIMLICH!

THE BLACK ROSE
"Jan Zimlich is an incredibly gifted storyteller. . . .
A sizzling hot story!"
—*New-Age Bookshelf*

HEART'S PREY
"Ms. Zimlich is a stellar light who plots intelligently
and creates complex yet consistent characters. . . .
Topnotch reading pleasure."
—*Romantic Times*

NOT QUITE PARADISE
"Ms. Zimlich presents her romantic premise in
splendidly convincing detail. . . . This is 'must' reading
for any fan of outstanding romance."
—*Romantic Times*

HER DARK CAPTOR

Lorienne frowned and turned her glare on the man who now claimed her as chattel. Her chin lifted a fraction higher. "So am I to warm your bed instead of your brother's?" she asked sharply, unable to stop the reckless words from tumbling from her mouth. "Will I find that you are his equal in that task?"

He stared at her for a swift moment, startled that anyone would dare speak to him in such an imprudent manner, especially a woman whose very life depended on his continued largesse. Then his fury rose and his mouth settled into a grim, dangerous line.

Lorienne cried out as he gripped her shoulders with iron-strong hands and dragged her to her feet, forcing her from the relative safety of the skins she'd been using to veil her nakedness. She shivered in the chilly morning as he stood her before him, his grip ungentle, and his strong fingers twining painfully around long tendrils of her hair. His dark eyes blazed, whether from fury or something else entirely she couldn't say.

"I have never been considered my brother's *equal* in any task . . . and never will be," he grated furiously. "You will stay here in the tower with me and tend to my needs. And make no mistake—you *will* warm my bed if I so desire."

Other *Love Spell* books by Jan Zimlich:
THE BLACK ROSE
HEART'S PREY
NOT QUITE PARADISE

THE SHADOW PRINCE

JAN ZIMLICH

LOVE SPELL   NEW YORK CITY

LOVE SPELL®

September 2002

Published by

Dorchester Publishing Co., Inc.
276 Fifth Avenue
New York, NY 10001

ISBN 0-505-52485-6

Visit us on the web at www.dorchesterpub.com.

THE SHADOW PRINCE

AUTHOR'S FOREWORD

Those of you who've read my futuristic romances will probably be surprised to find that I've written a book with a historical setting and time period. The simple truth is, I've always been interested in history, and writing *The Shadow Prince* afforded me the unique opportunity to indulge both my loves of ancient history and fantasy.

The genesis of this story began several years back, when I happened to find information about the Magii tribe, one of the six tribes of the Median Empire, which once flourished in the region to the west and south of the Caspian Sea. The Magii were described as sorcerers, priests, and magicians—a description that immediately piqued my interest. Then when I later found a mention of the Battle of the Eclipse, fought between the Median and Lydian Empires on May 28th, 585 B.C., the temptation was just too great to resist.

Although I've tried to include many historical details of the region and time period in the telling of the story, this book is still a work of fantasy and not meant to be taken as historical fact. I have, indeed, indulged myself immensely.

Special thanks are due to all those who've given me their support and guidance during the course of writing this book:

My friend and fellow author, fantasy writer Linda P. Baker, who believed in this story and these characters from the very beginning. The Deep South Writers Salon—Rebecca Barrett, Stephanie Chisolm, Carolyn Haines, Renee Paul, and Susan Tanner. And last, thanks also to Mark Drury of Sydney, Australia, who generously shared his knowledge of ancient history and cultures, providing me with information and guidance on research that proved invaluable.

I hope you enjoy reading *The Shadow Prince* as much as I enjoyed writing it.

Chapter One

Cinders from the funeral pyre danced and drifted on a chill breath of wind, hot specks of color spiraling into an endless sweep of night-dark sky. A log cradling the pyre suddenly collapsed in a shower of crackling wood and sparks, carrying with it the small body of Shalelle, high priestess of the Arizanti tribe. The flames leapt higher into the darkness, bathing the sheer landscape of the Median steppe in a hellish orange glow.

Lorienne cried out as the flames claimed her mother's lifeless body, a small, anguished wail that caught in her parched throat and faded into nothingness. She tried to wet lips leeched dry by a day of wind and cold but found she had nothing left to give.

In desperation, she tugged and pulled against the strips of hide lashing her to the wooden stake, testing their strength, her ability to break free. Dawn would soon ride across the eastern sky, cresting the jagged mountains and distant Caspian Sea. And with the morn would come another day of cold, stinging wind, so

1

fierce and sharp it felt like sand biting into her skin.

Lorienne forced down a frustrated sob and tried once more to break free of her bonds. If she didn't loosen them soon and replace the moisture stolen from her body, she would not survive the coming day. But Arkanna, the viper who'd slipped the blade deep into Shalelle's back, had wet the strips of hide lashing Lorienne's wrists and ankles to tighten them further, assuring there would be no escape.

A shrill bark of laughter pierced the darkness, and Arkanna stepped from the shadows of the makeshift camp. "You cannot hope to free yourself, Lorienne." A cold gust of mountain wind rushed across the flatness of the steppe, blowing the old woman's coarse white hair into a faded halo. In the glow of the funeral pyre, her sun-lined face looked more shriveled than before, her dark eyes more sunken and vindictive. "Do you not feel Death's approach?" she whispered to her captive. "He comes to claim you soon, daughter of Shalelle."

The woman lashed out with a bony hand and wrapped thin fingers through her captive's pale hair, tightening her grip until her fingernails cut into Lorienne's scalp. She jerked harder, forcing the girl's head back against the stake, her face to tilt upward.

"You still have it within your power to save yourself, young priestess," Arkanna whispered. "Your mother died because she refused to bend to my will. Renounce the thoughts of vengeance that dwell inside your heart and submit to me. Be my creature in name and deed, and I will spare your life."

Lorienne's eyes filled with tears as the flames guttered and her mother's pyre became nothing more than a smoldering pile of embers; and she squeezed their lids shut to prevent the downward passage of those tears. For a timeless moment, she remained motionless, allowing grief to cleanse her of all but the pain, all but the rage boiling inside her. Then her wintry gaze lifted and burned Arkanna's with fury.

"Never. . . ." Her chin tilted in defiance. "Let death come," Lorienne rasped. She forced her parched lips to move, her dry tongue to form sounds and words. "I welcome it. . . . I embrace it." Each word she spoke was accompanied by a sting of pain as the flesh of her lips cracked and split. "You are not fit to rule over a pack of dogs, Arkanna."

Blood welled from the web of tiny cuts on Lorienne's mouth, a trace sliding inward to settle on her tongue. Moisture of a sort. "Your feet are not fit to tread the soil of the steppes." Her eyes blazed with blue fire. "When my death finally comes, I shall die with a curse upon my lips . . . a curse upon you and all those who carry your blood."

The crone's thin lips stretched in a skull-like smile. "So be it. May your death be slow, Lorienne." Arkanna stared coldly at the young woman she'd condemned. "But if you should somehow manage to survive into the coming day, know this . . . there are some fates worse than death. Much worse."

She laughed again, a wild gleeful cackle. "You see, I've sold you, Lorienne. You were the tribute offered for the tribe's safe passage through the lands of the Busae . . . and the flames of your mother's funeral pyre the signal for their prince to come collect his payment."

Lorienne's eyes drifted closed, her rage and loathing replaced by a sudden surge of fear. Tales of sorcerers, dark magic, and the cruelty of Burian, the Busae prince, had reached far across the empire, all the way to the northlands where her tribe once lived.

She ceased her fruitless struggles and sagged against her bonds, praying that death would claim her soon. Very soon. Before the Busae prince claimed her instead.

3

Chapter Two

The wolves were singing to her, a chorus of low, plaintive voices calling out in the stillness of the predawn sky. Lorienne heard the crooning in the back of her mind and struggled to open eyelids thickened by tears of pain and grief. They were lonely sounds, soothing in a strange way.

She lifted her head slowly and frowned when she saw the Median sky. Dawn was fast approaching, and she was still alive. The thick blackness of night had given way to a deep shade of gray, a silvery hue that held the promise of a sunrise not long away.

Much time had passed judging by the fast-lightening sky, but whether she had drifted in and out of consciousness or simply slept, she didn't know. Arkanna was gone, and her mother's funeral pyre had long since burned down to smoky ash. The small camp was deserted now, save for a few sticks of wood left from the tribe's cooking fires.

Lorienne shifted the aching muscles in her neck and

tried to flex her bound wrists, but found she had no feeling left in her limbs. Her hands and feet had been lashed to the stake for so long that she felt nothing at all, not even a knife-jab of pain to reassure her that blood still flowed through those limbs.

A wolf howled suddenly, and Lorienne's heart gave a startled thud. The sound was much closer than before. She forced herself to concentrate, to try and track the creature's call back to its point of origin. From the east, perhaps? She knew from her memories of the day before that a chain of low hillocks snaked across the eastern landscape, swelling upward for a hundred steps or so, then receding into a thousand small dips and shadowed valleys. A thousand places for wolves to hide, and wait.

She pulled in a slow breath and expelled it in a resigned sigh. The wolves had scented her and would come for her soon: not the end she had envisioned for herself but at least it would be an end, a finish to her pain. They would come before the newborn sun had a chance to fully rise, as wolves were wont to do.

Lorienne waited, and stared into the distance as the sky turned a dull silver white. A thin layer of fog clung to the nearby hilltops like a gauzy veil, the haze swirling and drifting in the dawning light. Within the mist, a quick glimpse of furtive movement suddenly caught her eye. Her gaze sharpened and stilled. The wolves were there, dark wraiths standing sentinel atop the nearest hill.

Another hazy shape appeared atop the brow of the hillock. Darker, larger, and utterly still. A hole in the mist through which no light emerged.

Her heartbeat quickened, and a dank, deathly chill seeped through her bones. Lorienne stared at the shape, suddenly afraid. The wolves appeared to be surrounding it, as if they were guardians of the darkness contained within that black, lightless hole.

Death. It had to be. He'd come to claim her at last. He and his wolves.

The sun finally broached the foothills, and a blaze of early light fell across the somber landscape.

Lorienne watched, bewildered, as the shape began a slow transformation. Where only blackness had been a moment before, now there was substance and depth. And then abruptly the mist lifted and rippled away, revealing a dark figure sitting astride a pitch-black horse. Not Death then. Something else.

She stared at the apparition for a longish moment, trying to understand, to comprehend what her eyes told her was there. A man clad in black atop a jet horse was watching her from the hill with the same unswerving intensity that she now focused on him. How long had he been there? Since before the dawn? All night?

For all she knew he could have been there since time began, and would be there when time finally wound to an end. He seemed to be an integral part of the sweep of steppe and dun-colored hills, as if he belonged to the land as much as the wolves. But then her eyes might be telling lies. Man and horse remained completely still, frozen together like cool black stone without purpose or life. Perhaps he wasn't real, not in any known sense of the word. He could simply be a dark specter dredged from the depths of her mind.

To her surprise, the horse's tail suddenly twitched, giving motion to a tableau that had lacked any sign of life, save for the wolves. Her gaze widened as a sharp breath of wind curled across the hilltop, lifting a long strand of the specter's hair. She saw a thick black lock move gently in the freshening breeze, blowing loose across a lean shoulder to the back of his neck.

Metal gleamed in a burst of dawn light, and she spotted the hilt of a longsword jutting from a baldric slung across his back. The curving shape of a bow was visible as well. Lorienne tried to swallow her fear. The apparition was real then, but was it demon or man? Would wolves be in thrall to any mere man?

She felt as if a dark wind were blowing across her flesh. From all accounts, Prince Burian was no mere man. But if this was indeed the Median crown prince, why did he just sit there atop his horse, waiting and watching her like his companions the wolves? She shook her head slowly, unable to dispel the growing sensation that she had reason to be afraid. He could have helped her if he wanted, freed her from the prison of Arkanna's bonds, yet he did nothing. Nothing at all.

Lorienne tried to call out, to plead with him to free her, but her voice came in a raspy whisper, too weak and faded to reach him. Her head lolled forward.

There were sounds in the distance, the soft thudding of hooves across soil and grass, the jangle of mail, the creak and smell of leather and sweat. Had he decided to come for her then?

Confusion clouded her mind. What did it matter anymore? Her lids felt heavy. Thick. Too thick to hold open a moment longer. She was so tired. So very tired. All she wanted to do was sleep and put an end to the pain.

The Busae warrior reined his horse to a halt and lifted a gloved hand to shield his eyes against the glare of the rising sun. Behind him, a score of other soldiers halted as well, men and horses shifting impatiently as they awaited word that the escort column was safe from the threat of Arizanti treachery.

Vlada Sura, commander of the Busae prince's personal guards, scanned the nomads' abandoned camp with wary eyes, searching for any sign of betrayal or attack, but he saw nothing untoward there.

He leaned a forearm atop the high pommel of his saddle and studied the deserted camp once more. Only the ashy remnants of a signal fire and a few sticks of charred wood remained—and the girl, of course, the tribute left behind by her chieftain as payment for crossing the land of the Busae.

A frown touched the old soldier's sun-beaten features. The girl was tied fast to a wooden stake driven deep into the soil, her head sagging, a corpse by the look of her, which was a form of Arizanti treachery in itself. This tribute appeared to have been left in the sun and wind to die by her own tribe, a fate intended to cheat the Median royal house of any value she held as a slave.

"Yah." Vlada kneed his horse gently, forcing the animal closer to inspect her firsthand. He reached out and snagged a fistful of pale hair, dragging her head upward; then he lifted his brows in silent surprise.

She was unconscious, not dead. Though she'd been chafed and sun-reddened by the elements, she still lived. For how long, he couldn't say. Her chest was rising and falling in quick, shallow breaths, far too fast and noisily to bode well for her life.

Regret washed over him. A pity, that. She looked as if she might have once been comely. Vlada allowed the girl's head to fall once more and backed his mount away from her and the wooden stake.

He turned slightly as a horse and rider drew abreast of him, the heavy mail protecting both man and beast rattling as Prince Burian's gray tossed its head and twitched nervous flanks. Vlada dipped his head in acknowledgement of his prince's approach. "My lord."

Burian Kiryl unfastened his leather chin strap and tugged off the domed metal helmet and cap of mail beneath, shaking his head vigorously to cool his sweat-matted hair and beard. He was thirsty, weary, and eager to put an end to the long journey across such a barren stretch of land.

"Well?" His impatient word echoed like the crack of

a whip across the wind-scrubbed landscape. "Is she alive?" His nervous horse skittered sideways, and Burian retaliated by jabbing his heels into the gray's laboring flanks.

"She lives, my lord . . . barely. It appears Arkanna thought to cheat you of your prize." The gray's display of nervousness caused Vlada's eyes to narrow in renewed concern. The beast wasn't known for its skittishness. His suspicious gaze lifted to the surrounding hilltops, searching. Had he missed something that would cause the horse to act in such a way?

Prince Burian snorted and twisted his heavy features into an angry scowl. "The witch will pay for her arrogance someday, perhaps with her blood." His gaze swung toward his unconscious tribute, lingering on her slender form, the fall of pale, tousled hair that spiraled downward to caress the lush curves of her hips. The simple blue robe she wore was torn near the waist, revealing an enticing sliver of bared flesh from her hip to the top of a satiny thigh. For a brief moment, a gust of wind caught at the woolen fabric and widened the sliver to a delectable swath.

He wet lips that had suddenly gone dry and imagined the feel of that pale hair caressing his own bare skin. "She has the look of the northlands about her." Burian's mouth curved in a hungry smile, a movement all but hidden behind the coarse thickness of his russet beard. He liked fair women. "Such pale hair."

Vlada nodded absently and continued to study the harsh landscape; then his eyes stilled suddenly and he breathed a curse. *Gods.*

"My lord . . . look," Vlada whispered darkly, jerking a finger toward the east. "Atop that hill . . . the Shadow Prince!" Vlada's bowels turned cold and watery. Man and horse had seemed such a part of the hills and grass that they'd slipped past his view until now.

"Eh?" Burian ended his perusal of the girl abruptly

and turned in the saddle, his attention following the direction of Vlada's outstretched hand. His jaw sagged and his thick brows lifted in disbelief. There was no doubt about the identity of the watcher. Him or his wolves. "Adrik . . . here?" Burian asked in an ominous voice. He had seen nothing of the reclusive Shadow Prince for close on a year now, not even a glimpse from afar. "What strange hell is this we've found?"

Vlada grabbed for the bow and quiver slung over his shoulder, but Burian belayed him with a quick shake of his head.

"No!" Burian warned. The Shadow Prince was no ordinary warrior. If Vlada was fool enough to unsling his bow, it would be they who died this day, not Adrik. "He can fell us both with arrows before you even draw your bow! Even if you did manage to shoot him with a bronze-head, his wolves would set upon us for certain."

"But, my lord!" the soldier protested. "Why is he here if not to cause you harm?"

Burian shrugged and threw a suspicious glance at the shape atop the hill. Adrik's mountain fortress, Khorazm, was the better part of a day's ride distant, perched along the rocky coast of the great inland sea, yet he and the black demon he called a mount appeared well rested, as if they'd been standing vigil with the wolves atop that hillock for quite a long while. And there was nothing for him to see here except the Arizantis' abandoned camp—and Burian's pale-haired prize.

His heavy brows canted upward again, more in wonder this time than startlement. A sly, comprehending smile lifted the corners of Burian's mouth as his gaze trailed over the Arizanti's ripe young body once more. Could she be the reason for the darkling prince's eerie vigil?

"Ho!" Burian's bark of laughter startled both Vlada and the nervous gray. "It must be the girl!" The horse danced sideways. "The sorcerer's been watching her, for whatever dark purpose lurking in that mind of his!"

The hairs on Vlada's neck rose in response to that unwelcome thought. He suppressed a shudder. "I had heard women held no interest for one such as him."

Burian shook his head incredulously and grinned at the rider atop the hill. If he was right, surely the Magii's interest in the girl could be turned to his advantage. The very notion of Adrik being beholden to him would be ample compensation for the wearying ride and the girl's piteous state. "Females have never interested him before," he said, amused by the very possibility that Adrik's reclusive habits might have changed. "At least he's never been interested to my knowledge. But there's a first time for all things . . . even for him."

He nodded to himself. *Yes.* The unexpected turn of events could definitely be to his advantage. "Cut the girl down, Vlada." He smiled slyly as the soldier leapt from his horse to do his bidding. "Then bear her to the top of the hill. Since Adrik hasn't seen fit to come down to us, we shall just have to ride up and greet him."

Burian motioned for the rest of his column to hold their positions, then tapped his heels into his mount's sides and started toward the hill at a swift trot, clucking encouragement as the scent of the wolves caused his horse to snort in dismay.

He slapped the horse's rear several times to force it up the grassy incline. "Little brother!" Burian called to him. A large gray wolf rose from its haunches and bared a row of blade-sharp teeth. Tufts of fur lifted upright on the backs of two others. Burian eyed the snarling beasts warily as he crested the hilltop, struggling to subdue his panicked horse. "Will you not tell your creatures to rest easy?" he demanded in a petulant tone. "My horse is concerned that your wolves will make a meal of his flesh."

11

Adrik Kiryl threw a quick look in the wolves' direction and watched impassively as the beasts quit displaying their teeth and sat down to wait. He tilted his head slightly and studied his half brother through dark, hooded eyes. "What do you want of me, Burian?" he asked in a flat, cool voice.

Burian's lips curled as he halted his mount a good twenty steps shy of the watching wolves. He eyed his younger brother as warily as he did his brother's beasts. "I'm just curious as to why you're here . . . brother. You must admit it's not often that you deign to come down from your fortress lair. Even entreaties sent by our own father have failed to lure you into visiting Urmia in recent years."

For a fraction of a moment, Adrik allowed his gaze to slide downhill, to where Vlada Sura was attempting to drape the sacrificed girl's limp form across his saddle, and then he focused his attention on Burian once again. He stared at his brother dispassionately. "Urmia holds little fascination for me these days."

"And Father?" Burian asked carefully. "What of him, Adrik?" King Hedeon, who'd sired them by different wives, had grown more and more restive in recent months, brooding over his youngest son's refusal to pay homage to his father or the throne, especially now that his health had begun to wane. Hedeon had even hinted that if Adrik didn't come soon, he might journey to Khorazm himself, just to see his second-born once more before he died.

Burian clenched his jaw. That possibility troubled him greatly. His father, the Median king, could not be allowed to enter the gates of Khorazm, where he might fall under the spell of his sorcerer son, or worse, fall prey to the influence of some unearthly demon.

Burian's eyes narrowed and his features turned sullen. *He* was the crown prince, not Adrik. The ailing king's sudden display of favor toward a younger son was vexing in the extreme. "Does Father hold little fascination for you as well?" Until recently, Hedeon had rarely acknowledged Adrik's existence, much less any kinship of blood. This newfound interest in his second-born might well prove dangerous. For Adrik, at least. "He grows impatient with you." Burian studied his brother's stark features to weigh his response. "So much that his entreaties may soon be transformed into a royal command . . . or retribution."

Adrik glanced away and stared northward, to the snowcapped mountains of the Caucasus, his expression darker and more shuttered than it had been before. Burian's carefully chosen words carried with them a second, more veiled meaning, the hint of a threat only a fool would ignore.

The wind tugged at Adrik's long sidelock, blowing it toward the thick braid hanging down the center of his back. "And you, brother? Do you grow . . . impatient with me also?" Adrik asked in a voice as smooth and sharp as the edge of a blade.

Burian shook his head slowly. He'd pushed as far as he dared this day. No one knew for certain the sorcerer's powers. "Not I." The time might come, though. Someday.

Adrik's wary gaze settled on his brother's sun-ruddied face once again. "Then Father would do well to remember that I have freely given my fealty to you, not him. You are the crown prince, hereditary ruler of the Busae and rightful heir to the Median throne. I have no designs upon your title—or your future throne. I follow where you lead, brother. Your enemies are my enemies, your wars mine. If you tell me to wage war upon someone, I shall gladly lead the Magii tribe into battle against them, just as I've done before. Beyond that, I care nothing for the goings-on in Urmia, or for the king's demands. My life is of no concern to you . . . nor to our father."

13

Burian snorted. Anything Adrik did or did not do was cause for concern. Despite his reassurances, Adrik was still second in line to the throne . . . and a sorcerer of the first rank. "So you intend to keep ignoring his entreaties then?"

Adrik stared in silence at the wide expanse of blue sky. "Yes," he said quietly, "I do. He demands to see me because he wishes me to conjure a healing spell for him, and that is something I cannot give." His features tightened imperceptibly. "His current wife can attend him during his remaining days. He has no true need of my company . . . and I have no need of his. The king will simply die when his end time comes, without any interference from me."

The stiff set to Burian's shoulders relaxed slightly, and he nodded in acceptance of his brother's words. What Adrik had said could very well be true. Instead of displaying favor, Hedeon might simply be trying to force his sorcerous child into weaving a powerful spell that would enable him to live a while longer—something Adrik would surely never do. "Watch your words, little brother," he warned quietly. "They can be as knives to the wrong ears."

A slight smile touched the edges of Adrik's mouth. "Father's ears . . . or yours?"

It was Burian's turn to smile. "Mine perhaps, with enough provocation." Now that Adrik had proclaimed his fealty to him in no uncertain terms, he felt a curious sense of exhilaration. Even what might be termed a trace of affection for his much-maligned brother.

Vlada led his horse to the top of the hillock and paused, the unconscious girl hanging facedown over the well of his saddle. The soldier cast his suspicious gaze toward the watching wolves and waited for direction from his liege, carefully avoiding the Shadow Prince's fathomless eyes. It was said that the sorcerer could hold a man captive with a single glance, cast spells that caused animals and men alike to snarl and fight. He had no wish to tempt fate, or to fight with any wolves. Most especially since one of the sorcerer's wolves seemed to be watching him with disquieting intensity, a large gray beast with an unnatural glint in its golden eyes.

At a signal from Burian, Vlada swallowed and nudged his horse forward a bit more, though he was careful to keep the watching wolf in view at all times.

As Vlada approached, Burian's gaze slid to the fair-haired girl's slack form. Perhaps the declaration of fealty from his sibling was deserving of recognition, a reward of some kind that would curry favor with the sorcerer—and serve to amuse him as well.

He swatted the gray abruptly and moved toward Vlada. When his horse drew alongside the warrior's mount, Burian lifted one boot and shoved the limp body from its place atop the saddle.

Vlada gaped at Burian in shock as the unconscious girl landed in a boneless heap among thick stalks of grass. "My lord?" he whispered worriedly.

Adrik's gaze thinned as he stared downward to the grass: then his curious eyes flicked back to rest on his brother's face. He lifted a single jet brow in silent question.

Burian grinned back at him. "Consider her a gift, little brother. The Arizanti gave her to me, and now I give her to you."

The sorcerer's eyes grew darker, more veiled, and his features smoothed. "I don't want her."

The Median crown prince adjusted his reins and lifted his broad shoulders in an unconcerned shrug. He glanced down at the jumble of female limbs, blue robe, and pale hair, briefly regretting that he'd never feel those silky tresses brushing across his skin. He shrugged again and motioned for Vlada to mount. Urmia was filled with tempting women, even some with

15

fair hair; he would simply order Vlada to find one to warm his bed on future nights. "It makes no difference to me whether she lives or dies," he told his brother. "Leave her here to rot on the steppe if you wish. She's yours to do with as you will."

Then he laughed, wheeled the gray in a half circle, and thundered down the hill, with Vlada close behind.

Adrik watched as they rejoined the waiting soldiers. The column of men and horses slowly turned west, heading back in the direction of Urmia.

The gray wolf leapt to its feet and padded to where the girl's body lay in the low grass. The beast lowered its muzzle, snuffling curiously at the girl's tousled hair and slack face. When its curiosity had finally been sated, the wolf's yellow gaze lifted to its master, as if the creature were waiting for him to answer an unvoiced question.

The sorcerer stared back at the wolf for a moment, then sighed.

Chapter Three

Khorazm stood dark and silent in the waning light, a brooding stone monolith perched high atop a cliff fronting the Caspian Sea. From a distance, the battlements and gate towers appeared empty of life, but Adrik knew this was a trick of the eye. By now a dozen sentries were aware of his approach and would have sent out a hue and cry, sending word to the fortress's inhabitants that the Magian prince had finally returned.

Adrik paused near a bend in the narrow cart path cut into the side of the mountain, a track that eeled back and forth as it climbed to an abrupt apex at the fortress gates. His horse huffed wearily beside him. The walk back to Khorazm from the Arizanti camp had been long and tiring for him and his mount, as well as for the wolves that had accompanied him on his quest. But save for Sandor, the large gray wolf who was his constant companion, the remainder of the pack had melted into the lengthening shadows long before the fortress came into view. To rest, no doubt, and recoup from the journey home before they set out to hunt beneath a waxing moon.

With the unconscious girl draped across his saddle, Adrik had been forced to lead the horse back to the fortress on a circuitous, much longer route than the norm, through a winding series of rocky ravines and mountain passes to the seacoast rather than wending his way along the steep ridge lines he usually climbed. If his mount hadn't been burdened by the dead weight of the girl, he would have risked scaling the ridges, regardless of the poor footing and loose scree. As it was, the roundabout journey had lasted far longer than he had imagined. The sun was now low on the horizon, a great swollen orb bathing the quiescent sea with vivid streaks of orange and gold.

A gull squalled overhead, and Adrik closed his eyes for a brief moment, reveling in the flood of sounds and scents that heralded his arrival home. He pulled in a cleansing breath and allowed the thick sea air to wash the taste of dust and travel from his parched throat. He could hear the dull throb of the sea swells as they rolled against the rocky shore below, an achingly familiar sound that always enticed him into the quiet arms of sleep far sooner than the most potent of wines.

Beside him, the girl stirred slightly, moving a long leg, an arm, then quieting once again. Adrik checked to make certain that she was still secure across the breadth of the small saddle made of leather and felt, adjusting her torso a bit to distribute her weight more evenly. Not that she weighed very much at all. She was slender, reed-thin, the curve of her hips giving the mistaken impression that she was lushly formed. But after lifting her onto the horse, Adrik knew that was merely an illusion. In truth, she weighed little more than a child.

Misgiving slithered through him. This was no child,

not in any true sense of the world. Though young and slender, his captive was most definitely a woman fully formed, a troublesome fact he'd discovered when he had lifted her atop his horse and the ripe swelling of her breasts had pushed hard against his chest. The sensation had taken him by surprise. So soft, so achingly inviting it was that a wave of heat had stolen through his blood. He could almost imagine how those wondrous mounds would feel beneath his hands, his lips. . . .

He shook off such thoughts abruptly and clucked to his horse, his jaw tightening imperceptibly as he continued to make his way along the terraced pathway. What perverse notion had possessed him to succumb to his brother's meddling and saddle himself with this girl? She had no place in his life. No female ever could. He led his tired mount around the switchback's last winding turn.

Burian was a madman. He had simply pushed her to the ground and ridden away, leaving Adrik to choose whether she lived or died, which had surely been his sly intent.

For good or ill, Adrik had been forced to make the choice Burian thrust upon him. Now they would all have to suffer the consequences. Perhaps it would have been far kinder if he had simply left the girl on the steppe and let the gods have their way with her. If he bore her through the gates of Khorazm now, he would be condemning her to a life of misery akin to his own. A life in which she would die by slow degrees.

His wolf's snout nudged the back of his hand. Adrik glanced downward, a touch of sadness twisting the solemn line of his mouth.

"This is your doing," he whispered to the gray-furred beast.

The wolf made a deep-throated sound that was half whine, half growl.

19

Jan Zimlich

Adrik sighed. He was far too tired to argue such matters with the wolf. Tomorrow, perhaps. For now, he was in dire need of food, wine, and a long night's sleep. But he would have to tend to the needs and safety of his injured captive before seeing to himself, this captive whose mere presence in his life was disquieting in the extreme.

Torches flared in the gathering darkness, lighting the tall, arched gates that led into the fortress proper. Atop the battlements, more torches flamed to life, throwing a haze of orange light into the darkening sky.

The thick wooden gates groaned in complaint as they were heaved open by four burly guards clad in armor and mail. Sandor's rough tongue touched the back of Adrik's hand in a quick caress; then the creature vanished abruptly, loping off into the thickening shadows to join its brethren.

A stable boy rushed forward to take the reins of Adrik's mount but halted midway to his destination, his mouth falling open in surprise when he realized the lathered horse held a woman's body.

Wide-eyed, the begrimed youth gaped at Adrik uncertainly. "My lord?"

The tone of his question caused a muscle to bunch tight along Adrik's jaw. It was the first of many such questions, he knew—discomfiting questions about the Arizanti girl and why she had been brought to Khorazm.

A sentry peered over the stable boy's shoulder, squinting to see in the dying light. Others crowded near, staring. A few even dared to murmur amongst themselves in curious tones.

Adrik scowled and tossed the strips of leather to the stable boy. "Cool him well," he ordered gruffly, then slid his hands beneath the girl's slender frame, lifting her easily into his arms.

Ignoring the curious stares from his people, he

20

stalked through the gates into Khorazm's central courtyard, the girl cradled close against his chest. The soft leather boots favored by his tribe made little sound as he crossed an expanse of flagstones mortared with lime. High above him, sentries watched his progress from atop the battlements, peering downward curiously. Others appeared in open doorways lining the fortress's inner walls, soldiers and women with babes in arm, gaping children, their bodies silhouetted by the soft glows cast by torches and cooking fires. A hundred pair of startled eyes watched his every move.

Adrik glowered and quickened his pace across the flagstones. He owed no one explanations. He was their prince.

A flight of steps at the eastern end of the courtyard led to a wide terrace flanked by stone arches and fluted columns, the ornate entrance to the private residence of the Magian prince. Light spilled from openings cut high in the stone tower soaring above the colonnaded terrace. And far above, atop the flat apex of the tower, a smaller terrace and rooftop gardens faced the inland sea.

Adrik's gaze slid upward involuntarily. The tall stone tower with its sweeping vista of the Caspian Sea had been his home ever since he was an infant and had inherited the title of Magian prince upon the death of his mother. But the graceful exterior was only a facade, a mask worn to hide the foul truth secreted inside.

A frown touched his features. Darkness dwelled within the tower's thick walls, a darkness he could neither shed nor escape.

A servant bearing a torch rushed onto the terrace to light his way inside. As Adrik climbed the limestone steps, Jirina, the aged Mistress of the Tower, appeared beside the manservant.

Torchlight illuminated the human bundle in Adrik's arms, and a brief look of fear flickered over Jirina's

21

faded features. Then the old woman dipped her head in silent acknowledgement of her master's return, hiding her true reaction behind a show of respect.

"Welcome home, my lord," Jirina said slowly. Her gaze narrowed and lifted abruptly, as if she suddenly sensed danger lurking somewhere atop the tall stone tower. She shook herself slightly and nodded in the direction of the torchbearer. "Do you wish for Gobryas to relieve you of your burden?" A trace of fear was evident in her voice this time, a throaty quaver that betrayed her unease about the prince's unexpected guest.

Adrik caught Jirina's gaze and held it with his own. He wished someone could relieve him of his encumbrance, but he'd known from the moment he'd lifted the girl from the steppe that the burden he now carried would be his alone. Only he had the power to keep the girl safe within Khorazm's walls. Only he bore the responsibility.

He shook his head in resignation. "No . . . I will see to her needs. She will stay in the tower with me."

Relief washed over the old woman's stark features. She nodded quickly. "Yes, my lord." Jirina gave a signal to Gobryas, and the servant hurried into the tower's arched entrance. "Food and wine will be brought to your chambers at once, as well as water to wash your journey away."

"See to it," Adrik said quietly, and brushed past her into the tower.

Striding swiftly through the starkly furnished great hall, he reached the set of curving stone steps leading to the upper levels of the narrow tower. By the time he reached the third level, Gobryas had already left a torch in a sconce to light the shadowy corridor outside his rooms. Adrik kicked the wide door open and moved inside, depositing his burden on the raised wooden couch that served as his bed.

Jirina and Gobryas weren't far behind. They brought

with them a platter of soft breads and goat cheese, as well as wine and an urn of fresh water. The wicks of the oil lamps were lit, and a large copper brazier filled with glowing coals soon rested on a carved pedestal near the bed, spilling small wisps of warmth into the chilly night air.

The Mistress of the Tower also placed a stack of folded linens atop the low wooden table where the food and wine had been placed, along with a woven basket filled with the herbs and unguents Adrik often used for healing.

Once she had seen to her duties, Jirina bowed respectfully and backed to the door. "Will there be anything else, my lord?" she asked in a hushed voice.

Adrik shook his head. "No, Jirina. You and Gobryas may retire for the evening." They would be glad of that, no doubt.

As the door closed quietly behind them, Adrik shed himself of the heavy bow, sword, and baldric and dipped his hands into a basin of water, cleansing himself of the journey's grime. After a bracing cup of Ionian wine and a bite of goat cheese, he bent to his task, methodically stripping away the girl's torn robe and under-robe until she lay naked atop the bed's sheepskin coverings, her white-gold hair fanning out around her arms and shoulders like a silky veil.

For a sliver of time, Adrik did nothing more than stare, drinking in the sight of her ripe young body lying atop the fleece on his bed. He sighed finally and forced himself to concentrate on the chore at hand, blending and mixing the herbs and oils into a salve that would soothe and heal her body.

Before the moon had risen completely, he'd cleaned her windburned skin and rubbed the fragrant oils and unguents into the circlets of angry flesh marring her ankles and wrists, marks left by the tight bindings that had held her fast to the wooden stake. Once that was

23

done, he dabbed his fingers into the small bowl of soothing moisture and smoothed the slick mixture across her cheeks and lips; his fingertips glided gently over her sun-raw skin.

He studied her curiously as he worked. Her features were perfectly formed, her mouth full, her eyes deep and wide-set within an oval face. The sculpted lines of her nose and jaw were strong yet alluringly feminine, bearing a hint of her Arizanti parentage. Adrik found himself wondering what secrets lay hidden beneath those closed lids and feather-soft lashes. Would the color of her eyes be dark, much the same shade as his? Or as cool and pale as a winter sky, like the eyes of so many born of the lands to the north?

The thought struck him once again that Burian must be a madman. There was no other explanation. Why else would his brother have simply given away such a prize, to him of all people? The girl was truly magnificent, a tribute worthy of the Median crown prince— or of the king himself for that matter.

He allowed his fingers to stray lower, tracing the curve of her chin down the graceful column of her throat. His breath caught in his throat as a silky strand of her pale hair drifted over the back of his hand. Soft. Rich. Like the silken fabrics brought by caravan from the vast empires to the south and east.

The tips of his fingers moved lower, gliding past the hollow of her throat to lightly brush along the swell of her softly mounded breasts. To his surprise, she moaned softly and moved closer to his questing hand, as if her flesh sought the warmth afforded by his touch. He ran the pad of a thumb back and forth across the satiny flesh, testing her unconscious reaction, and was rewarded by a quick tossing of her head and another ragged moan. As though she were ready and eager for the heated caresses of one such as him.

Something hot and fierce suddenly moved through

Adrik's blood, a quickening of desire so swift and powerful that he gasped aloud. He closed his eyes a moment and shut his mind to the unfamiliar sensations, his hand pulling away from her burning flesh and clenching into a tight, tight fist. Was this what it felt like to hunger for a woman's touch? To *need*? His fist trembled. If so, he wasn't sure he wanted to feel such a thing.

A cold breath of air touched the nape of his neck with icy fingers. Dank, dark, and malevolent. Adrik stiffened and turned, his features hardening as a shape appeared near the foot of the bed. It was something there yet not there, as if he were gazing through a film of water at a tall, translucent form.

His fists bunched tighter, his nails biting deep into the center of his palms. He'd known the demon would come to him this night. The presence of the girl within Khorazm's walls was a lure the specter would find impossible to resist.

"Malkaval," Adrik whispered, the single word falling from his lips like a venomous curse. His nails dug through the flesh on his palms, drawing blood, but Adrik increased the pressure instead of lessening it. He concentrated on the pain, just the pain, using the stabbing sensation to veil his thoughts, hide the sudden, almost irresistible urge to draw upon the power within himself and cast a spell that would oust the demon from Khorazm forever. But he knew his chances of success were almost nonexistent, and failure would spell certain disaster. Perhaps even bring about the death of his body. Not that his death mattered a whit to anyone living. His fate had long been sealed, and the only one who would mourn his mortal passing would be the demon himself because that would surely cheat him of his aspirations.

For a short while the demon stared back at him, watching and waiting suspiciously, as if knowing what dark thoughts were slithering through Adrik's mind. Then the wraith smiled, and his sly gaze angled over the naked girl, his sharply angled features shifting and flickering in the orangish glow cast by the lamps. "What sweetly tender morsel have you brought me, my son?" he asked in a soft cunning voice. "Would she be a virgin, perchance?"

Adrik's gaze darkened and thinned. "I have not brought her here for you, Malkaval. She was a gift to me from my brother." His gaze stilled, grew more lethal. "And you . . . you are not my father."

The demon faded from view and reappeared on the far side of the sleeping platform, his eyes glowing like hot coals as he glared at Adrik. For a small space of time, he toyed with the notion of retaliating for the insult by striking the sorcerer with a searing bolt of energy. Instead, the demon rippled his thin shoulders in what might have been a human shrug and settled himself onto the soft skins directly across from Adrik—closer to the girl, too close, for he was smoldering with some dangerous emotion hovering somewhere between desire and murderous fury.

"You forget much, Adrik," the demon said in a voice that was dangerously calm. "Hedeon cared naught for you—or for the woman who shrieked in pain as you bawled your way into the world." His voice rose, and along with it his temper. "Your father merely sated his lust by emptying his seed into a female's loins. He had no need of you . . . you were—*are*—second-born, a shadow prince! The man sold you to me when you were newly born in exchange for wealth and power."

The creature laughed darkly. Cruelly. "I am the one who raised you from a squalling infant. I made you into what you are, Adrik. And I will soon make you into far more than you are now. You are mine . . . always."

Adrik stared back at the demon for a length of time measured more by the intensity of his emotions than the passage of mere moments. Malkaval had only spoken truth, but it was a foul, bitter truth that brought the sickening taste of bile to Adrik's throat. A demon had reared him from infancy, taught him all that he knew about life and the living world. Malkaval had taught him about death too . . . and of the desire for vengeance. Taught him well indeed.

"Yes," he said finally, his voice flat. "You raised me. How could I forget?"

The demon's form shimmered slightly, and his reddish eyes shone with an eerie inner fire. The sharp planes of his face shifted for a single tick of time, and he appeared almost to smile. He had spent more than a score of years shaping a human child into the most powerful sorcerer ever born of Magian blood, preparing Adrik for his future and the dark mantle he would be forced to wear before the heat of summer once more held sway.

Malkaval's attention shifted back to the girl, and his glowing eyes hungrily devoured her slender form. The filmy shape of his hand sped down the soft curves of her body, a breathy touch that the object could feel but he could not. Her flesh was like air beneath his nonexistent caress. Cold and dead and empty. Like him. But that would change in the near future. Soon he would be able to touch what lay beneath the tips of his fingers, to feel the living world. Very soon now.

The demon laughed, a sound devoid of humor or of any human emotion at all. When the grass sprouted anew and the skeletal trees awakened from their winter slumber, the long-awaited day would finally dawn. The sky above would slowly blacken, turn the color of the blackest pitch, a darkness so chaotic and complete that those who witnessed the turning would think the living world had been devoured by the Shadow Realm. They would be right in a way. Demons were born in such darkness. And sorcerers often died.

Malkaval's form rippled and shimmered, rose from the bed of skins until he appeared to be reclining on air. The demon's hot gaze flickered across the girl's bare skin once more. With the appointed day drawing nigh, what true harm would there be in allowing Adrik a taste of the fleshly pleasures he would soon be denied? "Keep your pretty gift." The course of Adrik's fate was set; nothing could change it now. And having this girl within Khorazm's walls might well prove to be an amusing diversion from the endless tedium of his immortal life. It would be a temporary diversion, to be sure, lasting only until she withered and died, either by Adrik's hand or his own.

A cadaverous smile stretched over Malkaval's angular features. He leaned closer, his glowing eyes burning above his skullish smile. "Ride her well, my son!" he hissed. "Let your body have its fill of her; then when you are done with that pretty outer shell, I shall feed on her essence. She will sate both our thirsts, in far different ways." The demon's cackling laughter still echoed through the chamber long after he'd vanished into the night.

Adrik continued to sit on the edge of the bed long after Malkaval's departure, staring at nothing, at everything, his gaze blank and unseeing. Why had he dared to bring her here? He knew what was likely to occur. It would have been far more merciful of him if he had left her on the steppes to die. Now she was doomed to share his miserable fate.

His shoulders sagging, the sorcerer climbed to his feet abruptly and paced the confines of his meagerly furnished chamber. He paused in his wandering long enough to refill his cup to the brim with fruity red wine and drank the liquid quickly, more to drown his doubts and worries than any thirst he might have.

His sword still lay on the table where he'd placed it. Sighing, Adrik freed the long blade from the leather baldric and scabbard, then studied the length of polished metal, his fingers curling and closing about the sword's engraved silver grip. He moved slowly back to the couch where the girl lay and closed his eyes. There were many, many forms of mercy.

His grip on the hilt tightened, and he lifted the double-edged sword upward until it rested at an angle nearly even with the bed.

"Do you plan to kill me?" a soft voice whispered.

Adrik's eyes snapped open, then he blinked in surprise. The girl was awake and staring up at him with a curiously calm gaze.

Lorienne's eyes slid to the sharpened sword held so near to her side. "If that is your intent, tell me now so that I might offer a prayer to my gods before I die."

He studied her openly, a single dark brow lifting in response to her words before he slowly lowered the sword. The irises of her eyes were much as he had imagined: pale, cool, like a morning sky. Large and breathtakingly luminous, their depths glittered like the glacial ice that wrapped the mountains in the north.

"I have no such plans, young Arizanti," he said carefully and eased his sword downward until its tip struck the cold tile floor.

He knew who she was, or so it seemed. Lorienne's gaze moved warily over the stranger's elegantly chiseled face. His features were bold-cut, aristocratic; the sculpted lines of his jaw and generous mouth were touched with a trace of brashness often found in those born of noble blood. His dark clothing was that of a nobleman as well, his long tunic, overvest, and pantaloons cut from a fabric far richer than any she had ever owned. She frowned as her gaze touched his hair. Save for a sidelock that fell loose to one shoulder, his jet hair hung in a thick braid down the center of his back.

A soft gasp escaped her throat. She had heard it said that sorcerers sometimes wore their hair in such a fashion. She pulled away from him, suddenly afraid when she hadn't been before. For the first time she realized, too, that she was without clothing, and she pulled frantically on the soft skins she lay upon to try and cover herself.

"You're a sorcerer!"

One corner of his mouth lifted imperceptibly. The term had sounded much like an accusation. "Yes . . . I am," he admitted.

A cold prickle of fear crawled over her bare flesh. She glanced around her new surroundings in dismay, trying desperately to tug the soft bed coverings around her torso. She was in a stone-walled room, alone save for a darkly handsome sorcerer, lying atop a bed heaped with warm skins. And she was naked.

Chapter Four

Lorienne awakened with a violent start, wrenched from a fitful sleep by the disquieting sense that she was being watched, observed from afar by an unnatural presence with cruel, glowing eyes.

The beat of her heart trebled as she glanced around. Full night had fallen since she found herself within the sorcerer's lair. The chamber was darker now, cloaked in a thick gloom silvered with the glow of the waxing moon. Thin traces of that pale moonlight were spilling through the arched window opening, streaming in fingers over the tiled floor to throw twisting shadows across the walls.

But no unearthly creatures appeared to inhabit those shadows. Either a dream or her own trepidation had brought about the odd sensation of being watched, an unsurprising reaction for someone in a like predicament, she supposed. She was the captive of a sorcerer, after all, a powerful stranger who now controlled every aspect of her life.

The thought of the sorcerer marred her brow with a quick frown. She hadn't seen him since moonrise, when she had first awakened. He had disappeared without much ado. Where was he now?

Her gaze narrowed warily as a shadow suddenly shifted along the wall. *There.* A tall, black-clad figure was standing near the undraped window, staring out of the opening into the moonlit night. Lorienne clutched a sheepskin tight against her chest, an instinctive gesture to shield her flesh from his piercing eyes. It seemed there had been a presence in the room all along, one as still and silent as the night itself.

She glanced at the shadowy form uneasily. It was the sorcerer she had sensed watching her. There was no one else here. No one else who could have watched.

Though she couldn't recall much of what had passed to bring her here, she did remember how she had awakened earlier to find herself unrobed in the sorcerer's bed, with him standing over her wielding a sharpened sword. Upon seeing that chilling look of intent strong on his hawkish face, she had truly believed it was Death cradling that uplifted blade, and that she was within a hairbreadth of beginning her journey to the Shadow Realm. With such a torturous vision playing out before her eyes, it had been no great leap on her part to imagine she would indeed suffer such a fate at his hands.

She frowned in confusion. And yet, that very same sorcerer didn't seem to be watching her at all. In truth, he didn't even appear particularly mindful of her presence. For whatever reason, the view of the night sky obviously held his rapt attention.

Looks could be deceiving, though, as Lorienne well knew. Arkanna had professed to be her mother's friend, and all the while she had been plotting to commit the foulest of betrayals. This sorcerer could very well be plotting her end even now.

A tear coursed down Lorienne's face unbidden, and she brushed it angrily away. She would not be so weak as to give in to fruitless tears. If she ever hoped to escape from this place and her mysterious captor, she would have to be strong. Strong and clever.

There was no doubt in her mind that she was indeed the sorcerer's captive. Such was a woman's lot within the empire. She was chattel, nothing more, of no more value than that of a strong-legged ass. A woman could be bought, sold, bartered, or stolen away on the slightest of whims. Even within her own tribe, no one would have mourned her passing if she'd died at the hands of Arkanna or Prince Burian . . . or now of the sorcerer himself. The only reason she hadn't suffered a like fate already was that her mother had been high priestess and seer of the Arizanti. But with Shalelle dead and gone, there was no one to protect or mourn her anymore.

She closed her eyes for a moment, squeezing the lids tight against the unknown future that awaited her. Surely the sorcerer would make his desires known to her soon. If he allowed her to live, was she destined to become a slave in his household—or was she simply to become his concubine instead of Prince Burian's?

"Are you in need of food?" a deep voice suddenly asked from the shadows.

Lorienne flinched and pulled the sheepskin higher on her chest, twisting an end up and up until it twined about her neck. The sorcerer's voice was dark and soft and cool yet eerily powerful, as though it carried within its depths a magical spell that would bind her to follow his every command.

She swallowed her burgeoning fear and forced her tongue to give answer. "Yes," she said curtly, and bit down on her lower lip to chastise herself for the sharp response. The single word had spilled from her lips in a tone that was shrill and overloud, much more

Jan Zimlich

brusque than she had intended. Antagonizing her new master at this juncture would not serve her in good stead. "Yes . . ." she repeated, more softly this time. Her gaze shifted to the view outside the arched window, to a silvery sky caught somewhere between morning and night. "I cannot recall when I last broke my fast."

A lamp flared to sudden life, and Lorienne flinched once again, her gaze widening with surprise when she realized the sorcerer was now standing by the side of the bed, mere steps away. She had neither seen him move from the window nor heard his tread across the glazed tiles, yet he was suddenly looming over her, holding a cup and a crust of bread in his outstretched hands. And the lamp now casting an orange glow across the chamber was sitting on a pedestal near the door, far from the window and where the sorcerer had stood. What dark magic had he used to accomplish such feats?

She shrank away from him, to the opposite side of the bed coverings, heedless of the hide slipping free of her neck. Suspicion deepened in her. She didn't much care for the unnatural ease with which he had managed to transport himself unseen, or the raw power she could all but feel emanating from his body. And those eyes . . . even in the gauzy light of dawn, those dark, dark eyes seemed to sear through her flesh, burrow through her skin, as though he were plumbing secrets from the depths of her that no one had ever known.

Regarding him with the same wariness she would show a serpent, Lorienne took the proffered cup made from beaten silver and sipped its sweet contents. He was watching her, too, a piercing, steady gaze that made her fingers fumble to grip the base of the goblet.

She cleared the uneasiness from her throat and glanced awkwardly away, unsure what he expected from her now. He appeared to be waiting for her to

34

speak, but what did one say or do in the presence of a sorcerer?

"This is good wine," she told him by way of making nervous conversation, then swallowed the remaining liquid in several swift gulps. It was said that many a warrior found courage in the bottom of a wine cup. Perhaps she would too, but whether that courage was false or not remained to be seen.

She closed her eyes a moment and savored the heady rush of the wine along with a forgotten remembrance. The fruity taste and scent had dredged up the pleasant recollection of a wine she had once sampled at a feast. She'd been very young then and had only been allowed a few small sips, but she remembered the taste well. "It has the taste of an Ionian wine." A trader journeying through the northlands had gifted her mother with a small carafe of the liquid, a rare and expensive gift that had brought with it dreams of faraway lands and a hot summer sun.

Adrik lifted a dark brow in surprise. "Yes . . . it's Ionian." Here was a child of the steppes, a nomad with little or no experience of life beyond the felt walls of the Arizantis' domed tents, and yet she had been swift to recognize the sun-baked taste of an Ionian wine? What other surprises did this girl harbor inside that tempting casement of flesh?

His dark gaze flicked downward, from the smooth lines of her unblemished face to her slender shoulders and chest, lingering on the softly rounded breasts bared to his view once more. The fall of pale hair that he had before admired appeared even more lush now that she was awake, a tumbling, curling mass of silk that draped the breadth of her shoulders to fall in loose disarray to the curve of her waist.

He clenched his jaw as blood began pounding in his ears once again. Hot. Demanding. A terrible heat coiled so tight inside the center of him that he thought he might burst into flame. He shook his head in a vain attempt to quench the fire suddenly raging within him. He had lain with women before—beautiful, willing women eager for the touch of one known to be a prince, even a prince who carried with him the taint of sorcery. But he had never felt the urge to lie with a woman so strongly before, an instinctual need to thrust himself deep within the soft folds of her silken flesh again and again until his body was sated and his manhood spent. The rush of desire was so unexpected and powerful that he wanted to throw himself atop her and take her now, to taste and feel and touch her beckoning flesh, heedless of any consequences.

"Take the bread," he commanded abruptly, his voice rough, impatient. He shoved the crust into her slender hand and backed away, wanting to distance himself from the source of such overwhelming temptation.

The sight and smell of the day-old bread made Lorienne realize how hungry she was. Though she was still suspicious of his motives, she shed herself of apprehension and devoured the sorcerer's offering in a few quick bites. Not that she had much choice in such matters anymore; but if he truly wished her harm, she did not think he would have slathered unguents over her wind-raw skin or offered her bread and costly wine. Or would he? He might be cruel and serpent-sly as well as powerful.

"Thank you," she said quietly, though her stomach complained bitterly that the single crust was all she had been given. She wanted more, much more, but instead she ignored her body's hunger pains and settled herself in a position to better study her captor, appraising the silent shape through curious eyes. For now, her hunger was best forgotten and her energies concentrated on the acquisition of knowledge—of him, this place, and her future, whatever that might be.

"I'm not certain of how I came to be here, or even

where we are," she said, and allowed her voice to trail away into uncertainty, inviting him to offer an explanation. "All I know is that I was condemned to die, or to spend my life as a concubine in Prince Burian's household." She lifted a hand in a gesture that encompassed the chamber and the fortress itself. "Instead I awoke here . . . a better fate, perhaps." She brushed a fingertip across her cheek, touching the slickness of the soothing balm that had been daubed on her face. "You obviously saved me. For that I owe you my life."

His gaze found hers in the dawn light. Did she truly think his motives had been born in such purity? "Do you know who I am?" he asked. Did she know *what he was*?

She frowned at his tone and studied his stark face curiously. There had been a trace of self-loathing buried in his voice, as if he despised who he was and knew she would as well. Though he wore his dark hair in a sorcerer's braid and sidelock, she knew nothing of him that would give her reason to loathe him. Fear him, perhaps, and justifiably so, but she despised no man without cause. "I know you're a sorcerer. . . . Is there more?"

The suggestion of a smile touched the edges of his mouth, then vanished without any proof that it had ever existed. He lifted a hand into the air, consciously imitating the gesture she had made a moment ago. "You are within the walls of Khorazm, fortress of the Magii. . . . I am Adrik, their prince."

Lorienne paled, her face turning the color of bleached bone. She stared at her captor in disbelief. This was *Adrik Kiryl* . . . the Shadow Prince. She'd heard tales of him before, legends whispered around many a late-night fire, dark tales of blood and battles and death, of a powerful warrior's daring in the heat of combat. Yet for all the accolades heaped upon him for his courage, it was also said that the reclusive Shadow

Prince bore a nimbus of evil about him, and that Death was never far from his side.

She shuddered inwardly. This was the man who would be her captor? Perhaps she had reason to loathe him after all. "The name of Prince Adrik is known to me."

His dark gaze never wavered from her face. She had spoken his name in such a way that it was tinged with vileness. "That is unsurprising. Many within the empire hold strong opinions of me."

A knot of unease formed in Lorienne's throat. Adrik Kiryl was more than a simple sorcerer, he was a man whose very existence invited strong opinions as well as fear. "It is also well rumored that the prince of the Magii is brother to Burian . . . and the second son of Hedeon, king of the six tribes." She didn't dare add that King Hedeon's second-born was also said to be in disfavor with his noble father. Was he in disfavor because he was a Magian sorcerer perhaps? The Magii were much despised, after all. Rife with priests and mystics and magic-users, the Magii had always been reviled and feared by the other tribes. "Are you truly a son to King Hedeon?"

His expression darkened. "An accident of fate, nothing more," he said in a quiet voice, then fell silent again. His thoughts mired in the past, in all that had been lost to him. All that could never be.

Lorienne watched his shuttered features closely, bewildered by the queer sense of sorrow and gloom that seemed to hang about him like a weighty mantle, as though he had long ago resigned himself to carry some terrible, unwanted burden throughout the passage of his life. A strange thought, that, for Adrik Kiryl had been born of the empire's noblest blood, guaranteeing him a life of ease and riches others could only possess in dreams.

The knowledge caused her unease to increase. She

cleared her throat, her fingers still wrapped tight about the base of the silver cup. "So, now that he has saved me, what does the son of Hedeon intend to do with me?" Such words from a woman might be termed as impudence by some, especially by one of noble birth. But few had ever accused Lorienne of being overly fond of prudence, especially not Arkanna, who had used the accusation of imprudence as a pretext for many a punishment. "Does the prince of the Magii plan to give me back my clothing and allow me to leave this stronghold . . . or does he intend to hold me here against my will?"

A look of uncertainty clouded Adrik's features. If he truly wanted to free her, it was well within his power to do so. She was an encumbrance, a tempting distraction who would surely bring disorder to what remained of his orderly life. And yet, even now, he could feel the blood boiling through his veins in response to her nearness. "You were a gift to me from my brother, Prince Burian. It would be an insult to him if I allowed you to have your freedom."

He glanced away, gazing at the blankness of a stone wall instead of her face, veiling the lie he was certain she would see in his eyes. The line of his mouth hardened with resolve. He would keep her for a while, just as Malkaval had advised.

"I see," she said in a rough whisper, a knot of dread wedging itself deep inside her. Prince Burian had made a gift of her? If that was so, her worst fears had come to pass because she was now considered the property of the Shadow Prince. He could do with her as he willed, and no one would dare question his actions.

Such was a woman's lot, she reminded herself, but she found no solace in the thought. She found no comfort in the remembrance of a vision Shalelle once had either, an ominous forewarning given by her mother the seer:

Jan Zimlich

The day will come when a darkling prince holds your fate within the palm of his hand. . . .

That day had obviously come.

Lorienne frowned and turned her glare on the man who now claimed her as chattel, the rancor she felt surely visible in her eyes. "It was clear that slaying me was in your mind when I awakened in the night to find you standing over me with your sword. Is that still your intent?" Could such an end by his hand be the fate foretold by her mother?

He turned slowly in her direction, his gaze filled with heat, a sweltering blaze he fought hard to contain. "I am not a fool, Arizanti. I would not weary my horse by bearing you through the mountains to Khorazm simply for the purpose of draining the life from your body. I plan to make you a part of my household. But if you would prefer my brother Burian as a master to me, then I shall see you safely delivered to his palace in Urmia. . . . I am certain he would be most pleased to welcome a new concubine into his bed."

Her chin lifted a fraction higher, and her eyes darkened with sudden anger. "So am I to warm *your* bed instead, my lord?" she asked sharply, unable to stop the reckless words from tumbling from her mouth. "Will I at least find that you are your brother's equal in that task?"

He stared at her for a swift moment, startled that anyone would dare speak to him in such an imprudent manner, especially a woman whose very life depended on his continued largesse. Then his fury rose to the forefront and his mouth settled into a grim, dangerous line.

Lorienne cried out as he gripped her shoulders with iron-strong hands and dragged her to her feet, forcing her from the relative safety of the skins she'd been using to shield her nakedness from him. She shivered in the chill of morning as he stood her before him, his grip ungentle, and his strong fingers twining painfully around long tendrils of her hair. His dark irises blazed, whether from fury or something else entirely, she couldn't say.

Adrik glared down into her upturned face. Her pale eyes were glazed with fear, and her features were drawn and white, drained of any hint of color. "I have never been considered my brother's *equal* in any task . . . and never will be," he grated furiously.

Her flesh felt hot beneath his fingers, her hair like the softest of silks. Adrik suppressed a shudder as an answering heat swept throughout his body. "You will stay here in the tower with me and tend to my needs. But make no mistake—you *will* warm my bed if I so desire."

Streaks of full-morning sunlight began spilling across the chamber, gathering in silver-white pools along the tiled floor. The light slanted across Lorienne's body, turning her fair skin and hair a ghostly winter-white.

Adrik saw the flesh on her arms shiver, from either the chill or her fear of him, or both perhaps. They were standing so close the tips of his boots were almost touching her toes. Temptingly close. He pulled in a ragged breath. If he wished, he could simply reach downward and explore the ripe contours of her body, or bury his face in the fragrant silk of her pale hair. He longed to trace his hands along the line of her slender hips, to pull her body hard against his manhood and allow his desire free rein. That's what his instincts told him to do. But the inhuman part of him was urging him to do other things . . . darker things, and to do them now without qualms or delay.

He closed his eyes a moment to quell those urges, and freed his fingers from her silken hair. "Let there be no misunderstandings between us," he said in a raw, strained voice. "I am your master now, and you will do as I say, Arizanti."

The girl's chin lifted sharply, and the line of her head settled at an angle that expressed her displeasure. "My given name is Lorienne, *master*. That is what I wish to be called, not Arizanti. I will serve you if that is your demand, but I serve no man while I am unrobed . . . even a prince." She knew those last were foolish words, but they couldn't be taken back now.

His fathomless eyes grew darker than before, so deep and flinty they appeared without life—as though they had been transformed into the eyes of some other-worldly creature, not those of a man. Lorienne swallowed and cursed herself for goading him.

Adrik stared back at her for a long moment, glaring darkly; then he turned on his heel and left.

Lorienne blew out the breath she'd been holding and watched in disbelief as her captor strode through the arched doorway and vanished. At the very least he should have beaten her for her impudence. What had possessed him to simply walk away?

With the dawning of the day, the fortress came alive. From the window opening high in the prince's tower, Lorienne watched and listened as those who lived within Khorazm's thick stone walls bustled about tending to their morning tasks. She could see only a portion of the flagged courtyard, a single section that abutted the southern side of the dark tower near the main gates, but the view was enough to give her an indication of the grand size and scope of the Magian stronghold.

And Khorazm truly was a grand thing to behold, larger and far richer than any fortress she'd ever spied. Though the mountains and steppes were pocked with a bevy of villages and strongholds ruled by various tribes, Khorazm was like nothing she'd ever seen or visited before. It sat high atop a wide cliff that fell away on one side to the chill waters of the Caspian Sea. Only a very foolish enemy would ever dare to try and mount an attack against the high-walled stronghold. The only visible way an invader could hope to gain access was by traveling up a precarious cart path that wound up the face of the cliff and ended at the gates, an approach that could be thwarted by a handful of archers with steady aim.

She continued studying the Magii tribe's fortress home from her vantage point atop the prince's tower. At the base of the stronghold, a large number of low openings were cut into the stone blocks: doorways that obviously led to a warren of storehouses and barracks built deep inside the walls and battlements. The outer walls, which looked to be more than twenty steps in width, apparently served as home to most of the residents of Khorazm, from the Magian soldiers and servants who tended the tower and their prince's needs, to the throng of workers who maintained the fortress, and all their families.

Lorienne angled her head to listen as the sharp echoes of metal striking metal reverberated from one of the open doorways below. She made a note of the location in her mind. These were the clangs commonly made in an armory, where swords and other weaponry were fashioned and honed.

As if to prove her deduction, a soldier carrying a glinting sword appeared in the doorway, hefting the weapon high and slicing the air with practiced movements to test the weight and grip. Several chattering women meandered past the soldier, all clad in the loose-fitting robes and simple overtunics of water bearers, the heavy clay urns they carried carefully balanced upon narrow shoulders. The soldier laughed in response to a teasing remark made by one of the women; then he too ambled out of sight.

Lorienne could hear other sounds as well—the muted calls of horses and other beasts, voices raised in

43

conversation, a soldier shouting orders—but with her limited view she could see little else of the fortress's activities.

She turned her head slightly and allowed herself to concentrate on the breathtaking vista that encompassed the remainder of her vision, a seascape so grand and sprawling that it overwhelmed her senses.

The silvery mantle of the Caspian Sea stretched to the horizon and beyond, the water glimmering like countless jewels in the morning sun. Directly below, the steady swells appeared to lumber into the base of the cliff the fortress was perched upon, the low rumble of sound created by the collisions rising upward until it carried into the tower itself.

Lorienne drew in a breath tinged with the smell of fish and sea, then tugged her sheepskin blanket close to her body for warmth. No wonder the prince had seemed so taken with the view from this window. She was taken as well. The sea and stars set against the blackness of a night sky would be a wondrous sight to behold.

A tiny sound within the chamber drew her attention from the sea to a whisper-soft swish of fabric from somewhere behind her. Lorienne turned abruptly, afraid the prince had returned to beat her for her words.

Instead, she found herself face-to-face with a small-framed woman of many years. Lorienne stared at the stranger in surprise, greatly relieved that she would have more time until she was forced to confront Adrik Kiryl once again. The aged woman's cap of gray-spattered hair was wound tightly about her head, and her faded features were lined by time and sun. Though the years had obviously stolen much of her beauty, she was still what the men of Lorienne's tribe would have termed a comely woman. Her eyes were her most striking feature. They were dark and well-deep, much like those possessed by the Shadow Prince. A trait common among the Magii, Lorienne supposed.

The woman dipped her head slightly and held out her hands. To Lorienne's surprise, she was holding the woolen robe her captor had taken from her, as well as a pair of soft gray boots made from felt and dyed doeskin. She touched the material in disbelief. The neatly folded blue fabric appeared to have been mended and scrubbed clean. "My robe . . ." No trace of the grime and soot and smoke from her days on the steppes remained.

"My name is Jirina. I am Mistress of the Tower and see to Prince Adrik's needs. He ordered that your robe be repaired and returned to you. I did the best I could in a short space of time. The wool was heavily soiled and there was a large tear low on one hip. But it will suit your needs until the fortress's weavers and seamstresses can make you another."

Lorienne pulled the fabric free of the woman's hands and clutched it to her chest. "Thank you" was all she could manage. Had her angry words brought about the return of her meager clothing?

Jirina straightened her shoulders and gazed at her evenly. "Do not thank me, Lorienne of the Arizanti. I simply followed orders given by my prince."

Lorienne gazed back at the other woman, masking her surprise with a feigned look of unconcern. Jirina already knew her name as well as the fact that she was Arizanti, and she could only have learned those things from Prince Adrik himself. She studied Jirina more carefully than before. This Mistress of the Tower might well prove useful in her quest for information about Khorazm and its inhabitants. Perhaps she had the ear of the prince himself.

"Then I shall thank your prince instead." She allowed her sheepskin cover to slip downward until it heaped itself upon the tile floor; then Lorienne shook the robe and pulled the heavy fabric over her head, smoothing the familiar material into place once it had settled.

She noted that Jirina was still eyeing her with a thin glance that could only be termed disapproving. Perhaps the old woman disliked concubines within the prince's household. Lorienne had heard it said that some servants grew resentful of their master's new acquisitions and would retaliate out of spite.

Perhaps the woman thought Adrik Kiryl had already staked his claim upon Lorienne's body and resented the deed. If so, Lorienne would find no ally in the woman and might even have need to guard her back against a sly blade.

Jirina's gaze suddenly shifted away from her face, though it seemed an effort to do so. "Prince Adrik has instructed me that you will not be staying in the outer walls along with the other household servants." Her slight shoulders stiffened, and her body stood taller and wood-straight. "You are to remain here with him in the tower, and you are to take your rest only within this chamber, nowhere else. Do you understand? You must abide by the prince's wishes at all times and without question."

Lorienne nodded reluctantly. "I understand." She understood all too well. "What of the prince's other women? Will they be here as well?"

The old woman glanced away, toward the vast sweep of the Caspian Sea. "The prince has no other women," she said sharply. She returned the full force of her glare to Lorienne's face. "Remember my words well. You now belong to Adrik of the Magii. As his woman, you are not allowed to leave the gates of Khorazm without his permission or without him as escort. There are many dangers outside these walls. . . . Wolves and other creatures roam the forest and mountains very near the fortress. Tigers can even be found deep in the forest upon occasion, and footing is treacherous along the cliff top as well."

She gave Lorienne a sharp look. "Many who've been fool enough to venture out alone have been found with a Scythian arrow in their backs. It would be wise to remember the fate that awaits you before attempting an escape."

Lorienne returned the old woman's stare for a moment but didn't answer. From the corner of her eye she had caught a glimpse of a curious sight atop a battlement. Though it was now full day, an armor-clad soldier was holding a smoldering torch high atop his head, waving it back and forth in a slow arc that trailed a giant plume of smoke. Then another soldier joined him, this one holding forth with colorful banners in each hand that swept back and forth through the air in time with his rhythmic movements.

She frowned curiously. "What are they doing?"

"They're signalists," Jirina explained. "Watchmen sending signals from Prince Adrik to a Lydian caravan nearing the base of the cliff. Our prince has given the Lydians permission to enter the lands of the Magii. Their emissary shall arrive here soon to have an audience with him."

Lorienne tried in vain to mask her surprise. "Have we not been at war with the Lydian Empire these few years past?" Why would the Shadow Prince agree to meet such an enemy? It was true she had no great love for the Median Empire herself, or for King Hedeon and his hated heir, but her own dislike would never take the form of betrayal.

Jirina gave her a small, chilly smile. "They may be enemies of our empire," she explained, "but that does not necessarily make the Lydians enemies of the Magii."

Lorienne nodded in sudden comprehension. The Lydians were not truly enemies of the Arizanti either.

What Hedeon, his administrators, and countless courtiers did was often not in the best interest of all six tribes that comprised the Empire. He only considered the arrogant Busae, of course, his own ancestral tribe, which was now ruled by his son. The Busae had fared very well indeed since Hedeon ascended the throne.

Given these thoughts, Lorienne could not pass judgment on Adrik Kiryl based solely on his willingness to meet with an enemy emissary. It was possible that her own mother, Shalelle, or even Arkanna might have done much the same. Prince Adrik's true loyalty obviously lay with his tribe and not the empire, nor with his father and brother, and she could not fault him for that.

A burst of movement high atop the battlements drew her attention back to the fortress's preparations for the Lydians' arrival. She watched as archers and lancers took positions along the main wall, their attention focused downward as they observed the approach of the Lydian entourage around the switchbacks that led up the cliff face to Khorazm's gates.

In the courtyard below, hundreds of Magian soldiers were forming ranks on opposite sides of the arched gates. Domed helmets, shields, and tunics of mail gleamed brightly beneath the morning sun, polished to a high shine in anticipation of a visit by their foes. The dark crests topping the officers' iron helmets dipped and bobbed among the assembled soldiers, adding an occasional glint of movement among the mass of black uniforms and shining armament. But despite the grand display of greeting, the Magian soldiers still clutched bows and bronze-tipped lances in full readiness, obviously mindful of the possibility of treachery.

Although her time with Adrik Kiryl had been short, Lorienne recognized him instantly as he walked through the troops marshaling in the courtyard below.

He was attired in similar fashion to hundreds of others, but the Shadow Prince's tall frame and confident stride were easily identifiable. An air of nobility seemed to radiate from him; he had a certain set to his shoulders that a lesser man could never possess. He wore his clothing nobly, too, though it was simple—from the loose black trousers blousing above soft boots that rode high upon his calves, to the simple, hip-length tunic and embroidered overvest that fell to his knees. Save for the golden embroidery decorating his sleeveless overvest, his attire could be the same plain fare worn by many a common soldier.

His dark hair was worn differently, however, not loose or capped or covered with a helmet like the others. His seemed forever bound in the sorcerer's braid that hung past his shoulders to the middle of his back. Only his long sidelock was loose, and that, she could see, was being lifted back and forth on the wind. The thick braid told its own tale, marking him a sorcerer for all to see—and fear. And perhaps that was the purpose of such a style, for the Lydians and others to see and fear as well.

The thick wooden gates swung open slowly, and the assemblage in the courtyard came to full ceremonial attention, their shoulders erect, their helmets and crests held proudly high. All eyes focused on the cavalcade of riders pouring inside the walls of Khorazm in double ranks, soldiers in the fore, servants and baggage handlers to the rear.

Stable hands leapt to take charge of the Lydians' horses and pack animals, while the Lydians themselves dismounted to stand waiting uncertainly. To Lorienne, they appeared wary and nervous like their Magian counterparts, as if they were unsure whether they were awaiting a formal greeting or a murderous attack.

A tall Lydian clad in the richly colored robes of a nobleman stepped to the forefront of the nervous sol-

49

diers and bowed slightly, directing his polite gesture both left and right, as if he too were uncertain who would receive him and how. Even from the tower Lorienne could tell that the Lydian was an imposing figure, rising above his countrymen by a full head or so. He was dark as well, with jet hair similar in hue to that possessed by most Magians, but with flesh the color of ripe olives, far darker than the tribe who'd allowed the Lydians entry into their small kingdom.

As if he had divined her presence from thin air, the richly garbed Lydian suddenly glanced up, his head lifting as his gaze climbed the stone tower until it came to rest on the window where Lorienne stood. He stared for a long moment, and then she saw the white flash of his teeth against the dark of his skin. Other Lydians began lifting their heads as well to see what had caught their leader's eye.

Beside her, she felt Jirina stiffen. "Come away from the window!" the woman ordered sharply. "The prince will not be pleased that you allowed yourself to be seen by enemy soldiers."

Lorienne continued to stare at the scene below with wondering eyes. This had been a day of firsts, and it had only just begun. "I have never seen a Lydian before."

The old woman gripped her arm with strong fingers. "Come away, or these will be the last Lydians you ever see! You will have time to see them later, if that is your desire. The prince has ordered that you are to act as servant and offer food to him and the ambassador here within the tower."

Lorienne wrenched her gaze from the courtyard to Jirina, yet she was still reluctant to move away from the window and the excitement below. "When am I to do this?"

"Come!" Jirina's grip tightened painfully. "We must hurry. And you would be wise not to do anything to cause the prince embarrassment or to insult his guest."

Lorienne suddenly felt the heat of another gaze fall upon her, one so dark and broodingly intense that she felt as if those eyes could sear the very flesh from her bones. She shivered inwardly. The Shadow Prince had followed the direction of the Lydian's gaze, and was now watching her from below. She pulled in a startled breath. Even from a distance she could feel the heat of his gaze linger upon her face and body, the touch of his eyes as strong and hot as any physical touch.

She pulled back from the window instinctively, the beat of her heart quickening in response to the heat generated by Adrik's piercing look. She should have paid attention to the old woman's words. Jirina had told her to come away from the window, but her impudence had caused her to delay, and now she might well be forced to pay the price of her foolishness.

The Shadow Prince had decided to stake his claim upon her body. Soon she would belong to him in more than name. She had seen the truth of it in his eyes.

Chapter Five

Adrik's dark gaze slid from the tower back to the tall Lydian standing beside him. The foreigner's bold stare had remained fixed on the uncovered window and the Arizanti captive for an impolite length of time, a view that Adrik found himself unwilling to share. But at least Jirina had seen to it that the girl had been reclothed. The insult would have been double-fold if she had been seen without her robe.

"I am Adrik Kiryl . . . prince of the Magii." His voice was flat and cool, bearing no hint of the anger smoldering inside him. "Why have you sought an audience with me?"

The admission of his identity caused the Lydian's brows to lift in obvious surprise. The man nodded once again, barely tipping his chin downward in acknowledgement of his host. "I am Pantaleon," he announced in return. "Younger son of Alyattes, king of the Lydian Empire." His glance shifted pointedly to the soldiers clustered so close about them. "I bear a private message for the Magian prince from my father . . . one destined for far fewer ears than these."

Adrik stared back, considering. Was this simply some Lydian ploy? A clever trick designed to separate him from the soldiers guarding his life? Perhaps, but Adrik didn't truly think this Pantaleon would be so bold or clever. Though the Lydian prince was striking in appearance, from his imposing height to the neatly trimmed beard that decorated his chin, he did not possess the look of cunning and fortitude needed to best a blooded soldier like Adrik, either in a battle of wits or arms.

The foreigner's long woolen robe and heavy outer tunic were too rich as well, the deep red hues too vibrant and costly to attire a seasoned warrior who would value comfort and practicality above all else. The son of Alyattes even appeared to bear the stain of paint upon his face, the rouges and powders and such worn by many of pampered blood, both male and female. He carried the cloying scent of a sweet perfume about his body too, just as Persian nobility ofttimes did. Had these Lydians been so foolish as to adapt the soft ways of that Median vassal state which lay to the south? Some within the Median royal house had done so in recent years, including his own father. King Hedeon was said now to act the Persian in all things at the behest of his present wife. If true, such behavior would inevitably spell the end to both the Median and Lydian empires alike, because no culture could long survive the corruption brought about by such an easy life.

Even so, he had to admit that he was greatly intrigued by the presence of this princely emissary. King Alyattes must consider his message to be of grave import to risk sending his own son into the teeth of an enemy stronghold.

Adrik lifted his gaze to the battlements, to the lancers and archers poised so anxiously above, then to the ranks of Magian and enemy soldiers massed within the confines of the courtyard.

"The prince of the Magii bids welcome to the son of Alyattes, king of the Lydian Empire!" he announced to all in a deep, commanding voice. "And to the soldiers of Pantaleon and his servants I bid welcome as well. Bring food, water, and wine to ease the weariness of the journey for our guests . . . and let no man among you break my vow of hospitality."

Serving women and water bearers scurried to do their prince's bidding, while the tense stances of the gathered soldiers slowly relaxed. Bows and lances were lowered; hands uncurled from sword pommels and the grips of wicker shields.

Adrik turned back to the man he had just declared his official guest. He would have no need to issue further commands or admonishments. No harm would come to Pantaleon or to any of his people within Khorazm or the lands of the Magii. His word was law, and the Magii treated it as such.

"Come," he told the Lydian prince, and motioned for the man to join him as he climbed the tower's wide stone steps. "We shall have food and wine to go with your father's words."

The brightness of the morning sun faded into cool shadow as they moved inside the entrance of the tower and made their way into the rectangular audience hall that comprised the lower floor of the narrow structure. Even in full day, small clay oil lamps placed in niches along the walls provided most of the lighting within the chamber, casting a hazy glow across furnishings that were sparse and functional, with no hint of the ostentation rampant in many a noble's home.

Jirina was waiting just inside the wide arched doorway. She bowed deeply to her prince and his guest, then lifted a thin hand to direct their attention to the center of the audience hall, where several simple couches with curved wooden legs were clustered around a long, low table cut and polished from a slab of limestone. "A meal has been prepared as you ordered, my lord," she announced in a carefully measured voice.

Adrik seated himself on one of the small couches, pushing aside the soft pillows and padding added for the comfort of a guest. He watched curiously as the Lydian prince settled his costly robes atop a couch directly opposite. If the Lydians were truly desirous of ending the long-standing war, their king should have sent his emissary to the Median palace in Urmia, where he could have clamored for an audience with Hedeon, not here to remote Khorazm for an audience with a disfavored son. Adrik was in no position to negotiate the terms of any treaty with a foreign power.

He continued to study his guest as Jirina placed bronze bowls, swaths of folded linen, and ewers of fresh water on the table for the cleansing of hands, a ritual practiced by most before any meal within Median lands.

As he dipped his hands into the bowl of water before him, Adrik heard a soft tread on the curving stone steps and glanced up to see his Arizanti captive making her way into the chamber, pausing uncertainly at the base of the staircase until Jirina motioned for her to begin her duties by placing serving trays atop the table.

His solemn gaze followed the girl's every move as she carefully positioned trays laden with fresh fruit, skewers of roasted meat, and rounds of warm black bread before them. Her movements were fluid and graceful, pleasurable to observe, even more so when she eased her body past him and her hip and thigh came so close to touching his forearm that he felt a stirring of expectation within his blood. But just as suddenly she withdrew, and he was left with only a vague impression of how her touch might feel along his flesh, because she had somehow managed to deposit the heavy tray and slip away without their limbs or eyes having any contact at all.

Adrik swabbed away droplets of water clinging to his hands with a strip of linen, noting, too, that the Lydian prince had also been watching Lorienne's every move. A muscle sprang to life along his jaw. The Lydian could feast upon Magian food and wine, but he would not live much longer if his eyes continued to feast upon the woman Adrik had chosen to take into his bed.

"I have freely given you my hospitality," he said in a lethally quiet voice, reminding the foreigner of his position as guest. "Speak your father's words before I grow impatient with your presence."

The Lydian prince appeared unfazed by the none-too-subtle threat. Instead of reddening with embarrassment and humiliation as Adrik expected, Pantaleon risked yet another lingering glance in Lorienne's direction before turning back to his host and lifting a rueful brow.

"Forgive my impoliteness," Pantaleon began, though he didn't appear penitent in the least. "It was not my intent to show disrespect or to abuse your hospitality." His teeth flashed white against his sun-darkened skin. "But pale beauty such as possessed by this woman is a rarity in my land and therefore much prized." He pulled a wedge of roasted meat free of a tray and chewed on it absently, his gaze straying back briefly to the fair-haired woman, who had retreated to the far end of the chamber when the subject of their conversation turned to her. "If she is more to you than a mere servant, I am doubly repentant for my rudeness, but I must admit that I suffer pangs of envy where she is concerned."

The Lydian glanced at Lorienne covertly once again before returning the full force of his eyes and voice back to his host. "We come from wealthy empires, you and I," Pantaleon said intently. "Riches of gold, silks, horses, and precious gemstones mean little when possessed in such abundance as ours. But surely there exists a thing of value I could offer that would entice the Magian prince to part with a pretty northerner. You have but to name your price and I would willingly pay. It would bring me great honor to return to my land with such a prize, especially a woman once owned by the man known as the Shadow Prince."

Adrik's eyes narrowed as the Lydian lifted one shoulder in a gesture meant to intimate that his offer was purely of a jesting nature and not meant to give offense. Even so, Adrik was quite certain the offer was rooted in truth. "She is mine," he said flatly, refusing Pantaleon's offer directly, and refusing to discuss the subject any further as well.

The Lydian's shoulder lifted once more, a regretful gesture this time. "Ah, well . . . I feared you would not be interested in selling her. I have seen the spark of desire flare in your eyes when you gaze upon her. And most likely I would be hard-pressed to keep her if she were truly mine. I would have to fight half the men of Sardis for the privilege of becoming her master, perhaps even my own father and brother Croesus as well."

Adrik glowered, and narrowed his mouth to a hard, straight line, angry with himself that he had so little control over the desires of his body that he'd allowed an enemy to sense his need for the girl burning hot and heavy inside him. Desire was a sign of weakness, one he could ill afford, and he had obviously bared it for all the world and his enemies to see.

His mouth thinned even more. The foreigner would do well to remember that a truce was a temporary thing. The war between their empires could continue now if he so desired. Here, in this very chamber. "It is my hope that the words chosen by the father are wiser than the son's. Hospitality is ofttimes a fragile thing."

To his consternation, Pantaleon simply laughed, a hearty, unexpected sound that echoed off stone and tile to fill every shadowy corner of the high-ceilinged chamber. It was a sound seldom heard within Adrik's tower, one that caused the Magian prince to stare at his guest in surprise. Perhaps he had misjudged the Lydian. The man was obviously perceptive, and any brave enough to merely laugh in the face of a threat made by a sorcerer possessed far more fortitude than most. Many men would have fled Adrik's presence long ago. But whether this painted nobleman possessed cunning as well as fortitude remained to be seen.

Pantaleon's laughter finally faded, but a bemused smile remained firmly affixed to his narrow lips. "Once again I find myself apologizing for my failings," he said in a placating voice. The Lydian lifted a silver rhyton fashioned in the shape of a crouching tiger and drained it of wine. "My father would surely be the first to tell you of the wisdom of his counsel over mine. And perhaps he is right." He smiled in a casual fashion, as though his father's thoughts of him were as insubstantial as air. "And it is my father who is of a mind to give you counsel this time, Prince Adrik, not I."

Adrik's jet brows pulled forward into a tight frown. Other than Malkaval, few had ever dared to offer him counsel of any kind, and certainly not an enemy king. "Yes?" The single word carried with it a softly voiced challenge, an invitation for Pantaleon to face the Shadow Prince's wrath should the father's words be ill-advised.

The Lydian prince cleared the dryness from his throat and leaned forward intently, the sleeves of his bloodred robe coming to rest atop the pale gray of the limestone. "King Alyattes proposes to make peace between our empire and the Magii. With the coming of spring, the battles to the west between our armies will surely begin anew—King Hedeon and your brother still thirst to create a great empire, an empire they would build atop the conquered bones of Lydia."

Pantaleon fell silent for a moment. "It has also been said by our spies that, with the coming of spring's warmth, your crown prince Burian plans to appease his father by sending a vast army of soldiers gathered from all the Median tribes into battle to defeat us . . . a great army led by his brother the Shadow Prince, with the feared Magii riding at the fore."

Adrik's features stilled, as if the stark lines of his face were carved from the same stone as the table. "I am not privy to the plans of my father or brother. But if my brother commands it, the Magii will fight. I have sworn an oath to Burian and shall follow where he leads."

Pantaleon eyed him carefully. "That is the crux of my purpose for coming here, Adrik of the Magii." He fell silent again, all trace of his earlier amusement vanishing. "My father the king is quite certain of the outcome of any renewed battles against the Median tribes . . . as long as the Magii and their sorcerer prince remain within the borders of their own lands and do not fight. But if a renowned sorcerer such as you chooses to lead Burian's army, the final outcome grows far less certain, and far more precarious. We know of your powers, Prince Adrik, and that you are now considered a sorcerer of the first rank, capable of bending men and the beasts of the forest to your will. We know too that your powers are said to make you capable of other things . . . strange affinities with demons and other undead creatures of the Shadow Realm. Though our own sorcerers can defend us from many of your spells, there are no spells or protective wards to fend off any vile creatures dredged from the belly of the Shadow Realm."

The Lydian clasped his hands together in front of him, his flesh and fingers all but vanishing inside the voluminous folds of his scarlet sleeves. "But know this, Prince Adrik, with or without your intervention, if the battles between our empires are not brought to an end before the first snows fly in the winter after this one, there will be no hope of an honorable conclusion. We will all be the losers for it, for we Lydians will never surrender. We will fight until our wealth is gone, our empire is in ruins, and the last of us is finally dead."

His jaw firmed and his chin lifted in defiance to emphasize his words. "We are prepared to embrace such an end with joy if it means defeating your father."

Adrik sat back from the table, his hands carefully folded before him in a nonthreatening pose meant to reassure the man he had granted his hospitality—despite the harshness of any words spoken between them. The unspoken message from Alyattes was clear and unambiguous: If the war continued and the outcome looked to go against them, the Lydians would willingly lay waste to their own empire just to ensure that Hedeon never possessed more than a burned-out husk, an empty shell of the once rich and thriving culture.

And the Medians might well be forced to suffer the same grim fate if the Lydians decided. Such things had happened before. Instead of armies meeting on the fields of battle, commands were sometimes given to burn fortresses and villages, slaughter animals, and lay waste to crops before they could be harvested, assuring that any who survived died slowly of starvation or exposure to the cold of winter.

Adrik gazed at the Lydian solemnly. There could never be a victor in such a war. "An end such as the one you envision would be a terrible waste."

"True," Pantaleon agreed in a soft, sad voice. "A bitter thing indeed." He sat back slowly and eased his hands into view, clasping them into a peaceful position that mimicked the careful pose Adrik had assumed. "This is why we have come to you, Prince Adrik. Without you, your father and brother cannot hope to defeat us in battle, not this year at least. We do not ask that you betray any blood oath in order to aid us—just that you do not bring your powers as a sorcerer to bear. We ask, too, that you consider delaying the addition of Magian strength to theirs for a short span of time. Only enough time to cause your father and brother to rethink their intransigence about negotiating a fair and equitable peace. They will grow concerned and uncertain if you delay taking command of their army and will instinctively waver in their plans. During that respite we shall try again to send an ambassador to Urmia to negotiate the terms of a lasting treaty, one that we hope will unite our countries as allies for many years to come."

Adrik blew out a short breath, his only outward reaction to King Alyattes' boldly conceived plan. The Lydian king was truly a formidable foe. Still, there were dangers here, the possibility of treachery foremost. He might delay assuming command of Burian's army only to find that the Lydians had used the time to prepare their forces for a lethal assault. But surely they knew the cost of such a betrayal. A sorcerer's wrath was not the sort of plague the Lydians wished to bring down upon their heads.

At least one element of the proposal remained unclear, though: the enticement offered to assure his cooperation with their plans. No proposal would ever have been made to him unless the Lydians planned to make it worth his while. And the enticement they offered would tell him exactly how serious they truly were about achieving this so-called peace with a sworn enemy. "In the event that I consider your father's proposal, what inducement would be offered for me to delay support of Burian and my father?" It was clear the Lydians knew little of his father or brother. Whether he fought at the head of the Median army would matter little to either of them. Burian would be eager to renew the war come spring, even if his army consisted of nothing more than a few thin ranks of serving women and bony old men. As for Hedeon, who knew what motivated him anymore?

His pointed question caused a look of satisfaction to cross Pantaleon's strong features. The Lydian emissary sensed that his diplomatic mission was nearing success. "Pack animals in my caravan carry plentiful chests of gold, silver, copper, and silks from eastern lands, as well as soft woolens dyed rich hues in the secret ways of my people," he announced in a self-important voice. "All treasures sent to you by King Alyattes. But the most valuable offering will arrive at the end of summer, when the unpleasantness between our peoples has been decided once and for all. My sister Aryenis is to be given to you in marriage by my father to forge a blood alliance between the Magii and the Lydian empire that will bind us together for generations to come."

A brief trace of sorrow suddenly shadowed the depths of Adrik's eyes. The Lydians were obviously unaware that with the arrival of true spring, any marriage bargain made between him and their princess would come to a cruel and certain end. His destiny lay elsewhere, whether he wished it so or not. His father and Malkaval had seen to that.

Pantaleon obviously mistook his silence for hesitation. The Lydian lifted an elegant hand and directed a finger toward Lorienne, who had approached the table at Jirina's prompting to pour more wine. "Rest easy, Prince Adrik, for Aryenis is quite pleasant to look upon, as dark as your woman is fair, but far more ripe—a sweet, heady fruit ready to be plucked from the vine. She would be a welcome addition to any man's bed and household."

The blunt talk of ripe women, beds, and plucking

fruit from the vine had caused a warm flush to stain Lorienne's cheeks a rosy hue. Adrik watched the color spread across her cheeks like a rising tide, then fade away into nothingness. He found himself wondering if the pleasant flush had traveled over more than just her face. He could not envision a woman more ripened and ready to be plucked. This simple nomad was far more appealing to him than any blood-born princess could ever hope to be.

Adrik picked up his newly filled rhyton and drained it of wine before turning morose eyes upon his guest. He would take Lorienne and bed her as he planned, but the end result would be much the same as if he married the Lydian princess—come late spring, any bond between him and a woman would be brought to an abrupt and unwelcome end.

The thought caused a dark frown to cut across Adrik's brow. If he were a mere man, he would be free to plan such a future—if he were truly a man. "You would see your sister married to a sorcerer?" he asked in a voice grown suddenly sharp.

Pantaleon's gaze stilled and turned earnest. "For the good of my people I would see my sister married to Adrik, prince of the Magii . . . second-born son to the king of the Median Empire. Whether that prince is a sorcerer is of little concern to either me or my father." He glanced at a fingernail and studied it carefully, giving the appearance of being distracted and indifferent to the effect of his words. "And if that second-born son ever aspires to become crown prince instead," he said offhandedly, "I think he would find his wife's people willing to render him any aid needed to achieve such a feat."

Adrik nodded slowly. So King Alyattes' true purpose had finally been revealed. A clever plan, that. One way or another the Lydians planned to rid their empire of the threat posed by his father and brother. It was likely that if Adrik were fool enough to try and take his brother's place atop the Median throne, he would most certainly become the next member of the royal house to die an untimely death. Perhaps the Lydians hoped a child born from the loins of Aryenis and his seed would then be next in line. What they failed to comprehend was that he would never live long enough for any of their plans to be brought to fruition.

Pantaleon lifted a brow in question. "So, now that you know the full of it, what answer do you wish me to take back to my father?"

The sorcerer steepled his hands and rubbed his pursed lips with the tips of his fingers. To refuse the offer outright would only serve to deepen the animosity between the Medes and Lydians, as well as put an end for all time to any possibility of a treaty.

He watched as Lorienne refilled his silver rhyton once again, the dark wine rising inside the narrow vessel until it almost touched the brim. The horn-shaped cup was a twin to the one used by Pantaleon, its polished surface sculpted in the shape of a crouching tiger. He ran an idle finger over the ornate cup perched on three legs, tracing the tiger's metallic head and ears. The Lydian proposal was much like the tiger immortalized on the cup—a beast crouching in readiness to slaughter its chosen prey. In this instance, he was the chosen prey; but as was the way of the forest and all wild creatures, in the blink of an eye, the hunted could suddenly transform into a dangerous hunter.

"Tell King Alyattes that I am eager for the end of summer . . . and the arrival of my bride."

Chapter Six

A freshening wind rode above the leaden waters of Lake Urmia and made its way across the wide tiled terrace and columned portico of the sprawling Median palace, a series of flat-roofed buildings cut from stone blocks bleached sand-white by time and the glare of the sun. The chilly breath of wind sighed through portals open to the terrace and sliced across the interior chamber, ruffling the thick mat of hair on Burian Kiryl's naked chest.

The Median crown prince jerked reflexively and opened his eyes, roused to a state of semiwakefulness by the unexpected chill rushing across his bare skin. He groaned and stretched his arms wide to flex the muscles in his shoulders and back, puckering his dry mouth in displeasure when he realized it was day already and the sun had almost reached midsky.

Burian blinked in the morning glare, then squeezed his lids shut to blot out the annoying light slicing like arrow points across the cool confines of his bedchamber.

"My eyes hurt!" he bellowed to any servant within hearing. The arrows of sunlight felt as if they were burning holes through his eyes to the tender spots where the painful vestiges of last night's wine resided. "Pull those coverings closed!"

A manservant scurried across the chamber to do his bidding and tugged long swaths of blue silk loose from holders on columns along the chamber's outer wall. The panels of light fabric fell free and drifted downward, closing the room off from the worst of the light pouring inside. Once the task was completed, the servant quietly placed a fresh ewer of wine and a silver cup on a pedestal beside the bed, then hurried into an adjoining chamber before Burian could take out his annoyance on him.

The crown prince finally risked reopening his eyes, gratified to find the chamber shaded from the worst of the glare. The daggers of pain still burned and stabbed behind his eyes, though, making it difficult to see. He groaned and lifted his stiff body onto an elbow, his mouth curling in a sudden, rapacious smile when his shoulder made contact with soft female skin. The touch of that womanly flesh roused an ember of desire within him, one that made him forget about the pounding behind his eyes.

The woman Vlada had found for him upon their return to Urmia was snoring slightly, yet to awaken from the wine and bedding of the previous night. Granted, she wasn't much to look upon. She was a thin little thing with a bone-hard body and a long face, not what he would call a beauty by any means, but she did have one particular attribute that Burian had made certain she possessed: her hair was a pale golden color, almost as pale as a northerner's.

He smiled darkly and lifted a strand of the golden hair streaming across the silken bed coverings, comparing its texture and hue once again to that of the tempting Arizanti girl he'd so foolishly given to his sorcerer brother. The Arizanti's hair had been paler, richer, and silkier, like nothing he'd ever seen, far more appealing than this whore's limp mane.

His wide forehead pulled into a web of furious lines. Why could he not free himself of memories of how that girl had looked tied to a stake out on the steppe, her robe ripped and dirtied, her hair streaming around her torso in a gust of wind? He'd even dreamed of her one night, of taking her just as she'd been, still tied to the stake, helpless to stave off his frenzied passion.

He sighed and brushed such thoughts aside. In the weeks since he'd made that impulsive gesture to his brother, he'd cursed himself soundly for simply giving the girl away; but the deed was done and there was no way to change it. For now, at least. Of course, for all he knew, she could already have met her death at Adrik's hands, so he would just have to satisfy his newfound craving for pale-haired women by dallying with such as this in his bed.

Still, his time hadn't been entirely misspent these past weeks. This woman Vlada had lured to the palace with the promise of gold had an agreeable temperament, and she'd eagerly worked to earn a scant few nuggets of the precious metal. A new concubine or consort would have cost him a far greater outlay of gold, effort, and frustration—especially when their eager caresses turned into ceaseless carping and complaints, which happened with all women given time. Here, for a pittance, the whore had gladly spread her legs without complaint, allowing him to mount and ride her whenever he felt the need arise, and he'd felt that urge countless times.

His manhood suddenly awoke from its slumber and grew rigid with need, brought to life once again by the thoughts roiling inside him. He reached out and squeezed the shiny peak of a nipple that had thrust itself in his direction.

At his touch, the whore instinctively rolled onto her back, affording him a clear view of her womanhood and surprisingly large breasts. Wordlessly, she opened her eyes and spread her legs wide, granting Burian easy entry to the pleasure awaiting him between her thighs.

He grunted and climbed atop her bony hips, his manhood jabbing deep and hard inside her. She made no sound as he pushed in and out at a frantic pace, eager for a swift release so he could rise and relieve himself. And if he closed his eyes tightly, he couldn't see her long face. Instead, he imagined that he was still out upon the desolate steppe, with the Arizanti tied fast to that wooden stake, her pale hair whipping around his naked chest. A pleasant dream, that.

He heard a sound nearby, like a quick breath blown out in a snort of disgust. His erotic imaginings faded abruptly, and his hurried movements slowed.

"Have you not yet grown bored with her?" The voice was sharp and feminine, shrill with an edge of derision. "I would have thought your member shriveled from distaste by now."

Burian glanced sideways, his eyes finding those of the dark-haired woman who'd strode uninvited into his bedchamber, but he made no move to pull himself free of the whore's loins. Instead, he pushed into her harder, his back growing slick with sweat as he tried in vain to achieve release. The woman pinned beneath him simply stared with wide, curious eyes at the intruder beside the bed. She didn't appear particularly perturbed by the untimely interruption, as if such an event had occurred before.

But Burian was growing more perturbed with each moment that passed. He scowled at Melina, his father's present wife, Hedeon's second consort since Burian's own mother had succumbed to some strange and unexpected malady when he'd been a young boy. It had been Adrik's mother, the Magian princess, who'd later died in the throes of childbirth, paving the road for Melina's ascension to her position as consort to the Median ruler, a rank she'd held for many a year. It was a lofty title for a woman considered outcast by her own people, the Parae-tak, a nomadic tribe that dwelled in the lands to the west.

"Well?" The Parae-tak had been wise to shun her as an outcast. The woman was like a poisonous thorn, deadly to all unfortunate enough to be pricked. "What is it that you want of me, Melina?" Burian demanded impatiently.

The woman's generous mouth parted in a slow smile, the dark expression of a predator eager for the taste of prey. She leaned toward him and ran a single finger along the length of his sweat-dampened back. "Poor Burian . . . I fear your manhood has indeed shriveled away. You cannot even satisfy yourself, much less this ugly lump of bones lying beneath you."

His features reddened, but instead of lashing out at Melina as he wished, Burian thrust himself into the whore even harder, unwilling for his father's wife to see him fail at such a simple task. He grunted in satisfaction as he felt the urge for release begin to burn inside his loins. Oddly, having a scornful Melina as an uninvited witness to the act seemed to be adding to his pleasure.

Melina watched in interest as Burian's heavy features stiffened with slow pleasure. Her smile darkened. Men were such simple, foolish creatures. A scrap of food, a few cups of wine, and a woman willing to spread her legs were all that was needed to keep them forever content . . . and firmly within her power. Her husband's firstborn son was no different in this regard. In truth, Burian was more easily swayed than his decrepit old sire.

"Ah . . . not so shriveled after all, I see," she whispered in a low, seductive voice. Her finger slid downward until her hand came to rest atop the roundness of his bare rump, remaining there as he ground his loins against the whore below him in a rhythm that grew more frenzied as Melina's hand stroked his shuddering flesh.

Her fingers dug into his skin, kneading, taunting, and teasing. "But I want to know why you waste your noble seed on nameless whores when you could have me in your bed instead. You know you still want me, Burian—you've wanted me ever since the first time I allowed you to bed me, when you were only a stripling youth eager for a woman's touch."

Burian groaned aloud in response to her words and the slender hand taunting his flesh. He did still want her, just as she'd said, a thirst he'd quenched numerous times since he was a boy of twelve and his father's wife had first come to his bed.

Her fingernail scraped along his skin and Burian groaned again. How was it that he still found her desirable despite the passage of so many years? She had to be a sorceress, a she-demon with power over the wills of mortal men. An ordinary female would have long since lost her physical beauty and been transformed into a wrinkled crone, but not Melina. She was still beautiful enough to hold both father and son in thrall. The unlined face, the rich black hair tumbling down her back, and the lushly formed body belonged to a woman half her age.

"You still enjoy my touch, don't you, Burian?" she prodded in a silky voice.

Unable to stand any more of her torture, he shifted swiftly and pulled himself up on one elbow in order to face her, though he was careful not to break the pounding rhythm of his strokes. "Yes!" he croaked hoarsely. He reached out suddenly and grasped Melina's breast through the silk of her robe, cupping and squeezing it within the palm of his hand while he continued to jab his member into the pale-haired whore.

Melina laughed, a hard, cruel sound, yet she leaned her body closer to his grasping hand.

Burian shouted his relief as his seed finally burst free, spilling fast and hard into the woman beneath him. He shuddered a final time and collapsed atop her, breathing heavily, his body wet with the sweat of his toil. His grip on Melina's full breast turned limp, then fell away.

Melina's dark eyes flashed and her lips curled in scorn, but she was careful not to display that emotion for Burian to see. Though the crown prince possessed a thick, well-muscled body envied by many a man, when it came to sating his needs he was no different than any smooth-skinned boy eager to rut with his first woman. It was a weakness shared in common by all men, one easily exploited by any woman cunning enough to recognize it. And Melina was nothing if not cunning.

"Your father wishes to see you," she announced, purposefully destroying his moment of male triumph.

Burian cursed and dismounted his whore, dismissing her presence completely by pushing her to the opposite side of the bed and turning his back. His face tightened in an angry scowl as he glared at his father's wife. "What does he want this time?" he demanded in a tone as hard and inflexible as his expression.

Melina lifted her chin and pushed a long tendril of black hair from the side of her face. She had enjoyed playing father against son and son against father all these years, a game that never failed to amuse her. "What he always wants these days."

Burian sat up abruptly, unmindful of his nakedness or his withered state. Melina had seen him thus many times before and would do so again. He slammed a clenched fist against the softness of the bed. "Why is my father so set upon seeing Adrik?" The frustrating question had been festering inside him for months now, a burning, pus-filled sore that threatened to erupt in a violent explosion of hatred and revenge. "Adrik means nothing to him! Nothing! I'm firstborn . . . not he! Why would Hedeon insist on seeing a misbegotten son when his time in the Shadow Realm is so near at hand? Does he think to replace me as crown prince? *Now,* after all these years?"

He remembered then that the whore with the curious eyes was still there, listening to their conversation. His gaze narrowed and his head snapped around. "Out!" he yelled at the woman, and lashed out with the quickness of an adder. "And stay out!" The sharp sound of his hand connecting with her flesh reverberated throughout the chamber.

She leapt naked from his bed and raced like a whipped dog through an open portal leading to the portico and terrace, managing to tear down a panel of the silk coverings in her haste to flee. "Leave the palace and don't return!" Burian shouted after her. Vlada could either pay her the promised gold or not, it didn't matter. He was through with her services. The whore's eyes were far too inquisitive for his tastes. Surely there were other, more desirable women with fair hair in Urmia, someone with a face to rival that of the Arizanti's. "Leave Urmia if you wish to stay alive!" he shouted, though she had probably run too far to hear his angry threat. Vlada would simply have to find him a dull-eyed whore with blond hair—one without bones so sharp they bruised his flesh.

The corners of Melina's mouth lifted in a satisfied smile. She'd been glad to see the whore's naked backside flee Burian's chamber. The crown prince's odd fascination with the blond-maned woman had begun to grow quite worrisome. She would have to root out the reason for this new obsession and stamp it out.

"I do not think your father means to replace you," she told him, though she was careful to add a faint note of uncertainty to her voice. Melina sank onto the side of Burian's soft bed and idly fingered the silken coverings. "You and Vlada were the ones who spoke with the Shadow Prince, not I. What was his reply when you told him of your father's desire to see him?"

Burian drew a deep, calming breath as he remembered the reassuring words spoken by his half brother. "Adrik vowed his allegiance to me, not our father. He swears the throne holds no interest for him. He also refuses to see Hedeon, or to come to Urmia at his request. He believes Hedeon only desires his presence because he's in need of a sorcerer of the first rank— one with the power to cast a spell that will cure him of his body's feebleness and renew his life."

Melina's features froze in an expressionless mask, though inwardly she seethed with sudden rage. *Renew* Hedeon's life? She would kill Adrik herself before she allowed the sorcerer to cast such a spell! The foolish old man had lived far longer than she'd ever imagined he would. Hedeon needed to move on to the Shadow Realm. Soon. She would grow ill with disgust if forced to lie beneath his shriveled old flesh many more times. In truth, she would sooner lie with Burian's ugly whore than spend another moment listening to the Median king wheeze and grunt from strain as he tried to force his enfeebled manhood to grow thick inside her.

She leaned toward her husband's son and lifted a hand, her fingers plying gently through the sweat-matted hair layering his broad chest. "And do you believe Adrik's vows?" she asked in a low whisper, deciding to expand her game to include brother against brother.

In years past, she had never truly considered that the reclusive Shadow Prince might pose a danger to her, not hidden away from sight and thought behind the walls of remote Khorazm. But now that Adrik had reached manhood and proved his mettle as both soldier and sorcerer, her husband's second-born son had become a very real threat indeed, both to Burian's future and her own. To ignore such a threat would be foolhardy. Vows such as Adrik's could be broken on the slightest of whims.

"Words are as plentiful as grains of sand . . . and just as unimportant," Melina told him. "Adrik is a sorcerer, after all, an adept of a very powerful demon . . . and demons are renowned for their lies."

Burian's features went pale and still. Had his brother's claims been as meaningless as Melina suggested? His own life and throne could very well depend on their veracity.

He shoved the bed coverings aside and climbed to his feet abruptly, pacing naked until he reached a bronze pot resting in a corner. Heedless of Melina's presence, he relieved himself, then walked back to the stone pedestal and the vessel of fresh wine. Pouring a large cup for himself, he then gulped it down, his eyes never straying far from Melina's watchful face.

"No, I suppose not," he said when the cup had been emptied, his voice as grim and hard as the line of his mouth. He replaced the cup atop the pedestal slowly and stared with unseeing eyes at the intricate design etched into the ewer. "I cannot afford to believe him, not when my throne and the very future of the empire are at risk."

"That is as it should be," she agreed, nodding in satisfaction. Melina watched without expression as Burian scratched at his chest and russet beard with a burly hand. It truly was unfortunate that Burian didn't share his half brother's darkly handsome looks. She would have enjoyed Adrik's company in her bed far more than the crown prince's clumsy attentions. But the sorcerer prince would have been far more difficult to control than the blustering Burian. Impossible, perhaps.

Burian turned slightly and studied Melina's cool features, searching her face for any sign of deceit or treachery. He couldn't afford to believe the honeyed words of his father's consort any more than those uttered by Adrik. She was just as dangerous to him as his sorcerer sibling, and wielded just as much power, especially over his foolish father.

As Hedeon grew more and more feeble of mind and body, Melina's influence upon him only increased. Every proclamation and decree issued forth by the king now bore the subtle stamp of Melina's influence, from the continuing war being waged against the obstinate Lydians, to the useless poultices and treatments requested from Hedeon's physicians. But when it came to the king's newfound obsession with his sorcerer son, Melina's influence carried as little weight as Burian's own. Hedeon was determined to see his estranged son, despite the combined efforts of his and Melina's to persuade him otherwise.

Melina leaned across the bed and lifted the silver ewer and poured Burian a fresh cup of wine. She held out the full cup to him. "And just what do you intend to do if your father does proclaim Adrik crown prince in your place?" she goaded. "Wish him well and vow your allegiance?"

Burian's features tightened, and he slapped the cup from her outstretched hand, spilling the contents and sending the cup tumbling noisily across the floor. "My father will not be allowed to make such a pronouncement! I will see to that! And I will tend to Adrik in my own way, without interference from you!"

For a short span of time, a cold smile appeared to touch her dusky features. "They hold both our futures within calloused hands, Burian, and they care not what ultimately becomes of us." She lowered her voice even further, until it was no more than a breathless whisper. "Perhaps it is time your father and brother learned there are deadly perils to wielding such power over us. Even kings and sorcerers die upon occasion."

He scowled at her for a long moment, and then clapped his hands once, signaling the servant waiting in a small antechamber outside. The same male servant who'd loosened the coverings to block the glare hurried in, his arms laden with the clothing his master would wear this day.

Burian grabbed the brown pantaloons from the servant's arms and shoved his legs inside the silky material, standing silently while the man bound them at his waist with a braided leather cord. Next came a long-sleeved tunic cut from the same bolt of cloth, then a heavy outer vest of silver mail. The tight metal links jangled as the garment settled into place over his arms, chest, and shoulders.

Once his feet and shins were encased within soft boots, Burian jerked a hand, dismissing the servant from his presence. He fastened a short stabbing sword to the clasp at his waist and crossed the chamber to stand directly before Melina, his hand resting purposefully on the hilt of the sword.

"Have a care, Melina. If you try to interfere in this matter, you will feel the cold touch of my wrath. Consorts come and go too . . . as you well know."

She glared back at him. "Are you threatening me, son of my husband?"

"Yes." The single word was as sharp and lethal as the tip of his sword. "I shall decide how best to handle my father and brother, not you."

Melina tossed her head angrily and swept out of his chamber, hurrying, no doubt, to ensconce herself in the throne room at Hedeon's feet before Burian's audience with him.

Burian snorted. He would simply have to watch and

wait—wait until his father succumbed to his various maladies, or Adrik proved his disloyalty by word or deed. In the meantime, Melina would bear careful watching as well.

Vlada frowned and glanced around the empty throne room. "My lord?" the soldier called, his voice echoing across stone and tile in the unnatural stillness. "Are you here?"

His hand moved instinctively to the pommel of his sword. It was too quiet, far too still within the immense chamber where the Median king held formal audiences and conducted affairs of state.

On an ordinary day at least a score of courtiers, servants, and supplicants could be found here, all dancing attendance upon their king. But today must not be an ordinary day, judging by the emptiness and echoing silence. Perhaps the summons he'd received to attend his king in the throne room at midday had been sent in error. Or perhaps the king had simply changed his mind, as was his right. And yet . . .

Vlada's wary gaze searched the length and breadth of the barren throne room, probing shadow-filled corners and small alcoves along the walls for signs of anything amiss. Such a summons would never have been sent in error, and he very much doubted that Hedeon would change his mind about seeing him. Not today. The king knew that he had just returned to Urmia this morning from clandestine meetings with several of the king's most able spies. Hedeon would be eager for any news he might impart.

The soldier walked slowly toward the far end of the room, where the Median throne rested upon a square dais in all its ancient splendor, a massive, high-backed chair carved whole from a single slab of stone sanded and polished to a uniform shade of grayish white. Steps cut from a darker gray stone climbed the dais on all four sides, affording access to the chair perched high atop the flat platform.

A single red pillow sat upon the throne to pad the king's frail body against the harshness of the stone, but there were no other decorations of any kind, no jewels encrusted in the surface or plating of gold or silver. The aged throne's beauty lay in its simplicity, not some grand display of wealth and kingly power. The fact that Hedeon had kept the simple throne when he rose to power was one of the attributes Vlada admired most about his master. A lesser man would have insisted on sitting atop a grand monument to himself.

The soldier frowned. All that was soon to change, however. It was widely known that Hedeon now sought to replace the ancient throne of Media with one more ostentatious, a magnificent golden thing being fashioned by Persian artisans and laborers commanded to accomplish the task. This old one, used by many generations of Median rulers, was to be chiseled and cut into smaller portions, then carried from the palace and discarded in a trash heap near the lake.

The line of Vlada's mouth turned taut and grim. Such a decision was surely the result of Melina's influence. The evil hag would not be content until all of Media rejected its past and adopted the ways and culture of the Persians she sought to emulate.

A flash of movement to the rear of the dais caused Vlada's grip to tighten around the hilt of his sword. He began to ease the blade from its sheath. "Who's there?" He'd seen a quick glimpse of fabric and an arm, enough to warn him that someone hid on the steps behind the platform, obscured from view by shadows and the throne itself. "Announce your presence!"

His fingers clenched reflexively, then relaxed as King Hedeon stepped from his place of concealment and tottered into view.

"My lord?" Vlada said, repeating his query from before, but this time his voice held a fretful note. Anxiety coursed through him. His frail old king appeared tired and unkempt, as if he hadn't rested or changed into a fresh robe in several days. "Are you ill?" Hedeon's skin looked pale and parchment-thin, an unhealthy pallor for even a man of advanced age like the king. "May I call a servant or your physicians to aid you in any way?"

Hedeon shook his head slowly and waved a hand in a vague gesture of dismissal. "No, no." He moved to the front of the dais and sank down onto a step to rest, rendered short of breath by the briefest of movements these days. He lifted his head to one side and stared at Vlada through glazed eyes of an unnatural shade and brightness.

"I need no help," Hedeon insisted. "Especially from the likes of servants and healers such as *them!*" A look of madness glittered in the depths of his eyes.

Vlada stared at his king in shocked silence. The soldier had left Urmia at Hedeon's bidding only two weeks before, as the moon began to wane in the night sky. When he departed, there had been no visible sickness in those familiar eyes, no evidence of the frailty and lunacy apparent now.

Hedeon's mouth trembled, working up and down for an uncertain moment before any sound escaped. A droplet of spittle collected in one corner. "The servants cannot be trusted," he said in a hushed voice, as though he were disclosing a secret of grave importance. "Did you know that, Vlada? We cannot trust them at all." His eyes shone even brighter than before. "They seek to have me look the fool in all things . . . and those traitorous physicians, well, they are the worst of the lot. They seek to poison me with their foul potions and hurry me into the Shadow Realm."

He shook his head from side to side. "But their efforts will be to no avail! Wait and see . . . wait and see. They will fall to their knees before me and seek my

Jan Zimlich

forgiveness, but I shall order them killed instead . . .
tied to a stake and flayed until their skin falls away into
my hands."

A thin snigger of laughter broke free of his lips, and
he raised a finger, flourishing it close to Vlada's face.
Whether the king sought to silence him with that finger or admonish him Vlada couldn't say.

"Not Melina, though, never her. . . . She would never
seek to harm me. She grieves for me already because
those treacherous physicians have tricked her into believing I will soon die. But you see, I've tricked them
instead, Vlada, all of them. They have all been foolish
enough to forget that my son is a Magian sorcerer. He
is an adept, and will smite them down with a terrible
spell if I but give the word . . . and I swear that I will
not hesitate to give that word."

A tremor ran through Hedeon's frail arm, and he
finally lowered the finger raised in Vlada's face, allowing his hand to fall limply to his lap. "Adrik will protect
me and make my body whole again," he announced
proudly. "His spell will make me young and strong, a
bull among women and a general feared by our foes.
My armies will then defeat those Lydian dogs once and
for all, and my empire will spread past Sardis to the
shores of the Aegean Sea!"

Hedeon glanced beyond Vlada to something unseen,
his luminous gaze suddenly cold and empty, drained
of rational thought. "I think I shall burn Sardis and
have King Alyattes and his bastard sons beheaded . . .
his daughter too. Yes, that's what I shall do."

He bobbed his head in agreement with his own cruel
imaginings: then his thoughts veered course once
more with deranged quickness. "You'll see that I'm
right, Vlada . . . Adrik seeks to bask in the goodness of
my presence. He will come to me soon and cast his
spell because he is grateful for all that I have done for
him. He must be. If not for me, the prophecy could

not be fulfilled. He would simply have died along with his Magian mother. But I made certain he never wanted for anything, and that he lived all these years so he could fulfill his destiny. Adrik knows this. He'll come soon. You'll see . . . you'll see."

Hedeon suddenly fell silent.

Vlada's armored vest clinked quietly as he bowed his head and sighed. Madness, pure madness. The king he had served and admired for so many years was obviously lost. The man Hedeon had been was gone forever now, the same as Vania, the Magian princess he'd loved so long ago.

Vlada's throat tightened around the knot of pain that had wedged in his chest when the king first mentioned Adrik's dead mother. He had loved Vania from the very moment he saw her, when the young bride and her caravan rode through the gates of the Busae fortress for the culmination of her arranged marriage to Hedeon. The Magian princess had been clad in her wedding finery that day, a costly robe of flowing red silk shot with gold. Even now Vlada could still remember the glint of the sun through her night-black hair, how she looked sitting astride that tall black horse, her back straight and proud.

But most of all he remembered the very first smile Vania had bestowed upon him, tossed his way when he'd stepped from the crowd of onlookers and grasped the reins of her horse so she could dismount. Her smile had been easy and kind, a gesture that clearly revealed her innate goodness and warmth for all to see. He had loved her from that moment onward, despite the brief marriage that allied Magian and Busae and consolidated Hedeon's power over all the tribes. Because of her vows to Hedeon, and the fact that Vlada was a simple soldier and she was of noble blood, he had never had the courage to act upon his love—but deep in his heart he knew that Vania had loved him, too.

And Adrik was her son, born on that terrible night when the black shadow of an eclipse had fallen across the moon, cloaking the world in sudden darkness. As the darkness reached its peak, Vania had died, her life ebbing away in a gush of blood as she thrust the infant free of her loins.

Vlada tried to forget, to unwedge the knot of pain from his chest, but he found that the wound to his heart had not healed with time. The hard, bitter truth of it was that he hadn't been near when Vania needed him most, and for that he would never forgive himself. He'd been gone from the fortress for several days before she died, trying to drown his forbidden thirst for the king's pregnant wife with endless cups of wine and the company of cheap whores.

To his eternal shame, he hadn't been there for Vania's child, either. By the time he had awakened from his drunken stupor and returned to learn of her death, a grieving Hedeon had already given permission for the Magians to take the child to distant Khorazm, granting them rights over his second-born son in accordance with Vania's wishes.

It wasn't Vlada's place to question the actions of his king, no matter how strange the decision to simply hand his own flesh and blood over to the Magii without protest. Hedeon's shock and grief over Vania's unexpected death had obviously caused him to make such an unfeeling decision. And Adrik was, after all, the fruit of an alliance between rival tribes. With Vania gone, the newborn infant had become hereditary ruler of all the Magii, so Hedeon had been right to respect their claim and give the child's rearing over to the Magii in accordance with their law.

That's what Hedeon had told him, and what Vlada had always believed. Yet there had always been tales of that unspeakable night . . . the gossip and rumors of midwives and servants who'd spread stories of demons and hellish bargains—and even worse things.

Ever since that night, it had been whispered among the tribes that the child had been born beneath a terrible shadow and was doomed to live out his life in darkness, a tale that soon gave rise to the name that followed Adrik to this day, that of the Shadow Prince.

Vlada shook off this hideous spate of thoughts and doubts he'd allowed to take root inside him, the same dark misgivings that had haunted his sleep many a night for nigh on twenty-five years now. The hushed tales of that fateful eve were simply that—tales without substance or truth, and any who gave credence to such talk was guilty of defaming the king's good name.

Vlada's spirits felt winter-bleak. He could not afford to entertain such doubts. To do so would be a betrayal of the king he both served and admired, and a stain upon his own honor. That, the soldier could not abide.

And yet, the uncertainties always remained, burrowing deep within the darkest recesses of his thoughts. Though he would kill the much-feared Shadow Prince if ever the empire or his king required it of him, Adrik Kiryl was still the child of his beloved Vania, the woman he had loved beyond reason or rational thought. A debt remained between him and the child, one that had gone unpaid since the night of Adrik's birth.

But would that debt still remain when he told Hedeon the news he brought with him from Sardis?

Arched doors swung open at the end of the throne room, the heavy wood propelled into motion by two of Hedeon's personal guards. Vlada's attention swung to the sound of many footsteps against the tiles of a mosaic decorating the central portion of the floor. The brightly hued mosaic was an immense depiction of a younger, armored Hedeon slaying a pair of massive bulls with mighty thrusts from twin golden swords held in each hand.

The footsteps quickened, and the courtiers, guards, and servants missing from the throne room before hurried past the mosaic, their heads and eyes cast down in formal obeisance as they neared the end of the chamber where their enfeebled king sat upon the steps of the dais.

Vlada soon glimpsed the king's consort among the gaggle and grimaced. Unlike the others, Melina's head was held defiantly erect, her shoulders unbowed. Burian was the only other who dared approach the throne without bending his head downward, but as crown prince, that was his right.

Melina bypassed Vlada without acknowledging him and dropped to her knees at Hedeon's feet. "Husband!" she said in a voice dripping with concern. "I have been searching for you! I grew worried when I failed to find you in your bedchamber."

Burian scowled and took a hasty step forward, as if he were about to mount the dais himself, then belayed his movements abruptly. He stood where he was and continued to scowl.

Melina glared back at him from the corner of her eye and rested her head upon Hedeon's thin knees, as would a loving, dutiful wife. Her arms wound themselves about the king's lower legs, like thin snakes coiling in readiness to strike.

For a brief moment, Hedeon's glazed eyes failed to grasp the identity of the woman clutching at him; then he suddenly lifted a gnarled hand to stroke her silken hair. "Melina, my beloved, forgive me for causing you concern."

"Let me help you rise, my husband. You should sit upon your throne, not these cold stone steps. I do not wish you to grow ill."

The king allowed her to help him stand and clung

to her elbow as she guided him up the steps to sit atop his throne. He settled onto the plush red pillow with a tired sigh and released his hold on her arm; then his ancient face stretched in an approving smile. "I am blessed by your presence, wife. The gods surely smiled upon me the day I brought you into my palace."

Melina preened and gave the nearby glowering Burian a small, smug smile. The crown prince had threatened her with bodily harm if she dared to interfere in the lives of his father and brother. Burian had blustered that he alone possessed power over their fates, but in truth, it was she who held title to that claim because the old king trusted her far more than any other. "The gods smiled upon me as well, husband," she told him in a honeyed tone, loud enough to be certain Burian and the others overheard. "But you must rest and not overtire yourself. I would grieve until the end of my days if you were taken from me. I prefer you to remain here, close to me, for many, many years to come."

Vlada cleared his throat and shifted uncomfortably, while the courtiers and onlookers simply smiled and nodded at such a warm display of affection between their king and his consort. The soldier risked a quick glance in the crown prince's direction, and found a red-faced Burian openly glowering at his father's smug wife.

Frowning, Vlada glanced from one to the other. Burian's rage was a tangible thing, a fierce layer of emotion that seemed to pour from his body in waves of scorching heat. An ill wind had blown between the two, but what had caused it he could not say. A fresh conflict to be sure. The crown prince appeared ready and eager to choke the life from Melina with his own bare hands.

The aging soldier cleared his throat once more to try and gain the king's wandering attention. The sooner this audience ended, the better for all concerned. "My lord . . . the report on my journey you wished me to give?" Vlada gently reminded him.

Hedeon's snowy brows pulled downward in confusion. "Report?"

"Yes—the journey I took at your behest? Spring will be upon us in a matter of months, and the battles for the lands to the west will begin anew. In preparation, you wisely sent me to meet with those who spy for us in the Lydian capital of Sardis."

"Ah, the report . . . yes." The king's brows drew upward again, reclaiming their normal position. "What did you learn from them?"

The soldier stiffened his shoulders. He had planned to impart his news in private, but the king's deteriorating condition had distracted him from his task. "My lord, such news was meant for your ears alone."

He saw Melina's gaze narrow with anger—with him undoubtedly, for daring to suggest that his words were not meant for her ears as well. Then she whispered something to the king, and Hedeon nodded in acquiescence.

"Speak your news now," the king ordered him. "All those present have gained my trust by their loyalty and deeds. There is no need for secrecy from any here."

Vlada was now more certain than ever of the king's growing madness. Secrecy was paramount when dealing with information uncovered by the empire's spies. Hedeon knew this, or he had known it at one time. Stranger still, his fresh words were in startling contrast to the disjointed natter about untrustworthy servants and physicians uttered just minutes before.

"I am waiting, Vlada," the king said testily.

Vlada raised his chin to a bold angle. "Remember, my lord, the Lydians have spies, too, possibly within the walls of this very palace. Would it not be better if we discussed the matter later?"

"I am your king, Vlada, and I have given you a command! If there are spies here among us, I will rout them from the shadows and have them put to death! Now speak!"

Vlada dipped his head slightly, acknowledging the king's impatient command. "As you wish, my lord." The soldier caught Burian's eye, but found no sign of aid from that quarter. He would just have to do what he'd been ordered, regardless of the consequences or any debts of honor left unpaid. "Our spies in Sardis have reported that King Alyattes' younger son, Pantaleon, is only recently returned from a journey made at his father's request."

The soldier paused for a moment, drawing a long breath to steel himself against the coming response to his revelation. "His journey took him to Khorazm, where Pantaleon sought and was granted an audience with the Shadow Prince."

A thick veil of stunned silence settled over the crowd clustered about Hedeon's throne.

It was Burian who first found his voice, though his broad face had grown pale and haggard with shock. "What is this? My brother has met with a Lydian prince?" The words exploded from his throat, laced with heat and fury. "Our enemy?"

Courtiers and servants alike muttered and shifted their feet, glancing at each other and their king with expressions of outright fear.

The paleness gradually faded from Burian's coarse features and was replaced by an angry suffusion of red. If this news was indeed true, then Adrik had already given the lie to his vow of allegiance, just as Melina had implied. "Where and when did the spy say this audience occurred?" he demanded furiously.

"It is said the meeting took place two weeks past . . . within the very walls of Khorazm. The substance of the talk is not known, but the courier who carried the news from Lydia reports that rumors have begun to spread in Sardis that the king's daughter will marry a foreigner in late summer."

Vlada said no more. The implication of this announcement was clear to all who were present.

"No!" The old king leapt to his feet so unexpectedly that Melina lost her grip on his legs and fell to one side. Hedeon clapped his hands to his ears. "I do not believe these lies! I refuse to hear any more!" Hedeon sped down the steps of the dais and hurried toward a rear door, his hands still clapped to the sides of his head to blot out the sound of their voices.

"Hedeon!" Melina shouted after him, but the king wasn't listening. He was muttering to himself as his aged body sped to a doorway that led to the private areas of the palace, moving more swiftly than anyone thought him able.

As he vanished through an open archway, Melina pulled herself upright and glared at Burian through narrowed eyes. "I warned you this would happen!" she hissed. "Now what are we to do?"

Vlada closed his eyes and waited. He knew what was coming even if the others did not. The repercussions would now begin.

Burian's features knotted with rage. Everything was clear to him now. His future was set, and the path he should take had finally been revealed to his eyes. Adrik had betrayed him, and for that he would die.

Chapter Seven

Seabirds soared overhead, circling high above the rock-strewn shoreline as daylight faded and the sun eased toward the chain of mountains huddled along the western horizon. Lorienne sat atop a moss-covered boulder and watched the setting sun grow huge and orange, bathing the quiescent waters of the Caspian Sea with a mantle of vibrant color.

She breathed deeply, grateful to be finally free of Khorazm's confining walls, even for a short while. She had spent the better part of the afternoon walking the thin strip of beach, enjoying the fish-tinged scent of the sea, the rush of sound the cool waters made as they lapped and pulled at the rocky shore. The sounds and scents were new to her and far more pleasant than those found in the musty tower where her time was now spent.

Though the Shadow Prince had finally granted permission for her to leave the fortress in the company of a guard, she knew he marked her progress from within his tower. She could feel those brooding eyes upon her even now, still sense his presence somewhere near, as if he were watching her from only a few steps away, not from the fortress high atop the cliff rising behind her. It wasn't the first time she had sensed such a gaze upon her, either. She had awakened more than once in the night to the feeling of eyes observing her every move. Could this be more of the same?

She glanced around her in puzzlement, studying the desolate shore for signs that Prince Adrik was somewhere nearby. To the left of her, the strip of sand and small stones along the tide line ended abruptly, replaced by a tall outcropping of rock that jutted into the sea.

Her confusion deepened as she perused the jagged tumble of stones. For a brief instant, she thought she had seen the dark shape of a wolf watching her from atop the outcropping, its muscular body cast in shadow by the glare of the waning sun, but the shadow quickly melted away, leaving only a view of rock and sky.

A sudden chill touched her skin, and Lorienne folded her arms about herself, unsure if the chill had originated from within or without. Had the eyes she felt resting on her been those of a wolf or a man? Adrik Kiryl was said to possess a special affinity with the creatures of the forest and night. Perhaps the wolf had been sent to watch her in his stead. If the sorcerer were indeed capable of such a peculiar feat, he was far more dangerous than she had first imagined, and she had imagined many, many things in the preceding days.

It had been weeks now since the sorcerer brought her to Khorazm, but the passage of time had not led to any greater understanding of him or his abilities. He had revealed little of himself beyond the fact that he was the Magian sovereign and that he considered her to be his possession. Yet he did not treat her as though she were a mere belonging to be used or discarded.

She touched the rich fabric that now robed her, part of the clothing he'd ordered made for her. The long under-robe of dyed wool was soft and warm, its hue the deep, pleasing green of spring leaves. A heavy outer vest made from lamb's wool fell in a straight line almost to her feet, protecting her from the cold of winter that had begun to sharpen the air. It was the finest clothing she'd ever owned or worn, fit for someone born of noble blood. So why would he make such a gift to a woman he considered no more important than chattel? The clothing of a servant would have sufficed in its stead.

Stranger still, Adrik Kiryl had made no real attempt to stake his claim upon her body, despite the words he'd exchanged with the Lydian prince and his refusal to sell her to him. But ever since she had been obliged to sleep upon a pallet next to the sorcerer's bed, and had not been allowed to leave his chamber or the tower itself without permission from him.

Her features clouded with sudden worry. Surely he wouldn't command that she continue to sleep on that little pallet once he wed the Lydian princess . . . would he? The marriage was set to take place in the summer. She and Jirina had both overheard the bargain struck between the sorcerer and the Lydian prince, and the sorcerer's soft-voiced acceptance of a Lydian bride. The wedding ceremony would occur in a matter of months, after winter and spring lost their holds upon the land and summer began in earnest.

And once that marriage took place, her position within Prince Adrik's household would become even more tenuous than now. At present she was neither concubine nor consort. Nor was she one of the low women who dwelled in the cities and traded their bodies for a few hides or a bit of gold.

But the sorcerer's princess bride might well treat her as a harlot. No wife would take kindly to the notion of

91

Jan Zimlich

another woman sleeping beside her marriage bed, and the Lydian might seek revenge upon her in the cruelest of ways.

Lorienne didn't particularly relish the idea of being an unwilling witness to their beddings, either, a humiliating thought that carried with it sudden, heated memories of her first encounters with the Shadow Prince.

Although many days had passed since then, she could still remember the searing touch of his eyes upon her naked flesh, how his firm hands had sought to hold her in place. And yet somehow his iron grip had carried with it the feel of a heated caress. She remembered, too, how her own body had betrayed her on that morn, the strange eagerness inside her to feel the caress of those hard hands upon her skin.

She leapt from the rock abruptly and walked along the tide line, angry with herself for allowing her thoughts to veer down that path. Why should the very memory of the sorcerer's touch fill her with such an aching sense of need? She should be content that he had not sought to claim her. But instead of relief, she felt an odd sense of urgency growing deep inside her, as if her body craved that which her mind warned her to reject.

Resolve suddenly burgeoned in her: She would no longer allow herself such wanton thoughts. Whether the Shadow Prince wed the Lydian or not should be of no true concern to her. He was simply her captor, and she his unwilling slave, one determined to regain her freedom when the opportunity arose. By the time the Shadow Prince's bride arrived, Lorienne planned to be gone from Khorazm. If the gods smiled upon her, she would be far from the fortress and its darkling prince before the chill hand of winter tightened its grip upon the land.

She cast a covert glance over her shoulder, to the

young guard assigned to watch over her. Garbed in the black uniform of a Magian soldier, he remained some ten steps behind, granting her at least the illusion of a solitary walk. But his watchful gaze never strayed far from her or their immediate surroundings, and his hand stayed firmly affixed to the hilt of his sword, as though he sought to protect her from the possibility of attack as much as to prevent her escape. But that protectiveness might simply be a display of youthful bravado, because she couldn't imagine any enemy fool enough to stage an attack within sight of the Magian fortress.

"My lady!" the guard called out to gain her attention.

Lorienne halted her progress across the rocks and turned as the lower portion of the sun finally vanished in a blaze of orange light. "Yes?"

The guard stared first at the fast-darkening sky, then gazed up at the fortress perched high above them. "The day grows late. We must go back to the fortress now." He gestured toward the steep pathway they had used to reach the shore. "Prince Adrik will be angry if we delay."

Lorienne dipped her head in acknowledgment and sighed. "Very well." She started up the sloping path, dutifully picking her way past rocks and prickly scrubs sprouting from crevices and the sandy soil.

If she tried to dally, the prince might well blame it on the young guard and punish him when he had done nothing to merit such ill treatment. She had no wish to see Damek suffer in her place, nor for the prince to grow so angry he denied her the freedom to venture outside the fortress again. That would indeed be unfortunate. It had taken much time and effort on her part to convince Jirina to intercede on her behalf in order to gain permission for a simple walk upon the beach. If she ever hoped to flee, she needed to acquire as much knowledge about the surrounding landscape as possible, and the only way to do that was to see it firsthand.

Until today, when Adrik Kiryl placed her in Damek's charge, she had not even been allowed outside the tower itself, much less the fortress walls. Nor had she been given the chance to converse with any within Khorazm other than Jirina or the prince himself. And the Shadow Prince had said very little to her in the preceding weeks. In truth, he appeared intent on avoiding her company as much as possible, leaving her with Jirina each morning while he, in turn, remained absent from the tower until late in the day. A strange occurrence, indeed, since he had seemed so determined to bed her scant weeks ago.

Yet she knew he still desired her. She could see his need burning like flame in those flinty black eyes. She could sense it in the way he held himself when she was near, so watchful, aloof, and still, as if he feared the consequences if their bodies happened to touch in some way.

The pathway grew steeper, the footing more treacherous as the rocky trail narrowed even more, winding back and forth up the face of the cliff. The scrubby grass clung to the bottom of her under-robe, and loose sand shifted beneath her boots, making each step seem an arduous task. Her foot caught in a small mound of scree and she stumbled slightly, sending a storm of small rocks, sand, and debris careening down the side of the cliff.

Damek grasped her arm tight to help hold her upright. "Have a care, my lady!" the guard said worriedly. "Prince Adrik will flay the skin from my bones if you come to harm."

She leaned into him until she regained her balance, then gave him a shy smile. "Thank you. I promise to be more careful." She continued climbing the winding pathway at a more measured pace, glancing down every now and again to judge how much distance they'd covered. The steep ascent to the base of the fortress was far more wearying than the downward climb had been.

She halted her progress for a moment to draw a breath and to wipe away the thin beading of moisture dampening her brow. Damek stood close and waited for her to continue, obviously unaffected by the harshness of the familiar climb.

Her gaze shifted from the shore below and settled on his youthful face, probing his thin features for answers to the questions that had plagued her for weeks. "Tell me of your prince, Damek," she asked in a quiet voice. "I fear I've learned little of him in my time at Khorazm."

"There is nothing to learn," Damek said warily.

The soldier's look of suspicion told Lorienne to proceed with care. "Please, Damek, I have had no one to speak to other than Jirina, the Mistress of the Tower, and she either speaks in vague riddles or tells me nothing of value."

He was silent for a long moment before he answered. "What do you wish to know?" he asked finally, though he still seemed reluctant to speak at all.

"Is he truly a sorcerer?"

"Yes," the soldier said uneasily, his gaze drawn upward instinctively. "He knows we stand here and speak of him. He knows all within the fortress, and all within the fortress know that. There are no secrets among the Magii. And what he does not know from us, what he does not know of the forest and mountains beyond our walls, the wolves and other beasts are quick to tell him."

A frustrated frown crossed her features. This soldier spoke in riddles too, the same as Jirina. "But what of the *man,* Damek? What of Prince Adrik?"

His uneasiness increased, and a shadow of worry passed through his eyes. "What is there to tell, my lady? The Magii know the ancient prophecies, and what

95

shape the future holds for our prince. The change is coming . . . very soon now. Nothing can prevent the coming darkness. It was written in the stars long ago."

Anxiety knotted the center of Lorienne's brow. The answers Damek provided were even more elusive than Jirina's. The old woman had also spoken of prophecies and a coming change, but when pressed she fell into a stubborn silence and would give no further details. Perhaps the change of which these two Magians spoke was the prince's forthcoming marriage to an enemy princess, an event sure to spark anger among the Median royal family as well as a few other tribes.

The very thought of the upcoming wedding caused Lorienne's fears to rise and taunt her once again. "You said there were no secrets among the Magii. If that is so, then tell me why Prince Adrik continues to hold me inside his tower. Why must I remain in his chamber? Why can I not live as the other servants within the fortress walls?"

Damek's gaze shifted from her face, as if he could no longer look her full in the eye. "To keep you safe, perhaps," he answered quietly.

"Safe?" She exhaled a disbelieving breath. "I think more dangers await me within his tower than here outside."

Damek glanced nervously at the dusky sky. "You do not yet know what dangers lie in our land, my lady. If you wish to remain safe, you would do well to heed the prince's commands." He looked at the sky once more. "Hurry. The pathway will soon be cloaked in darkness."

She had no choice but to obey. The sun had all but vanished behind the mountains, and night was descending swiftly. To delay her return longer would prove fruitless anyway. Damek obviously had no intention of answering more questions.

A few moments later they reached the narrow ledge where the dark gray stone of the fortress and the dun-colored cliff butted one against the other. High above the walls, the tower that had been carved from a much darker stone rose into the night, like a thin black finger reaching toward the heavens.

As Damek signaled their return to the guards atop the battlement, Lorienne gazed up at that black tower. She felt the Shadow Prince's eyes upon her again, and knew he waited for her return.

A small wooden doorway cut into the base of the fortress swung open, and a guard carrying a torch appeared to light their way through the short tunnel running through the thick outer wall.

Lorienne followed the torchbearer in silence, ignoring the tunnel's dank, musky scent and the scurrying of small creatures through the dark. Behind her, she heard Damek closing and bolting the wood door with a heavy iron bar. Before the torch bearer moved too far and the torchlight faded to nothingness, she threw a quick glance over her shoulder to peruse the details of the portal, taking careful note of the latch and the amount of noise made as the bar dropped into place.

If needed, the small doorway and the trail to the shore might well provide her with a path of escape. Fleeing through the wooden door in the dead of night past a troop of guards would be difficult, but not impossible. Yet if she were fortunate enough to make it through the door, far greater dangers awaited her outside. Indeed, footing on the pathway leading down to the shore might well spell her end. In pitch-darkness, without Damek or a torch to guide her steps, she might slip and plunge to her death from the steep cliff. And if she were to believe Jirina and young Damek, unspeakable perils lurked beyond the fortress walls, unknown beasts and creatures lying in wait for her to try and escape.

But if she were truly destined to die here, such an end might be preferable to countless years spent as a

97

prisoner inside this dark, lonely tower, her only company the stiff-faced Jirina and the prince's future consort.

The tunnel ended abruptly, and Lorienne stepped past the narrow entrance into the courtyard beyond. Pleasant smells drifted from numerous doorways surrounding the courtyard: the scent of meat spitted over cooking fires, fresh bread warming in the ashes in preparation for evening meals. She heard sounds of laughter as well, the bawling of hungry infants, and the quiet conversations of soldiers, servants, and wives.

Familiar sounds. Comforting smells, the same sorts found within any Arizanti village when darkness fell and the women began to make ready the evening meal.

She longed to linger in the courtyard, to walk among the villagers' number and join in their preparations and repast—yet she didn't dare attempt such a thing. These were Magians, not Arizanti. Strangers. Her company would not be welcome here. Indeed, scores of suspicious eyes were following her progress across the wide courtyard even now, searching her face for answers to questions better left unvoiced.

Her cheeks flamed with heat and color. Most were simply the stares of the curious, but a few of those watching faces were stiff with censure. Lorienne lowered her head instinctively to shield herself from view and fastened her gaze on the flagstones instead. Damek had told her that there were no secrets among the Magii. If that were truly so, all present this night knew she slept in their prince's tower. They probably thought her a whore.

The steps leading into the tower appeared beneath her, and Lorienne mounted them quickly, relieved that she would soon escape the view of those censorious eyes. Even the walls of the prince's tower were preferable to the scorn of the Magians outside.

The arched doorway swung open slowly, and Jirina

motioned her through, the small torch the woman carried lighting a path into the darkened hall beyond.

Damek and the other guard retreated instantly, retracing their steps to the courtyard.

"Thank you, Damek," Lorienne called after him, but the young soldier failed to respond.

A cinder from Jirina's torch sparked and fell to the stone floor. "Come . . . the prince has been awaiting your return," the old woman told her, and stepped aside to allow Lorienne inside. She redirected her light toward the winding staircase leading to the upper levels of the tower. "You are to cleanse your body in the way of the Magii this night."

A sudden dread touched the nape of Lorienne's neck with icy fingers. She had been in the tower long enough to comprehend that cleansing of the body was often the harbinger of a Magian ritual. Her sense of foreboding increased. "What does this mean?"

Jirina met her gaze for an instant but remained silent. The torch held before her, she began climbing the steep staircase. "Follow me."

Lorienne hesitated at the base of the steps and followed the old woman's movements with her eyes instead.

"You *must* come," Jirina said over her shoulder. "The prince has ordered it."

Sighing, Lorienne trailed after her, though she was loath to do so. The command issued by the Shadow Prince was further proof of her precarious situation. If she refused to obey him, even in a small matter like this, he might well have her put to the sword, and no one would care.

To her surprise, once they reached the prince's level, Jirina kept to the staircase and continued her upward climb. The steps narrowed and grew steeper, just as the pathway up the cliff had done.

She glanced about curiously, although there was little to see. Until now, she had not even been allowed to climb this high. No windows or portals were cut through the tower walls, preventing even the faintest glimmer of moonlight from falling upon its dark interior.

Save for Jirina's tiny torch, they were mantled in pitch-darkness as they ascended, the steps winding in a dizzying pattern that ended in a sudden apex when the ceiling appeared to reach down to touch their heads. Then they stepped through a small hatchway mounted into the ceiling and emerged atop the tower's long flat roof.

Lorienne halted in midstep and gaped at the view from atop the tower. True night had fallen across the sea and mountains, veiling the sky in a hue as black and deep as that found in the winding staircase. Above her, stars shimmered in the darkness, a thin ribbon of cold light curling across the night. She felt as if she had been lifted whole from the world she knew and set down inside an enchanted realm where magic held sway.

Closer at hand, the tower's roof stretched before her, the long expanse broken by the placement of massive urns and pottery vessels large enough to hold a plethora of flowering vines, small fruit trees, and sweet-smelling bushes. She could hear the peaceful sound of falling water nearby as well. The steady sound was cool and compelling, even though a chilly foretaste of winter hung in the air.

Jirina walked behind a tangle of vines and leaves and directed the glare from her torch to a huge square-shaped cistern embedded in the roof itself. Another cistern formed a partial wall behind the first, the huge vessel rising to a height several steps above that of an adult male. Water trickled from an ornate spout jutting from the side of the clay vessel, the thin stream falling gently from the open mouth of a stone fish that continuously replenished the liquid held in the cistern be-low.

"You may cleanse yourself here," Jirina announced as she waved a bone-thin hand toward the lower cis-tern.

Lorienne stared into the maw of the cistern silently. The water looked deep, as deep and bitingly cold as any river or mountain stream she'd ever bathed in. But she doubted Jirina would allow her to leave the roof without immersing her body as the Shadow Prince re-quired.

Sighing, she quickly shed herself of her fleecy outer vest and the woolen robe beneath, then stepped over the lip of the cistern and began lowering her body in-side, gasping in stunned surprise as the warmth of heated water closed around her naked legs. The water wasn't truly hot by any means but it wasn't mountain cold, either. Tepid was perhaps a better word, the same sort of warmth found in a pot left to cool over the embers of a dying fire.

"It's warm," Lorienne exclaimed, and laughed aloud in delight. She clung to the lip of the cistern and plunged her body deeper, lowering herself until all that remained above the surface was her head and shoulders. Her toes brushed against the curved bot-tom, and she relaxed her grip on the side slightly, no longer afraid that she might slip so deep into the cis-tern that she would drown. "How is this possible?"

The old woman smiled in response to Lorienne's amazement. "There is a small clay oven in the chamber directly below the cistern. In the cooler months, Prince Adrik has the servants keep the fire in the oven stoked so the flames lend a bit of warmth to the water in the cistern above."

Lorienne shook her head in disbelief, luxuriating in the feel of her long hair sliding through the warm wa-ter. She had heard of such things before but had

101

thought them a lie. "Your prince truly is a sorcerer," she mused aloud, and thrust her head beneath the surface, rising again a moment later to shake away some of the moisture clinging to her hair. "What other wonders does his tower hold?"

Jirina's gaze suddenly drifted from hers and settled upon something unseen. She cleared her throat and handed the girl a small bronze jar filled with a blend of fragrant herbs and oils. "This is to help cleanse your skin."

Lorienne sniffed at the contents and tilted the jar over her shoulders, breathing deeply as the thick liquid slid downward along the surface of her skin. In truth, the scent was quite pleasant. She rubbed at the oily mixture, spreading it along her face, arms, and chest, and massaged what still clung to her palms through the lengths of her hair. "This feels wonderful," she said, more to herself than Jirina.

When she was done, she dipped her head beneath the surface of the water again and again to rinse the wet strands free of the oil. Her eyelids tightly shut against the sting of the oil, Lorienne finally broke the surface sputtering for air, laughing aloud at the sheer pleasure afforded by the bath. She hoped other Magian rituals were as pleasurable as this.

She rubbed at the moisture wetting her face and clung to the side of the cistern with one hand, still unable to reopen her eyes. "I hope you have some linen for me to dry myself, Jirina," she said, laughing, to the servant. "I fear my clothing will become sodden if I try to put it on now."

In answer, a soft length of cloth touched the side of her face. Lorienne clutched at it greedily, dabbing the remaining water and oil from her face and eyes. Smiling contentedly, she reopened her lids and gasped, her pale eyes widening in horror.

"I—" Her cheeks flooded with scalding color. The

Shadow Prince was kneeling beside the cistern, a mere step away. It was he who'd pressed the linen cloth to her cheek, not Jirina. She glanced around wildly, but the old woman had vanished completely, leaving no sign that she had ever been atop the roof at all.

Lorienne felt weak and ill of a sudden, the beating in her chest so loud and painfully swift that she thought she might faint away. Only Adrik was here with her, watching with those darkly burning eyes.

"Jirina . . . she was with me," Lorienne finally said in a quavery voice that grew weaker with each word. She knew she sounded foolish, but she couldn't seem to find her tongue.

Adrik rose to his feet abruptly and continued to watch her, unable to force his gaze from the enticing vision before him. For weeks he had tried to bury the wellspring of desire burgeoning inside him, ignored its very existence until he found he could do so no more. Now, after so long, the torrent of need he had carefully hidden away was threatening to burst free of all constraint. And where was the harm in that? It was time he cast aside worries of the future and allowed himself to feel at least a small measure of pleasure. The change would be upon him soon enough, and when it came to him, he would no longer feel anything at all. It was long past time to grant himself permission to savor the sweetness he'd been hoarding for this day.

"I sent Jirina away," he said in a voice suddenly grown hoarse. He allowed his gaze to slide along her naked skin. Her pale hair and freshly oiled flesh shimmered with droplets of gold cast by the torchlight, as though her body were sheathed in a patina of gold. "The ritual does not concern her . . . only you and me."

Her grip on the cistern's curved edge tightened reflexively. *Oh, gods.* After all the waiting and fear, the moment she had dreaded most had finally come to her like a thief in the night from the shadows atop the

Jan Zimlich

tower. When Jirina first told her of the ritual cleansing, she had suspected what this night might hold, and the heat burning in Adrik's eyes had proven those suspicions true.

She stared up at him mutely. After tonight, she would no longer find safety in the little pallet beside his bed. The sorcerer intended to claim her now.

Lorienne could think of nothing to say, no words that might sway him from the course he had chosen, and in truth, she no longer knew if she wished to sway him from that path. Though she feared what was to come, she felt as if this moment had been preordained long, long ago.

Lorienne pulled in a deep, calming breath and lifted a submissive hand, waiting for Adrik to aid her in rising from the cistern so she could accompany him to his bed. But to her surprise, the Shadow Prince ignored her uplifted hand and shed himself of his boots and overvest instead. Then he quickly stripped off his silky tunic and pantaloons and stood before her, his powerful body bared for her to see.

"I have denied myself long enough," he said hoarsely. "I intend to bed you this night."

Lorienne tried to swallow away the sudden tightness in her throat. With each moment that passed she found it more difficult to breathe. Though she longed to do so, she found herself unwilling and unable to glance away. Adrik stood before her unashamedly, his lean body gleaming in the light cast by the little torch Jirina had left standing in an iron holder.

Lorienne stared at him in silence, awed by the strength and power contained in his chiseled form. The Shadow Prince had the appearance of a statue carved by the hand of a master stonecutter, each sinewy muscle in his broad shoulders and arms shaped and molded to perfection. The smooth expanse of his chest tapered downward to a narrow waist that joined slender hips and corded thighs, the lines and muscles revealed in stark relief to her eyes. If any male could be said to possess great physical beauty, it would surely be this one, for his lean face and body were truly magnificent to behold.

She drew in a sharp breath as her gaze suddenly brushed over that which she had sought to avoid: His manhood stood ready, thick and heavy with the proof of his desire, far larger than she had imagined it. Color stained her cheeks once more, and the fluttery beat of her heart trebled. He planned to lance her with that thickened length.

She bit down on her lower lip, her tongue and mouth useless and dry. It required an effort of will to force her gaze from the spear rooted between his muscled thighs. She stared upward and waited for whatever was to come, her gaze fixed on his finely chiseled jaw, the sharply angled lines of his face.

He was watching her in return, the heat of his gaze searing a fiery trail down her neck and throat. Lorienne longed to plunge herself deeper into the cistern, to tamp out the flames burning across her skin, but she could no longer move or think or see anything beyond those smoldering eyes.

The Shadow Prince's hot gaze was relentless, holding her firmly in place as he lowered himself into the cistern beside her, the warm water rippling around him as it closed about his naked form.

A rush of anxiety gripped her. Did he plan to take her here and now, immersed in a cistern of water? She had never heard of such a thing, yet the very thought of it made her heart beat even faster than before.

The jar of fragrant oils still sat beside the cistern. The Shadow Prince picked it up and poured a stream of the liquid onto his own shoulder, then lifted Lorienne's hand and placed it atop the shimmering patch of oil. "You must cleanse me," he whispered huskily,

Jan Zimlich

his enigmatic eyes darkening with desire, "and I shall finish cleansing you. It is what my people do to prepare themselves so that our bodies may know each other . . . even if our minds do not."

Her hand trembled mightily as her fingers plied the oil, slowly rubbing the slick liquid onto his shoulders and neck. His softly spoken words had wrapped themselves around her like the costliest silk, as though his hoarse voice held a rapturous spell that compelled her to obey.

As her fingertips slid across his skin, Adrik closed his eyes and gave himself over to the rush of sensations generated by her touch. He had wanted to possess Lorienne since the very moment he had first seen her, and yet, for reasons even he did not fully fathom, he had denied himself the pleasure of her body for interminable weeks. Was his refusal to take her intended to spare her in some way? Or was it a punishment of sorts, a form of self-torture intended to inflict even more misery upon himself?

He drove the disquieting thoughts away. The reason for his reticence was of no consequence now, for he had finally made the decision to act upon his desire, no matter the price he would pay. Watching her walk upon the beach this day had somehow unraveled his intentions and set him on this dangerous path.

A tremor of fear suddenly moved through her body, one so powerful he could feel it through the tips of her fingers, but he felt no remorse or shame for bringing that fear about. She belonged to him, and it was his right to claim her if he wished.

To prove he had that right, perhaps to himself as well as her, he reached out suddenly and pulled her hard against his chest. The abrupt contact of his flesh caused her to draw in a startled breath, a little sound of shock mingled with pleasure that only served to increase his desire. He wanted to hear that sound again, to feel her pressed hard against him.

Adrik poured a dab of the fragrant oil down the center of Lorienne's back and began slowly massaging it into her skin, his hands caressing, touching, and exploring her. She gasped as his fingers slid downward, gliding beneath the surface of the water to caress the hollow of her lower back. He bent close and breathed in the fragrance of the herbs and oil still clinging to her hair, a fresh scent somehow reminiscent of wildflowers and a cool spring day.

Lorienne's eyes, huge and round, remained fixed on Adrik's face as he explored the contours of her back. He could feel the quick rise and fall of her chest against his own, a feathery sensation akin to the panicked fluttering of a bird's wings. Her fear was so strong he could almost touch it, almost smell its presence swirling in the air around them, as though it were a living creature about to take flight.

The temptation was irresistible, and so he eased one hand around the curve of her hip and placed it between them, his slender fingers dipping lower to move within her. But the feel of his hand and fingers exploring that secret flesh increased Lorienne's fear to a fevered pitch. She made a frightened noise and struggled to pull away, flailing blindly in a desperate desire to escape.

Instinctively, Adrik wound his arms about her to keep her from fleeing his embrace. "Are you still a maiden?" he asked in a probing voice.

She dipped her head once in a fearful nod, still seeking a way to free herself.

"You have nothing to fear from me," the sorcerer said quietly, his softly spoken words laced with a soothing spell conjured to ease the worst of her fears. The number of lovers she'd had mattered not to him, but a maiden required gentle care if he were to bring her pleasure.

"I will not harm you, Lorienne." Often lies were best hidden amidst a forest of truth. "I seek only to pleasure myself . . . and you, this night." He added power to his sorcery and shaped his words so that they wrapped around her like fleece.

His mood darkened and he fought an almost irresistible urge to ravage her now, to thrust himself inside her loins again and again, riding her body with the mindless abandon of some wild creature. The urge was like a fever, a black heat festering in the blood.

He clenched his jaw tight and fought to stem the darkness rising inside him. With each use of magic, he lost yet another tiny sliver of his humanity and moved ever closer to transforming into the thing he was destined to become. The rising tide of darkness would soon swallow him within its horrid depths, and he would become a creature of the Shadow Realm.

The black urge to savage Lorienne gradually faded, and Adrik heaved a ragged sigh. The price he had paid for this soothing spell was far steeper than the last. Soon there would be nothing left of his soul to lose. Perhaps there was nothing left already.

Lorienne's trembling slowed, and she felt an odd sense of warmth spread throughout her body, as if the warm water within the cistern was somehow flowing inside her as well. She knew she should be frightened, should flee from Adrik if possible, yet deep inside, she was aware on an instinctual level that the sorcerer did not plan to harm her. He sought pleasure, nothing more, and she no longer possessed the will to resist.

The tension in her shoulders faded abruptly, and her arms and legs turned leaden, useless, as if they belonged to another. She leaned into Adrik's embrace, unable to support the numbing weight of her torso and legs. His arms wound tighter, drawing her close against him.

Lorienne gasped aloud as her breasts were crushed against the Shadow Prince's chest. Without conscious thought, she thrust herself against him even more, the heat generated by the feel of her flesh on his causing a wave of desire to build deep inside her. She could feel his manhood pressed against her, hard and demanding, thick with need, but oddly, she found that she no longer dreaded what would soon come. In truth, the feel of him hard against her abdomen made her almost giddy with anticipation.

Adrik made a tortured sound low in his throat as he sensed her beginning to yield. Something hot and fiercely primitive flared to life inside him, a terrible ache deep in the core of him only Lorienne could take away. Suddenly, he no longer cared if he lost his humanity. He would conjure a score of spells if he must. All that mattered was this single moment in time and the woman who would bring him pleasure this night.

On impulse, he bent his head and kissed her, brushing his lips across the warm softness of her mouth until the taste of her was imprinted on his mind forever. Slowly, he felt her begin to respond to his gentle exploration, her lips quivering beneath his as she tentatively sought to explore him in return.

He groaned again, unable to prevent the sound from slipping free of his throat, then deepened his kiss, caressing the ripe contours of her mouth with his lips.

His hands locked around her hips, and he cupped her pliant flesh within his palms, dragging her so tight against him he could have slipped himself inside her if he wished. But he stopped himself just shy, his member throbbing with eagerness. *Soon,* he promised himself.

He could hear himself breathing faster, panting with need like a wolf about to mount its mate, yet he managed to cage the beast within him by sheer force of will. He wanted to savor this night, to sate both his own desire and hers with long hours of gentle bedding, not spend his seed in some mindless animal frenzy. For this one night, he wanted to live the life of a mortal man.

Adrik lifted his lover swiftly and seated her on the cistern's edge, revealing her womanhood and breasts in such exquisite candor he found their nearness hard to resist. His mouth and hands ached to explore her, to plumb the secrets of her body with his fingers and lips. He wanted to suckle at her breasts, to taste the droplets of water clinging to her thighs with the tip of his tongue.

Instead, he backed away from the edge of the cistern, distancing himself from the overwhelming temptation of such lush breasts and velvety thighs. He had sworn to pleasure her virginal body as well as his own, and it was a vow he intended to keep.

Soon now, he promised himself again. And when he was done, he would need no further spells to ease her path into his arms. She would come to him willingly for all the time he had left.

His dark eyes sought and found hers. "Go. . . ." he instructed, his voice raw with need and passion. If he continued with the ritual cleansing, it would inevitably end with him taking her in the mindless frenzy he had hoped to avoid. "Take the torch and return to my chamber . . . prepare yourself."

The very thought of what would soon transpire turned the heat inside him into an all-consuming flame. He needed time away from her, a span of solitude to collect his thoughts. Otherwise, the torrent of black heat boiling inside his body might finally break free of its shackles and gain release. "I shall join you after I see that the gates are secure and the night watch is on duty."

Lorienne nodded woodenly. The pounding in her

chest had grown so loud it was almost deafening. Did Adrik hear the beating too and know he was the cause? "I shall be waiting for you," she finally managed to whisper, and swallowed hard. She had only spoken the truth. Despite everything, despite her fear of him, she would indeed be waiting for him, her breast pounding with expectation. She wanted the pleasure he had offered as much as he.

Trembling, she climbed to her feet quickly and gathered up the dampened linen to shield her body from those relentless eyes. She clutched the sodden linen to herself and grabbed her discarded clothing as well as the little torch, then fled barefooted across the tower roof to the small hatchway and stairway beneath.

Once she reached the safety of the stairwall, she paused in her downward flight for a short moment and pulled in a great gulp of needed breath. How had she come to this? Her legs and hands wouldn't cease shaking, and she felt as if she couldn't draw the proper amount of air. Desire had done this to her. Despite all she knew of the Shadow Prince, all that she feared, she desired him as a man, and would soon give her body over to him. And she would do so willingly, even eagerly.

The door to his bedchamber loomed before her, the heavy wood dark and brooding in the thin flicker of the guttering torch. She eased the door open and stepped inside, relieved to find herself in familiar surroundings once again, though she knew she should feel awkward and discomfited within these rooms.

She dipped the dying torch into a clay lamp to light the oil and wick within. The lamp flickered and caught, casting a welcoming glow across the dark. A second lamp stood lit on a pedestal near the tower window, the haze of yellow light brought to life by Jirina, no doubt, before the woman had left for the night. A silver ewer and tray holding cups, bits of fruit, and a loaf of dark bread sat waiting atop the table, left for them by the Mistress of the Tower as well.

The sight caused Lorienne's mouth to twist in a grimace. She had no appetite for either wine or food just now. Her stomach felt tight and quivery, as if she might soon be ill, and her legs refused to rest, carrying her this way and that about the tenebrous chamber at a nervous pace.

Her hands still trembling, she paused long enough to quickly don her robe and overvest, and smoothed the rumpled fabric back into place. She remembered then that she had forgotten to finish drying herself with the damp linen. Beneath the woolen robe, droplets of water still clung to her skin, the liquid trailing down the length of her body to gather in little puddles upon the stone-tiled floor.

Her restless limbs sent her into motion again and she found herself lying atop the Shadow Prince's bed, as though he had woven a spell to direct her body to recline itself in just such a way. Once she realized where she had finally settled to rest, she wanted to leap into motion once again, to place as much space between herself and the softly piled hides as possible. But oddly, she couldn't seem to gather the will to rush away, so she simply lay among the fleecy skins, anxiously watching the play of shadows along the walls. Waiting for him to arrive.

The lamps within the chamber suddenly guttered, their once comforting glows sputtering and shrinking until all that remained were thin tongues of flame. And then the yellowish light vanished entirely.

Lorienne froze, the hammering in her chest transformed from anticipation to fear. Her frantic gaze was drawn instinctively to the sliver of light cast by the tiny torch in a sconce near the door, the only shield that remained between her and the dark. Then it too sputtered from existence, and a thick, heavy darkness descended with a suddenness that left her fighting for air.

The only light was a thin haze of silver from beyond the tower window, but even that was so muted to be almost nonexistent, the moon and stars obscured by gathering clouds.

Lorienne lay in the cloying darkness and tried to convince herself that her fear was misplaced. The Shadow Prince had told her she would come to no harm, and she believed his soothing words. Too, in the past she had already noted how lamps appeared to mysteriously light and extinguish themselves whenever the Shadow Prince was near. This was just more of the same.

She shivered in the darkness as a chill breath of wind rode across her flesh. Then suddenly he was there, his fingertip trailing along the length of her arm in a feather-soft caress.

Lorienne gasped as his hand moved lower, down to touch her thigh, then upward once again to explore her heated loins. At his touch, she whimpered and shifted restlessly, eager to feel his hand hard upon her, to be free of the constraining robe once more.

Outside the tower, the clouds thinned and parted, lifting from the slivered face of a newborn moon. A pale finger of moonlight slanted through the window and lit a narrow path across the shadowy chamber, illuminating a shimmering form hovering above her, its eyes burning in the dark like hot red coals.

It laughed, a harsh, cruel sound.

Lorienne screamed.

Chapter Eight

Mocking laughter echoed across the shroud of darkness, a monstrous cackle of sound that stabbed through Lorienne like the sharpened blade of a knife. The shape's eyes gleamed malevolently, bloodred holes seething with rage and loathing.

"Are you not pleased to finally see me?" it whispered in a dark insidious voice. The creature shimmered, vanished, and reappeared again, its translucent form having no more substance than that of a puddle of water spilled upon the floor.

Lorienne tried to scream again but terror choked her throat so that the only noise to slip free was a breathy little whimper.

"Why act the terrified virgin?" it asked slyly. "You know I have watched you these past weeks. You've sensed my presence before."

Lorienne shuddered. It was true. She had felt a presence in the shadows many times, something observing her with cruel intent, but she had thought Adrik responsible in some way, not this inhuman thing. And it *was* inhuman. She was certain of that. This creature had been born of the Shadow Realm, not of the earth.

"Begone from here, foul creature!" she managed to croak. "Return to your own realm and leave the living alone!" She lifted a hand and quickly made the warding sign her mother had taught her to fend off evils from the darkness beyond. This was surely an evil from that darkness, a demonish creature that didn't belong in the company of the living.

It simply laughed, obviously amused by her feeble attempt to produce a ward. "You cannot evict me from my own abode!" the thing said gleefully.

The words caused Lorienne to feel as if her bones had turned to ice. What did they mean? "Your abode? Khorazm is the fortress of Adrik Kiryl, Prince of the Magii," she retorted with as much confidence as she could muster. "The Magian prince is also a sorcerer, and he will soon come to cast you from his tower!"

She glanced at the shadowed doorway, hoping against hope that the sorcerer prince would indeed come to rid his fortress of this evil monstrosity.

Unconcerned with the possibility, the demon seemed to drift on a blanket of air. The thing was beside her now, a cadaverous smile slashing across skull-like features that wavered as if they were made from water. "I think not," it whispered back to her. "Who do you think trained your heroic young prince in the ways of sorcerers?"

Its eyes darkened, turning a red so deep and bloody that they gave the appearance of holes set within a grinning skull. "Adrik is my son, you see, and no son would ever cast out his own father. The truth is, he brought you to Khorazm for me. Adrik knows I have a certain . . . predilection for tender little virgins like yourself."

The demon touched her with a single finger, and she felt as if a serpent had slithered through a coil of her hair. She shrank away from the foul caress, pushing herself downward into the skins piled on the bed, but she couldn't escape the shadow's fetid presence or those glaring red eyes.

"Lies!" Lorienne said vehemently. "All lies!" She didn't want to think about the possibility that the Shadow Prince might have been spawned from this hideous thing, didn't want to consider that the prince might have truly offered her body to this creature like a tasty bit of meat heaped upon a platter. And she never wanted to feel that slithery touch again.

The demon's smile stretched wider. "The truth of it is before your eyes—I am here, and Adrik is not. Have you not wondered why that is so? My son simply wearied of your presence and sent me to dispense with it. In his eyes, you are but a foolish little mortal, a bothersome annoyance, whereas he is a prince of the dark realm, destined to become the most powerful demon ever known! He cares not what becomes of you and your pathetic kind."

The shadow creature's snakelike finger eeled through Lorienne's hair once again. "I have come to pluck the flower of your maidenhead in his stead, young virgin. And when I am done, I am afraid you will be withered and dead."

Lorienne bolted from her bed and raced headlong to the door, swinging it wide as the sickening sound of gleeful laughter filled the darkness behind her. She raced madly down the curving steps without benefit of a torch or boots, her bare feet slapping and scuffing across the chilly stones.

Tears scorched her cheeks and stung her eyes. She had to get away, to escape this terrible evil that sought to kill her in the prince's bed. Her only hope was to run, run as fast and far from Khorazm as her trembling legs would carry her, and to do so without delay. And when she could run no more, she would cast herself from a mountain ledge rather than give herself over to that demonish thing.

A haze of light from a wall torch lit her way to the tower's arched entry. Lorienne barely slowed, pausing only long enough to fling the heavy door wide so she could escape. And then she was down the limestone steps and running swiftly across the flagged courtyard, a small sweeping figure rushing instinctively toward the opening in the fortress wall that she had entered only hours before.

A sentry shouted from the darkness atop the battlements, and Lorienne quickened her pace, plunging into the narrow tunnel as the tramp of boots rang across flagstones somewhere behind her.

Darkness engulfed her, thick and rank with the scent of must and decay. Chest heaving, she came to an abrupt halt and began feeling her way along the grimy tunnel wall. She could see nothing in the utter blackness, not even the pale flesh of a hand when placed directly before her eyes. All that pierced the still blackness were the sounds of her strangled breathing and the squeak of scurrying vermin. Her questing fingers found fur and movement on the wall and instinctively recoiled, but then she collected herself and moved on, feeling her way through the pitch-dark with only her fingers as guides.

There were other sounds behind her now: muffled shouts near the tunnel entrance, the stomping of many feet. The sentinels standing watch had been mustered and were now in close pursuit.

Suddenly, Lorienne found the tunnel's end. She ran trembling hands along the small wooden door, trying to retrace the workings of the latch and bolt from only a sliver of memory. Then her fingers closed around the heavy iron bar and she jerked it upward, crying out in relief when she heard the workings of the latch give way.

A moment later, she was free, the chill breath of a night wind whispering across her cheeks. The clouds shading the moon and stars lifted again, throwing a soft haze of silver across the cliff and seascape below.

In the glow of that pale light, Lorienne found the narrow footpath leading down the face of the cliff. Heedless of the danger, she lifted her robe and plunged down the path, running and stumbling along the precarious trail as she sought the shore below.

Rocks and scrub tore at her bare feet but she ignored the pain. Her tears fell in earnest now, channeling down her face to wet her neck and jaw. She was free. Whether she died this night or another, no one would ever imprison her again.

The shouting came from above her now. Torches flared, bright, harsh orange, as the guards exited the tunnel and held their flames aloft, searching the darkness along the side of the cliff. Lorienne raised her face and saw the sentries' shadows hulk along the top of the cliff, cinders from their torches lifting and swirling on a gust of wind. Then she lowered her face and veiled her features with blowing strands of hair, lest the guards catch a glimpse of her pale flesh in the moon's glow.

As she struggled down the treacherous path, the sounds above her grew. Several guards were now on the pathway behind her. She could hear their heavy breathing, their curses as they stumbled and slid on the dangerous path.

She increased her speed, her bare feet gripping the rocks and gravel where boots would not. Soon the sounds above her dwindled away, swallowed by distance and the slow rumble of the sea below.

And then the cliff fell behind and Lorienne found herself on the thin strip of beach once more, wending her way across the sharp stones piled along the shore. She winced as a rock dug into the sole of one foot but she didn't dare come to a halt. Time was of the essence. If she thought to make good on her escape she needed to be far from the fortress by first light.

She needed to keep her wits about her as well. Though another pursuit by the guards was inevitable, it would likely arrive from a direction never expected; thus she couldn't afford to rest or hesitate now. To the east, the shoreline and wide sea lay directly beneath the cliff and fortress walls, preventing any hope of escape by that route. Instead, she would have to wind around the outside of Khorazm to either the north or the south and make her way into the surrounding mountains. Perhaps she could then head north into the towering sweep of the Caucasus, once the forbidding home of the Arizanti tribe. There, she might find a deep cave high in the mountains where she could hide herself until the Magii wearied of searching or spring finally came, whichever was first to arrive.

But before that occurred, she somehow had to bypass any pursuers leaving the fortress through the heavy main gates. By now, a company of guards would have likely exited Khorazm's main entrance to lie in wait for her when she rounded the fortress walls. So she would have to avoid them somehow, perhaps flee farther south than they expected, into the deep forest, and then she could double back on her path and head north to safety deep within the mountains.

She darted up an embankment, across a rocky field, and into a thick wood south of the fortress walls, ignoring the stabs of pain from her bleeding feet. South it would be, at least for a while.

The flares of many torches were visible atop the battlements now, tiny splotches of orange high above the tops of the surrounding trees. She could see that a few moved along the brow of the cliff, searchers still threading their way along the treacherous path, but their numbers were few, and she began to feel em-

119

boldened by the dearth of guards engaged in active pursuit.

It was full dark now, the darkest part of the night, when her chances would be greatest to flee through the woods without detection. Above the treetops, a thick roof of sullen clouds was riding across a black sky heavy with the promise of rain. As if to fulfill that promise, a fat drop of moisture suddenly fell upon the back of her hand, then another and another.

Lorienne breathed a sigh of relief. The gods were watching over her this night. The guards wouldn't be able to find her near as easily in the dark and rain. Her footsteps would vanish soon after their creation, and any crackle of sound she might make would be lost in the fall of the rain.

A sudden memory of what had transpired in the tower caused the flesh along her nape to rise. The Magian guards were not all she needed to fear. What if one of her pursuers was a demon, not a man? Would mere wind and rain cloak her presence from its inhuman eyes?

Torches lit the night, throwing twisting shadows across the watchtowers and stone battlements. Adrik glowered down at the guards filing slowly into the courtyard below, their gazes cast downward to the flagstones beneath their feet, as if they sought to avoid his eyes. What had begun only an hour before as a casual task to retrieve their prince's wayward captive had now transformed into something else altogether. Failure was clearly written in their listless pace, the sag of armored shoulders once held proudly erect.

Against all odds, Lorienne had made good her mad escape.

Young Damek glanced up to where Adrik stood atop the battlements, the guard's misery apparent in his worried expression. It was he who'd shown the girl the way down the face of the cliff that very afternoon.

The expression on the face of Adrik's second in command looked as miserable as Damek's. "Forgive us, my lord!" Harpagus called. "We have failed you! She appears to have made it down the cliff path to the shoreline and vanished into the wood. But she cannot be moving fast! The tracks we found on the path prove her feet are bare. Unless she carried boots tucked beneath her arms, she is completely unshod."

Adrik's mouth tightened grimly, and he slammed a fist against a slab of stone in frustration. He didn't blame Damek or any of the others. It was his own failure, not that of his soldiers, for he himself had given permission for Lorienne to walk with Damek upon the beach. It was he who'd been foolish enough to leave her unattended once she knew a pathway to flee the fortress.

He cursed himself silently. The responsibility lay with him, no other. When Lorienne was near, he had thought of nothing save her enticing scent, the lure of her full mouth and silken thighs. He had allowed himself to become enamored of her, besotted by the very notion of bedding a tender young virgin while he still wore the body of an ordinary man. For a short while he had pretended to be a prince like any other, but Lorienne had given the lie to his hopeless fantasy.

"Have my horse readied!" he ordered suddenly, and watched in satisfaction as several of his chastened soldiers leapt to do his bidding. "I shall hunt her myself . . . alone."

No one dared quibble with his pronouncement. All knew their Magian prince was well equipped to carry such a plan to fruition. With the aid of his beasts, he could track her through the deep forest far more swiftly than any mortal man, whether she was unshod or not. Which he would do. He would hunt as long and far as needed to reclaim that which was his.

121

As the quarter moon reached its apogee and began its slow descent toward day, Adrik returned to his chambers to prepare for his journey north. Northward was the direction any Arizanti would surely go, to the Caucasus, and Lorienne was no exception. The rugged mountains and hidden chasms of her childhood would beckon like a mother's teat to a hungry child.

He wrapped himself in his heaviest overvest and thickest boots, and made ready a small bundle of fresh clothing for Lorienne as well, frowning as he added the doeskin boots she had left behind. Only a fool or a half-wit would have raced headlong into a cold fall night without benefit of boots or preparations of any kind. And from the little he knew of Lorienne of the Arizanti, she was neither dull of wit nor a fool. Her mind and will were as strong and able as any man's.

So what had possessed her to act so precipitously? One moment she had seemed ready and willing to yield herself to his attentions, the next she had fled both him and his fortress with a suddenness that defied explanation.

Adrik slung his baldric and sword over his shoulder and sheathed a short stabbing blade at his waist. As he lifted the bundle of spare clothing and prepared to leave, a faint shimmering of light near the window caught his attention.

The sorcerer half turned, his eyes narrowing with sudden comprehension and all-consuming rage.

Malkaval.

It was all very clear to him now. The reason for Lorienne's flight was no longer a mystery. After an absence of long weeks, the demon had returned to Khorazm to wreak his cruel havoc upon them both.

Adrik's gaze narrowed even more. The apparition was there yet not there, a water-thin shade whose very presence filled the chamber with a cloying presence of unease and dread. "This is your doing," Adrik accused.

His voice was deathly quiet. "You have caused her to run away."

Malkaval laughed in response, his filmy eyes shining with glee. "Fear not, my son, you shall have her back soon enough. This is only the beginning of an amusing game. I plan to hunt her in the forest tonight. You may join me if you wish. The sport of such a hunt will pleasure us both."

An eerie calm stole though Adrik's body, a calm so cold that he felt a trace of wonder at its cause. In all his years he had not been filled with such a powerful sense of resolve as this. For the very first time he felt he possessed the ability and strength of will to defeat the demon Malkaval at one of his own merciless games.

He drew in a breath and gathered himself to work a powerful spell that would cast the demon from Khorazm forever. The magical energy wove around him like the silken threads of an insect's web, drawing closer and tighter, growing in intensity as he prepared to lash out with all the force at his disposal.

"If you bring harm to her in any way, I shall cast you from my fortress and my life forever!" the sorcerer threatened. "And then I shall refuse to make the transformation when the time comes . . . dooming you to remain as you are for all time! Is that what you desire?"

Malkaval's skullish smile melted away. The holes that were his eyes darkened and crackled with rage-red fire. "You dare to threaten me?" he bellowed, each word like separate peals of thunder crashing across the shadowy chamber. "You will do as I command or I will smite you from the face of the earth!"

Adrik stiffened his shoulders and gazed directly into those terrible eyes. "Then do so."

The demon's gaze widened and turned a liquid crimson. The shimmer that clung to him grew brighter and stronger, incandescent with rage.

Adrik met the demon's maddened gaze with a steadiness he had never known he possessed. "I care not if I die a mortal's death," he told the demon. "But you, on the other hand, you care greatly—for if my mortal self dies too soon, you will be condemned to live as you are for another thousand years."

Time passed, and still the demon glared at his human charge, his anger deepening as he realized the ominous depths of Adrik's resolve. "You would threaten me with that which I most desire . . . just to protect this one mortal girl?"

Adrik's mouth was flat and hard. "Yes."

Malkaval glared malevolently. He longed to strike out, to obliterate Adrik from the living world, to burn the skin from his body a finger's-length at a time, then peel away the crisped flesh and gorge upon it as the sorcerer was forced to watch himself slowly devoured. Yes, Adrik would pay for these ungrateful words. Pay a hefty price indeed for his mortal arrogance.

And yet . . . if he were to truly deal the ingrate such a killing blow, the ramifications would fall upon Malkaval himself as well. There would be no human host to take his place when that brief portal opened between the Shadow Realm and the living world. He would then, just as Adrik had said, be condemned to a miserable spectral existence for another hundred hundred years.

Have a care, he warned himself. He could not cast away a thousand years of scheming for the sake of a careless gesture of revenge.

A glint of slyness flared inside the demon's reddish eyes. He would seek his revenge in other ways. Far more subtle ways. The demon's deathly smile slashed across the width of his shimmering features. "Then go find your puny female, *human*." The demon hissed that last word as if it were a terrible curse. "I care not anymore. But you shall have no help from me in your fool's quest."

And then he was gone, swirling and condensing into a smoke-thin curl of light that collapsed upon itself and vanished.

Adrik stared at the now empty shadows, a sense of foreboding twisting through his thoughts like a poisonous vine. Malkaval would return. Soon. The demon would not just slip quietly into the shadows until it was time for the exchange. And when he did return, Lorienne would pay the price for Adrik's rebellion.

He hurried from the chamber and down the steps, unsurprised when he found Jirina waiting for him near the tower doors. The old woman held out a felt pouch filled with hard bread and a round of cheese, as well as a goatskin flask of wine. Wordlessly, he slung the straps to the pouch and flask over his shoulder and made for the open door.

"Be wary, my lord," Jirina said quietly. "May the back of your head grow new eyes upon it so that you see all that hides in the darkness."

Adrik met her gaze for a moment, then left the safety of his tower behind and descended the steps. A cadre of guards waited below with lit torches and glum expressions. His horse was waiting for him there as well, its hooves beating nervously at the flagstones as the dark beast danced and twisted with impatience.

The sorcerer leapt atop the animal and settled himself into his small saddle, draping his pouch and flask around the high pommel in front of him. A soldier then handed him his bow and a quiver of bronze-tipped arrows. As he slung them across his shoulder with the baldric, he nodded a silent acknowledgment to his soldiers and reined his nervous horse into motion.

Adrik soon left the arching gates of Khorazm behind, following the winding cart path as it snaked gently down the side of the mountain toward level ground. With each curving turn in the switchback, his eyes searched the northern landscape for any sign of Lorienne, but he saw nothing to draw more than his casual attention.

As the pathway wound lower and lower, the dark gray shapes of wolves began appearing in response to his silent call, the creatures slinking out of the night to fall into swift step behind his horse. Their numbers gradually increased, the pack growing ever larger as they neared the edge of the thick forest.

Adrik glanced at the wolves gathering around him and frowned. Though he recognized many of the creatures that had come in answer to his call, the wolf most familiar to him wasn't among their number.

"Where is Sandor?" he asked the others worriedly, and closed his lids for a short moment, opening himself to the profusion of tenuous images that suddenly drifted through his thoughts. He saw trees and darkness and a cloudy glimpse of Lorienne's pale hair streaming through dense brush. Like shades drifting through the afterlife. He could sense something else as well . . . an ominous scent curling on a breath of wind.

His lids snapped open and he nudged his horse southward. "Find them," he told the other wolves, and watched grimly as the creatures loped into the forest and vanished. He just hoped they caught Lorienne and Sandor before something else did.

Lorienne's footsteps grew more hurried, despite the bite of briars and branches that lashed at her from the darkness like barbed whips. Without the thick protection offered by her woolen robe and fleecy overvest, most of her flesh would surely be torn and shredded by now. Even so, her face, hands, and bloodied feet burned like fire from numerous encounters with the forest's grasping limbs. The whip-thin branches had torn at her head as well, ripping away long strands of hair from her scalp.

Above her, the wood had grown so dense and thick the glow of the moon and stars had all but vanished, replaced by the blackened shapes of huddled trees and skulking brush. But at least now there was a carpet of fallen needles and decaying leaves beneath the soles of her feet, not the sharpness of briars and rock, so she was able to increase her speed, even though she could barely see in the heavy darkness to take each step.

She'd once seen a man who'd been blinded in battle, scars and half-healed wounds where his eyes had been. His children had been leading him about the camp, directing his every step lest he fall and further injure himself. That was how she felt now, blinded and risking injury with each blundering movement.

The droplets of rain she'd felt earlier began again. A moment later the rain came down from the sky in earnest, falling in a light shower that beat upon the leaves and dark trees with a muffled wash of sound.

Lorienne pulled her sodden fleece tight about her and shivered against the growing chill. Her clothes, already damp before leaving the fortress, were now saturated and heavy, and felt as if they were a weighty bundle upon her body.

Even worse, her feet were bare, numbed by cold and pain, and her hands and cheeks stung from the lashing from limbs and rain. But there was little she could do to fend off the ill effects of the growing downpour. She had nothing dry and warm to cover herself, and unless she were able to obtain boots and fresh clothing from somewhere, that state wasn't likely to change. She reminded herself more than once that she had been raised an Arizanti, a nomad of the high mountains and steppes long familiar with exposure to the sting of cold and rain.

The loud snap of a twig in the dark nearly caused

127

her to flatten herself against the trunk of the closest tree. Her breast pounding with renewed fear, Lorienne glanced around wildly, unable to discern much of anything in the black and rain. Another twig suddenly crackled, as though it had been crushed beneath a boot or paw.

Damek's admonitions came back to her, and she had cause to wonder if the sounds had been created by the very dangers the young soldier had warned her against.

She remained still and tight against the trunk of the tree, waiting and watching her surroundings. There was a scuttling, scuffing sound nearby, closer than before, as if some creature were padding quietly through the fallen leaves.

Her gaze thinned in the darkness, targeting the dense undergrowth that had given rise to the threat. She could hear panting now, the quick huffs of some doglike beast pulling in air.

Wolves, she thought uneasily, and flattened herself against the wet tree even more. Memories of another place, another terrible night shivered through her thoughts.

The glint of beastly eyes shone briefly, and Lorienne felt a sudden rush of relief. Those eyes had glowed yellow, not the red she had come to dread most. A solitary wolf then.

A bewildered frown touched the center of her brow when she realized she was no longer afraid. Oddly, her fear had melted away like rainwater dripping from the trees the moment she realized it was a wolf hiding in the wood. It hadn't been hunger or hatred she sensed in the glint of those golden eyes; it was curiosity instead.

A large gray wolf suddenly broke free of the brush that had veiled it from view, but came no closer to where she stood. Instead, it threw one last yellow glance her way, then padded off on a path that would run parallel to hers, as if the creature sought to accompany her from afar. It was a comforting notion somehow.

Lorienne expelled her breath in a weary sigh, then pulled away from the tree and continued on her way, still moving southward, into the heart of the deep wood.

The rain was falling heavily now, a great wall of moisture that made finding her way through the darkness even more difficult than before. She stumbled over a decaying log, a limb or branch or some other bit of debris jabbing into the side of her foot like a wooden dagger.

Wincing from the searing pain, she propped her foot on the log and carefully explored the area until her fingers found the splintered wood protruding from her flesh. Lorienne jerked it free and placed the weight of her foot flat on the ground, gritting her teeth as the pain immediately increased.

She bit back a frustrated sob. She could ill afford such an injury now. Her pace would surely be slowed, and the journey would become far worse when she turned to the north and began climbing high into the mountains, barefoot across rocks and uneven ground. She would have to stop and rest before that time, and somehow fashion makeshift coverings for her feet.

She hobbled on through the woods despite the pain, unwilling to give up now, not when she was so close to being completely free. Even though storm clouds still boiled overhead, the sky was growing lighter, signaling the pale beginnings of a new day. If she tarried, the Shadow Prince or his guards would surely find her with the dawn.

As she walked she could feel the sticky wetness of blood seeping from her injured foot, and was gladdened once more by the presence of the pounding rain. She was leaving a blood trail, an easy path for both men and beasts to follow. Hopefully, the rain would wash that away, too.

It was then that she heard the first growl, a low rumble of sound from somewhere deep in the brush. Lorienne froze, listening and waiting. The beating of the rain filled her ears. So did the pounding of her heart. The beast that had given that low growl had sounded far larger than any wolf.

She swallowed the fear rising in her throat and glanced around the rain and darkness with wary eyes. It growled again, from the right somewhere. The trees were thicker there. Taller. Like blackened sentinels arrowing up into the night. Underbrush filled the narrow spaces between the rain-dampened tree trunks, shielding from view any creature clever enough to secret itself there.

Brush rattled—not the dry movement of leaves and wood, but wet sound, like the slap of soggy leaves as something large pushed them aside. From her left, she heard a snuffling, snorting sound as well, as though the snout of some creature was rifling through damp leaves after a scent.

Two directions. Two beasts. More than likely the wolf was one, but the other, the source of those terrible growls . . .

The pounding in her breast grew louder. Damek and Jirina had both tried to warn her. Tigers prowled the forest floor in the lands bordering the seashore, a forbidding place where few humans dared to venture. The Caspian tigers were the true rulers of the deep forest, bearded kings large enough to devour a small child whole. Those gaping jaws and knife-sharp fangs could even tear the limbs from the torso of even the mightiest warrior.

Fear became a living thing inside her, coiling in the pit of her stomach like a serpent preparing to strike.

She didn't need to see the creature to know it was indeed a tiger.

She could hear it moving now, sounds louder than the rainfall as it pushed aside the dense brush and slinked in her direction. The tiger was stalking her, preparing to make a meal of her flesh. If she wanted to live, she would have to run, even though the blood leaking from her foot would leave a clear scent the creature would surely follow.

Her body shivered from the terror brought on by the thought of death within the maw of a tiger. She forced her leaden feet to move, small steps at first, then faster and faster as she started running headlong through the forest, heedless of the limbs grasping from every side, the heavy, padding tread of the tiger close behind her. She could hear it huffing, feel its enormous form drawing closer, gathering itself to spring. But that moment never seemed to come, as if the beast were playing a game with her, stalking her though the woods out of some perverted sense of pleasure.

An unseen limb hit at her cheek, the impact almost felling her. She kept running, though it was an effort to do so. Her chest was burning, as if she were breathing fire with every panting gasp. She was tired and winded, almost to the end of her endurance, but she knew if she stopped, the creature would be upon her in an instant.

The urge to turn and face the danger head-on was overpowering, an instinctual need driving her to toss a single glance over the top of her shoulder, to gaze just once upon the face of her own approaching death.

She fought the urge, that terrible instinct to know, until she could fight it no more. Her head snapped to one side, and she strained to see the tiger racing through the darkness behind her. For an instant, she caught a glimpse of a lumbering shadow, a huge mass of orange and black striping and red . . . bloodred eyes boiling with hatred.

Lorienne wanted to scream but could spare no breath for that purpose. She ran on instead, driven by an even deeper terror than before.

And then something crashed through the brush beside her and leapt into the rainy air, snarling furiously as it hurtled into the creature behind her. Lorienne heard snarls and growls and screams as the wolf and tiger slammed one into the other, the collision throwing both animals off balance and sending them crashing into the dense scrub in a rolling tangle of teeth and claws.

After a second's hesitation, Lorienne kept running, crying in fear and relief as she dashed madly into the night, unmindful of the cold and rain or the pain burning in her foot. The wolf had saved her, thrown itself into the tiger's path in her stead, if her pursuer was indeed a tiger. She was no longer certain. She'd seen those glowing red eyes before. Unearthly eyes.

Her tears fell steadily. She wondered if the wolf had survived.

Chapter Nine

A copse of elms stood tall and unbending beneath a bright morning sun, their thin skeletons stripped of leaves by the approach of winter. Beneath the bare trees, a pair of wolves snuffled through decaying leaves that had blown into low drifts, sniffing to find a scent. Any scent. The wind-driven rain of the night before had washed much of Lorienne's trail away.

Adrik reined his horse to a halt beneath the branches of an elm and allowed the weary animal a few moments' rest. At the urging of the wolves, he had turned northward well before the dawn, altering direction abruptly to try and keep apace of Lorienne's change in course. She was heading for the Caucasus now, just as he'd suspected, her night flight south into the deep forest no more than a circuitous route designed to confound any pursuers. But he doubted she had considered the possibility that some of those pursuers might well be wolves, able to track even the faintest of scents.

He watched silently as the wolves suddenly loped through mounded leaves and headed northward once again, following her trail with the unerring tenacity of hunters hard on the scent of wounded prey. The wolves' excitement was a tangible thing. Lorienne was close, very close. Even he could feel it now.

The sorcerer surveyed the landscape carefully. The woods were sparse here, stands of elm and oak and black walnut sprouting from hillocks running the length of a narrow valley walled by jagged mountains. To the north, the chain of mountains visible along the distant horizon soared far higher than those closer at hand, the granite peaks and ridges of the Caucasus cloaked in a mantle of early snow.

Beyond the closest hillock, he could see the bright glint of sunlight reflecting upon water. He knew the lay of the land here well. A chill stream fed by mountain snows wandered along this portion of the valley floor, its course snaking around low hills as the stream meandered back toward Khorazm and the great freshwater sea.

He nudged his black horse back into motion, allowing the animal to set its own pace in the direction of the stream. Once they began the harsh climb up dry and dusty mountain trails, there would be little in the way of drink until they reached the high mountains. The weary animal needed time to rest and take its fill of the crisp mountain water here in the valley before making the ascent.

Lorienne would likely do the same.

As they neared the curving stream, a wolf loosed an excited yap and bounded into the trees. Adrik turned his horse to follow. Both wolves had run into the thick shadows beneath a stand of oaks bordering the rock-littered stream. The creatures were leaping about and prancing in joy, performing a wild dance of greeting for one of their own.

Relief washed through the sorcerer when he spotted the source of the animals' joy. *Sandor*.

When he had found the ominous print of a tiger's paw embedded in mud a ways back along with the bloody signs of some fierce beastly battle, he had been certain either his wolf friend or Lorienne lay dead from the attack. Possibly both.

He leapt from the saddle and led his horse beneath a canopy of limbs and winter-browned leaves, dropping the reins and his bow and sword before hurrying to his fallen friend. The huge gray wolf was curled in the shadows at the base of a tall oak, panting wearily. A thin coating of dried blood stained the fur on a hip and rear leg, but the injuries didn't appear overly serious. Several deep gouges ran in straight lines down the wounded haunch, slash marks left by the claws of a tiger. But the bleeding appeared to have ended mostly, leaving the wolf's thick gray fur stained with flecks of brownish red. Sandor had obviously spent the better part of the morning licking her wounds to halt the loss of blood. A good sign, that.

"What of Lorienne?" he asked the creature quietly.

The wolf's tail thumped tiredly against the loamy ground. Then the creature lifted its great head and glanced deep into the shadows of a nearby tree, directing Adrik's attention there as well.

He saw Lorienne's small form huddled in the sun-dappled grass and blew out a sigh of relief. If she were dead or gravely injured he knew he would have known instantly, or Sandor would have informed him somehow. Instead, she appeared to be sleeping peacefully, from exhaustion no doubt, her body curled like an infant's, her head pillowed on a mound of fallen leaves. She had even had the foresight to cover her feet and legs beneath a thick carpeting of leaves, warming her body against the chill.

"I knew you would see to her safety," the sorcerer

whispered to the courageous wolf. He ran his fingers along the creature's injured haunch, then gently stroked the soft muzzle and ruffled the upright ears. "Fortune surely traveled with you. I doubt many wolves could have survived a battle with a hungry tiger."

The wolf blinked slowly, her liquid yellow eyes intent upon his face. She nuzzled the back of his hand, pushing against him with her snout as if to thank him in some way. It was a tender gesture, one that spoke of fierce devotion and abiding faith.

Adrik closed his eyes and touched his palm to the top of Sandor's furry head, his lips moving in a soundless chant. The wolf would survive, with or without his healing spell, but his small conjuring would take away her pain and help ease her way back to health. It was the least he could do considering he owed her Lorienne's life.

A moment later, he withdrew his touch and rose, gazing fondly at the beast that had been his companion for more years than he could remember. "Thank you, my friend."

The other wolves edged closer and settled around Sandor protectively, knowing the sorcerer would soon move away. They would watch over her in his stead.

Adrik lifted his gaze and sought the small form lying so still and quiet in the cool gloom beneath the sprawling canopy of a nearby tree. He made his way swiftly to where Lorienne lay and dropped to his knees beside her, assessing the sleeping woman's injuries with a practiced eye. Her hair and robe were in disarray, and small scratches marred the perfection of her features, but like Sandor, fortune had truly smiled upon her the previous night. Though numerous, her cuts and scratches had been brought about by the scraping of briars and brambles, not a tiger's claws.

He brushed leaves from her legs to examine her fully, frowning when he saw an ugly tear in the flesh along one side of her foot, the sort of wound created by an arrow or the jab of a dagger.

He peered at the angry red flesh on her foot. Bits of splintered bark still clung to the edges of the gash, leading him to surmise that a limb or branch had caused the injury, not the point of a blade or an animal claw. And though the wound was beginning to swell and fester, it appeared to have been well cleaned. Before falling into an exhausted sleep, Lorienne obviously had maintained the forethought to tend to her injuries, most likely by rinsing herself in the cold mountain stream of the mud and grime on her robe and legs.

Yet despite her tousled state, to Adrik she appeared much as she had when he last saw her atop the tower roof. She looked just as desirable to his eyes, just as appealing, with those pale tresses tumbling about her body. There were differences, though. He could see that dark crescents of fatigue now smudged the hollows beneath her eyes. And even in sleep, her features were pinched and drawn with worries absent just the day before.

Still, the mere sight of her made him burn with need and desire once again.

The sorcerer suspended one hand over the wound in Lorienne's foot and closed his eyes, concentrating on the reddened circle of flesh, the webbing of scratches marring the pale, perfect beauty that had awakened within him a need so powerful he feared he no longer possessed the will to stave off the darkness spreading inside him.

Without thought to the consequences, he brought the full force of his powers to bear upon Lorienne's fatigued and battered body, his only goal to end the pain and suffering of her human flesh. He soon felt the outpouring of energy through his fingertips as his strength seeped into her body, heating and healing her flesh from within.

She moaned in her sleep and twisted beneath his hand, trying to pull free of the unearthly heat, but he stilled her unconscious thrashing by will alone. The webbing of cuts and scratches on her face and hands began to fade, the lines turning red, then pink, then pale before dissolving from sight. Bruising along her foot and ankle vanished as well, the darkly mottled flesh turning a rosy, normal hue as the blood beneath her skin leeched away.

He gasped suddenly and pulled his hand away from her flesh, his trembling fingers bunching into a fist so hard and tight his nails bit into the center of his palm. The conjuring was causing the darkness to rise within him once more, a thick black tide threatening to drown him in its malefic depths.

He wanted . . . so many things.

Sweat dampened Adrik's forehead, and the hard line of his jaw clenched as tightly as his fists. He tried to concentrate, to will his remaining humanity not to slip away. But the toll exacted for this conjuring refused to fade. He felt as if he were standing upon the edge of a terrible precipice. If he shifted his thoughts, or moved in the slightest of ways, he would fall headlong into a morass of shadows, allowing the darkness within to finally hold sway.

The part of him that had long since become inhuman awoke and whispered from those shadows, an insidious voice telling him the only way to end his terrible need was to ravage the girl now, to take her unconscious body and have his way.

The light around him dimmed, then grew as black as night, and he knew the shadows had clouded his eyes, veiling the living world from view. His blood turned to dark flame. He ached for her. He burned like the sun. He wanted to savage her as a demon would.

He bunched his fists hard against his thighs and shouted in sheer frustration as he fought the temptation to simply be that which he was destined to become.

At the sound of his anguished shout, Lorienne flinched awake, her arms and face twitching in startlement from the abrupt change to wakefulness. Yet once the shock had passed, she had presence of mind to crack her lids slowly and hold herself very still, unsure of what she might find with open eyes.

Somehow, she was unsurprised to find the sorcerer kneeling beside her. She had known he would be the one to come for her. And on some odd level, she had been aware of his presence from the very moment he stepped into the wood beside the stream. She was aware, too, of some internal struggle raging inside him. She could sense it, feel it thick in the air around them, a cloud of anger and unease that refused to dissipate.

A frown touched her brow. She couldn't help but feel a surge of pity for him. His harsh features were shadowed with pain, torment and utter hopelessness, and a hundred other emotions that had no human name. His was the face of a man haunted by a darkness she could only evoke in her worst imaginings.

No, she amended silently. Imaginings played no role in his torment. After encountering the cruel specter lurking inside his tower, she knew the evil nature of the darkness that had etched such torment upon the Shadow Prince's chiseled features. She knew it all too well. And in some small way, she understood the purpose of the war being waged. Instinctively, she knew the Shadow Prince was battling for possession of his very soul, and that long-fought battle was nearing a climactic end.

"You found me," she said softly, a statement of fact,

not a question. But her words failed to gain a response from him. His gaze had stilled upon something unseen, and his thoughts seemed far removed from both her and the narrow valley, as if he were caught in the throes of a waking dream. It was unsettling to witness him in such a state.

"My lord?" she asked, and found that her hand had moved of its own volition to cover his clenched fist. Strangely, his flesh was like fire beneath her touch, not chill as she expected. After a moment's hesitation, she tightened her hold upon his hand, seeking to ease the sorrow so visible in his face and eyes. "Can you hear me speak?"

He heard her voice calling to him, a magical sound that he followed back toward the world of the living. Light pierced the shadowy darkness around him, and he saw the dim gray shapes of trees, mountains, and Lorienne's welcome form and features appear before him. "Yes." Even to his own ears, his voice sounded distant, hollow. "I can hear you."

The darkness finally receded, not entirely so, but enough that he felt a part of the world around him once again. Yet deep in his heart he knew that he had lost another fragment of himself forever, an irreplaceable part of his humanity that had kept him from tumbling from that precipice into the abyss below.

When the next time came, as it surely would, there would be no turning back from the darkness yawning inside him. Nothing could delay his fall from humanity now. Not Lorienne. Not anyone. He had been wrong to believe that he could savor his last days through her, to live with her as an ordinary man if only for a little while.

He pulled his fist free of her touch. Her very nearness might be the catalyst that sent him over the precipice forever. He knew that now, and he knew what he must do to correct his mistake in judgment.

Adrik sensed rather than saw that Lorienne was studying him through guarded eyes. Worried eyes. She didn't know what to expect of him, and in truth, neither did he. He tried to relax his balled fists but found it a difficult task. This protective stiffness in his limbs seemed an integral part of him now.

He watched as she frowned in sudden wonder and explored her face with the tips of her fingers, then stared curiously at the unmarred flesh on the backs of her hands. "I am no longer hurt." Her voice was edged with the same incomprehension inscribed on her brow.

"I know," he answered simply.

She touched one hand with the other and flexed the foot that had been injured the night before, amazed by the transformation. At daybreak, scrapes and cuts had covered her skin, more numerous than she could count. Now there was nothing, and the same held true for her foot. No trace of the painful wound remained. Even the stinging numbness from the cold and wet no longer prickled the bottoms of her feet.

The guardedness returned to her eyes. "Did you do this by way of sorcery?"

"I had no salves or healing unguents," he offered in explanation, though he wondered why he did so. He had sacrificed much to conjure that spell. "You should be content with the knowledge that you've been healed and not question that healing's origins."

She turned her head from side to side, testing her ability to move her neck without the soreness that had resided there at dawn. "I am not discontent that you healed me. I just don't understand why, especially after last night. . . . A creature appeared to me in your chamber. It . . ." She didn't know how to finish the thought, how to speak of the unspeakable.

The Shadow Prince met her gaze steadily. He could tell her an untruth that might satisfy her for a while but in the end, she would know it for a lie. And all he

141

had ever known were secrets and lies. The truth had long been a thing to be avoided and feared, hidden from the world lest he be seen for what he truly was. But even among his people few comprehended the real truth. Through the centuries, the Magii had given rise to many sorcerers, magicians, and priests, all supposedly born with the ability to call upon the power of demons. It was common knowledge, known and celebrated by all—but the terrible reality was that the reverse was actually true. The demons called upon the sorcerers and kept *them* in thrall.

For a moment, Adrik was still and silent, utterly so, and then he drew in a shuddering breath and gazed at her with the certitude of conviction. He would do what he must. "Leave here, Lorienne . . . now."

A blend of shock and pity flashed in the depths of her wintry eyes—but it wasn't pity he desired from her. Never that. "Your body is healed, and you'll find bread, water, and clothing in a pouch hanging from the pommel of my saddle." He glanced toward the north, to the snow-tipped mountains crowding the horizon. "Go where you will and never return to this land."

She sat up abruptly and stared into his solemn face, trying to ascertain if he had spoken truth. After all that had passed between them, he would heal her body and send her away? After their time upon the tower roof, he knew full well that she desired him, too, and would not resist if he tried to finish what had begun between them last night.

Lorienne frowned and worried the center of her lip with her tongue. She didn't understand, neither him nor his reasoning, yet she found she couldn't simply walk away, no matter the risk. Not yet. She had to know the why of everything first. "Why would you grant my freedom now?"

He was still gazing at the mountains, his mouth tense, his eyes somber and unfathomably black. "Creatures such as I do not often suffer bouts of generosity. Go from here. Accept the offer and leave before my black nature reasserts itself!"

She could do naught but stare. He had yet to rise from his knees, but she could see his trembling, the shivers running in waves through his hands and arms. His hands were bunched as before, rigid against his thighs. His face, usually so cool and detached, was worried and angry, as if the gentle offer of a moment before had come from another. As if at times he did indeed possess a different nature entirely.

Yet knowing these things, she still couldn't accept his unexpected offer of freedom. A foolish decision, she knew, but her heart and mind were not of one accord when it came to this man. "I do not understand you."

"Do you not understand that which is before your eyes?" he nearly shouted. The trembling spread to his legs. The shadows were calling to him. "I am not entirely human, Lorienne. Leave me while you have the chance . . . before a specter such as the one you saw last night rises from the darkness within me." He wanted to climb to his feet, to run from her presence, but he found that his legs refused to accept his commands. "Please . . . I no longer have the strength to ward it off."

She continued to stare, unwilling to understand. Adrik's eyes were great burning holes set within his tortured features. They were haunted eyes, filled with torment and self-loathing. But it wasn't evil she sensed within him; it was need and aching pain. "I know your nature, even if you do not, my lord."

With a gentleness born of uncertainty, she lifted a single hand and touched her fingers to his trembling arm, again offering comfort in the only way she knew. "I see nothing within you so dark and evil that I must flee its very presence. I see only a man in terrible pain . . . a human man."

143

Adrik flinched from her touch. "Please . . . just go," he begged in a raw, uneven voice. "I've given you your freedom." Her fingertips were like tongues of flame against his skin, searing his flesh. "If you continue to touch me, I will be lost."

She saw the naked need shimmering in the depths of his burning eyes, and knew he would ravage her body if she didn't pull away as he asked. His need was so powerful she could feel it thrumming beneath her fingertips, as if his shivering flesh were about to erupt into flame. There was nothing soft or gentle about the man kneeling before her. The Shadow Prince's features had settled into hard, remorseless lines. If she didn't flee, he would take her, and he would do so without a smidgen of pity or regret.

A shiver of awareness stirred within her, and she made a small, helpless sound in the back of her throat. Perhaps he wasn't entirely human. Perhaps he would soon take a Lydian consort into his bed. This one moment could be all the time she would ever have solely with him. He was a prince, after all, and she was less than nothing. Yet none of that truly mattered to her anymore. Even if he were a demonish creature with glowing red eyes and a score of wives, she knew she would still want him, still burn to feel his demanding flesh pressed tight to her naked skin.

The decision made, she lifted a hand to his face and allowed her trembling fingers to wander along the firm line of his jaw. Her pale eyes caught and held his heated gaze. Time froze between them, but she refused to release his tormented eyes. Her own need had become a living thing inside her belly, a scalding, twisting flame searching for a pathway to the outside of her body.

"Take me," she whispered raggedly, and lifted her chin to an angle that spoke of boldness and sudden certainty. Like him, she would feel no regret or shame

144

for what they were about to do. She ran her fingertips along the corded muscles of his arm. Whatever demons were loosed between them could have their way. "Do so now . . . here, in this place."

Adrik closed his eyes and drew a shuddering breath, reveling in the sweet sensation of Lorienne's fingertips drifting so lightly across his skin. His blood quickened with a need as fierce and hot as the sun riding across the sky above. The maw of the abyss beckoned from the shadows behind his eyes, but he no longer cared if he tumbled from that precipice. If he lost the last slivered fragments of his humanity while buried inside the warmth of her body, he would enter the Shadow Realm forever content.

She ran a slender finger along the edge of his lower lip, teasing the softness with the tip of a nail. It was an innocent exploration, not a wanton gesture by a woman practiced in the ways of men, yet the simple contact elicited a gasp of such torment from him that Lorienne pulled her hand away, suddenly afraid.

Adrik's eyes reopened and he pulled her upward, forcing her to rise upon her knees until they were face-to-face, their bodies separated only by their clothing and a narrow space of air. He stared with blank, unseeing eyes at the woman now kneeling before him. His trembling grew, sweeping violently through his torso and limbs. He could feel his skin begin to burn, and he ripped the confining tunic away, his breathing coming faster and faster with each moment that passed. He had to possess her, had to bury his manhood deep inside her before his body burst into a mass of flame.

She was gazing up at him with wide, fearful eyes, as if she regretted the offer she'd so impulsively made. But it was too late, too late for such uncertainty now. He no longer had the strength or will needed to halt himself now.

145

He tore the vest of dampened fleece from her shoulders, umindful of her little whimper of fear, then swiftly pulled the woolen robe over her head, freeing her naked flesh to his touch and view.

With a groan of pleasure, he cupped the soft heaviness of her breasts within his palms, crushing the taut peaks beneath his hands. His palms moved in fevered circles, exploring and kneading the sensitive flesh until he felt her surge against his questing hands, eager for more.

His manhood strained against the silky pantaloons, thick and pulsing with desire, so achingly full that he thought the seed it contained might spill itself now. He released her abruptly and reached for the cord cinched at his waist, working the knot loose so that the black fabric fell and pooled at his knees. A moment later, his legs were free of the soft calf boots and clingy trousers.

A cool breath of wind rippled over his thighs and swollen member, and Adrik moaned deep in his throat, the light touch of air like a score of chilly fingers against the newly bared skin. He drew Lorienne to him, shuddering as her unresisting flesh settled firm and warm against the hard lines of his chest and hips. She was trembling as much as he, delicate shivers of maidenly fear and newborn need that rode up her thighs and belly to quiver in her chest.

His breathing became swift and harsh, the panting of some maddened beast eager for release. Adrik knew that his tenuous control was fast slipping away. He could feel the shadows lengthening and swirling inside him but it mattered little to him anymore. All that mattered now was his throbbing manhood and her beckoning flesh.

He grabbed her hand roughly and pulled it to himself, groaning as her fingers wound around his pulsing length. "I need you to hold me," he told her huskily, then abruptly bent his head and lowered his mouth to suckle at a breast.

Lorienne gasped as his lips tightened around her. She lost herself in the sensation, in the sudden, driving need to feel those lips tugging at the sensitive flesh. And then she felt the moist caress of his tongue circling the tip of her nipple and never wanted the embrace of his mouth to end.

Instinctively, she wrapped her shuddering fingers tight about his turgid flesh, exploring and caressing the hot length of him as he'd done with her breast. She could feel a sense of urgency building deep inside him, a rigid heat that threatened to set her hand afire, yet she couldn't seem to stop herself from caressing him, though she knew full well where such an intimate touch would lead.

His suckling grew more fevered and needful, and her hold upon him turned more urgent in response. He dragged her hips closer, tighter to himself, and she felt his silken heat push against the base of her abdomen, the rhythmic movement of her hand drawing him ever closer to the hot, secret place between her thighs.

He cried out suddenly, a harsh sound muffled by the swell of her breast, and flung her backward roughly, forcing her down and down until the mounded leaves crackled and scattered beneath her back. His weight followed swiftly, the hard planes of his body molding effortlessly to her curves and hollows until she felt as if they were one being, not two. And still he suckled her, as if he couldn't bear the thought of freeing her peak from the confines of his mouth.

She made a noise, a desperate little sound, and thrust her breasts upward, pleading for more.

Adrik freed the rose-hued peak and lifted his head, gasping for a breath of air, and then he shifted his attentions from one breast to the other, his tongue and

147

lips drawing fast, heated circles upon the ripeness of her mounded flesh.

Lorienne whimpered again, and she felt her body begin to unfold of its own accord, her thighs drawing open in readiness to receive him. She found that her fingers were still wrapped about his taut manhood, and her steady caresses became swifter, more frantic, eliciting a harsh sound deep in his throat.

The primal sound of pleasure he made gave her a sense of power and mastery she'd never known, and she reveled in the newfound knowledge that it was she, a lowly Arizanti, who'd evoked such a passionate sound from a man as formidable and foreboding as the Shadow Prince. The knowledge was heady, intoxicating, increasing her desire to a feverish pitch. Her body began to unfold even more, her limbs loose and languid, heavy with desire.

Through the swirl of darkness gathering around him, Adrik heard Lorienne's sharp little gasps of need and knew he could wait no longer. He lifted his head slightly, and shifted his body, his hands moving to cup the sides of her head. He found himself staring into her cool blue eyes, so deep and vast he thought he might drown in their sensuous depths. For a brief moment he wondered why that was so, how this one young maiden could have had such a profound effect upon him and throw his life into disarray. But the thought vanished as quickly as it had come, and all that was left to him was the driving urge to bury himself deep inside her and fulfill his animalistic need.

His fingers wound and tangled themselves in her pale, silky hair, whether to draw her closer or hold her in place he couldn't say. She stared up at him with those well-deep eyes, a look of utter innocence quivering along the curve of her lips. But another look was etched into that perfect face as well, a sultry wantonness that promised endless nights filled with twined limbs and cries of passion.

Adrik knew then that he was lost. "I must have you," he whispered in a raw, strained voice. "And once I am done, I will have you again."

Lorienne moistened her mouth, her hands drifting upward to explore the curve of Adrik's narrow hips, the sinewy muscles of his sweat-dampened back. Freed from her grasp, the Shadow Prince's manhood surged closer to the moist heat between her thighs, the warm end of him demanding entrance to her core.

"Yes . . . please," she whispered back. She was burning inside, a sweet, hot ache that rushed through the center of her body and set her afire. Her features twisted in a grimace of pleasure. "I know only that I burn inside, and I can stand no more."

He lowered his mouth to hers, covering the softness of her lips with a ruthless kiss. A pulse at her temple quickened beneath his fingers, and his kiss turned more insistent, almost savage in its intensity. Her breasts thrust hard against the firmness of his chest, and he wrapped his fingers tight within her bounteous hair, pulling her so close he could feel the wild beating of her heart against his skin. His tongue explored the moist cavern of her mouth, and when he felt the silky tip of hers begin a timid probing in return, his kiss deepened even more, his lips grinding hard against the fullness of hers to claim possession of her lithe body once and for all.

Her slender hips arched against him in readiness, and the little fragment of himself that had remained intact shattered into countless pieces and fell away.

Groaning with pleasure, he forced her thighs to spread wider, and he buried himself inside the hot tightness of her sheath, driving deeper and deeper with every thrust, uncaring of her cry of pain or anything save his own primitive need.

The blackness closed around him like a featureless void, and he stepped willingly from the edge of the precipice. The abyss beckoned, the shadows swirling black and violent within him, and he tumbled headlong down into the darkness. He felt the malignant presence of creatures hidden deep within the void, evil things not born of the living world. He could sense their rage and utter loathing closing around him. Blackened shapes raged and screamed in the darkness, their curving fangs and sharpened teeth snapping from the shadows. They had come to welcome him.

Adrik buried himself deeper, his hips surging against hers in a mindless rhythm that he couldn't halt, didn't possess the will to control. Each wild thrust drove him farther and farther into the tautness of her flesh, pushing him into the very center of her until the heat inside him turned to molten flame.

His body shuddered, a violent trembling, and he shouted in feral joy, an animal-like cry of release. Then with his one final, burning thrust, his seed burst free, spilling endlessly into the depths of Lorienne.

Darkness filled him, thick and still, fraught with the unearthly stench of the creatures gathering around him, waiting for one of their own.

And then the gloom and shadows suddenly parted like mist, and he saw an unexpected light, a bright thing of beauty and goodness and purity shining from the center of the darkness, a lamp to light his way from the abyss. The shapes and hatred and fangs retreated from the light in fear, screaming in outrage as they melted back into the accursed shadows that had given rise to them.

He reopened his lids slowly and found himself staring down into Lorienne's limpid gaze, the brightness of purity and purpose he had sensed before shining like signal fires from the depths of her eyes. It was she who had drawn him back to the living world, forced

the darkness to retreat. Though she lay as still as stone beneath him, her slender hands were wrapped tight about his head and neck, as if she had sought to hold him to the living world by her strength alone.

A great sense of peace washed over him. With Lorienne's aid, the battle within him had been waged and won. He would remain a man—at least for a while. She had clasped him to herself instead of pushing him away, lent him the strength of purpose needed to salvage the tattered remnants of his humanity. He was free now, for as long as his will to hold the darkness at bay remained strong and resolute.

Adrik knew then that he could never let Lorienne go far from him. Not now. Not until his time among the living was at an end. She was the light to his darkness, his other half, an alluring vessel that held a substance as essential to him as life-giving water. Without her near, the abyss would claim him.

But the strain of what she had done was written clearly in the stark lines that knotted her brow. He had taken her with demonish intensity, uncaring of her pain or pleasure, a hideous way for any maiden to be brought to her first joining.

He paled with the shame of what he had done. Fresh bruising purpled the side of her neck, and her throat had been marred by a small crescent wound: the teeth marks of some wild beast.

Adrik sighed and lowered his eyes. He had done this. Yet despite all that he had inflicted upon her, he could still see the twin lights of caring and concern shining within the wells of her eyes, emotions as foreign to him as the affection of a father or mother.

"Forgive me . . ." he whispered raggedly, and buried his face in the curling mass of her tangled hair. He pulled himself from her with care, freed her of the coarse invasion of his maleness, and rolled his weight to one side, drawing her close against his chest.

Jan Zimlich

Already he felt the first faint renewed stirrings of desire within him, and knew he would take her again soon. But he would be far gentler this time, displaying the care necessary to give pleasure to another as well as receive it. "It was not my intent to bring you pain."

She gazed at him for a long moment, sensing his regret, his uncertainty—strange emotions for a sorcerer or a prince. And then Lorienne touched his face gently, her fingers splaying across the width of his cheek, letting him know by touch alone that she understood and accepted him as he was. "There is nothing to forgive. I gave myself to you willingly. There exists a bond between us, whether we wish it were so or not."

Adrik's muscled body was still hard against her, and she was aware of him in a way that she had never been of any male. She could feel every sinewy line, every muscle pressing upon her flesh. His night-black eyes burned with an intensity that took her breath away, and a tremor rushed through the center of her in response. Despite the aching tenderness between her thighs, the irresistible need to take him within herself still simmered in her blood.

Lorienne understood with sudden clarity that this same need would dwell in her always, and she would desire Adrik until the end of her days. "I fear our futures are twined together now, my lord."

He breathed in the heady fragrance of her hair, committing the sweet scent to memory. He was the sorcerer, not she, yet it was Lorienne who'd cast such a powerful spell over him that he knew he never wanted to be free. For however long a future he had before him, he wished to spend it entwined with hers. "You speak as a prophetess. How could you know this?"

She smiled sadly, a small lifting of her mouth rather than a full-fledged smile. "I have known it since I first awoke within your chambers . . . since I remembered

152

how my mother first told of the darkling prince who would hold my fate within the palm of his hand. She was a great seer, trusted by all the Arizanti. You are that prince, my lord. I am certain of it now."

He pulled himself up to an elbow, his fingers idly threading through a length of her hair. Such a fate was a pleasant dream, but it could never truly be. He stared at her gravely.

"Lorienne, any future I have will be fleeting at best. The change will be upon me soon. You brought me back from the darkness this day, but I am destined to find my end there."

She frowned. "Damek and Jirina both spoke of some coming change. What meaning does it hold for your future?"

"I have no future," he told her harshly, his voice and mouth both hard and grim. "With the arrival of late spring, the shadowed sun will blacken the earth. At that moment, I am destined to become a creature of the darkness much as the demon you encountered last night. So I cannot possibly be the man your seer mother saw in her dreams, for I will no longer be a man."

A sudden chill raced across Lorienne's skin, and she frowned in fresh terror. He'd mentioned that cruel specter in such an indifferent way, as if it were a common experience to encounter demons in the night. "The demon . . ." she said in a terse whisper, her body rippling with unease at the very memory of that hateful creature. "It told me things about you . . . terrible things." A look of revulsion passed over her features. Could those taunts have possibly been true? "It even claimed to be your father."

"His name is Malkaval." Adrik broke contact with her eyes, unwilling to meet her gaze, not about this. The demon's name was meant only for surreptitious whispers and curses in the night. Just the mention of it befouled everything in some way. Yet saying it in the bright light of day seemed somehow to lessen a measure of its hold upon him. He hoped that was so. "In a way, he is my father," Adrik sought to explain. "The only one I've ever known."

Lorienne stared at him in shock, aghast that any man would entertain the notion that a demon could indeed be his father. "That cannot be. You are the son of Hedeon, king of the empire."

Adrik was silent for a long moment and then he sighed, and with his sigh seemed to come a release of sorts, a grudging acquiescence to tell Lorienne as much of the truth as he dared. "Only by manner of blood. On the night of my birth, Malkaval came to King Hedeon and demanded that I be given to him. My mother had died giving birth, and Hedeon had no desire to raise an unwanted second son, so he struck a bargain with the demon—my life for the Median throne, and the continued health of Burian, the king's appointed heir. Malkaval readily agreed. He had been awaiting my birth for many centuries. He said it was written in the stars long ago that a Magian prince was to be the fulfillment of an ancient prophecy."

His solemn gaze lifted to the sky, to the snowcapped mountains huddled to the north. "Ever since that time I have been under the care and tutelage of my mother's people—and of Malkaval, who trained me in the ways of sorcerers." He shrugged one shoulder, a gesture filled with hopelessness and resignation. "So you see, in a fashion he is my father."

Sadness touched Adrik's face and eyes as he continued, "Your mother was wrong. The path to my future was written long ago. With the coming of the eclipse, I am fated to take Malkaval's place within the Shadow Realm. I cannot hope to change that now."

Lorienne shuddered. The whispered legends of the Shadow Prince's beginnings had never mentioned how

King Hedeon had cruelly handed his own blood into the care of a demon. How could any father do such a thing? Never before had she heard of such a despicable act. "No man can have two differing futures written in stone. One must be wrong, the other correct. I believe in the prophecy my mother envisioned for me, and that future includes you, though what shape my destiny will take I cannot say. But if it is true, the king and this Malkaval must then be wrong. The gods would not allow anyone to be so cruel-hearted. Destiny is not a thing that can be bartered or sold."

Adrik sighed, a sad, mournful exhalation of air. He wanted to believe. There had been such conviction in Lorienne's voice and words, such overwhelming certainty that they were destined to have a life together. Yet he didn't dare give himself permission to believe in her dream. To do so would surely wreak havoc upon them both. In her innocence, Lorienne knew little of the cruelties of men—or demons.

"Lorienne . . ." he began in protest, but could think of nothing that might dissuade her from her mistaken belief, and so he fell into silence. He longed to whisper words of reassurance, of caring, even commitment, but he knew they would be untrue. He could commit to nothing. But he could savor the time they had to them, relish it each and every day. And so he sought to reassure her in the only way he knew, with his hands and lips, vowing to himself that he would do so in a gentle manner unlike any he had ever shown.

He brushed his mouth across hers, an undemanding exploration utterly at odds with his prior possession. Then he nuzzled her cheek and throat, his lips grazing her silken skin like a breath of wind.

She sighed against him and wriggled closer, her slender hands drifting along his shoulders and neck, sliding beneath the thickness of his braid to ease across his back. Lorienne liked the feel of him beneath her fingertips, how the muscles in his body rippled in response to her slightest touch.

The proof of his rekindled desire now rested heavy against her inner thigh. She smiled to herself, reveling in the knowledge of her sensual power. He was eager to have her again. His manhood was already thick and swollen, pulsing with barely restrained need.

His lips roamed from her cheek down the line of her neck, settling against a small hollow at the base of her throat. His sidelock slowly followed, the deep black strands of hair teasing along a path that matched the trail of his lips.

Her fingers threaded through that night-dark hair, pushing the loose strands behind his ear. She wound her arms about his shoulders, pulling him close, eager to feel the smooth expanse of his chest crushed against her own. Her own lips sought and found the outline of a scar upon his shoulder, a small circle of puckered flesh that told the tale of an arrow loosed in some battle long past.

She allowed her questing hands to wander lower, running down his back to the firm line of his hips and buttocks. Lorienne explored every curve and hollow of his well-muscled flesh, delighting in the steady sounds of pleasure escaping from the depths of his throat.

His hips were pushing against her now, his manhood probing to regain entrance. Yet he seemed almost hesitant, as if he were denying himself that which he desired most of all. Instead, he continued to ply her flesh with the soft caresses of his hands and lips, lighting a storm of desire within her to equal any of his own.

He cupped the fullness of her breasts within his palms, and Lorienne bent her knee, instinctively lifting one leg to afford him access between her thighs.

He groaned and slipped himself inside the moistness of her, slowly, gently easing his manhood into the depths of her tender flesh. He eased a hand between their bodies sliding it down her abdomen until he reached the silken warmth between her legs. And then he delved into the mysteries of her womanhood with sure fingers, heating such a fiery trail of desire along the sensitive flesh that she let loose a plaintive little cry for him to do even more.

He obliged her growing need by pushing himself deeper, then deeper still, but with none of the brutal impatience he had earlier shown. This time he neither demanded nor took from her any part of herself that she was not willing to share. Adrik labored to share himself as well, whetting her sensual appetites with gentle caresses and fresh embraces to stoke the fires of expectation being kindled inside her.

Lorienne moaned softly as the pain and tenderness from before faded away, replaced by a sudden sense of urgency gathering within her body. She knew he had woven some sort of spell about her, one that had soothed the aches from her body and prepared his way, but she didn't care. If his magic felt like this, he could weave a thousand spells about her.

She thrust against him in impatience, increasing the pace of his rhythm. He was buried so deep inside her, so achingly deep, yet she desired even more, needed to feel him burn a pathway up into her very center.

The trees and grass faded from her view, and her world narrowed in scale until all she could see was the sorcerer's darkly burning eyes and sharp-angled features. Her body suddenly stiffened and she pushed her hips hard against him, her neck arching as his manhood plunged even deeper, filling her with feverish heat.

Her features knotted, and she stared at him in silent wonder as an endless wave of tremors shivered through her body. She gasped, moaning with pleasure. And through it all, his dark eyes held fast to hers, a heated caress as intimate as any she had known from his hands or lips.

Adrik felt the storm of quivering tighten around him, and he thrust himself deeper, his mouth asserting its possession of hers as his body shuddered and he claimed his own release.

Afterward, the two lay together in silence, clinging one to the other, their bodies still wracked with the aftershocks of rapture.

In the sunlit silence, Adrik folded Lorienne's fragrant warmth within his arms, cradling her close against his chest. His hawkish face settled into resolute lines. She was his now, in name as well as in deed, and he would allow neither man nor demon to come between them.

Chapter Ten

The idyllic days of fall had proved all to brief, those warm afternoons and chill nights Lorienne had spent twined in Adrik's arms.

Now, winter had swathed the high mountains in its cold embrace, and the slopes of jagged peaks were mantled in a veil of white and the bluish shimmer of glacial flows. A thick layering of snow blanketed the endless valleys and hollows nestled between ridges. Streams that had been clear and inviting when she'd arrived in the fall were now clotted and frozen with thin sheets of ice.

Atop Khorazm's stone battlements, Lorienne shivered in a gust of wind and drew the heavy folds of a fleecy greatcoat tight about her shoulders. Yet it wasn't so cold that she shivered and grew numb from the exposure.

Here along the Caspian, the clime was far more temperate than high in the mountains, cold to be certain, but not dangerously so. Occasionally, a touch of brown-

ish green could even be seen scattered across the harsh
landscape, clumps of weed or scrub unaltered by the
change of seasons.

But the transformation to winter had wrought many
changes within the fortress walls. Unlike Lorienne's
own tribe, which grew staid and complacent with the
coming of winter's chill, the Magians appeared to increase their activities to a frenetic pace. From dawn
until the fall of dusk, ranks of soldiers drilled and
marched across the courtyard below, honing their skills
with swords and lances, while archers formed lines atop
the battlements and loosed countless practice arrows
into the surrounding forest.

The women of Khorazm weren't idle either. They
hovered over cooking fires day after day, smoking great
haunches of venison, ibex, or strips of meat cut from
giant sturgeon pulled whole from the inland sea. The
fruits of their ceaseless labors were then left to dry inside storage rooms within the fortress walls.

Lorienne had even joined the women's efforts on
many occasions in the preceding weeks, adding her
sweat and toil to theirs as they cleaned and cut great
portions of carp and sturgeon to bury beneath the
ashes of the cooking fires. Lorienne smiled to herself,
remembering the renewed sense of belonging she'd
felt when she had joined the Magians' daily activities.
She knew they had sensed the same as well, for the
women of the sorcerer's tribe had begun to cast welcoming smiles her way instead of suspicious glances.

But it was the other activities taking place within the
fortress that gave her the most reason for pause. Horses
were curried on a daily basis, their hooves and coats
meticulously tended by a phalanx of young stable boys.
Manes were clipped and fitted with decorative covers
made of felt and leather appliqued with all manner of
gold and colorful beading. Eventually she knew the Magians' Nisaean horses would be fitted with leather

masks as well, their surfaces painted with images of tigers and deer and other creatures of the forest and steppe.

Lorienne shivered from an inward chill. The Magians proudly decorated their horses in such ways before waging war, in much the same manner as the Scythians. They were preparing to give battle soon.

The clangs of metal striking metal now echoed continuously from the armory, the sounds more urgent than when she had first arrived, as if all were being placed in readiness for some calamitous event. And the Magian prince was directing the preparations to inflict death and destruction with a singleness of purpose that was frightening to behold.

At any given time, Adrik was certain to be found within the midst of the soldiers practicing within the courtyard, either hurling a lance to perfect his own skill or wielding the flat of his sword in mock battle against one of his men.

She shivered again, her gaze turning back to the snowcapped peaks of the Caucasus visible in the distance. It was still an alluring sight, one she found difficult to resist, especially in the face of such ominous portents taking place around her.

Adrik mounted the battlement steps on silent feet and approached her from behind, his eyes clouding with suspicion when he saw the northerly direction of her glance. Anger and fear warred for possession of his features. He had found her thus far too many times since the end of fall. Thoughts of flight still dwelled within her heart . . . flight from him.

He grabbed her forearms and spun her toward him, blocking her view of the northlands with his body. "Do not be tempted, Lorienne." A flash of anger deepened the hue of his eyes. "I will not allow you to leave again."

Lorienne stared up at him in dismay. How was it possible that she had neither seen nor heard his ap-

Jan Zimlich

proach? Though she should have long since grown accustomed to his stealthy tread and sudden angers, he had managed to take her by surprise once again. "Am I no longer allowed to gaze upon the land of my birth for fear that it will anger you in some way?" Her voice held a mild note of reproach but not of overt anger. "I have given no cause for your mistrust." She had learned enough of Adrik Kiryl in the past weeks to know that the roots of his mistrust were buried within his worries over losing her. So were his maddening displays of proprietorship.

She laid the flat of her palm against the smoothness of his cheek. "I made my choice many weeks ago, when we joined together beside that mountain stream," she reassured him. Her fingertips traced the curving length of his jaw and angled back to brush the lobe of his ear. "The gift of my body was my vow that I would willingly remain with you."

She heard him draw a sudden breath and knew her touch had achieved the desired response. Their passion had yet to fade or dwindle, despite the passage of time. In fact, it seemed to grow stronger with each night they spent twined in each other's arms.

"I have no intent to leave you, Adrik . . . nor could I even if I wished. The passes have filled with snow by now." A sadness touched her eyes. "And where would I go even if that were not so? Hide myself forever in the bowels of some dank northern cave?"

It had been foolish of her to ever entertain such a plan. "I have no tribe to go to anymore, no home." The chieftain of the Arizanti had slaughtered her mother with less care than that given a goat or sacrificial lamb, then left her to die on the steppe in the cold and wind. And the rest of the Arizanti had done nothing to halt Arkanna's murderous actions. "I have nowhere to go but here." Knowledge of her people's betrayal had served to quash any thoughts she might

162

have once harbored of one day returning to her tribe.

Adrik's grip on her forearms gentled, and Lorienne stepped closer, allowing him to fold her within the warmth of his embrace. She sighed against his chest, thoughts of her dead mother carrying a fresh onslaught of grief and pain.

The day will come when a darkling prince holds your future within the palm of his hand.

Shalelle's vision of the future had turned out to be far truer than she could have ever imagined. A darkling prince did indeed hold her future, her very life, within the palm of his hand, but what that future would entail Lorienne didn't know for certain. For now she was content to spend her nights wrapped within his arms.

But his fate and his empire's will be yours to command.

The second verse of her mother's prophecy came to mind with a suddenness that prickled the nape of her neck, the seer's words rising from the past to rush through her soul like a chilly wind.

Lorienne gazed into her sorcerous lover's somber face for a longish moment. She didn't fully comprehend the meaning of Shalelle's words, but she did understand that her own fate was no longer hers to command. It now lay firmly within the Shadow Prince's grasp, and would remain thus evermore.

"We are bound together, you and I," she told him in a gentle tone, "our futures locked as surely as the blade of a sword to its hilt."

The tense watchfulness faded from his features abruptly, and his arms enfolded her slender form. He had been wrong to doubt her. To be afraid. "I am your home now, Lorienne," he told her quietly. "The Magii are your tribe for as long as you live."

Perhaps they truly were bound together, Adrik reasoned, as what tied them one to the other felt more powerful than any force he'd ever known. But even swords were known to break. He hoped the force bind-ing them together was stronger and more lasting than the metals used to forge the finest longswords. The very thought of losing Lorienne brought such a sense of fear and aching loneliness that he knew he would not survive their parting.

Yet he knew they would soon be forced to do just that. In a matter of weeks the mountain snows would cease their fall, and the first of the couriers from Urmia would begin to wend their way toward Khorazm. With spring's approach, messengers riding swift horses would be sent from the royal palace, bearing missives and royal commands from both the king and Adrik's brother. Burian would order him to collect the best of the soldiers from the Magian ranks, pack supplies and horses and weaponry, and quick-march to a chosen plain somewhere between Amida and the distant Halys River, where the next battle would likely be waged in the long-fought war between the Median Empire and the obdurate Lydians.

It had been much the same come every spring for the past five years, a bloody, never-ending war of attrition that had exacted a heavy toll on the Medians and their foes alike. There was no reason to believe this year would be any different.

The contents of the messages sent to him by King Hedeon would be just as familiar, though far less bellicose than those sent by his brother. Once again the king would demand new and higher taxes from Adrik's vassals in order to pay for his wars and excesses. Hedeon was also sure to demand his presence at the imperial palace again, a command Adrik would continue to ignore, but most likely at his peril this time. Hedeon wouldn't countenance his refusals much longer.

His arms tightened firmly about Lorienne's slight form, and he silently wished that they could remain just as they were forever. But that wasn't possible. With the easing of winter's throes, far greater perils than any royal summons would soon arise. Once spring was firmly entrenched across the land, the time of the change would be upon him. And Malkaval would expect him to hold to the foul bargain made by his father many years before—a bargain Adrik now felt unobliged to honor. But what would that change?

There was the matter of the Lydians, who fully expected him to keep to the alliance he had forged with Pantaleon. His agreement to seal that alliance by accepting a Lydian bride had been based on the foreknowledge that the eclipse and his transformation would already have occurred by the time the marriage party arrived, and that he would no longer be alive. He had fairly reasoned that the Lydians would not be inclined to ally a princess of their blood to an unliving demon.

But what of that bargain now? If he truly were fated to find a common future with Lorienne, to overcome his evil destiny, then he would have to seek new agreements where he could, and somehow thwart Malkaval from his ultimate goal of changing places with him. And he would have to do so while preventing the enraged demon from engaging in a murderous rampage to inflict vengeance for his thwarted plans.

Adrik sighed heavily and brushed a pale strand of hair from his beloved's face. The goals before him would be neither simple nor easily attained. "I shall be leaving Khorazm soon," he announced in a solemn voice. "I must meet with the Lydians again." If he didn't, the war would never end. His father and brother would never end it.

Lorienne stiffened against him and lifted her face to meet his gaze. "No," she whispered. Fear, stark and fever-bright, glittered in her eyes. Once he rode away through the fortress gates, she knew all the preparations and practice for battle would be brought to swift use. "Please, Adrik!" The possibility that he might never

165

return made her feel dead inside, dead and empty. "I don't want to remain here without you."

She couldn't help but stare around the fortress with the eyes of a stranger as she had when she first arrived. The brief sense of belonging she'd earlier felt fled entirely, and a sense of dread rose within her to replace it. "Without you here, I fear Khorazm . . . and I fear what will happen if we are parted."

Adrik's brows drew together as he watched a tangle of emotions play across Lorienne's features. Her eyes were unnaturally bright, brimming with moisture, and a tremor of some fierce emotion quivered along the edges of her mouth, ready to burst free.

To his surprise, a single tear then slipped from the corner of her eye and ran down her cheek. Adrik's bewilderment grew. Had fear for her own life loosened that tear, or was it fear for him instead? "There is no need to be frightened, Lorienne. You will be safe here." The possibility that she might have shed that tear for him tore at the fabric of his soul. No one had ever cared enough to do such a thing. "The people of Khorazm will guard and protect you as if you were born of this tribe. This is truly your home now, the Magii your tribe."

She shivered in his arms. "And what of Malkaval?" she said in a hushed tone, as if she were afraid to say the name aloud. The thought of having to face that foul specter again made her feel weak and watery inside. It had made her feel that way since she returned. "Does the demon not reside here as well? What if he returns to Khorazm while you are gone?"

He squeezed her tightly, then placed his hands on her shoulders, pushing her slightly away. His mouth turned firm and resolute as he tipped her chin upward and held her captive with his eyes. "Malkaval will not return or cause you harm. I will make certain of that before I leave."

Her fingers wound through the dark strands of hair blowing loose down one side of his head. "And what of you, Adrik?" She tried to swallow the lump of fear gathering deep in her throat. Her mother's prophecy of the future suddenly seemed far less reassuring than before. "Who will see to *your* safety? You leave here to go into battle for a father who betrayed you, in a war not of your making or desire. All this against an enemy you would rather forge an alliance with than continue what has become a ritual spilling of blood."

The corners of her mouth dipped lower, the line turning as firm and unbending as his had been. She hadn't even mentioned the demon's hideous plans. Adrik had told her enough that she understood the mortal dangers that awaited him come spring. "If you fail, you will die."

Adrik sighed. "Yes," he said. "Then I will die."

The day was dawning soft and cool, with a taste of winter still clinging to the damp sea air, yet at the same time it was filled with a sense of expectancy that seemed to linger on the wind, a subtle hint of a change in seasons.

Spring was riding on the wind, and once the mountain snows began to melt, Lorienne knew that Adrik would depart from Khorazm, perhaps to never return. She couldn't imagine a life that didn't include him now.

Only three weeks had elapsed since they had spoken atop the battlements, but in that space of time she had grown more enamored of him with each day that passed. She didn't know the nature of what it was that had bound them so tightly together. Perhaps it was something as simple as hope. But the very thought of losing him now, feeling as she did, was far more difficult than it had been before. If she lost him now, she would lose herself.

Jan Zimlich

Lorienne blinked away the threat of tears and continued to stare at the predawn shadows spilling through the latticed covering that had blocked the worst of the winter winds from the chamber's only window opening. She burrowed deeper beneath the pile of fleecy hides that warmed the sorcerer's bed and curled closer to the heat engendered by his body.

He made a contented sound in his sleep and pulled her even closer to his chest, his arms settling about her in a gentle embrace she found poignant, yet somehow reassuring. Her darkling prince could be either tender or warrior-fierce, though she doubted if few other than her had ever thought a tender, gentle side even existed within him. But she knew. She had seen the proof of its existence more than once now.

As if she sought to hold him firmly to herself, Lorienne pressed her body tighter against him and allowed her mouth to taste the fullness of his lips. At the first touch of her lips to his, her body quickened with desire. Even in sleep the Shadow Prince could kindle such a storm of passion within her that she found it impossible to resist.

She needed to feel him inside her, wanted him to take her while the silvery hues of dawn were slowly easing across the chamber that had become so familiar to her.

Her fingers delved through his night-black hair, the long, loose strands newly freed from the prison of his braid after the two of them had bathed in the warm water in the cistern the evening before. She sighed against his lips and reached down the muscled length of him, her hand easing along his abdomen until she cradled his maleness within her palm.

She heard the change in his breathing: One moment soft and steady with sleep, the next a sudden exhalation of surprise. Yet his lids remained firmly shut, his lashes long and sooty-black in feigned sleep, as if he intended to do nothing to interfere with the predawn wanderings of her hands and lips. And so she took advantage of his strange reluctance and explored him at will, her hands roaming his muscled flesh in ways that might have once caused her to redden with shame. But she felt no sense of embarrassment now, only the dull throb of desire growing deep within her belly.

"You have woven a spell around me, sorcerer," she whispered against his cheek, knowing that he listened. "It is one I fear I will never want to escape." She nuzzled his neck, her lips trailing downward to caress the smooth expanse of his chest.

She breathed in the heady, masculine scent of him and knew it was one she would never forget. The smells of leather and herbs and fragrant oils clung to his skin and hair, as well as a scent she couldn't identify, which for some reason teased along the edges of her memory. Something intoxicating. A hint of something wild and untamed from deep within the primeval forest.

His manhood was hard now against her hand, rigid with the proof of his need. Yet he still did nothing, allowing her hands to roam where they may.

The sense of power afforded by his acquiescence filled her with a desire like none she had ever known. She wrapped her legs about him and guided him inside her, eager for the joining to commence. She gasped aloud as he filled her with his heat, and she thrust against his hips in a mindless way, her movements growing more frenzied as the silvery hues of dawn were replaced by the brighter shades of day.

She found then that he was staring at her with open eyes, though he continued to hold his body utterly still. Submissive and complacent. As if he were the captive and she the lord and master. Lorienne knew then that this was his gift to her, his avowal that he would remain with her, just as she had done with him weeks before. For this one moment of time the Magian prince belonged to her, body and soul, not the other way around.

Their eyes locked, his dark and unfathomable, hers hazy with desire. "Adrik . . ." she breathed against him. Then her features knotted with pleasure, and she lost herself in rapture.

Lorienne cried out sharply, and Adrik knew she had found her release. Only then did he grant himself permission to search for his own. As her tremors tightened around him, he cupped the soft bounty of her breasts within his palms, cradling her gently, and plunged himself deeper into her silken flesh. He groaned against her tangled hair and wrapped his hands tight around her buttocks, thrusting into her until the shudders of ecstasy wracked his body and he let out a cry of relief.

As his breathing finally steadied, Adrik drew her into his arms, a sense of joy and contentment strong within his heart. He smoothed her tousled mane and rained small kisses along the side of her face, thanking the fates and the gods in their heavens for sending Lorienne his way. All the beauty and brightness of the world could be found in her eyes.

"May all our mornings begin in such a fashion," he whispered against the thickness of her hair. For the first time in his life, he dared to hope. Dared to dream that this could truly be his future life.

A voice pierced the early morning silence, the sharp call of a soldier from outside the tower walls.

Adrik sat up abruptly. The joy he had felt only moments before withered away. A sentry atop the battlements had called out to the soldiers in the courtyard below, warning of a courier's approach.

"What is it?" Lorienne asked worriedly. The call of the sentry so early in the morning sent a shiver of dread down the center of her back. She clutched at Adrik's arm, unwilling to let him go. He was staring at the latticed window covering with a remote expression, as if whatever lay beyond that opening had already stolen him away. "Adrik?" she asked, his name a dread-filled question.

He turned himself until he was sitting on the side of the couch, the soles of his feet flat against the coolness of the tiles. He gazed downward for a moment, staring at nothing, and released a pent-up sigh. So it would begin.

"The first of the couriers from Urmia has arrived."

Lorienne squeezed her lids closed and laid her head against the bareness of his back. Far too soon. "When must you leave?"

He climbed to his feet and strode to the window, throwing its lattice panel aside in order to gaze across the courtyard. Already the gates were being opened in order to allow the courier entry inside Khorazm's walls.

"Soon," Adrik answered quietly. "Before the full of the next moon for certain."

The horse's hooves sounded loud and hollow against the flagstones. That and the creak of leather were the only sounds Vlada could hear within Khorazm's central courtyard.

In fact, his was the only trace of movement to be seen within the fortress's walls, as if all within had been turned to stone the moment he had ridden through the fortress gates.

The soldier lifted a graying brow. Not the sort of reception usually given a courier for the king.

A phalanx of Magian soldiers appeared to be awaiting him near a set of steps leading to an imposing stone tower. The armored soldiers had come to swift attention when he rode through the gates and were observing him from beneath the visors of iron helmets, the butts of their lances resting easy against the stones, yet obviously held in readiness for any sign of attack.

From all appearances the Magians would fight to the

171

last to defend the occupants of that tower.

Vlada took a steadying breath. He had no desire to challenge the Magians on that score, especially since he had entered the gates alone, without benefit of any guards of his own.

In truth, he had no desire to be within the walls of Khorazm at all, and would have refused the commission from Prince Burian if a way to do so had presented itself. But it hadn't, and now he was here, a single emissary sent to deal with the treachery of a sorcerer prince in his master's stead. Not a task he relished.

His gaze flicked left, then right, sweeping over his new surroundings. Though he had heard much of Khorazm and its people through the years, this was his first visit to the Magian stronghold. Tales of this fortress and its inhabitants were as plentiful as the stones in a riverbed. Stories of demons and magic and unnatural spells.

He stiffened his shoulders. If he managed to survive, Vlada hoped this visit here would be his last.

As he crossed the courtyard to the tower steps, he slowed his horse's gait until its hoofbeats were almost silent against the surface of the flagstones. He glanced up warily, studying the activity above. Battlements ran the length of the fortress walls, their solid line broken only by the placement of watchtowers, an occasional staircase, and the tall black tower that faced the Caspian Sea. Magian sentries and archers gazed back at him from atop those battlements and watchtowers, their eyes as wary and suspicious as his.

Vlada frowned, still a bit taken aback by the cool reception. He had not thought the Magians would treat the arrival of a royal messenger with such overt suspicion. It was he who should view them with dire misgivings, not the reverse. After all, they were the ones who had a sorcerer for a prince, one now known to be in league with the enemies of the empire.

He pulled on the reins abruptly, and his horse came to a weary halt, its head hanging tiredly as the beast huffed out steam in the chilly air. Vlada dismounted, each movement slow and exaggerated so that his intentions would not be misconstrued by some nervous archer.

He stretched the stiffness from his legs and shoulders, glad to finally feel the ground beneath his feet again. The days spent in the cold atop a horse had taken a harsh toll upon his aging body. He now creaked as much as the leather of his saddle.

The doors to the tower opened suddenly and the Shadow Prince strode onto the landing, his darkly piercing eyes holding Vlada as much a captive as any contingent of guards. The old soldier shivered beneath the force of that penetrating gaze. The sorcerer was clad in Magian black, his tunic and overvest as dark and foreboding as his eyes and unbraided hair.

Adrik Kiryl paused at the top of the steps and dipped his head slightly to acknowledge the presence of his brother's second in command. Though they'd had little cause to meet face-to-face through the years, he knew the soldier by reputation and admired him for his skill and loyalty. "Welcome to Khorazm, Vlada Sura. I trust your journey from Urmia proved uneventful."

Vlada bowed deeply in a careful show of respect. "It proved uneventful, my lord," he told the Magian prince, though the last day had been anything but. The sorcerer's wolves had trailed him and his escort column for a full day and night, watching and glaring as they rode across Magian lands, giving them great cause for trepidation. Stranger still, he had thought he recognized one of those wolves, a large gray beast with piercing yellow eyes like the one that had stared at him so boldly out on the steppe.

But he didn't share those observations with the sorcerer, or the knowledge that his escort awaited his return in a dense wood near the sea. More than likely the sorcerer already knew, as it was said he knew all that went on in his lands. "Though the journey was uneventful, I fear I've grown too old to act the messenger. The cold and mountain snows do my body little good these days."

A trace of suspicion flickered in Adrik's mind. Indeed, this soldier's shoulders were stooped with fatigue and his face appeared haggard and weary. And why would his brother risk the health of his second in command by using him as a lowly courier? Any soldier or trusted servant could be utilized in such a way.

Adrik motioned toward the arched door embedded in the wall behind him. "Come . . . you may warm your bones within my tower."

Vlada nodded eagerly and rubbed the chill from his hands. He would dance attendance upon the foulest of demons if it meant warming his body for a little while. "Your offer of hospitality is greatly appreciated, my lord." He mounted the steps quickly. "I can hardly remember when I was last warm."

Adrik led him inside the dim coolness of the tower's great hall. Oil lamps flickered within the niches cut into the walls, and embers glowed inside several bronze braziers sitting atop pedestals, sending small wisps of heat wafting across the chamber.

Vlada eyed the small stone table sitting near the doors, then shrugged and removed the domed helmet and cap of mail protecting his head. Tradition decreed that a guest remove his armament and leave all weaponry upon a table near the door. To do less might be construed an insult by his unlikely host.

He laid both his sword and his helmet atop the table, the meeting of stone and metal sounding loud in the gloom of the hall. Once he had done as the strictures of custom demanded, he followed the Shadow Prince to the far end of the chamber, where several low couches surrounded a long table cut from native stone.

He took a seat and waited nervously, too uncertain of the prince's hospitality to risk alienating him in some real or imagined way.

A servant appeared at Vlada's elbow and the soldier glanced her way, blinking in surprise when he realized the woman bending to pour him a cup of wine was the very same one who had served as handmaid to Adrik's mother before the Shadow Prince was born. Despite the intervening years, the Magian woman still possessed a certain beauty that was both compelling and rare.

"Jirina?" he asked quietly, still not quite believing it was really she. Being in the handmaid's presence brought back memories of Vania he preferred to forget. "Is it truly you?" His gaze had not fallen upon Jirina's face since the weeks before Adrik's birth. By the time he had returned to the palace and learned of Vania's death, both Jirina and the infant had been spirited away to Khorazm.

Jirina finished pouring his wine into a cup made of hammered silver, then dipped her head and stepped aside. "Yes, my lord Vlada. Much time has passed since my eyes last rested upon you." She gazed at him steadily. "The Fates have not been unkind to you these years past."

The soldier snorted. "They have been unkind enough to make me long for my lost youth." He smiled at the servant, thoughts of his youth and his beloved Vania strong in his mind. A shadow of pain moved through him. "But the past is past and can never be relived once it has gone to its grave."

Jirina lowered her gaze abruptly. "Perhaps not, unless the past was sent to its grave before its true time." She eased her head downward in a short bow and withdrew from the table to a dim corner of the chamber, where she joined another servant to await their master's pleasure.

Frowning, Vlada lifted his brows in response to her cryptic words, but he made no further comment. He turned his attention to the Shadow Prince, who had watched the exchange from across the table with darkly curious eyes. Vlada drank his fill of sweet Ionian wine and studied the design etched into his cup to avoid those questioning eyes. He did not want the son asking painful questions about his knowledge of Jirina—or her long dead mistress.

After an uncomfortable silence, the soldier straightened his shoulders and looked directly at the Magian. "My lord, Prince Burian has sent word that you are to immediately choose the best of your soldiers and journey westward to Amida and the Tigris River. Soldiers from the other tribes have been ordered to join you there, but the prince has issued a decree that his army is yours to command. Once our forces have gathered near Amida, you are to lead them to a plain near the Halys River, where you shall meet the Lydians on the field of battle no later than the last week of May."

Adrik nodded to himself. The orders were much as he had envisioned. "And the king . . . what are his orders to me?"

Vlada sighed heavily and leaned forward, resting his elbows atop the polished stone. "The same as last spring, I fear. He has commanded that you attend him in Urmia immediately."

The mere thought of his next words filled the soldier's mouth with an ashy taste. Once he had loved Hedeon as he would a brother, but that had begun to change in recent months. Vlada lowered his voice to a near whisper, not wanting anyone except the Shadow Prince to hear the message he had carried so far. "Prince Burian commands that you continue to ignore the king's wishes, and to journey westward as he requests. He said to remind you of your vow of loyalty to him, not the king."

The soldier was quiet for a moment, his reluctance to impart such news clearly written on his features. "Prince Burian also said to tell you that the madness now has the king well in hand, and that your father is no longer capable of ruling an empire of ants, much less all of Media. As crown prince, Burian asks for you to keep your pledge of loyalty and to support any future decisions he makes in your father's stead."

Adrik leaned his head to one side and studied the soldier through hooded eyes. The message from his half brother was abundantly clear. Though his father's body continued to live, the time of his reign had finally come to an end. Burian now virtually controlled the throne and the empire, not Hedeon. And once Burian firmed his hold on that power and purged the empire of those disloyal to him, the mad king would most likely be sent to an untimely end.

He nodded slowly. "You may tell my brother that I plan to keep my vow of fealty to him. Nothing has changed between us since we last spoke. He is the rightful crown prince. As second-born, I simply follow where he leads. Because he commands it, I shall lead his army to meet the Lydians." Adrik shifted his head and the long strands of his hair dipped lower to brush across the shoulder of his tunic. "Tell my brother that his enemies are my enemies, and his wars shall always be mine."

Vlada masked a frown. He had not expected such treacherous pledges of fealty from one who it was clear to all planned to betray them by allying himself with the Lydians. The information relayed by the empire's spies in Sardis had been unambiguous: A marriage was in the making, one that would solidify the birth of a formidable alliance between King Alyattes and the Magii. If such a thing were allowed to come to pass, neither Burian nor Hedeon would survive the summer. When winter arrived again, the empire itself might rest in Lydian hands, with the Shadow Prince seated upon his brother's throne.

The worried frown he had veiled a moment before suddenly broke free and harshened Vlada's features. And yet, he still found it difficult to reconcile the whispering of spies with the seemingly honest vows uttered by the man seated across from him. Could the spies have been wrong in their assessments?

His frown deepened. If so, Burian's plans of vengeance could be both ill-timed and undeserved. But the orders given him by Crown Prince Burian had been implicit, and Burian was the rightful heir to the Median throne. As his second in command, Vlada could do no less than obey those orders.

"How soon shall you leave for the western lands?" the soldier asked, careful not to let his uncertainty flavor his voice.

Adrik masked his expression more than before. "Very soon." But not until he saw to it that Lorienne was protected from Malkaval. "Perhaps as early as tomorrow."

Vlada heard what sounded like a tiny sob in response to the prince's pronouncement, a startled gasp that echoed from the shadowy corner where Jirina and the other server awaited orders. He turned his head toward the sound, curious to see if it had been Jirina who'd cried out in such an unseemly fashion, but he found the old woman's features devoid of any visible emotion. The same could not be said of the other servant, though. Her oval-shaped face was awash in grief and worry.

Vlada's brows lifted in surprise. The young woman who'd sobbed aloud was the Arizanti he had found near death on the barren steppe. He recognized her instantly. A torrent of pale hair still fell in curling waves long past her shoulders. It was the same blond hair and comely face that had haunted his dreams for weeks after Burian had left her to the Shadow Prince's merciless care. But the memory of that pale hair had haunted Prince Burian's dreams as well, leading the crown prince to excesses and a worrisome obsession that Vlada had found impossible to curtail.

He gazed sharply at the young woman who'd caused such turmoil in his prince. When he'd seen her last, she had been bedraggled and near death. Now she appeared pampered, well tended, and was clad in the rich woolens of a noblewoman. She had also cried out when she heard that the Shadow Prince would soon leave, as though she worried about a lover's fate.

Vlada frowned again. As amazing as the prospect seemed, it appeared that the chaste Prince Adrik might actually have taken her to his bed, an unexpected turn of events to be sure. If true, Burian would be furious.

"I see the gift made to you by the crown prince still lives," he told Adrik, reminding the lesser son of both his benefactor and the girl's lowly origins. "When I return to Urmia, Prince Burian will be gladdened to learn she did not die in your care."

Adrik rose slowly from the narrow couch and directed his gaze toward Lorienne, warning her with his eyes to be still and silent. His own unease was apparent in the sudden bunching of muscles along his jaw. Vlada's last words had carried more than one meaning. Whether Lorienne had survived the past months or not should be of no true concern to his uncaring brother. So what was Burian's game? Why would he be interested in what had become of her?

The possibilities tumbled through his thoughts, vying for attention, but he couldn't settle on any one possibility. Whatever had prompted Burian's renewal of interest in Lorienne, the reason did not bode well for either of them.

Chapter Eleven

Clouds raced across the night sky, wrapping the sea and waning moon in a black so deep the glare of a single torch glowed as hot and bright as a signal fire. Adrik stood atop the tower roof and gazed into the darkness that surrounded Khorazm. Even the mountains were cloaked in shadow, their snow-tipped peaks veiled by low scudding clouds.

Below him, the courtyard was alive with the drumming of feet and animal hooves, hammering from the armory, and the voices of soldiers and nervous women. The final preparations for a dawn departure had been made, and the ranks of Magian soldiers chosen to journey northward were now bidding loved ones farewell.

Time was growing short.

Adrik closed his eyes and stretched his arms wide, focusing his thoughts on the tower he stood upon, the heavy entrance doors, the window openings, even the cracks between the granite stones. For the briefest of moments, a webbing of energy flowed around him, one that spread and poured across the tower roof like a river of milky water. Invisible to human eyes, the sorcerer's protective ward spilled down the sides of the tower to the courtyard below, spreading outward until the energy had engulfed all of Khorazm within its protective embrace.

Adrik sighed finally and lowered his arms. He had done all that he could. Malkaval had proved too strong to simply cast out, forever, as Adrik's own powers weren't potent enough to sustain such a spell. But as long as this temporary ward remained in place, the demon would be barred from returning to Khorazm or harming Lorienne. Until Adrik had time to settle matters between them, Malkaval would have to expend his rage elsewhere.

"Adrik?" Lorienne called softly, and stepped through the hatchway leading to the tower steps. She knew she would find him here. He was standing near the edge of the rooftop, facing away from the night-dark sea as he surveyed the muddle of activity taking place in the courtyard below.

He turned toward her slowly, and she was struck once more by the solemnity of his expression, as if nothing in his life had ever held a trace of humor or light. Then, to her surprise, he appeared to smile, the corners of his mouth lifting in an unexpected gesture of feeling and warmth.

She blinked away the sudden moisture burning in her eyes. She cared for him, and she knew he cared for her in return. To lose him now, short months since they first joined, seemed wrong somehow. Terribly wrong. As if Shalelle's prophecy had been mistaken after all. "Jirina said to tell you that the messenger from Urmia has gone, and that all is now in readiness for your departure."

Adrik nodded and crossed the last few steps between them to fold her lithe body within his arms. Vlada's leaving presented him with one less difficulty to surmount. The ward he'd created would temporarily protect Khorazm and its inhabitants from unearthly perils, but it would do nothing to prevent danger from mortal sources. "I didn't have the strength needed to cast Malkaval out completely, so I have erected a protective ward around the fortress instead. It will last long enough. No demons or other unliving creatures will trouble you while I am gone."

Lorienne bit her lip until she tasted blood on her tongue. Did he not know that she had grown to worry more for him than the wrath of some demon? What good would any ward prove if he were never able to return to her? "I will miss you greatly in the coming days," she admitted, unable to prevent a quaver from entering her voice. "How soon will you return to me?"

He smoothed her wind-tousled hair then straightened himself abruptly, his shoulders growing rigid with resolve. Whatever came to pass in the coming weeks, he had done as much as possible to assure Lorienne's safety. But what should he tell her of his return? Though he had dared to hope he might have a future with her at his side, the cold, bitter truth was that he probably wouldn't survive the month of May. His end would come to pass either at the hands of the Lydians, his own father and brother, or the angry demon who had raised him.

He decided to lie to her, to protect her from the truth for a little while. "I will be with our army in the west until the summer campaign draws to a close. No matter what happens between us, the Lydians will eventually have to allow their soldiers to return home in order to plant crops to see them through the next winter, and we must do the same. We will return to our own lands before the rains of fall begin."

Her hand moved from the sleeve of his tunic to the flat of her belly, an unconscious gesture. "Fall is such a long time away," she whispered, commanding herself to be as strong as the Magian women she had watched bidding a safe journey to their men. She brushed her fingertips protectively over the soft wool covering her abdomen. "Far too long." By fall the seed she felt growing inside her would be an ungainly mound. Would he still find her desirable then? Would he acknowledge a child born of her loins?

"The months will pass quickly enough." A melancholy smile struggled to find purchase on his lips. For him, fall might never arrive. "Come, Lorienne." He led her toward the hatchway leading to the staircase. Around them, the sky had lightened to a grayish hue. "It's nearly dawn."

They descended the winding staircase in utter silence, both preoccupied with their own thoughts, their own worries. Lorienne clung tightly to his arm, drawing strength from his presence.

A blaze of orange light and flickering shadows greeted them upon their arrival on the lowest level of the tower. Every lamp and torch within the great hall had been lit, causing curls of smoke to rise like wisps of fog to linger in a cloud that hovered along the high ceiling.

Jirina was waiting near the arched door, just as she always did. The old woman bowed deeply in a show of respect, far deeper than was her norm. One by one, she handed Adrik his baldric, bow, and quiver, which he lifted into place atop his armor and tunic of mail. Last she gave him his helmet and watched while he snugged it atop his head.

She regarded her master steadily. "I have known and served you many years, my prince," she told him quietly, "and throughout all those years I have been as proud of you as any mother, and I know that Princess Vania would have been proud of you as well. Your rule has given strength to all the Magii, and we shall be able to endure whatever may come because of the sacrifices you have made for us. We will not forget you or your generosity."

Adrik dipped his head in acknowledgment of Jirina's words. "And I shall not forget you or your service, Jirina, either to me, or to my mother." He drew a felt pouch from within his tunic and placed it in her hand, the hard edges of the lapis, rubies, and other costly stones it held outlined against his fingers. He said nothing to her of the pouch's contents, merely pressed it deeper into her palm.

"Live well, Jirina," he told her in the customary farewell of the Magii. Other pouches had been distributed throughout Khorazm as well. He had made many such arrangements with trusted members of his tribe. If need be, they would see to Lorienne's care.

The old woman stared in wonder at the pouch resting in her palm, then lifted her gaze to meet the Shadow Prince's solemn eyes. She knew what the pouch held. "Die well, my lord," she said in a hushed voice, the traditional rejoinder told to a Magian soldier about to leave for battle.

Lorienne flinched when she heard Jirina's words. How cruel the custom sounded when delivered at a time such as this. But she knew even Jirina was not unaffected. She worried for Adrik, too. Though the old woman's features remained devoid of expression, Lorienne could see the fear buried deep in her eyes, a sight that only served to increase her own fright of what might come.

She clutched at Adrik's forearm even more, as if she could hold him within the tower by the force of her will, though she doubted he could feel her touch beneath the thick leather armor and tunic of mail.

"I wish . . ." she began, then fell silent again, suddenly uncertain of what to say to him.

Adrik touched a finger to her lips, hushing any

words before they spilled from her mouth. "I wish many things as well, but it will do us no good to dwell upon such things." He caressed the curve of her mouth with the end of his thumb. "Just know this, Lorienne of the Arizanti . . . in these past months, you have brought me more happiness than I have ever known. If I am to die now, I will die not as you found me, and for that, I thank you."

He caught her chin with his thumb and forefinger and drew her toward his lips, angling his head so that the visor of his helmet didn't impede his kiss. His mouth captured hers in a tender caress that spoke far more loudly of his feelings than could any mere words. After a timeless moment, he pulled away, releasing her entirely as he turned and strode into a rush of dawn light outside the tower's entrance. And then he took the steps two at a time and hurried across the courtyard to his waiting horse, hurling himself atop the saddle before her proximity caused him to have a change of mind.

As the dawning sun threw a blaze of light across the quiet waters of the Caspian, the Magian army prepared to depart. All was in readiness, and a strange, other-worldly air hung about the column as the sunlight revealed the profusion of horns and feathers and animal snouts decorating the masks worn by the Magian horses.

Adrik's own horse turned in a nervous circle, the sound of its hooves striking the flagstones just one noise among a cacophony of others. He soothed the anxious beast and kneed it into motion toward the fortress gates.

Double rows of mounted soldiers as well as ranks of spearmen and archers fell into step behind him, a long train of bawling pack animals being led by baggage handlers at the rear of the column. Black Magian pennants snapped proudly in the freshening breeze, the banner poles held high by strong-armed bearers not yet wearied by their constant task.

Adrik increased the pressure of his knees and forced the horse into a trot as he exited Khorazm's massive gates. He knew that Lorienne had followed him out of the tower and watched his departure from the top of the steps.

He never looked back.

By the time the sun fully broached the horizon, the column had already made its way down the winding cart path and had turned toward the north and west, moving inexorably toward the high mountain passes still partially blocked with drifts of melting snow. The journey west to Amida would be treacherous, and this was only the first of many weeks of travel through perilous terrain.

The pennants weren't waving quite so proudly by midmorning. Though Adrik could still hear the lively notes of a marching tune played by a baggage handler on a bass reed pipe, his soldiers had lost much of the vim they had exhibited with the leaving at dawn. He drew his horse to a momentary halt atop a rock-strewn ridge and surveyed the surrounding landscape for a likely place for men and beasts to take a short rest.

From his position high atop the ridge, he could see in all directions. The Caspian was now a silver glimmer to the east, and Khorazm a dark sprawl of stone near its closest edge. His gaze moved to the south and suddenly stilled. Adrik frowned and lifted a hand to shield his eyes from the glare of the sun. Along the spine of another ridge, he could see specks of movement, men and horses making slow progress toward a different chain of mountains. He could see the dark green pennants of the Median Empire flying as well.

His second in command drew abreast of him, his horse clambering for purchase among the loose rocks. "My lord?" Harpagus said breathlessly. He, too, was staring at the movement atop the distant ridge.

Adrik watched carefully as the small column began to vanish down the far side of the ridge, moving farther to the north of their position, and more importantly, farther away from Khorazm. Only then did he allow himself to relax.

"Rest easy, commander," he told the officer. "There is no need for alarm. Those soldiers carry the imperial pennants of the empire. The crown prince's messenger and his escort column are simply returning to Urmia."

"Yes, my lord," the officer replied without question, and spun his horse back to inform his men.

As the last of Vlada's column vanished from sight, Adrik finally lowered his hand, but his gaze remained fixed on the top of the empty ridge for a longish span of time. He frowned into the distance, trying to quell the odd sense of unease that had sprung to life inside him.

The constant thrum of the sea was like soft music, a sound so ingrained within her now that Lorienne knew she would miss it if it were gone one day. Around her, the beach beneath the fortress was awash in movement, banter, and laughter as the women of Khorazm worked together to cut and clean heavy slabs of sturgeon freshly pulled from the sea by fishermen who'd braved the chilly waters atop flimsy rafts made of reeds. The results of their morning's work were then tied and wrapped into linen-covered bundles, the succulent roe extracted from the fish carefully deposited in clay pots that would later be carried up the face of the cliff by a bevy of servants.

From her place atop a rock, Lorienne watched the Magians' activities, still a bit uncertain about joining in, but gladdened by the opportunity to accompany them on their trek to the beach. She knew Damek still watched her, a task the young soldier surely found onerous by now, yet he never complained, even when she had insisted on the trip to the beach this day. He had finally relented when she told him how lonely and bored she was without the company of his prince.

Lorienne sighed. It wasn't a lie. Adrik had been gone nearly a week now, and she had found it increasingly difficult to fill the empty days. Without him, she felt as if she had been cast adrift atop one of those flimsy reed rafts and would never find her way to shore again.

The seed ripening inside her was causing changes to her body that only made her feelings of emptiness far worse. She found it nearly impossible to eat more than an occasional bit of bread and sip of water without growing ill. And without Adrik's warmth beside her in the night, she had found that sleep escaped her as well.

She needed him desperately, needed the reassurance of his arms around her, the protection of his embrace. Yet she knew that couldn't be. If the fates favored her and she did indeed see him again come fall, he might even be wed to the Lydian princess by then. What they had already shared together might be all there would ever be.

Her hand was suddenly drawn to her ripening belly. Even if Adrik never returned, she would still have his child to fill her arms and ease the emptiness of her days. Perhaps that would be enough.

Hoping that was true, Lorienne smiled sadly to herself and climbed to her feet. She turned toward the cliff and spotted Damek standing sentinel atop a scrub-covered rise. The soldier would be happy to learn that even she had had enough of the beach for one day. She lifted a hand and waved to him, signaling that she was ready to return to the fortress, but instead of walking toward her as expected, the young soldier suddenly spun in the opposite direction and grabbed at the heavy sword sheathed in a baldric across his back.

Lorienne froze, bewildered by Damek's frantic motions. Somewhere atop the battlements a sentry shouted a warning. And then she heard the thud of many hoofbeats pounding through the sandy soil.

A horse and rider suddenly crested the rise Damek was standing on, and she watched in horror as the young man was felled, trampled beneath those thundering hooves before he could fully draw his sword. Other riders appeared from the north and south, rushing toward them along the shoreline, geysers of sand and water thrown into the air by their horses' flailing hooves.

Behind her, the women screamed and dropped their bundles of fish, running in all directions as they sought to flee the surprise attack. She heard the angry shouting of the fishermen, but they were still out on the rafts upon the water, weaponless and too distant to defend the women on the beach.

Arrows loosed by guards atop the battlements cut through the morning air, only to fall harmlessly to the sand shy of their intended targets. One finally hit its mark, and an attacker tumbled from his saddle, his body rolling to a stop facedown in the water. Blood pooled around him and washed onto the sand.

Her heart hammering wildly in her breast, Lorienne finally broke free of her paralysis and started to run. There was no choice for it now. The attacker who'd trampled poor Damek had topped the rise and his horse was sliding downward through the mounded sand, obviously heading toward the spot where she'd stood frozen. But she didn't know in which direction to run. The rider was between her and the cliff path now, blocking any hope of escape from that quarter. She considered running into the water itself but rejected the idea at once. More riders had appeared along the beach, shouting and charging their horses through the midst of the screaming women, forcing them to dart this way and that as they tried to flee.

She angled toward the south, running parallel to the beach and the cliff to try and reach the front of the fortress and the main entry gates. Even now, Magian soldiers were likely pouring through those gates and rushing to their aid. She would meet them as they rounded the fortress walls.

Struggling against the sand and the voluminous folds of her robe, Lorienne tried desperately to increase her speed. Behind her, she could hear the hooves of the attacker's horse digging into the sand, the creature's snorting and huffs for air. She choked back a frightened sob. The rider was intent on running her down as well.

An arrow dug into the ground beside her, but she knew instinctively that it hadn't been meant for her. For an endless moment, she could feel and smell the hot breath of the horse blowing upon her neck, and then the beast was beside her and she felt herself lifted into the air. She screamed in fear as the rider slung her across his saddle, its high pommel driving the breath from her in a painful rush.

Bile rose in her throat as the pommel slammed into her belly this time, and the upside-down landscape passed in a sickening flash beneath her eyes. She squeezed her lids tightly shut as the horse broke into a full run, its body lengthening as it raced down the beach. A man's strong hand pulled her backward slightly, preventing the pommel from hitting her again, but now her hip was tight against him and his powerful hand was holding her firmly in place.

The sounds of the Magian women's screaming began to fade with distance, but the rider didn't slow his pace. Instead, the horse seemed to increase its thundering speed. She heard the hollow thudding of more horses as well, and realized that the others had broken off their frenzied attack and were now heading away from Khorazm on a path similar to the one she had taken when she fled into the forest so many weeks before. But that didn't make any sense at all. Why attack if they planned to break off their assault without storming the fortress or capturing anything of value?

Suddenly she understood it all with dizzying clarity. *She* had been the intended target, the only target. Lorienne tried to swallow the fear gripping her throat but found that she couldn't with her body suspended.

She cried out sharply as a piece of brush clawed at her face and hair. She fought to lift her body upright, her hands scrambling for purchase on the horse's sweaty hide, but could do little to help herself other than pull her flowing hair out of harm's way. In response to her frantic struggles, her captor's arm merely tightened its hold about her, gripping her waist and hip in a painful embrace.

The ground still sped beneath her at a dizzying rate, forcing her to keep her lids squeezed shut lest she give in to the sickness and lose what little sustenance remained in her roiling belly.

Time passed; how much she wasn't certain. Then without warning, her captor's horse finally slowed, its gait dropping from a dead run to nothing so suddenly Lorienne thought she would be thrown over its neck and head. But her captor's arm still held her firmly in place.

For a moment, the only sounds she heard were the laboring breaths drawn by the horses. Then her captor barked an order to someone beyond her. A chill rode up her spine. It was a familiar voice, one she had heard quite recently.

She struggled to rise again, and this time the arm restraining her lifted out of the way. Finally, she was able to scramble and slide to her feet on the opposite side of the lathered horse. But the ground shifted beneath her feet and she staggered into her captor's leg as a renewed wave of dizziness swept through her body.

191

She clung to both his leg and the horse's braided mane for a long moment, trying to regain the sense of balance she had lost, but the effort was in vain. Still clinging to her captor's leg, she bent double and retched, heaving until the world around her turned dark and utterly still.

The same powerful arm grabbed on to her shoulder and pulled her upright before she could slide to the ground.

"Bring me a skin of water!" the familiar voice ordered. "Quickly!"

From what seemed like a great distance, Lorienne heard murmuring and the shuffling of booted feet, the occasional clang of armor. She knew her captor had dismounted and was now easing her toward the ground, but she could do nothing to resist. In fact, all she wanted was to lay her head down upon a pillow of grass and sleep the rest of the day away.

A cool cloth soaked in water gently bathed her face and throat. Lorienne moaned, and a dribble of water fell onto her lips. She used her tongue to capture the moisture, and then someone lifted her head and neck, enabling her to take slow sips from the mouth of a skin.

Her eyes reopened, and she blinked herself back to reality, slowly focusing on the face of the man holding the skin of water. She stared, frowning uncertainly. The face above her belonged to Vlada Sura, the messenger from Crown Prince Burian who'd come to Khorazm the week before. But he had left the same morning as Adrik, hadn't he?

"I don't understand . . ." she managed to croak.

Her accusatory stare caused Vlada to blow out an uneasy breath and grimace in self-disgust. Stealing women wasn't the sort of chore he normally performed for his prince. "Forgive me, my lady, but Prince Burian ordered me to retrieve you, and I could think of no other way to do so without spilling a great quantity of Magian blood."

She shook her head, not comprehending what he had said. "Why?" she finally asked, her voice a bit stronger now.

He cleared his throat and prodded her into a sitting position. "I was ordered to bring you back with me to Urmia with all haste. Crown Prince Burian has decided to revoke the gift he made to his half brother and to keep you for himself." The soldier grimaced again. His own words filled him with loathing for what he had done. "You are to become a concubine in the prince's household."

Lorienne stared at the soldier in shock. She had considered many possibilities, but never this. She had been unconscious when the prince had seen her on the steppe, then given her over into Adrik's care. Why would he plot to steal her back and take her as a concubine? He was the crown prince of the Median Empire, and she a lowly Arizanti who had shared his brother's bed. She couldn't imagine why he would even want his brother's leavings.

Tears brimmed in her eyes. And what of Adrik? She had grown to care for him more than life itself, and she knew he cared for her as well. If he survived the coming days, would he not go to battle with his brother over what Burian had now done?

Her heart stilled and she felt sick inside. The message for Adrik to go west to meet the Lydians had come from Prince Burian himself, the very man who plotted to steal her away! It was even possible that Adrik was not meant to return to Khorazm, that this was all some sort of clever ploy designed by Burian to dispose of Adrik once and for all.

If so, she needed to be strong and just as clever as those who had stolen her away. To that end, she knew that fear and suspicion of the Shadow Prince and his motives were widespread within the empire. She would now use that very same fear and suspicion against those who sought to bring harm to him.

She lifted her chin in a small show of defiance. "I will not submit to the attentions of your prince. A man as weak and pathetic as he holds no appeal for me at all." Her eyes narrowed and her chin tilted even higher. "I am the property of his brother, the Shadow Prince, and he will not take kindly to you stealing me from his bed."

The sounds of uneasy mutters and whispers came from the soldiers behind her. She even heard an angry curse, though she wasn't sure if it was directed toward her or the sorcerer they feared so much.

Lorienne's mouth curled in a defiant sneer. "Do not be surprised when the sorcerer takes his revenge by casting a spell that causes your manhood to shrivel and boils to grow upon your face." She had told the threat to Vlada but it was obvious her words were meant for all those who'd participated in her kidnapping.

The crown prince's soldiers shuffled uneasily, their mutters growing louder and more worried. But to her dismay, their leader only laughed.

Vlada climbed to his feet abruptly and took a swig from his skin of water. When he was done, he shook his head and laughed again, amused by the girl's un-expected display of verve, but also laughing in the face of her threats for the benefit of his frightened men. They had already grown nervous the week before when it was discovered a pack of wolves had followed them across Magian lands. But if their commander could find amusement in such hideous threats, then so should they.

Vlada had thought the girl would simply cry and cower and act the part of a mewling victim. Instead, she had clearly shown that she possessed the heart of a warrior. He said, "I salute your cunning, little one.

But your hopes of sowing dissension among us with your threats of dark magic have fallen on deaf ears."

Lorienne continued to stare at him, her gaze fixed on her captor's rugged features. "I make no empty threats. When Adrik learns what your prince has done, he will come for me. This I promise."

The soldier broke contact with her angry eyes and motioned for his men to mount. "We shall see soon enough, Lorienne of the Arizanti." He bade her to rise as well, then tied her hands in front of her with a strip of leather. "For now we go to Urmia. And if you wish for your mouth to remain ungagged, you will make no more threats in Prince Adrik's name."

Vlada hid a sudden frown by glancing toward the midday sun. His greatest fear was that the Shadow Prince *would* come for her, arriving at a time of his own making, not of Burian's. If that occurred, they might all end up with dried-up members and a bevy of boils.

Chapter Twelve

The underside of the silver tray had been shined and polished to a fine sheen, a chore Melina forced an unlucky palace servant to perform each day. She held the flat tray high to catch the sunlight slanting into her chamber from the open terrace. The silvery surface was free of smudges or other imperfections, just the way she preferred it. Perhaps she would give the servant a piece of fruit as a reward for his diligence, unlike yesterday, when he had felt the bite of a whip for leaving behind the outline of his thumb.

Melina lifted the tray higher and preened, pursing her lips to make them appear as plump and ripe as those that belonged to a girl of no more than sixteen. She stared at her silvery reflection for a long span of time, angling her head from side to side to achieve the most flattering view of herself.

She adjusted a length of dark hair, flicking it from her face to reveal the pale expanse of her unlined neck. Squinting, she carefully checked her throat and the curve of her jaw for any sign of age or weathering, but there were no lines or wrinkles to be found anywhere. Her face and skin were still youthful and flawless, perfect in every way.

She posed herself at an even more attractive angle and smiled at her reflection in contentment. She looked remarkably seductive today, so much so that Burian would not be able to resist coming to her bed this night. Her plans would finally be set into motion.

"Ah, such a pretty illusion," a voice whispered from behind her.

The serving tray slipped from her nerveless fingers and clattered against the tiles. Startled, Melina gasped and spun toward the sound of a voice she hadn't heard in many, many years. Her eyes widened slightly. Until now, she had thought never to see that face again either.

"Malkaval!" she breathed, half in fear, half in wonder that the demon had returned to Urmia after all these years. A suspicious frown suddenly marred the smoothness of her brow. But why had he returned now? Unless . . . Her hands flew to her face to check for wrinkles and sagging flesh. She breathed a sigh of relief. He hadn't taken her beauty away.

A thin smile crawled across the demon's skull-like features. "Yes, my sweet, I have come to visit you once again. But fear not, I do not intend to remove the spell I cast so long ago. You will remain young and beautiful . . . as long as you are willing to do my bidding."

Melina's dark head dipped in a quick nod. "Of course. Whatever you wish." What choice did she truly have? She couldn't lose her beauty now, not when she was so close to achieving her goals. Without the spell the demon had wrought so many years ago, she would become nothing more than an aged crone, as wrinkled and withered as her decrepit husband. "Tell me what

Jan Zimlich

it is you want of me!" she said, desperate to please him in some way.

The demon's mouth thinned in a malicious smile, his form shimmering like a reflection upon water. "I knew I could still count upon you, Melina."

Smiling, she picked up her fallen tray and placed it atop a table. "You may always count on me, Malkaval." As long as her illusion of beauty remained intact, the demon could count on her for anything he wished. Hedeon would soon be dead, either by natural means or Burian's hand, and then she would be free to marry the son. She would not stand idly by while Hedeon's death caused her to lose the power, wealth, and privilege it had taken her a lifetime to accumulate. She would never be the pitiable wife of a dead, mad king. She was meant for far grander things than that. With the aid of Malkaval's illusion, she would bind Burian to herself and become the new king's wife. Like father, like son. Foolish weaklings both.

She crossed to stand before the demon, as unafraid now as she had been when she saw him last, before the death of Vania, Hedeon's second wife. They had struck a bargain between them then—she would keep her youth and beauty for all time, enabling her to entrap a besotted Hedeon, while in exchange, she would aid Malkaval in claiming the king's second born son for his own.

The task had proved simple enough, especially since Hedeon had been so eager and amendable. A few nocturnal whispers of encouragement in Hedeon's ear, a few threats of banishing him from her arms and bed, and Vania had quickly found herself dead. Surely this new task the demon wished of her would be simple as well.

"Tell me what you wish of me," she said to the demon, her lips curling with enthusiasm. Perhaps their goals would again be mutually beneficial.

Malkaval glided closer, his eyes burning red. "I will allow no one who interferes with my plans for Prince Adrik to do so and live! I let him keep that puny girl so that he would know and taste the mortal world that he was about to lose forever. I wanted to give him something pleasurable to remember for the next thousand years! But she has somehow turned him from me, and for that she will die!"

Melina's dark brows lifted. "And what am I to do about this 'puny girl' you speak of? I am days distant from Khorazm."

His cadaverous eyes turned so deep and red they seemed to bleed. "She is no longer at Khorazm!" His voice crackled with fury. "Burian has seen to that! He has sent his lackey Vlada Sura to steal her from Khorazm and bring her here so that she can become his new concubine! The fools are going to destroy everything it has taken me a hundred hundred years to plan!"

Melina's ripe mouth flattened into a tight, angry slash. "His concubine?" she hissed. Rage glittered like fire in the depths of her own eyes. What had Burian planned? "His *concubine*?"

The silver tray that gave her such endless pleasure sailed across the chamber, flying out the terrace entrance to crash and clatter along the polished flagstones.

Many things that had gone unexplained for long months made perfect sense to her now. When Burian returned from seeing the Shadow Prince, he had become suddenly enamored of fair-haired whores, an obsession that had appeared to grow over time, not fade as she had hoped. "Is this the same Arizanti captive Burian gave to his brother to amuse himself?" Her mouth flattened even more. "And does she possess the pale hair of the northlands?"

"Yes . . . to both your questions."

Jan Zimlich

Melina screamed in fury and frustration. *No one* was going to prevent her from becoming consort to the next Median king. "And you say he sent Vlada to claim her as his concubine?"

"They return to Urmia even now. You must kill her quickly when she arrives . . . before Adrik learns she has been stolen by his foolish brother."

She clasped her hands before her and paced her chamber angrily. "Why have *you* not killed her yourself?" she demanded of the demon, a niggle of suspicion surfacing in her thoughts. "Surely a demon could smite this girl with a single glare. Why have you not done this?"

Malkaval shimmered orange, then white, and his features appeared to settle into a rage-filled glare. "The time of the change is almost upon me . . . but Adrik *must* enter the gateway willingly for the transformation to occur between us. He has vowed that if she comes to harm by my hand he will not allow the exchange. He even went so far as to weave a protective ward around Khorazm to keep me from entering the walls of my home!"

Melina's gaze narrowed in sudden understanding. "Ah . . . you wish me to kill her in your stead so you cannot be blamed for her death. Is that a correct assumption?"

"Yes!" the creature said quickly. "You must do it so that Adrik never knows my part in it! The girl—this Lorienne—must die!"

Melina stared out at the wide terrace and the sunlit lake beyond, thinking of ways in which to dispose of the girl before Burian could take her as concubine. He could jab his member into countless fair-haired whores if he wanted, but a bound concubine was another matter entirely. As his consort, Melina would allow no such competition to live within her own household.

She nodded slowly. "Our goals just so happen to co-

200

incide on this, Malkaval," she said tersely. In truth, she couldn't care less if the demon ever achieved his goal of becoming human, but if his quest was actually successful, then Adrik would be dead and gone, one less claimant to the Median throne. "I cannot allow Burian to take a concubine. I plan to marry him soon, you see—as soon as that deranged old man finally meets the death he so richly deserves." She smiled, a cold little lift of her mouth that never penetrated her eyes. "So I shall gladly think of a clever way to rid us both of this interfering girl."

She moved even closer to the demon, closer than any mortal had a right to dare, gazed at him speculatively. "But if I do this for you, what more will you give me in return?"

"Eternal beauty is not enough?" He touched her face with a clawlike nail, wishing he could feel his fingertip brushing across her skin. Soon, he reminded himself. Very, very soon now. "Do not anger me, my sweet. I could remove the spell from you if I so desired," he threatened casually. "Do you wish Burian to see you as you truly are? I fear your intended husband would not wish to share his bed with a withered old crone with loose breasts and sagging skin."

Melina tried not to react, though she knew a quick little glint of fear had rushed through her eyes, giving her thoughts away. But she would ignore his threats and hold to her ground because she knew just how desperate the demon was to make the coming exchange. In the end he would give her what she wanted because he had no other choice, not if he wanted the assurance of success. "I'm weary of the role of consort to a king . . . I want to rule the empire as Burian's queen, to share his power equally!"

Malkaval laughed, a malevolent sound that slithered around the chamber like the hissing of a serpent. If he gave her what she wished, poor foolish Burian would be dead within the year. "A woman ruling as queen? Your ambitions have grown through the years, Melina."

She lifted her head haughtily. "Why not? I am far more capable of rule than any male born of Hedeon's blood. With your aid I shall build an empire that will rival Egypt's!" she said fervidly.

Malkaval gazed at her in amusement. Melina was as mad as her sickly husband. Did she truly believe that a mere woman could rule an empire in place of a male? The line of his shoulders moved in a gesture that would have been construed as a shrug if he possessed a living body. This woman's paltry delusions were of no significance to him. If she did as he instructed, he would gain all that he had ever desired. The empire could crumble to dust beneath Melina's pretty feet for all that he cared; he would soon be mortal, and far away.

"So be it," he said in a display of munificence. "You shall be queen if that is what you desire. When the girl is truly dead, I shall ensure that Burian finds you so alluring that he asks you to rule at his side as queen. But what happens after will be entirely up to you, for I shall be gone from here by then."

A look of utter panic swept over her face. "Gone? Where?" If his quest was successful and he left Median lands, what would become of her? Would his spell hold until the end of her days?

The demon laughed again, amused by her overwhelming conceit and selfishness. It was a pity she could not make the exchange in Adrik's place. She would make a fine demon. "Do not worry, my sweet. If you send the girl to her death for me, I shall see to it that your beauty is as eternal as your greed."

His red gaze thinned, grew as narrow as cracks in a wall of stone. "But be warned, Melina. If you fail me in this, I shall make you suffer in ways you have never imagined. The loss of your beauty will pale in comparison to what else I will take in revenge."

* * *

The chamber was dark and still, the air heavy with the scents of sickness and approaching death. Only a glimmering of sunlight reached through the thick layers of fabric hanging along the wide opening to the king's private section of the terrace. A breath of wind finally managed to wend its way through the material, ruffling the bottoms of the costly blue silks.

For a brief moment, the air smelled fresh and alive.

"You wished to see me, father?" Burian said, barely managing to keep his voice free of impatience. He had better things to do with his time than to dance attendance upon a mad old man. His nose wrinkled. Especially a mad old man who smelled as if he had spent the last week buried inside a tomb.

Hedeon managed to lift his head from a silk cushion, then let it fall backward again. "Burian, my son . . . yes, I did want to see you." His face had grown emaciated. Sunken. And his eyes were filmy with age. "I wanted to ask you about your mother. How is she these days? She never comes to visit me."

The crown prince arched a heavy brow. "My mother has been dead many years. Melina is your consort now."

The king looked puzzled for a moment. "Melina?" His frown deepened. "I do not know any Melina."

Burian snorted. Hedeon had been wed to Melina for a score and five years, ever since the untimely death of Adrik's mother. It was a sign of the madness, Burian decided. Otherwise, how could he have forgotten such a lengthy span of his life? "You do not remember her?" he asked quietly, wondering how this new development could be used to his advantage. "You wed her after the death of your Magian wife."

Hedeon closed his eyes a moment and nodded slowly, his frail head moving up and down on the cushion. "Yes, that's right. I remember the Magian now.

Her name was Vania . . . an ugly woman, not beautiful like the Parae-tak I took to my bed. I wed the Magian to gain control of her tribe."

His eyes suddenly became clear and lucid and his thin mouth curled in disgust. "I remember Vania well. She was tall, with a long face and small breasts, and she was a powerful sorceress. Very powerful. Did you know that?" The set of his lips turned into a grimace. "Yes, I remember now . . . I was afraid she might turn me into a goat or a swine. She was capable, you know, and she threatened to do so on one occasion. She might have even turned me into an insect if I had allowed her the chance."

Burian sighed. "Is this what you wished to tell me?"

The king frowned, thinking. "I cannot find Vlada. No one will tell me where he is, and I want to know. I am the king—it's my right to know these things!"

"He will return to the palace very soon," Burian said quickly. "He went to Khorazm at your behest, remember?" Burian didn't see the need to tell his father of the orders he had given Vlada in the king's name.

"Ah, that's right." Hedeon nodded in satisfaction. "Good. Adrik will be coming to see me soon. Vlada will make certain of it."

Burian glowered at the old man lying upon the bed. He was weary of this nonsense. And weary of hearing about the treacherous Adrik coming to visit his doting father. "Spring is almost upon us, father. You sent Adrik west, beyond Amida, to lead our army into battle against the Lydians." Hedeon was beyond knowing what was truth and what was not. "If he comes here, it will not be until our army returns at the end of summer."

The crown prince veiled a look of sudden satisfaction. He had sent his traitorous little brother into a pit of offal that he would find difficult to escape. Adrik would either have to fight the Lydians as duty required, or reveal his treachery for all to see. One way or the other, the problem of his sorcerous brother would soon be resolved. Either the Lydians would kill Adrik for betraying their alliance, or soldiers loyal to Hedeon and the Median Empire would put him to the sword for his alliance with a hated foe. There would be no marriage to a Lydian princess. The final result would be Adrik's death, and an end to Hedeon's sudden strange show of favoritism.

A chilly smile touched the edges of Burian's lips. All the wrongs in the world would soon be righted, including his foolish mistake in giving the Arizanti girl away. His smile turned darkly contemplative. A gift given could be taken away, which was exactly what he had done. Even if his monastic little brother had been first to thrust himself inside her loins, so be it. In this they would share as true siblings.

The haunting notes of a pipe drifted through the night, the soft sounds like a woman's voice lifted in a plaintive song. Vlada leaned his back against a tree trunk and listened as the soldier continued to play, his gaze fastened on the crackling flames of the campfire.

He yawned. Another day's journey and they would be in Urmia, and he would no longer be responsible for the young Arizanti. That would surely be a relief. The girl's presence had been making him increasingly uneasy, so much so that he feared the future more with each passing day.

Each time she refused the food offered to her, each time he caught her retching quietly behind a tree or bush, his uneasiness grew to a level he had never experienced before.

To make matters even more difficult, he had found that he actually enjoyed her company, and was gladdened by the days they had spent on the journey together. Not only was she so beautiful as to be a distraction, she possessed both the courage of a tiger and the gentleness of a lamb. Add a quick and agile mind to that blend and he could well understand both the sorcerer's and Prince Burian's attraction to her.

He glanced sideways, to where Lorienne lay sleeping on the ground beside him, her fair head pillowed upon the saddle of his horse. His nights had been spent in much the same way ever since they had set out for Urmia—long, sleepless hours with her near his side, shame for what he had done stealing away any hope he might have had for true rest. If he did manage to fall into sleep's embrace, the time was spent fighting off violent dreams about Vania, vengeful sorcerers, and dying and death.

Sighing, Vlada shifted his neck against the tree and tried to settle into a more comfortable position. He feared there was no such thing as comfort anymore, not for him, at least.

The tune finally ended and the pipe fell silent, the last tender notes echoing through the surrounding wood. The soldier who'd been playing lay down to sleep on the opposite side of the fire. Soon the only sounds in the makeshift camp were the snoring of a soldier and the flames licking at the charred wood glowing in the fire.

At the edge of the small clearing, he could see the silhouette of the sentry standing watch, his helmet slowly angling from side to side as he surveyed the dense stand of trees. Vlada took one last careful look around, then folded his arms across his chest and tried to close his eyes in what would surely be another vain quest for sleep.

Beside him, Lorienne stirred restlessly, her body shifting slightly in his direction. By the sound of her breathing, he knew she had awakened and was lying in the darkness, wakeful like him.

Vlada pursed his lips. After a long, silent moment,

he finally decided to give voice to the concerns and worries that had plagued him for days. He swung his head toward her, unsurprised to find those pale eyes staring back at him in the dark.

"You are with child," he said in a hushed voice, careful lest his men overhear.

Lorienne stared back at him, startled by his pronouncement. He seemed so utterly certain. "Yes," she finally answered, just as quietly.

He held her gaze to his. "The Shadow Prince is the father?" As unlikely as that possibility, he had to know the truth. If it were true, the child she carried would be third in line for the Median throne.

Lorienne sighed, uncertain if she should trust the soldier with such information. But instinct told her that Vlada Sura was an honorable man. Adrik had thought so, too, and what the soldier didn't know already, she was sure he had mostly guessed. And perhaps his knowing the truth might somehow aid her plight in some way. "Yes . . . Adrik is the father."

"Does he know?" Vlada asked, more worried than ever of the repercussions of what Burian had done. The girl was breeding, and Burian had stolen her from his own brother. Worse still, he planned to make her his concubine.

Lorienne shook her head in regret. "I didn't tell him before he left, though I wish now that I had." A troubled frown passed over her brow. Though her belly was slightly rounded, she had not thought the evidence visible to any eyes but her own. "How did you know?"

The old warrior blew out an amused breath. "I am not entirely ignorant of the ways of women. You have not been eating much, your face is always white and drawn, and I have caught you secretly retching on more than one occasion."

Lorienne grimaced. She had thought she could mask her state for a very long while. "I see."

Jan Zimlich

It struck Vlada then that the babe she carried within her would be the child of Vania's child, a direct descendent of the woman he had loved. It occurred to him also that this infant was the offspring of a powerful sorcerer and would someday grow to become a formidable foe of the future Median king.

His unease grew even more. What would Burian do when he discovered Lorienne carried Adrik's child? Whether Adrik lived through his encounters with the Lydians or died in the thick of battle would make no difference to Burian where the girl was concerned. Even unborn, the child posed a monumental threat to both the crown prince and his future heirs. Burian was still childless, despite all his years of excess with scores of women. If he discovered the truth, he would dispose of Lorienne immediately. Burian would never allow his brother's seed to grow in any woman's belly. He feared Adrik and his powers too much for that.

Vlada closed his eyes and drew a shaky breath. Gods. What was he to do? He had chafed at the task Burian set before him, but now that task was even more odious than before.

Danger lay in all directions. He was about to deliver Lorienne into Burian's hands—a man who would surely kill her once he knew the truth. And if that occurred, would he ever be able to find sleep again? The child would carry Vania's blood in its veins, and he would never be able to live with himself if he spilled that blood. The debt he owed both her and her son still remained unpaid.

The soldier sighed, a deep, troubled sound. The day he had stolen Lorienne away she had said that the Shadow Prince would come to retrieve her once he knew. "You said that Prince Adrik would come for you once he discovered you had been taken. . . . Was that the truth?"

She nodded slowly. "He will come if he can. . . . We

. . . care for each other." But there was more to her relationship with Adrik than simple caring. She left unspoken the single word that had echoed through her thoughts for many weeks now, the one little word she could no longer deny, though she had tried many times. *Love*. She loved him, and she hoped he loved her as well.

Vlada turned and stared at the guttering fire. The question was, would Adrik be able to arrive in time to rescue Lorienne from his brother? If they had traveled swiftly, Prince Adrik and his forces would be nearing Amida by now. The Magians would surely have dispatched a messenger to him after Lorienne had been stolen from Khorazm, but their prince was already far away, and the message might not reach him for many more days.

He sighed again. It was too great a chance to take. To see to the safety of the Shadow Prince's child, he would have to act on his own.

"I will do all that I can to protect you once we arrive in Urmia," Vlada vowed to her solemnly.

Lorienne stared at the soldier in shock. He sought to protect her from his own master? She had never expected such from him. "Why would you do this?"

"I owe a debt to Princess Vania, the mother of the Shadow Prince." He was quiet for a moment. "It has gone unpaid long enough."

Lorienne's pale brows lifted in amazement. She knew little of the Magian princess who'd died giving birth to Adrik. "You knew his mother?"

Vlada nodded and smiled sadly, his thoughts drifting backward in time. "Yes, I knew her well. She was proud and kind, with gentle eyes, a warm smile, and a way about her loved by all who ever knew her." He glanced at the star-strewn sky. "I miss her still."

Lorienne suddenly understood. "You loved her, didn't you?"

Vlada blew out a surprised breath but echoed her conclusion with a slow nod. No one had ever guessed the truth of his feelings for Vania before. "I loved her," he admitted. "But I was a simple soldier and she was a royal princess wed to the leader of my tribe. I could do nothing to change that."

Lorienne clearly saw the pain etched into his face and pressed no more. Though she knew little of the dead princess, she was well aware of Adrik's peculiar origins and the hideous price he had been forced to pay for his father's vile bargain. "Jirina told me little of the princess, and Adrik only spoke of her rarely." She shook her head in disbelief. "I know she died after giving birth to Adrik, but I have never understood how King Hedeon could have been so cruel as to hand over the care of his newborn son to a foul demon in exchange for power over the tribes. Was his throne worth the life of an innocent child?"

Vlada's gaze snapped around, and a sudden frown cut deep furrows across his weathered brow. A grieving Hedeon had simply given responsibility for his motherless son over to his dead wife's people, as was customary with the Median tribes. And Adrik had become the hereditary ruler of the Magii at the moment his mother died. "What is this you speak of?" His voice rose sharply, so loud a sleeping soldier grew restive and tossed his head from side to side.

She stared at him blankly. He sounded angry almost, as if her words had badly startled him in some way. Did he not know? "Adrik was second-born . . . an unwanted son, but the demon Malkaval wanted him desperately. Ancient prophecy had foretold the birth of a powerful Magian sorcerer beneath the shadow of an eclipse, and once this sorcerer grew to manhood, the time would come when he would be able to change places with the demon. Malkaval knew this and had been awaiting Adrik's birth for a thousand years. He struck a bargain with Hedeon to fulfill his every desire in exchange for the child—and Hedeon readily agreed." The line of her mouth turned flat and grim. "Adrik has grown to manhood at Khorazm with a demon acting the father to him because his own would not."

"No," Vlada said heatedly. The muscles along his jaw bunched with anger, shock, and disbelief. "It cannot be true!" And yet, somewhere deep inside himself, in a black and miserable place, he knew the truth. He knew. There had always been whispering, unspeakable tales of demons and hellish bargains made. And Hedeon had become king within mere days of the child being taken to Khorazm. Soon after that he had wed the devious Melina.

His sun-weathered face paled, and his eyes stung with the salt of unshed tears. Ever since Vania's death he had believed Hedeon had simply given the child over to the Magians' care to fulfill the wishes of his dead wife. He had wanted to believe his king, hadn't wanted to know the truth because it was too horrifying to contemplate.

"Oh, gods," he whispered. If this had been a lie, Vlada was sure there were many, many others. What other dark secrets had been hidden away on that accursed night? "The young prince has lived all these years in that tower with a demon?"

Lorienne nodded woodenly. "Jirina saw to his bodily needs, and Malkaval comes and goes. . . . He seems to relish returning just to inflict his cruelty upon Adrik and the Magians. He even goes so far as to call himself Adrik's father."

Vlada's jaw went slack. "You have actually spoken with this creature?"

She shivered from the memory. "Yes, it was my misfortune." A grimace twisted her features. "He is vile and cruel, no better than the foulest of vermin!"

His baldric was lying on the ground beside him.

211

Vlada reached for it instinctively and pulled his sword halfway from the sheath, his fingers tightening in readiness around the grip. He glanced at the night sky worriedly. Before, he had thought he might have to do battle against mortal opponents if he sought to protect Lorienne and her child, but now he knew danger might await them from an unearthly foe as well.

His hold on the sword tightened even more. Yet protect her he would. He had failed Vania once, and would not do so again.

"Sleep, Lorienne," he warned her. "You will need your strength in the coming days. Tomorrow we reach the palace and you must keep your wits about you and be on your guard at all times."

She shifted her head within the well of the saddle, trying to ignore the smell of horse and sweat embedded in the leather and felt. She didn't feel much like sleeping, but for the sake of the child she would do as Vlada asked.

"Whatever happens," she told the old warrior quietly, "I would like you to know I am grateful for your aid and protection. Adrik respected you. He told me you were a man of honor. Now I know he was right."

Vlada couldn't find the words to respond. Instead, he stared into the night. A log crackled and spat embers in the fire as the night watch changed, the first sentry grunting in pleasure as he laid himself beside the dwindling fire.

Eventually he heard a subtle shift in Lorienne's breathing, a steady, quiet rhythm that told him she finally slept. And still he stared into the night, watching and thinking.

As the first pale hints of dawn touched the night sky, Vlada was still sleepless, his gaze fixed on a point among the dense trees on the other side of the clearing. Spots of light glittered in the wooded darkness.

The soldier blinked. There were two spots of gold in

the dark, an eerie gleam that caused the hairs along his arms to lift in apprehension. His gaze narrowed, and his hand worked to slide the sword from the remainder of its sheath.

He pulled away from the tree trunk, slowly shifting his idle body into battle readiness. His mouth hardened with resolve as he laid the sword across his knees and waited for the wraith to make its move.

The sentry had his back to this part of the camp, and Vlada knew he could not call out. Chaos would reign if his soldiers awoke, and in the confusion, the yellow-eyed specter might slip away. And he would not charge blindly into the wood and leave Loriennne unprotected. So he would just sit and wait for the threat to reveal itself.

The splotches of yellow finally moved closer, creeping nearer the fire from the cover offered by the trees. Embers suddenly sparked, throwing scores of flaming cinders into the air. For a brief span of time, the clearing was lit with orange and flickering shadows, and in that moment, Vlada knew what manner of creature it was that gazed at him from across the fire. He had viewed the beast far too many times now for the memory to grow stale.

The familiar gray wolf was staring at him with those gleaming yellow eyes, the very same eyes that had gazed at him so intently upon the steppe. The beast was watching him now, as carefully as he watched it. His frown deepened. There was something unnatural about those eyes. They were far too clever and cunning to suit him.

He held the wolf's gaze for a long while, just how long he couldn't say for certain. The fire guttered even more, smoking and crackling as the glow of the wood faded with time. Still the wolf watched, as though the creature were taking his measure in some way. Oddly, he sensed that he was in no mortal danger from the

213

wolf. The beast's stare left him only with a vague feeling of disquiet. But why would any wolf display such a profound interest in him, even one that belonged to a sorcerer?

After a while, Vlada reached slowly for the bow and quiver at his side, notching a bronze-tipped arrow and pulling the string. But the wolf didn't move or break that eerie stare, as though it did not fear him either.

He released the tension in the bow carefully and placed it upon the ground. Killing the wolf now seemed wrong somehow.

Vlada lifted a hand and motioned toward the safety of the trees. His men were beginning to stir with the approach of dawn. If one awoke and found a wolf in their camp, the beast would be slaughtered instantly. "Go!" he told the wolf in a hushed voice. "Hurry!"

For a moment, the wolf simply gazed back at him, and then the great eyes broke contact with him and the creature vanished into the shadows, disappearing without a trace that it had ever been there.

Vlada shook his head in disbelief. He didn't know why he had done that. By all rights he should have killed the wolf on sight. But he hadn't—and strangely he was glad of that.

Chapter Thirteen

Amida stretched before them, dry and dusty and dismal against a rolling landscape beginning to green with the arrival of spring. Flat-roofed houses made of mud or blocks of basalt were stacked one upon the other in mismatched rows that ran down a narrow central road barely wide enough for three men to walk abreast, much less allow the passage of a full military cavalcade.

Adrik frowned as he made a quick survey of Amida's outer fortifications. The crumbling basalt walls surrounding the village offered the only protection from invaders, whether the danger came from bandits, marauding Scythians, or a direct assault by the Lydian army. In sections, the stone walls had been allowed to fall into utter disrepair, many areas no more than piles of broken bricks decaying into powdery dust. Worse still, no sentries stood atop the remaining walls to watch any comings and goings along the Tigris or the surrounding hillocks, leaving the entire village open to attack from even the weakest of enemies.

Jan Zimlich

"See to the village's defenses," Adrik snapped to his second in command, certain that he would not have to give the order twice. Harpagus had served him well for half a score of years. The man was loyal to a fault, and would follow the orders given him exactly or die in the trying. "Set men to rebuilding the walls, then start training their people to begin standing watch. The villagers are too close to the empire's western boundary. If they wish to survive, they must learn to defend themselves."

The backbreaking labor of rebuilding the village's fortifications would also serve to keep his soldiers occupied and out of trouble until he met with the Lydians again. The time for such a meeting was almost at hand. Soldiers sent to probe the borderlands to the west had reported back that the Lydian army was massing only several days' ride away.

"All those whose labors are not needed in the village can begin erecting our encampment a few hours' ride to the west of the village," Adrik instructed, "where we will have open ground on which to assemble our forces. Our army will also be half a day's march closer to the Lydians." The soldiers from the other tribes that Burian had ordered to join his own forces would soon arrive. The Budii, Strukhat, and Parae-tak were sure to obey the crown prince's command, while the Busae, Burian's own tribe, would remain behind to defend Urmia and their prince. But he doubted very much if the Arizanti would add their strength to his, regardless of any royal command. Their leader Arkanna's desire for vengeance upon Lorienne had overridden her judgment and caused her to try and cheat Burian of the tribute she had agreed to pay; by now she had probably hidden herself and her tribe away somewhere in the mountains, fearing retaliation.

"Choose a place for our base camp on high ground, Harpagus," he continued, "with fresh water and space

216

enough to accommodate the armies of the other tribes. I will meet with those in command once they arrive."

The officer lowered his head in a quick bow. "At once, my prince," he said, and swung his horse toward the rear of the column, shouting out a series of orders to the rest of the Magians.

Adrik turned his attention back to the windswept village. A bevy of pale faces had appeared in open doorways and portals lining the central road, their eyes carefully following the progress of the Magian ranks through their midst. He could see fear in some of those faces, while the intense curiosity of others was clear. The colors and black pennants of the Magii tribe were known throughout the empire, but Adrik doubted if these simple villagers had actually set eyes upon a Magii warrior before, much less the infamous Shadow Prince.

He caught the gazes of a cluster of frightened women huddled before a row of crudely built houses of mud and straw. As if to prove his infamy, a mother suddenly turned her head to one side and pushed her infant's face to her breast to shield the child from the sorcerer's view. She made a quick warding sign over the infant's head, as though she sought to protect her offspring from some demon's wrath. Other mothers did the same, turning their children away, or forcing them back into the bowels of their windowless homes.

Adrik scowled and kept riding. The village's market lay directly ahead, where the road suddenly emptied into a large square. Amida's few vendors either dozed in the sun or were busy hawking their wares in the shade of makeshift awnings, selling fabrics, wine, animals, and choice fruits plucked fresh from fields farther to the south. A small cart pulled by goats rumbled past, its cargo of empty amphorae destined for filling at the village's only well by two burly young water bearers who trailed after the cart.

His scowl grew more pronounced. Amida was far too

large to be dependent upon a single well. It would be a simple matter for an enemy to poison the village's only source of water. He would have to correct that failing along with the crumbling walls.

As he sat upon his horse considering where to dig a second well within the nearly deserted square, the thudding sound of hoofbeats pounded down the narrow road that cut through Amida and ended in the square. The pounding echoed and reechoed as the rider raced past the rows of mud and limestone buildings.

Adrik turned toward the sound, just in time to see a lathered horse run though the entrance to the square, the bedraggled rider leaping from the saddle before the animal could even slow. Magian soldiers moved forward swiftly, grabbing the reins of the exhausted horse and clearing a pathway through their midst for the begrimed rider, who gave the appearance of a man who'd just ridden a great distance with little food or sleep.

The messenger ran toward Adrik on stiffened legs, his gait wobbly and uncertain after days spent in the saddle. As he neared the man sitting astride the tall black horse, the young Magian threw himself to his knees, his chest still heaving for needed air. "My lord!" the soldier called out breathlessly.

Adrik's gaze hardened instantly, darkening with foreboding and a terrible sense of dread. Part of the young soldier's face was tinted a purplish gray, as if he had been badly injured in weeks past and the color was only now beginning to fade.

"Damek?" The single word cut through the air like a blade. His sense of dread turned to utter certainty.

Lorienne.

The soldier gulped air, his eyes wide and filled with grim resolve. "Lord Vlada returned a week after you left. . . . His soldiers attacked our people on the beach as they cleaned and bundled fish!" Another soldier tried to hand him a cup of water to ease his parched throat, but Damek waved him away. "They came to steal your lady, my prince! The beach was full of women but she is all they stole from us, the only one the attackers even appeared interested in. There were no demands for a bounty for her return, no negotiations of any kind. They simply stole her and were gone."

Adrik closed his eyes, and a tremor passed through his body, a violent shudder of fury and grief and aching loss. Burian had done this. His greedy brother had stolen back that which he had given away.

"We tried to follow their trail," his soldier continued in a rush, "but Commander Vlada was very cunning. . . . He sent riders in all directions to throw us off the scent." Damek shook his head miserably. "He planned the theft well, my lord. It was definitely prearranged."

Adrik's hands knotted into fists of rage. Burian had sent him west to meet his end at the hands of their enemies, while he took for himself the only thing of any value to his younger half brother. His anger grew. By now, Lorienne had been in Urmia for many days, held prisoner in the palace by a cruel madman and a vengeful thief.

"This will not stand!" Adrik hissed. Even if he had to destroy Urmia stone by stone, he would gladly see the city razed and burned to a mound of ashes, and when he was done, he would seek his revenge upon his perfidious brother. "They will pay for their treachery with their blood!"

He fell silent for a short moment, his mouth setting in a hard, terse line. Adrik turned then to his second in command, his gaze as hard and brittle as the line of his mouth. "The soldiers of the other tribes will soon be here. . . . I give command of our combined armies over to you, Harpagus. I shall leave you detailed instructions on dealing with the Lydians, but when the time comes, you will know what to do. An omen will show you the way."

Harpagus bowed shortly. "As you wish, my lord."

"I leave tomorrow for Urmia with the bulk of the Magii." Adrik's fists knotted tighter. "If my foolish brother wants to wage war against me, I will gladly oblige."

Torches set in wooden sconces flared brightly in the night, ringing the sprawling encampment in a blaze of light. Scores of silken tents marched across the camp's interior in careful ranks, the colorful fabrics shivering and trembling in a quickening breeze. The silhouettes of countless soldiers shifted back and forth near the torches and cooking fires, a great army taking its ease after a hard day's march. The sounds of laughter and muted conversations drifted on the wind. Horses called and nickered from the darkness where they had been hobbled for the night.

Atop a nearby rise, Adrik sat upon his horse, watching and listening as the Lydian army settled onto the plain far west of the Tigris for what appeared to be a stay of long duration.

It was not a welcome sight. He hadn't anticipated the Lydians crossing the disputed borderlands into Media so soon, especially not this far east of the Halys River. Was this a sign of the treachery he had earlier feared? It was no matter, really. The bones had now been cast, and he would have to play the meager lot he had been doled.

He kneed his horse into sudden motion, trotting down the rise to enter the Lydian encampment. He lifted a single hand and the sentries found themselves inexplicably turning away, their movements jerky and unwilling, but the end result was that his approach was unseen by mortal eyes.

Light from the Lydians' torches and fires finally

pierced the cloaking spell, revealing a shadowy figure trotting through their midst astride a tall black horse, the creature's great head and nose adorned with the mask and horns of an ibex.

Sentries cried out belated warnings, and frightened soldiers fell back, fumbling into others as their numbers parted before the specter like a tide rolling away from the shore. Pale-faced soldiers grabbed for swords and lances, fear of the mounted wraith alive in their eyes.

"The Shadow Prince!" a voice cried out from somewhere in the crowd, and others soon took up the fearful call, their whispers spreading through the Lydian encampment like the flames of a grassfire. Their fear grew as others spotted the sorcerer and the horse that wore the fearsome face and horns of a forest creature. The fact that the Magian had ridden into their camp alone and unseen only served to increase the air of mystery that clung to him.

Adrik kept riding, aloof and alone, his gaze fastened on the royal pennants flying above a collection of bright red tents squatting in the center of the camp. The Lydian pennants and the fabric of the tents snapped and shifted in the freshening wind, the sounds advancing and receding with the strength of the breeze.

He shifted his knees as he approached the royal tents, bringing his horse to a slow halt directly outside the largest of the silken dwellings. Word of his coming had preceded him. Already Lydian officers and nobles were spilling from the narrow entrance of the tent, rushing into the darkness to see for themselves the specter that had ridden so boldly into their midst.

Adrik surveyed the Lydians warily, then slowly dismounted, allowing his reins to fall untended to the ground. The antlered horse stood stock-still, content to

221

remain where he was until his master took up the reins again.

Prince Pantaleon strode through the entrance and paused, his expression glum and bitterly cold when he saw the Magian standing before his tent. The Lydian's dark eyes flashed with anger. "I had thought not to see you before the summer, Prince Adrik, perhaps not even until my sister was safely delivered to Khorazm," he said in a sharp tone. "Bargains made by the Magian prince are obviously of no more value than those made by the Median king."

Adrik refused to react to the insult in any way. In truth, Pantaleon was well within his rights to be suspicious of his sudden appearance in their camp before the battle was even joined. "Circumstances ofttimes change and when they do, we must adapt ourselves . . . or chaos will continue to reign."

The Lydian prince lifted his head to an even more imposing angle and studied the sorcerer standing before him through narrowed eyes. "Indeed," Pantaleon said at last, and dipped his head slightly and pointed to the opening in his tent, offering the Magian his hospitality, though he did so grudgingly. "Chaos has reigned supreme for five years now. Perhaps that is long enough."

Adrik strode boldly through the Lydians who'd clustered around to stare, and entered Pantaleon's spacious tent. Costly fabrics and silken hangings formed the walls and floor of the lamplit dwelling which shivered in the wind. Soft cushions and piles of thick hides beckoned invitingly. Even his boots fell upon a layer of fabric far too rich and delicate to tread upon.

Pantaleon motioned him toward the cushions and skins piled in the center of the tent. "Come, take your rest, and tell me what matter brings you and your army to us before spring is even fully upon the land."

Adrik seated himself atop a mound of fleece and

took a cup of wine offered by a pretty young servant. He sipped at the dark red wine, lifting a brow as the tart liquid puckered his mouth and throat. The Lydian's taste in wines was obviously far different than his own penchant for a sweeter blend. "Your spies were remarkably well informed as to my brother's intentions. He has indeed been gathering the tribes into a vast army that he has commanded I lead against you."

Pantaleon couldn't suppress a small smile as he settled his lanky body upon a cushion. "Our spies are never wrong." He stroked the elegant little beard adorning his chin. "But I must ask again, what matter is it that brings you to us so soon? We had thought not to see you until the first of summer, if then."

"My circumstances have changed," Adrik admitted, studying the Lydian with care. Though Pantaleon's attire and manner were as graceful as they had been when he visited Khorazm, there were now no traces of the rouges and powders that he had worn upon his face. Perhaps the wearing of them depended on the occasion. But the Lydian and his clothing still carried the sweet scents of Persian perfumes, overpowering any smells of sweat or grime or travel in the confines of the tent. "I now find myself in the unexpected position of renegotiating the terms of our agreement."

Pantaleon's face flushed with anger, and several of his nobles muttered among themselves. "Continue."

Adrik held his gaze. "I cannot wed your sister this summer or any other. . . . My future lies elsewhere. I know that now."

The Lydian's narrow features turned scarlet. "You seek to disavow our bargain?"

Adrik shook his head slowly. "No, not exactly . . . but if I am fortunate enough to live through the coming weeks, I wish to spend any future I might have with another. And I fear King Alyattes would not be satisfied if I were to take his daughter as my consort, then forsake the royal princess for a woman who was common-born." He gazed at the Lydian intently. "I simply hope to restate the terms of any alliance between us in a mutually acceptable manner."

Pantaleon stared back in anger and surprise. "Simply? There is nothing simple in what you request, Prince Adrik! If you reject my sister as your consort, you reject an alliance sealed with the blood of our families. Are we to 'simply' accept that dishonor as our due? Your request diminishes us all and destroys any hopes we might have had for peace."

It was Adrik's turn to stare, long and bitterly hard. They must think him an utter fool. The Lydians sought only a temporary alliance, one fraught with perils that would end in his own death the moment a new Magian heir had been pushed from Aryenis's loins. If the war between their empires could not be won upon the battlefield, the Lydians would use his seed to bring about the end of the Medians by seating a child of their own blood on the throne in place of an heir from his father or brother.

Adrik leaned forward slightly and dropped his voice to a harsh whisper. "And what if I were to arrange for your sister to wed Crown Prince Burian instead? Would that bring dishonor upon your family? Surely a match with the future Median king would serve the interests of both empires far better than a marriage to a lesser son."

Pantaleon gaped at him in stunned surprise, then motioned for his nobles and officers to leave the tent. A moment later the silken flap was sealed, and they were alone save for two serving women and the flickering shadows cast by torches and lamps.

The Lydian drained his cup of wine and held it out for a servant to pour more. His voice dropped even lower than his guest's, a hushed whisper that only carried a step or two away. "We approached King Hedeon with that very offer some two years ago, but he rejected our overture. He sent word back to us that he sought no alliance with our empire, only our deaths, and would return us the head of any future emissary unfortunate enough to be dispatched to his palace." The Lydian shrugged lightly. "Hence the continuing war, and our request of you instead."

Adrik nodded, understanding now what he previously had not. It was of no concern to Hedeon that Burian was still without an heir because the Median king had no intention of ever truly giving up his throne, which was why he so desperately wanted to see his sorcerer son. His father needed him to weave a spell that would enable him to live longer, so he had the time and inclination to continue his efforts to create an even greater empire than he now possessed, one built upon the wealth and toil of others that would rival any other in size and scale. And he would never stop until he had either achieved that goal or finally gone to his death.

Adrik's gaze darkened, dangerously so, black and utterly still, like the murky waters found at the bottom of a well. The latter result held far more appeal to him. "I doubt Prince Burian was ever informed of your offer. But your people were wise not to doubt threats made by my father. He seeks your lands, your wealth, and your deaths. He truly would have returned the head of any emissary—even you—and would have arranged to have it delivered to your father sitting atop a serving platter. He has done worse things to his enemies before. Now he is even more dangerous because his greed has driven him quite mad."

He stared unseeing at the shadows twisting across a wall of the tent. "Never doubt what my father might do," Adrik continued absently. "Hedeon would even strike a bargain with the foulest of demons if he thought he could have what he most desired."

Pantaleon cleared his throat uneasily. "The words of the son paint a disturbing picture of the father." He pursed his lips grimly. "If these things are true, what makes you believe that King Hedeon will now agree to the very bargain he refused two years ago?"

Adrik's eyes never left the wall of the tent. The shadows were moving and shifting with the fabric and the wind, like thin black figures dancing madly before a flickering fire. "I leave tomorrow for Urmia," he announced. "If my father still lives when I reach the palace, I shall deal with him, and my brother as well. They will either agree to the terms of the alliance, or face attack by me."

Pantaleon physically drew back, his shoulders stiffening. His face turned a deathly shade of white. "You would attack your own blood?"

There was no forgiveness in the set to the sorcerer's features, no hint of any misgiving. "My father holds no feelings for me," he said quietly, "and my brother . . . My brother has stolen something of great value to me, and I intend to take it back. When that which I seek has been returned to my care, Crown Prince Burian will agree to the alliance and wed Aryenis. I will see to that. Nothing of our bargain will change save for the name of your sister's husband and the place where she will wed at the end of summer. Would changes to our agreement such as these be acceptable?"

Silence reigned for a short moment, thick and fraught with expectation. A thin smile finally lifted the edges of Pantaleon's mouth. He nodded. "Changes such as you envision would indeed be acceptable to us, even welcomed, perhaps."

Adrik blew out a relieved breath. He had hoped the Lydians would readily agree—having Burian take the Lydian princess as his consort put King Alyattes one step closer to the Median throne.

"But what of your father?" Pantaleon reminded him

quietly. "Burian might agree, but what the king rejected two years past would be no more palatable for him today."

The mere thought of his father caused Adrik's features to turn as hard and cold as stone. "Hedeon's wants and needs are of no concern to me. The king is old and sickly, and from what I am told, quite mad. Burian rules now, in fact if not in name, and he is in need of a suitable consort and an heir." His features hardened even more. "As I am in need of the safe return of that which he stole from me. I will not stand idly by and leave her to such a fate."

Comprehension lit Pantaleon's eyes. "Ah, I see now." He touched a fingertip to his manicured beard. "The girl in your tower . . . your brother has stolen away the pretty little northerner who made your eyes flame with such desire."

His gaze met Pantaleon's directly. "Yes," he said tersely, daring the Lydian to question him further.

Pantaleon returned his cold stare solemnly. "I, of all, understand your need for the fair-haired northerner's return. Remember, it was I who would gladly have given you anything you asked in order to possess such a prize. When you refused my offer outright, I knew you planned to keep her in your bed." He sighed deeply and shook his head. "Though I understand why Prince Burian felt compelled to steal her away, he was an utter fool to do such a thing."

He lifted a hand and signaled one of the serving women to move closer. Pantaleon caressed her thigh possessively. "Many an empire has risen and many have fallen to ruin because of a man's longing for the touch of a single woman," he said quietly. "It is the one weakness that lies within the hearts of all men. And it is the one thing that fate and empire can never hope to bind."

Adrik turned his stare to a wisp of smoke curling

from a lamp. Around him, the wind shivered through the fabric of the tent, and the shadows continued to dance and twist across the silken walls. Once, before that fateful journey across the steppe, he too would have considered his lust for a single woman to be a terrible weakness. Now, he thought it might very well be his greatest strength.

"And what of our war, Prince Adrik?" Pantaleon suddenly asked, drawing his thoughts back to the here and now. "What will become of it? Two great armies will soon be gathered and readied on a nearby plain. There will be far fewer questions asked if our armies meet in battle once more, just as they have these five years past. If we do not fight, some may even brand us as traitors to our own cause. We cannot simply walk away and declare that we will no longer fight. Both our empires would fall."

Adrik sighed. The Lydian was right on that score. The sorcerer was quiet for a long moment, and when he finally spoke, his voice was edged with grim resolve. "Come the last week of this month, there will be a great omen, one that cannot be denied by any who bear witness to its arrival. On the appointed day, the afternoon sky will darken to the blackest night as the shadow of the moon falls across our lands."

Pantaleon shivered and glanced around. "An eclipse?" he said in a frightened whisper. "You know this to be certain?"

A nod was Adrik's only answer.

"I have heard legends of such things," Pantaleon continued, "but I have not seen one for myself." He shook his head in disbelief. "Truly a great omen."

"But it is not necessarily an ill omen," Adrik suggested gravely.

Pantaleon's dark brows lifted in sudden comprehension. "Yes, I see. My people are a superstitious lot, as I am sure yours are as well. A great omen such as this could be a portent of many things to come."

Adrik nodded again. "Even peace."

Chapter Fourteen

The small column had made its way through the outer rings of Urmia's fortifications, a series of three distinct walls of varying sizes strategically placed at intervals to help defend the city. The king's current palace sat like a great white jewel atop a small hillock behind the third and final wall, the lake an endless shimmering of blue visible just beyond it.

The familiar sights sent a dagger of dread through Vlada's breast. Dread and foreboding.

As the carved gateway leading into the palace grounds loomed large before him, the soldier pulled in a steadying breath and straightened the line of his shoulders. He was still an officer in the service of his empire and would endeavor to present himself as such, despite the difficult choices thrust upon him of late.

Above them, lining the perimeter of the palace walls, at least a score of archers and spearmen stood at the ready, watching curiously as the column of Busae soldiers and the female captive began crossing beneath the final gates. Sunlight glinted off the domes of their iron helmets, which did nothing to allay Vlada's unease. The palace guards were well trained and well armed, prepared to give battle to any foe at a moment's notice. Vlada had seen to that himself.

"Remember, be wary at all times," he whispered to the woman riding beside him. "Your wits must remain sharp, and your body strong if you wish to survive what will soon come."

Lorienne swallowed and nodded surreptitiously, her pale eyes wide and worried as she studied her new surroundings. She clung to the high pommel of the saddle as Vlada led her mount toward a sprawl of flat-roofed buildings huddled along the leaden waters of a lake gleaming a brilliant blue beneath the midday sun. The buildings were huge and white, scrubbed so bright by the glare and time that the mere sight was painful to her eyes.

Ahead of them stood the massive entryway to the Median palace, the arched doors flanked by matching columns of polished limestone. Raised carvings decorated the length of the tall columns, elaborate depictions of Median wars and warriors, and scenes of what might pass for everyday life within a noble household. To Lorienne, raised as she had been within a poor, nomadic tribe, the overt display of wealth was both strange and disquieting. In sharp contrast, Adrik and the Magii lived simple, austere lives devoid of most outward trappings of wealth.

The war column finally drew to a halt before the massive doors of the palace, where a horde of servants and slaves stood waiting, many with sun-darkened features or eastern eyes that revealed exotic origins.

Lorienne found herself staring. She had never seen such variety in looks and coloring before. The differences reminded her all too clearly of the vast size and scale of the empire. Her own tribe, the Arizanti, was small and insignificant when compared to the count-less peoples held in thrall by the Median throne.

Soon she found herself being aided to dismount, lifted bodily from the horse and set upon the bright white steps leading to those massive doors. Vlada appeared at her side and she clung to him tenaciously, her fingers digging into the mail covering his forearm. Her feelings for the weathered soldier were strange, indeed. She should fear the man who had stolen her from the safety of Khorazm, yet instead, she was cling-ing to him in desperation, as if he and he alone could bring about her salvation.

Vlada leaned close to her ear, so close she could feel his breath upon her skin. "Remember, too, tell no one of the child!" he whispered tersely. "No one! Don't speak to either the king or the crown prince unless you are ordered to. And do not eat or drink *anything* that has not first been tasted by the servant girl that I send to you. Her name is Mandane, and she can be trusted with your life. You will know her by the scar that runs down one cheek ending near her jaw."

Lorienne nodded woodenly and clutched at his fore-arm even more tightly than before. Treachery such as Arkanna's she understood. A blade slipped deep into the back when one was distracted was the most com-mon form of taking another's life among the Arizanti. But this—to fear the simple eating of a round of bread lest it be baked with poison—she would never under-stand. Vlada had told her that she could die from even the slightest sip of tainted wine or water. The soldier had said for her to trust the girl named Mandane and to let her serve as taster. Lorienne supposed she had no choice if she wished to live until Adrik came for her.

She blinked away the haze of tears gathering in her eyes. He would come for her. She knew he would.

A woman suddenly stepped from the cool dimness

beyond the palace doors. She was dark and lushly formed, her hair and skin as smooth and flawless as the costliest of silks. But her eyes were what drew Lorienne's swift attention. They were black, blacker than a moonless sky, and alive with malice so fierce Lorienne could almost feel the heat of it upon her body.

A shudder moved through her limbs. The evil and hatred that filled those eyes were aimed at her like the tips of poisoned arrows.

Vlada cleared his throat and bent his head in a curt bow. "My lady." He gazed at Melina warily. It wasn't like the king's consort to greet anyone on arrival to the palace. The fact that she had done so did not bode well for them. "How does the king fare?"

The woman's plump mouth flattened as her gaze flicked briefly over the woman hanging on to the soldier's arm. "He fares the same as always, Vlada Sura." Her voice held a sharp note of contempt. "He has been demanding to see you . . . and he has commanded that his second-born come to him now—or suffer his wrath." She lifted one shoulder in a careless shrug. "As I said, the same as always."

Vlada nodded. "I will attend him at once and give him my report."

Melina's mouth tipped in a cold, thin smile, and her gaze flicked over the fair-haired Lorienne again. "Then you must attend Prince Burian. I have heard that he has been awaiting your return as eagerly as his father waits upon his sorcerer son."

"I shall see them both without delay," Vlada agreed quickly. He tried to ease Lorienne past but the king's consort stepped forward to delay their passage through the palace doors. Vlada met her gaze steadily. "My lady?"

The consort's eyes turned as flat and rigid as the line of her mouth. "You have yet to tell me of our guest, Vlada. If she is to be given the hospitality of my palace, do you not think that I have the right to know her name?" Her gaze passed over Lorienne's pale mane of hair, then moved back to the soldier's face, as if what she had seen wasn't worthy of her undivided attention. "I see she is from the northlands. Why have you brought her here?"

Vlada stiffened. Melina's obvious interest in Lorienne was truly an omen of impending evil. "She is Lorienne of the Arizanti, my lady. Crown Prince Burian commanded that she be brought to the palace without delay. He has . . . plans for her, I believe."

That last he added almost as an afterthought, one calculated to possibly disrupt Melina's planning, at least for a time. If the woman still feared Burian's wrath, she might well be leery of bringing harm to the woman he had ordered brought to his bed.

Vlada finally angled past and led Lorienne inside.

Melina watched intently and listened to their footsteps as the pair hurried away across the palace's great audience hall, finally vanishing into a side corridor that led to the king's and the crown prince's private chambers.

Her eyes turned as dark and flinty as obsidian. Once the two had left her sight, she signaled a waiting servant with a wave of her hand. The man who hurried toward her was small and thin and dark, a fellow outcast from the Pare-tak who'd sworn allegiance to Melina many years past.

She pulled a gold and lapis armlet free of her forearm and slipped it into his clammy hand. For a moment, she could see the gleam of gold and bright blue stones shining between his fingers; then his fist closed tight around his prize.

"You have seen the northerner for yourself now," Melina whispered in disgust, "just as you asked." She herself had been shocked by the sight. The girl was small and puny, with a face as pale and wan as her

tangle of fair hair. Not the sort Burian usually wanted
to warm his bed. "I expect you to keep to our bargain.
Let there be no mistakes."

The man nodded quickly. "It will be done, my lady,"
he said in a low, cautious voice. The armlet disappeared into the sleeve of his robe. "Soon."

Melina's eyes glittered with black fire. "See to it!" she
snapped, her mouth twisted in an angry grimace. The
crown prince's obsession for the pale-haired Arizanti
had caused her no end of trouble in recent months,
most of all the return visit by Malkaval, who would
surely take his revenge upon her if the skinny Parae-
tak failed in his task. "And make certain her end is
anything but peaceful. It will please me to know that
she suffered."

Lorienne clung to Vlada even more fiercely than before, though she knew the soldier could be of no real
protection to her now. The man ogling her from across
the chamber was large-faced and burly, with russet hair
and a thick, unkempt beard of the same hue. Even his
hands were overlarge and unappealing, like the sturgeon the Magian fishermen pulled from the depths of
the sea.

She hid her grimace so that he didn't witness her
aversion. Crown Prince Burian bore no resemblance
whatsoever to his younger half brother. Where Adrik
was slender and handsome in a darkly sensual way, his
brother was ruddy and ungainly, as if the seed that had
given rise to them both was as dissimilar as the appearance of their bodies.

Prince Burian's stare turned salacious, openly so, as
though he were considering ordering her to disrobe
and spread her thighs here and now, with Vlada and
several servants as witnesses to her ordeal.

She tried and failed to suppress a shudder of distaste.

"Ah, Vlada, I see your quest proved successful!" Bur-

Jan Zimlich

ian said gleefully and strode toward them. He cupped his hands behind his back and circled them, regarding his pale-haired prize with heated interest. He had waited long for this moment. The memory of how she had looked tied to that stake had haunted his dreams long enough.

He lifted a strand of her fair hair and pulled it near his nose, sighing with pleasure as he took a deep breath of the scent that hung about her like a fragrant cloud. She smelled of the deep forest, horses and leather, scents that never failed to arouse him.

Lorienne flinched away from him, shifting toward Vlada to free herself of his pawing touch.

Burian laughed aloud. She would be eager for his touch soon enough. "Stealing her away from Khorazm could have been no easy task, Vlada. Your efforts are deserving of a reward. Would a chest of gold and gemstones be to your liking?"

Vlada shook his head slowly and regarded his master with wary eyes. "I require no such reward, my lord. If you wish to give compensation for delivering Lorienne safely into your hands, perhaps you should direct the bounty to your brother instead."

He redoubled his efforts to watch every twitch of Burian's hands. For one so large and burly, the crown prince could move with the speed of an attacking tiger when he wished. "This venture of yours is sure to bring the Shadow Prince's wrath down upon our heads. Perhaps the wrath of all the Magii as well."

Burian's restless movements stopped abruptly, and his face froze in a heavy frown. The reminder of his brother had destroyed his pleasure in this moment he had eagerly anticipated for so long. He eyed the soldier angrily. "You dare to question my judgment?"

Vlada lifted his chin. He had dared more already than he ever dreamed he would. "Yes, my lord, on this matter, I do. I fear by taking the girl you risk all-out war with the Magii."

Burian snorted and strode angrily toward the opening leading to the portico and terrace. "Adrik and his army are weeks away by now. Weeks! He readies our troops for the pending battle against the Lydians! He will not come to Urmia. . . . I doubt if he'll even live to see the next full moon! The Lydians or our own army shall see to that!"

Lorienne's face paled and her lips curled with horror. Adrik was right to hold his family in contempt. It was clear that his elder brother schemed and wished for his death.

"Do not doubt that Adrik will come!" she told Burian in a low voice, even though Vlada had advised her against speaking. "When he learns what you have done, no army will be able to stop him from coming."

"Lorienne!" Vlada hissed, and warned her to be silent with his eyes.

But it was too late. Burian was across the chamber in a moment, fury etched in cold lines across his features. His thick hand lashed out like a striking serpent and closed around her chin and jaw, forcing her head up and back until her heels lifted from the tiled floor and the bones in her neck threatened to snap.

Enraged, the crown prince stared down into her face, his anger so strong that his arm trembled and a trace of spittle appeared at one corner of his mouth.

Vlada held his breath. Though his hand had settled around the pommel of his sword when Burian rushed across the room, to draw his weapon now, upon the crown prince, would be inviting instantaneous death for him and Lorienne both.

A bead of sweat dribbled from Vlada's brow. Lorienne didn't know how close she was to dying. Burian would snap her neck without a shred of remorse. She didn't know how close she was to bringing about both their deaths.

"You are but a slave!" Burian raged. "Slaves do not speak in my presence unless I command it!" He lifted her head higher, his fingers wrapping themselves about the column of her throat.

Lorienne struggled to breathe, clawing desperately at the powerful hand choking off the air to her chest, but her efforts were to no avail. The crown prince was too strong, too angry to respond to her feeble attempt to free herself from his iron grip.

She felt her body rise until all that held her weight upright was his choking hand and the tips of her toes. A mantle of darkness began to settle around her. A few moments more and she knew she would die.

"My lord," Vlada interjected in a calm and soothing tone of voice, though inwardly he feared Lorienne was about to die, "the girl is not entirely to blame for her ill manners. The Magii and your brother obviously did not train her in the ways of slaves. She has never received proper instruction, but such a failing can soon be rectified. She can be properly trained in a matter of days if you so desire."

But the soldier's calming words didn't seem to penetrate the veil of anger that shrouded the crown prince. His grip on Lorienne's neck had yet to ease, causing the hue of her face and lips to turn a sickly shade of grayish blue, as if she was swiftly approaching the moment of death.

Vlada leaned close to his master. "I will see to her training personally, my lord, and vow to have her ready for you to bed by week's end! I swear to you she will be respectful, willing, and silent."

Burian took several deep breaths. Finally, the angry flush that had ruddied his features began to subside. Then without the slightest hint of warning, he shoved

238

Lorienne away from him, slinging her body halfway across the chamber toward the entrance.

Lorienne tumbled across the tiled floor, gasping and choking for air as her body finally slid to a stop in a boneless heap. She gagged and clutched at her throat, struggling to draw breath.

"Then see to it!" Burian commanded. "And if she ever dares to mention my brother's name again, I will cut out her tongue, then feed the rest of her to the palace rats!"

Vlada hurried to Lorienne's side and pulled her to her feet, half dragging her limp form to the open doorway. "Yes, my prince. I will see to it immediately."

"When she has learned the proper behavior of a slave girl," Burian raged on, "you will send her back to me! But if she continues to be defiant at week's end, kill her and bring me her head instead!"

Vlada jerked downward in a compliant bow, then rushed Lorienne into the corridor, half carrying the still gasping girl as they made several quick turns and entered a section of the palace that was darker and less ostentatious, with plain stone walls pocked with an endless procession of doorways leading to the main chambers of the palace servants.

He finally pushed his way through a wooden portal and dragged Lorienne inside, taking a deep breath to steady himself once they were safely sealed inside the small chamber.

Trembling, Lorienne sank atop a hard, narrow couch, the only furnishing in the chamber other than a low table pushed against one wall. A small window stood at head level, the slitlike opening covered with a latticed panel made of wood inlaid with iron. Lorienne knew instinctively that the window opening had been barred with the panel to prevent escapes by any of the palace slaves.

Her noisy gasps for air finally slowed to a healthier

sound and rhythm. She winced as she touched a hand to her throat, knowing she would bear the bruising marks of Burian's fingers upon her flesh for days to come.

Vlada leaned himself wearily against a wall and stared at the terrified girl. She had ignored his counsel and almost died as a result. "Do you understand the reasons for my warnings now?" he demanded, unable to halt the impatient edge that had slipped into his voice.

Lorienne nodded miserably, her eyes filling with salty moisture. If not for Vlada's intercession, the crown prince would surely have killed her, with no more thought than he would have given the lowliest of vermin—simply because she had dared to speak Adrik's name in his exalted presence. "I understand," she managed to croak in a raw whisper, the mere act of trying to speak bringing on a fit of coughing and a great amount of pain.

"He will kill you next time. Do not doubt that." Vlada folded his arms across his chest. "But his fury has brought about an unintended result—he will not order you to his bed until you have been taught to show him proper respect. That will give Prince Adrik more time in which to make his way to Urmia, a few days at the least. If the Fates favor us, he will arrive before Burian orders you to attend him in his chambers."

If Adrik comes at all.

The same grim thought hung unspoken in the air between them, but their eyes relayed the message even if their tongues did not.

The old soldier frowned suddenly and his gaze filled with worry. Even though Burian had been momentarily appeased, there was still Melina to contend with—as well as the Median king.

* * *

Lorienne lay upon the hard little couch and stared morosely through the small window of her chamber. A wisp of clouds was visible against the blue of the Median sky, the scene broken into an intricately woven pattern of circles and squares through the lattice that shuttered her into the sparse room.

It was a view she had grown familiar with in the past days, the only one she was allowed. Any doubts she might have harbored about her ultimate fate had ended long ago. If Adrik didn't come for her, she would die in this terrible place.

The door to the tiny chamber was locked tight at all times, the bar released only with the brief comings and goings of Mandane with her food or of Vlada, who felt obliged on occasion to try and instruct her to behave as a proper slave as Burian ordered.

But even those visits were a welcome respite from the utter sameness that had become her life. Other than the small slice of clouds and sky visible through the narrow window, she had nothing to view, nothing to fill her time but dark thoughts of her future, and her child's. And other than the occasional visits of Vlada or Mandane, she had not set eyes upon another human since the day she arrived.

A frown passed over her brow. At least she had not had to look upon Prince Burian again, but she knew that day would soon arrive. The week Vlada had gained for her was almost gone now. The crown prince would not be patient for much longer.

She brushed a stray lock of hair from her face and touched a hand to the gentle swell of her belly. At times she still felt ill and weak, as if all trace of strength had been drained from her body, but with each day that passed, she grew stronger physically. She knew the seed inside her was growing stronger, too. In the days since she had been confined here, she had felt the first,

241

faint stirrings of life within her. Soon she would not be able to hide the truth of her condition.

The heavy wood door suddenly scraped against stone, and Lorienne bolted upright, aware that someone was about to enter her tiny prison. The door finally swung wide and Mandane stepped through carrying a platter laden with black bread, a large round of goat cheese, and an urn of fresh water.

Lorienne smiled feebly in greeting as a guard closed the door again. In the past few days, she'd grown used to the company of the quiet serving woman, and looked forward to her daily visits to break the boredom of her days, even though they had shared only a few words. After almost a week, Lorienne still didn't know what had happened to Mandane to leave her face so scarred.

She had even considered the prospect that Prince Burian might have left her in that state. Judging by his violent behavior toward her, it wouldn't be beyond the realm of possibility. The Median crown prince was quite obviously a crude and loathsome beast capable of most anything.

But Lorienne had never acted on that belief by asking the serving woman what had happened to scar her cheek. Mandane kept her own counsel, and Lorienne had decided not to intrude. The woman had yet to even whisper Vlada's name, as if no special relationship existed between the two, even though the soldier had made the arrangements for her to deliver Lorienne's food.

The serving woman nodded in return and placed the platter upon the low table pushed against a wall. "Good day, my lady. I hope you rested well last evening?" She poured water into a small bronze cup, then lifted the vessel to her lips, sipping the liquid into her mouth.

"My rest was peaceful . . . and long," Lorienne replied carefully, in a raw and breathy voice still weak from Burian's ill treatment. Though Vlada was never mentioned by name, after her first meeting with the servant, Lorienne had soon realized that her answers to Mandane's questions about her well-being were relayed directly to the soldier's ears. "I have no reason for complaint."

Mandane nodded again and broke a piece of cheese from the round. "Good." She chewed slowly. "You must rest to keep your strength. There are trying times ahead."

Lorienne gave her a cautious look. Had a message from Vlada been hidden in her words?

Before she could give the matter further consideration, a sudden frown passed over the serving woman's brow, ridging her aging face with deep lines. Mandane staggered slightly, knocking the cup of water from the platter. The water spilled and puddled on the stone floor.

"Mandane?" Lorienne asked worriedly, and leapt to her feet. The woman had suddenly grown pale, so pale the scar on her cheek stood out starkly against the deathly color of her skin. "Are you ill?"

Her breathing quickened, short gasps that did nothing to quell Lorienne's rising fear.

The serving woman suddenly staggered past the table and slumped against the wall, her fingers clutching vainly for purchase on the stone.

Lorienne rushed to the woman's side and grabbed her by the shoulders as she started sliding toward the floor, her fingernails scratching down the blocks of stone.

"Mandane!" Lorienne cried, the frightened pounding in her breast growing louder and louder inside her ears.

She eased the woman's limp body to the floor and gently cradled her head. Mandane's gasps for breath had grown more ragged, more uncertain, and her skin had turned an ashen shade of gray.

She stared up at Lorienne with wide and frightened eyes, and then the glimmering of life slowly ebbed away, her gaze turning dark and black, then blank. Her limbs loosened, grew still, and her mouth sagged open, revealing a sliver of half-eaten cheese.

Lorienne stared into the woman's slack face, the fearful thrumming in her chest turning into a pounding roar. "Gods," she whispered. The woman was dead.

Her frightened gaze swept toward the platter resting so innocently upon the table. The servant Vlada had assigned to taste her food had died after a single sip of water and a bite of cheese—food and water meant for her.

Poor Mandane had died instead, poisoned by someone within the palace, a madman who wanted her dead.

Lorienne swallowed away the sudden dryness in her throat. Which had carried the poison? The water? The cheese? Mandane had yet to even taste the round of bread. All three could even be tainted. She had no way to know the truth of it.

"Guard!" she called out hoarsely, aware that one of Prince Burian's sentries stood watch just beyond the door, but no one answered her frightened cry, though a small scraping sound outside told her clearly that someone was there.

In truth, Mandane was beyond receiving any sort of aid, but Vlada needed to know what had occurred.

"Guard!" she called more forcefully, but again silence was her only answer. She carefully placed Mandane's head upon the floor and moved to the door, beating on the wood as loudly as she could.

After long minutes, Lorienne understood there would be no answer to her pleas for help. She blinked to try and halt the rush of tears beginning to slip from the corners of her eyes.

She was alone, sealed inside the small chamber for an unknown length of time with the body of a woman who had died in her stead.

"Oh, gods." The tears fell free, sliding down her nose and cheeks to fall upon her trembling hands. "Adrik . . ."

Chapter Fifteen

Guards atop Urmia's outermost wall stood frozen at their posts and simply watched as the long column of black-clad Magii passed through the first of the entry gates leading into the city.

No one thought to stop them. In truth, no one dared to try, for the Shadow Prince rode at the head of the column, and all who witnessed the arrival let them pass into Urmia unmolested.

Even the Magians' horses were fearsome to behold, wearing antlers and other strange masks covered with the images of various forest creatures. The jet-black horse the Shadow Prince rode was no exception, with the horns and face of an ibex jutting outward from its head.

As the Magians entered the first of Urmia's gates, the prince's black horse snorted and tossed its masked head about but didn't slow its steady pace. The beast seemed unmindful of the pack of wolves trotting companionably alongside its legs, as if the gray-furred predators were friends and guardians of the armor-clad prince and his mount.

Some who witnessed the arrival lifted hands to form warding signs, while others turned their eyes away from the man and his wolves. They knew who the sorcerer was, and they were afraid.

As the Magii made their way through the outskirts of the city toward the palace, the narrow streets emptied before them. Crowds that had milled in the marketplace or outside neat houses built of mud bricks or stone melted away upon sighting the prince, his wolves, and the disciplined ranks of armored Magians marching through the city.

Vendors grabbed their wares and fled. Women herded children inside homes, shutting and barring doorways to try and hold the sorcerer's spells at bay.

Adrik's dark gaze swept back and forth, surveying his surroundings as the column neared the thick stones of the middle wall, the second of three rings of fortifications protecting Hedeon's palace.

The street running along the outside of the wall was empty now save for a single vendor desperately tugging on the halter of a recalcitrant donkey. The beast was overburdened with baskets and amphora, but finally gave in to its master's urging and hurried on its way.

Once the vendor and his donkey rounded a corner and fled from sight, the city fell into a strained silence, one fraught with an air of tension and fear. Other than the slow thudding of hooves and boots upon packed dirt, the occasional jangle from mail or the iron fittings of a halter, no sounds intruded on the now desolate streets.

Though Adrik longed to quickly storm the palace gates and demand Lorienne's immediate freedom, he allowed the creatures accompanying him to set their own pace. Behind him, the travel-stained column did the same, whether the soldiers were mounted or marched on foot. They were all weary and begrimed, strained to the point of their endurance by the exhausting journey back to the east from the region near Amida, a distance traveled in half the normal amount of time.

When Adrik was less than ten steps from the city's closed middle gates, he brought his horse to a slow halt and turned his attention upward, to the Median soldiers forming a protective line that stretched the length of the center wall.

The wolves stood or paced restlessly about his horse's long legs, Sandor among them, who had been waiting with the others in a wood beyond the edges of the city, standing in a patient vigil for him to arrive from the west.

His dark gaze met the beast's familiar yellow-eyed stare. Words had never been necessary between them. Sandor already knew how grateful he was for her aid, and how much their friendship meant to him. The wolf had trailed Lorienne and the Busae who'd stolen her all the way from distant Khorazm. She had done so for him, simply because Sandor knew he would wish it.

Adrik turned his attention back to the gates barring him from what he had come to retrieve. He shifted his legs slightly and lifted himself in the saddle, his angry gaze passing over the pale faces of the soldiers lined above him, finally coming to rest upon an officer wearing the insignia of the Busae tribe.

Their eyes met, and the man appeared to take a hasty step backward, as if he wished to flee from the searing rage visible in the sorcerer's eyes.

"You know who I am!" Adrik called up the officer. "Open the gates and allow us entry!" His expression was cold and flint-hard. "Open them now or die!"

The officer stared down at him for a long moment, considering, then glanced away and muttered to a guard beside him. Soon the heavy arched gates swung outward, unbarred to allow the Magians entrance into the heart of the city. The officer had obviously decided that his life was far more valuable than a set of wooden gates.

Adrik kneed his horse back into motion, and his column slowly advanced, its soldiers alert for any sign of treachery or attack. The inner streets emptied as swiftly as those on the outskirts, the inhabitants of Urmia fleeing to the safety of their homes or the refuge they thought to find inside the palace walls.

Soon the confines of the city were behind them, and the land turned grassy, with small clusters of trees and shrubs forming decorative plantings. The narrow, dusty street widened to a grand road made of crushed limestone that led to the third set of gates and the walls rimming the palace itself.

Adrik knew that if Burian or his father planned to offer resistance, here is where it would occur. The open area in front of the final wall spread before them in a gentle, upward slope, affording the palace's defenders a distinct tactical advantage. If he were forced to wage battle here, he would have to do so while climbing uphill, while the protectors held to higher ground. These last fortifications were also under the protection of the palace guard, skilled warriors who were certain not to abandon their duties as easily as those guarding the city's outer walls.

At his column's approach, grim-faced archers and spearmen began racing along the battlements, taking positions to protect the palace from the Magians advancing toward the gates.

Adrik signaled his officers, and his soldiers began fanning out in both directions, mounted warriors to the fore, his own archers and lancers lining up to the rear of the ranks. Within moments, the Magian soldiers had prepared themselves for an assault upon the pal-

ace walls and gates. Swords were pulled from scab-
bards, bows drawn and readied.

A breeze laden with moisture from Lake Urmia
breathed across Adrik's face, lifting the dark sidelock
that fell to his shoulder. He glanced at the May sky, a
blue so deep and bright it hurt the eyes. Though
windy, it was a clear, pure morning. If he was to die,
he could not have chosen a better day.

Above, the guards suddenly shifted, parting to make
way for someone to approach the wall. The head and
upper torso of an officer appeared, and Adrik's eyes
narrowed in response. The weathered face gazing
down at him was all too familiar.

The sorcerer's face turned hard as stone, and his
hands knotted into tight fists. Vlada Sura. He longed
to pull the bow from his back and loose an arrow into
the man's treacherous heart. He had thought the soldier to be a man of honor, but in that he had been
sorely mistaken.

"I should kill you where you stand!" Adrik shouted
up to him angrily. "You came to Khorazm in the guise
of a messenger and I gave you my hospitality, when all
the while you planned to steal that which I value most!"
His eyes sparked black fire. "Give Lorienne back to me
now, and I shall leave here and never return!" A cold,
deadly look passed over the sorcerer's face. "Refuse me
at your peril, and the peril of all within the palace
walls!"

Vlada frowned and shook his head slowly, so slowly
his movement seemed laced with regret. To Adrik's
eyes, the soldier appeared almost hesitant, as though
he was aggrieved by something unknown that had
taken place. Even stranger, the officer didn't appear
surprised or fearful like the others to see the wolves
accompanying him.

"I cannot return to you what is not mine to give,
Prince Adrik!" Vlada responded finally. "The girl be-

longs to your brother, not me—and it was at his order
that I spirited her away."

The old soldier fell silent for a short moment. When
he spoke again, his voice was lower, more earnest, as
if he was conveying a message meant for Adrik's ears
alone. "I would not have taken her if I had known . . ."

Puzzlement shadowed Adrik's mood. It was clear to
him that Vlada had left something unsaid between
them, something of grave import. "Is Lorienne well?"
he demanded, his anxiety over her physical state rising
to the fore. If she had come to harm, all who dwelled
inside the palace would suffer his wrath.

Vlada nodded slowly but his features remained devoid of all expression. "Well enough."

Adrik's eyes thinned even more. The answer was curiously lacking in information. His horse shifted beneath him, stomping a hoof upon crushed limestone.
Sandor whined unhappily. "I want to see her *now*."

The soldier stared back at him and again his face
and voice seemed tinged with regret. "I was unable to
locate Prince Burian within the palace to inform him
of your arrival, and I am uncertain how long he will be
unavailable. In his absence I have been given strict orders to follow." Vlada's gaze met and found Adrik's.
"Those orders do not include allowing the Shadow
Prince entrance to the palace in order for him to see
the captive the crown prince has claimed as his property."

Adrik stared back at him intently. Curious. Much
had been said as well as unsaid by the soldier. Almost
as if . . .

Suddenly Adrik understood the message Vlada had
been trying to convey without giving voice to the actual
words. His gaze sharpened, and he probed Vlada's face
with his eyes, but found no answers there, only more
questions. Curious indeed.

"If I am not permitted to see to the welfare of the

girl," Adrik shouted, loud enough for all present to hear his words, "then I demand that you open the gates and allow me entry to see my father, King Hedeon, who has commanded that I attend him immediately! I shall present my demands to him instead."

Vlada pulled his helmet from his head and bowed shortly, a gesture filled with the respect due the son of the ruling king. But there was something else in his expression as well—relief, perhaps? "Open the gates!" he ordered the guards. "Prince Adrik has arrived to see his father, as commanded by the king!"

Adrik suppressed a chilly smile as the carved gates swung open before him, revealing the cool shimmer of the lake in the distance and the sprawling mass of white stone that formed the palace itself. He didn't know what game Vlada was playing or where his true allegiance lay; all that mattered now was that the soldier had cleverly presented him with the means to enter the palace grounds. Somewhere within these walls, Lorienne had been hidden away.

He swung his glance toward his present second in command. "As long as Prince Burian's whereabouts are unknown, our flanks and rear are endangered," he told the officer. "He could have left the palace with his personal guards in order to stage a surprise attack upon us from outside the walls. Send scouts to search the area and report back immediately if he's found, but in my absence, do nothing to provoke attack by the palace guards."

The Magian officer clapped a fist to his breast in salute. "Your orders will be carried out at once, my lord." He motioned toward the now opened gates. "But what of you? You risk your life if you enter those gates without protection, and we cannot protect you from outside the walls."

Adrik's features settled into hard, grim lines. "I enter

the palace gates alone. If I do not return by nightfall, leave here at once for Khorazm."

"But, my lord!" the officer protested. "We cannot leave you at the mercy of your enemies!"

Adrik belied his protest by lifting a hand. "If I do not return by nightfall, I will be dead, and will be at no one's mercy."

He lifted his head into the quickening breeze and gazed up at the sharpest, bluest sky he had ever viewed. It would definitely be a good day to die, if that were truly to be his fate.

The sorcerer threw a quick glance at Sandor and the other wolves. "Wait here," he instructed. The wolf growled in protest, but settled upon her haunches to wait as he had ordered.

Once he was certain the wolves would remain where they were told, he walked his horse beneath the curving arch of the gates, determined to meet his fate unflinchingly.

Lancers on the battlement above him stood at the ready, prepared to throw their iron-tipped spears with but a moment's notice. A score of bows had been pulled and drawn, a rain of arrows ready to be loosed upon him. Yet the attack he expected never came, and he was allowed to enter without harm.

As he neared the main entrance to the palace, Vlada appeared atop the steps, waiting with a veteran soldier's patience for him to dismount. All was silent around them, as if the two of them were alone in the midst of so many. The only sound to be heard was the crunch of gravel beneath his horse's hooves.

Adrik watched him carefully, still trying to puzzle out Vlada's game. If it had been the soldier's true intent to kill him, he had missed a prime opportunity.

A moment later Adrik drew his horse to a halt and lowered himself from the saddle. Still leery of what might come, he climbed the palace steps one at a time until he found himself face-to-face with Vlada Sura, a man he considered neither friend nor foe, but somewhere in between.

He inclined his head slightly, acknowledging Vlada's presence as well as his unexpected aid. But was it aid that he had rendered? In actuality, the soldier might very well have lured him into a deadly trap that would soon fall upon him.

Adrik's gaze darkened with a mix of suspicion and curiosity. "I do not know whether I should place my trust in you, Vlada Sura."

The soldier blew out an amused breath. "Nor I you." He met the darkling prince's solemn gaze with unswerving intensity. For the first time he noted the son's resemblance to the mother. Though his face possessed none of Vania's gentleness and warmth, the Shadow Prince's harsh features were imbued with an air of strength that evoked memories of his dead mother.

Vlada frowned suddenly, and his gaze grew even more intense than before. There was nothing of the father about him, and for that he was grateful this day.

"I was not within the palace on the night of your birth." Vlada shook his head regretfully. "I was told that Hedeon gave your care over to the Magii because your mother wished it." His frown deepened. "Until now I never knew that for a lie."

Adrik stared back at him curiously, wondering what had prompted the soldier's strange admission. Was this newfound knowledge somehow responsible for the old soldier's belated attempt to render him aid? "Where is Lorienne?" he said in a commanding tone.

"Keep your voice down," Vlada warned. "The palace walls have many ears. She is safe enough for a time."

Adrik's expression tightened. "Does Burian have her?" he asked in a harsh whisper. The very thought of his brutish brother pawing and clawing at Lorienne's tender flesh made him wild with anger.

Vlada shook his head. "Not yet. I managed to keep him from her these past days, but that reprieve will soon end." He leaned close to the Shadow Prince's shoulder, his voice urgent and intense. "She must be freed from the palace without delay! I found the servant I sent to act as her food taster dead inside her chamber yesterday. Lorienne had been locked in with the body for a day and a night, and no guards would answer her pleas for help. Since then she neither eats, nor drinks, at my order."

Vlada glowered angrily. "I cannot protect her anymore. Whoever sent the poison will surely try again."

A cold, deathly chill swept through Adrik's blood. "Who would have done this?" he demanded through clenched teeth.

A helpless shrug was Vlada's only response, but he had his suspicions. "You have many enemies within these walls. It could have been most anyone, my lord . . . anyone." But *Melina*, most likely.

The sorcerer's mouth turned as flat and cold as his eyes. Burian had best pray to his gods that Adrik never discovered the poison had been sent to Lorienne by his hand. "I will free her somehow," he said vehemently, "or die in the trying."

Vlada lifted a graying brow in surprise. The sorcerer's words had been spoken from the heart. From the first, Lorienne had been insistent that he would come for her. Could it truly be that there was a measure of caring between the two? If so, then Vlada knew his decision to finally pay the debt he owed Vania by aiding her son had been fitting and proper, the only choice a man of honor could make.

"Come," he urged the young prince quietly. He led the son Hedeon had abandoned to such a grim fate into the entrance of the palace, a place Adrik had seldom visited in his life, and then only at the behest of his erstwhile father. But those brief stays had lasted only a day or so and then the king had inexplicably ordered him returned to Khorazm, far from sight and mind.

As the unlikely pair entered the palace's immense audience chamber, servants, bureaucrats, and courtiers stared at them in stunned surprise. Most had never set eyes upon the Shadow Prince but knew who he was nonetheless.

Startled whispers trailed in their wake, echoing in the cavernous silence, as did the ringing sound of their boots striking the polished tiles.

Adrik glanced neither left nor right. He stared straight ahead as they strode across a huge mosaic of a godlike king slaying two massive bulls with twin swords forged of gold. The son grimaced as he glanced down at the fanciful mosaic, then forced his eyes away. The godlike image painted upon the tiles was allegedly of his father.

Instead of the painted rendering, he concentrated on the dais visible at the far end of the chamber, on the huge throne made of polished gray stone standing tall atop the square platform. Guards stood at attention along the walls, there to protect their lord and master from any type of threat.

Adrik's eyes thinned with anger as his gaze swept over the dais and throne. A frail, tiny form rested atop that mighty chair, a figure whose image had been emblazoned on Adrik's memory forever. No one needed to tell him who sat huddled upon that throne. Though he hardly knew Hedeon the man, he had seen the king's image often enough, carved into stone and painted upon tiles across the length and breadth of the Median Empire.

It was an image he despised.

The robed figure upon the throne suddenly took note of their approach and came to swift attention, sitting stiff and tall within the chair. A thin crown ringed Hedeon's grizzled head, the golden band holding wisps of whitened hair in place.

Vlada bowed before his king, not as deeply as he would have done only a month ago. "My lord, I have brought you a visitor."

Frowning, King Hedeon studied the soldier and the stranger with him carefully, and then rose from his throne to stand on uncertain feet. He stared at his uniformed visitor, the sidelock and neatly tied braid.

Recognition suddenly flared to life inside Hedeon's faded eyes. A sorcerer's braid.

He staggered down the short steps that led from the dais, almost falling when he tripped upon the last of the stone steps. His long white robe and wispy hair wafted around his thin figure like gauzy clouds, exaggerating the gauntness of his appearance.

"My son!" the king called out joyfully. A smile creased his sunken face. "My son has finally come to make me whole again!"

Adrik halted in midstep and remained where he was, refusing to approach any closer. The man who had caused him a lifetime of pain and anguish and misery now stood before him, as unrepentant and demanding as always.

"Greetings, *Father*." Adrik's voice and face were etched with contempt.

The king tottered to him and wrapped thin arms about his long-lost son. "I told them you would come! I told them all." He glared at the gaggle of courtiers gathered at the opposite end of the chamber, too fearful to approach any closer than they had. "You see how they fear you? They shall feel my wrath now, won't they, my son?"

Hedeon laughed aloud, a raspy sound that soon caught in his throat and chest. The king released his hold on Adrik and clutched at his breast, fighting to draw in needed air. He staggered back from his son and lowered himself to the steps of the dais to rest.

For a moment, the king sat like one dead, his body unmoving, his eyes blank and unseeing. Then a tremor rode up his sticklike arm, and his head swung back toward Adrik, proving he still lived. Though life still flowed through his blood, his face and skin were pale, as white as bone, and a line of drool glistened on one side of his mouth.

"Heal me!" he croaked between gasps for breath. "Make me again the man I was!" His gaze caught and held that of his sorcerer son, demanding that which he most desired. "My seed is what gave you life itself. You owe me this much!"

Vlada stiffened. Now that he knew the truth of what Hedeon had done to his own flesh and blood, Adrik's grim existence was even more horrifying to contemplate. "My lord . . ." he whispered, trying to ward off the confrontation between father and son that was certain to come. "Perhaps it would be best if you were to—"

"Silence!" the king commanded, and chopped a thin hand through the air dismissively. "Your interference is not wanted in this!"

Vlada glanced sideways, to where the Shadow Prince stood so quietly beside him. Adrik's expression was unreadable; his face had gone as still and hard as the stone of Hedeon's throne. But he knew that quietness masked something far more dark and dangerous than a simple block of carved rock. The sorcerer was out for vengeance, for many, many wrongs.

"I owe you?" Adrik finally managed to say, his voice low and deadly. He tamped down on his rage, forced it deep into the pit of his stomach, where it gathered itself, dark and searing, awaiting the time of its release. "I owe *you*?"

The fire in his belly grew even stronger than before. "For what, Father—for giving me into the care of a demon who desires my death above all things?" His voice rose with his rage, echoing in the silence of the audience chamber. "For denying me the life granted any ordinary man, much less the son of a king? I owe you for this?"

He walked slowly toward the figure seated upon the dais, a pathetic old man maddened by greed and envy and the pursuit of power. Adrik stared at him coldly. Any trace of pity or compassion he might once have felt had withered inside him long years ago. He shook his head, his mouth curling downward in contempt. "I am here to reclaim my life, Father, not to renew yours."

Hedeon glared back at him, refusing to believe that his demand might fall upon deafened ears. "You must cast me a spell! I have been waiting all this time, hanging on to life only because I knew you would come to me. I am your father . . . your blood."

Adrik lowered his head and shut his eyes a moment, drawing strength from the quiet in his mind, from the belief that he could and would reclaim the life that had been stolen from him—his as well as Lorienne's.

"You are nothing to me," Adrik finally whispered. "Not blood, and certainly not a father." He lifted his head and glared at the old man, his chin lifting in defiance. "Malkaval has been more a father to me these past years than you have ever been . . . and he isn't even alive."

The king leapt to his feet abruptly, his wrinkled brow clouding with anger and desperation. "Cast your spell, and I vow you will someday have my throne in return!"

The smile Adrik gave him was as cold as the ice of winter. "And what of your firstborn, your precious crown prince? You would give me your throne over him?"

"Yes!" Hedeon shouted. He grimaced in disgust and lifted his hands, gesturing to his frail and failing body. "I am trapped in this withered shell. . . . I want to live,

to be as strong as I once was. You can give that to me!
I know you can."

He moved closer to Adrik and clutched desperately
at the sleeves of his tunic. "Name your price . . . anything!"

Adrik stiffened beneath his touch. "Give me back the
woman Burian stole from me." The dark smile that
tipped the edges of his mouth was a terrible thing to
behold. "Give her back to me and I will weave you a
spell," he said in a tantalizing voice. "One you will not
soon forget."

"No!" The shout came from beyond the throne, the
single word reverberating across the cavernous chamber.

Adrik turned toward the sound to see his brother
striding angrily toward them, tugging at the cinch of
his pantaloons as if he had just thrown them on. The
scabbard at his waist was askew as well, hanging so that
the sheathed sword slapped against the top of his thigh
with every step he took. The woman rushing along in
his wake appeared just as disheveled as the crown
prince, her hair tousled, the costly silk of her robe rumpled, as if she had leapt from a bed only a moment
ago.

Comprehension flickered in the sorcerer's eyes, and
the dark smile that had touched his lips returned once
more. No small wonder that Vlada had been unable to
find Burian within the palace. The woman hurrying
after the crown prince was the king's current wife, the
consort Hedeon had wed before Vania's body could
even be placed in a tomb.

Burian came to an abrupt halt, his face red with fury.
He glared at his father. "The girl is mine! I am your
heir. You have no right to make a trade of my property
to anyone."

The king gazed blankly at his firstborn son, per-
plexed by the turn the argument had taken. "Who is

this girl you speak of? Who is she that my sons would both seek to claim her as their own?"

Melina stepped away from Burian and hurried to her husband's side in a flurry of mock concern. As she offered her arm to support him, the errant thought crossed her mind that it was indeed ironic that her husband sought from Adrik the very same spell she herself had received from Malkaval all those years ago. "The girl is nothing but a pale-haired whore, husband." She presented him with the most flattering view of her face to try and gain his attention but there was something within Hedeon's eyes that gave her pause, as if he, too, would become enamored of the girl if he gazed upon her. "You should have her killed immediately, my husband, before she causes even more trouble among your sons!"

Adrik saw the glimmering of interest flare to life inside his father's eyes and knew Melina's callous words had had the opposite effect than what she intended. The king would demand to see Lorienne now and such interest from the Median king spelled danger for all concerned. "She is an Arizanti whom Burian is holding prisoner within the palace, and I want her returned to me."

"In exchange for my spell?" Hedeon asked anxiously.

Burian could see that his father was wavering. If not stopped, he would soon give in to Adrik's demand. A look of cunning eased over the crown prince's burly features. "The king of Media certainly cannot agree to such a trade with a known traitor! The very same man who seeks to betray you by making bargains with our enemy, the Lydians!"

He stared coldly at Adrik. "We know of your plans, sorcerer, but they will never come to fruition. There will be no alliance between the Magii and the Lydians. I will see to that! Do you deny the bargain you made, brother? Can you?"

Adrik shook his head slowly. "You may call it treason, but the only bargain I sought would bring peace to both us and the Lydians . . . before we destroy each other completely with our constant wars and never-ending battles."

Hedeon leaned his weight against Melina's shoulder to hold himself upright. His strength was fading away, ebbing like a trickle of water from a broken urn. It was clear to him now that Adrik had no intention of granting him a healing spell, not willingly at least. But if the sorcerer didn't cast him a spell soon, he would fade from the living world into the Shadow Realm, and that was something he was determined not to do.

His eyes glittered far too brightly, like jewels glinting beneath a fierce sun. It was time to force the sorcerer's hand. The king stepped close to his second-born, his gaze fixed on Adrik's face. "Do as I command and give me a spell," he whispered threateningly, "or I shall have the head of this woman you seek returned to you upon a silver tray. Yes . . . that's what I shall do."

A triumphant smile curled across Melina's full mouth. "A wise decision, husband," she gloated.

Where Hedeon's eyes glittered brightly, Adrik's became lightless, devoid of any mortal life, black, black holes burning in his face. His fury at his father's threat was a tangible thing, an ominous feeling clinging to the very air. He longed to lash out at Hedeon, to kill him here and now, but to do so would invite swift retribution against Lorienne.

"Harm her in any way," he threatened in return, "if you even dirty her robe with your foul touch, I shall transform you into the filthy swine that you are."

The king's gaze turned blank and empty, and he frowned in sudden bewilderment. The sorcerer's threat had brought a memory to the fore of his mind, a remembrance of the same warning given to him in another place, another time.

"Like mother, like son," the king finally said in a hushed tone. "Yes, she said she was going to turn me into a goat or a swine for taking a pretty Parae-tak outcast into my bed. She said she might even shrivel my manhood if I didn't send Melina away, but I couldn't do that . . . I couldn't. And Melina would only have me if Vania were dead and she herself was my consort."

Melina gasped and tried to pull her husband toward a doorway to leave the chamber, but he shook free of her and refused.

"Husband!" she snapped angrily. "No one wishes to hear your imaginings!"

The king shook his head several times, trying to clear his mind, but his thoughts were still mired in the distant past. "You see why she had to die, don't you?" he explained, staring at no one in particular. "She was a danger to me, to my future throne, and Malkaval wanted my second-born for his own. He needed a noble child of Magian blood, and so we struck the perfect bargain between us. He was given the infant, and with Vania dead, all of my dreams were made true . . . All of them!"

Melina paled and gaped at the king in horror, then from one to the other of the men who had witnessed Hedeon's long-delayed admission. "He knows not what he says!" she told them frantically. "Don't listen to his lies. He's mad . . . you know he is!"

Vlada lowered his eyes and gazed at the tiled floor, anywhere but at the face of the man who'd betrayed all those around him in such a horrifying way. "Oh, gods," the soldier said beneath his breath. The terrible tales and rumors whispered by servants and midwives for so many years had been true after all. Vania had not died pushing the child from her loins. She had been the victim of the foulest of betrayals—murdered by her own husband as she lay helpless in her childbed.

Even Burian appeared startled by the revelation, and

gazed with eyes suddenly sharpened by distrust at the woman who had often shared his bed.

The Shadow Prince simply stared at his father, his dark gaze filled with the promise of death. He understood now. Understood all the odd portions of his existence that had never been clear to him in the past. Before this day, he had thought Hedeon only partially responsible for the circumstances of his life, but now he knew the truth of it. His father had murdered his mother and given his infant son away, all in exchange for Malkaval's aid in achieving both his throne and his freedom from a marriage that had given rise to his power.

"How?" Adrik asked without any trace of emotion in his face or voice. "How did she die?" He had to know, had to discover the total truth, though each word of his father's crazed confession was like a wound inflicted upon his body.

Hedeon frowned for a moment, trying hard to remember. "Why—I stabbed her, of course." His bland pronouncement carried no hint of regret or shame for what he had done, nothing that could be construed as remorse at all.

Vlada rubbed at his brow with a trembling hand and fought against the moisture threatening to gush from his eyes. "All these years . . ." His voice trailed off miserably, and he choked on the knot of emotion in his throat. "All these years I believed the lie."

Adrik continued to stare coldly at his father, his back and shoulders rigid, his eyes dark and dangerous with the promise of death. "Give Lorienne back to me now," he demanded, his own voice sharp and brittle. "Give her back and I shall leave this place and gladly never return. If you continue to refuse . . ."

He allowed the promise of his vengeance to hang in the chamber like an upraised sword.

Something in his second-born's bitter stare finally

penetrated Hedeon's mind. He pulled his thoughts back to the present, away from the flood of memories dredged from the past, and blinked to focus on the here and now. "What of my spell?"

Adrik stiffened with anger. Even if he made the bargain and did what Hedeon asked, Lorienne would never be set free. His father was madder than he had ever imagined and might just kill her out of venomous spite. "There will be no spell, and no bargaining between us. Not now, not ever." His eyes burned with the heat of his rage. "Release her and I will allow you to live. If you do not, I will destroy you, your palace, and your entire empire!"

Fury and madness competed in Hedeon's gaunt face and glittering eyes. "You dare to threaten me?" he croaked in an angry whisper. "I am your king, your master, your father!"

Adrik blew out a breath laced with hostility. "You are nothing to me." He had his answer now. Hedeon would never willingly free Lorienne, simply because he knew his son desired it.

He turned his back on his father and walked slowly toward the distant entryway, watchful for any sign of treachery from those still inside the audience chamber.

For a moment, the only sound to intrude was the beat of his boots across the endless expanse of tiles.

"I'll have her killed!" Hedeon shouted feebly. "I swear it!"

Adrik kept walking.

Chapter Sixteen

As the sorcerer's footsteps faded away, a thick, heavy silence descended over the audience chamber. No one spoke, and Vlada knew few would even dare to draw a deep breath until the king's rage had passed.

"I want this Arizanti woman brought to me now!" Hedeon ordered, and several guards hurried to obey. "I want to see the creature who has cost me the aid of my son!"

Vlada closed his eyes. In his present frame of mind, the king would surely have her killed. He glanced at Burian, to see if the crown prince planned to intervene, but Burian was staring at Melina warily, not reacting to the order his father had given.

The old soldier's disdain for his masters grew. Burian knew what his father would do, and he had the power and the will to countermand any order given by the ailing king, yet he simply stood there and did nothing, as if possession of the girl had never held any meaning for him at all.

And if that were so, then the crown prince's command that Lorienne be stolen away from Khorazm had been no more to Burian than an amusing distraction, a means to inflict torment upon his half brother in some way.

Vlada blew out a weary breath. Lorienne's very life was beginning to weigh heavily upon his shoulders, the life of the child within her as well. Soon he would be forced to make a decision whose consequences would bring either death or life to all concerned.

But he had no other choice, none that he could foresee in his mind. A grimace passed over his features, and his mouth settled in a flat, pain-filled line. Despite what he'd thought, the debt he owed Vania remained unpaid.

There was a commotion near the throne chamber's rear doors, the shuffling of feet, a woman's sharp cry of pain and fear.

Lorienne.

The guards returned, dragging her between them. Her feet were bare, and her pale hair was in a tousled state, the curling locks tumbling down her shoulders and back. Forced to accompany the guards at a moment's notice, she was clad only in a woolen underrobe, the sort used for warmth beneath a heavier gown in winter.

The mere sight of her fair hair, such an oddity in southern lands, was enough to cause Melina to glare—and to catch and hold King Hedeon's undivided attention.

The guards finally flung her to her knees, depositing her at the feet of Hedeon.

Lorienne glanced up slowly, her heart pounding with the fear that had become her constant companion these past days. The wizened old man with mad eyes standing before her was wearing a golden crown—the crown of a king.

She studied the Median monarch speculatively. His face was skeletal, almost as thin as the demon's had been, and it appeared just as cruel. No hint of warmth or mortal feeling softened the sunken lines of his cheeks and jaw. Whether he was a king or a commoner, she knew the man who wore this face was utterly pitiless, possessing none of the emotions experienced by normal men. What he had done to Adrik had proved his lack in that regard long ago.

Could it have been this man or his minions who'd tainted her food with poison and killed poor, hapless Mandane, whose only crime was to eat a bite of cheese? Or had it been one of the others? Prince Burian and the woman with such darkly evil eyes both watched her now, and either appeared fully capable of doing such a heinous thing.

Lorienne shivered and tried to shunt thoughts of Mandane's death away, as well as the vile memory of the long day and night she had spent locked inside her chamber, her only company the woman's deteriorating body.

She gazed up at the king, wondering anew whether he was the one responsible, and why he would so fervently wish her dead.

As he stared back down at her in sullen silence, Hedeon's withered face ruddied, turning scarlet with growing rage. Adrik had refused him a spell, betrayed him because of this Arizanti girl.

"Give me a sword!" he ordered the guards, and the nearest soldier pulled his free of its scabbard and placed the hilt within Hedeon's thin hand.

Lorienne rose to stand on trembling legs. Though she feared what would soon come, she would meet her fate upright, with her head and chin held defiantly high.

Vlada eased his own hand toward the scabbard

strapped to his waist, trying to slip the short stabbing sword from its sheath surreptitiously.

The king's eyes glittered dangerously as his gaze swept down the girl's lean form, narrowing slightly as they came to rest upon the slight swell of her abdomen visible beneath the woolen under-robe.

Instinct caused Lorienne's arm to slip downward, where her hand wrapped itself about her abdomen protectively.

For a moment, the king did nothing but stare in surprise, and then his gaze thinned even more. He had seen that same swelling many times through the years, an event that had heralded the swift end of many a satisfying relationship. He had seen the sudden shifting of her hand to protect herself as well.

A tremor shook the narrow line of his mouth, and he lifted a bony finger, pointing to the telltale bulge of her belly. "Do you think your king a fool?" he hissed angrily. Spittle ran down his chin, a reaction he couldn't seem to control anymore. Soon there would be yet another vying for possession of his throne—a throne he would never willingly relinquish.

But now that had changed. Without the spell of his sorcerer son, death would surely come to him quickly, enabling Burian to finally claim his throne. Or perhaps even the bastard seed growing in this girl's swollen belly would one day lay claim to the Median throne. It mattered not which son had planted that seed. The end result was the same. Adrik had refused him a spell, and a child pushed from the loins of a common whore might someday rule his empire.

"Her fault . . ." Hedeon mumbled to himself. "Her fault."

The Median king gathered his strength and lifted the heavy sword. He had striven through the years to prevent just such as this, refusing all offers of arranged marriages for Burian, and forcing his healers to taint

269

the crown prince's wine with an herbal potion that robbed his seed of vigor.

"Which of my sons has managed to fill your belly with his seed?" he demanded, though he knew the answer to that already. The potion flowed through Burian's blood even now, rendering him incapable. The child in her belly belonged to the sorcerer. "Speak!"

Melina gasped in horror, and Burian's face turned as red with rage as his father's. Adrik had managed to do that which the crown prince had never managed to accomplish, despite the countless women he had taken to his bed. And now, the Shadow Prince had bred an heir. Even if Adrik died today, the child could conceivably rise all the way to the Median throne.

"Kill her, husband!" Melina yelled in a shrill voice. "The whore carries the sorcerer's child! Kill her quickly! He plots to steal your throne!"

Hedeon hefted the sword over his head, his arms trembling from the strain to lift the heavy weapon.

Suddenly he was struck. The blade bit deep, and a bright gout of blood welled from a wound between the shoulder blades. And then the sword drove deeper, twisting hard and fast to make a quick end of it.

Hedeon staggered slightly, his body lurching forward. His eyes, thin with rage a moment before, were now round and startled. The upraised sword slipped free of his hands and fell to the tiles with the sharp clatter of stone striking metal. The sound was still echoing as he turned his head, angling it to the side so that he could see who stood behind him. See the one who had betrayed him.

His mouth sagged, and a tiny rivulet of blood seeped from the left corner of his lips. Disbelieving lines puckered the center of Hedeon's brow as he gaped at the man who'd driven the blade deep into his back, burying it in his flesh all the way to the hilt.

"You!" the king whispered incredulously, his eyes

growing cloudy and vague. He tried to touch a hand to the sword buried in his back and failed.

Vlada squared his chin and stared into his king's glazing eyes. "You have destroyed too many lives already. I could stand by no longer and see the past repeated." He lifted his shoulders, and the weathered planes of his face turned stiff and grim. "It's fitting and just that you should die the same way as you killed poor Vania," he said bitterly.

Hedeon gaped at the old soldier in disbelief. Blood was running freely from his mouth now, and he found he could no longer speak. The darkness of the Shadow Realm was beckoning, drawing closer with every wet breath he drew.

His gaunt features grew taut and pinched. He didn't understand, didn't understand at all. Vlada had buried a blade in his back, condemned him to death because of his dead Magian wife? What did the life of one long-dead woman matter to anyone?

He collapsed in a boneless heap, rasping for air through lungs swiftly filling with blood. Pale-faced guards and courtiers simply stared at their dying king in shock, as did Burian and Melina. No one moved or spoke. No one tried to render him aid. Not even a whisper stirred in the chamber.

Lorienne finally found her feet and took a stumbling step backward, away from the dying man. She gazed at Vlada in shock. The soldier had vowed to try and protect her, but never in her wildest imaginings had she thought he might do so by killing the Median king.

Vlada calmly grasped her arm and began walking her toward the chamber's rear doors, their movements slow and measured. In moments the shock would pass, and the guards would fall upon them in a vengeful frenzy. But for now their startlement was too new, too unexpected, giving him and his ward a brief opportunity to make an escape.

Around them, the onlookers still stood frozen, rooted in place by what they had just witnessed.

The old soldier increased his pace, tugging Lorienne along with him, and then he broke into a sudden run, sprinting through the doors into the corridor beyond. He hurried her toward a seldom-used wing of the palace, one that held a secret passageway that had been dug beneath the earth in case Hedeon ever needed to make a swift escape. No one had thought to stop them yet, though they had hurried past numerous guards standing watch.

Vlada actually began to believe that they might well survive this day with their heads intact. They had already lived far longer than he ever imagined.

Hedeon gasped, fighting to pull air into lungs choked with blood. His eyes grew faded and distant. A moment later he gasped again, a quieter sound this time, and then his struggles for breath abruptly ceased. Blood welled from his back and mouth, pooling in dark red puddles upon the white tiles.

Burian blinked, still dumbfounded by the unexpected turn of events. "The king is dead," he announced into the silence.

And then a sound intruded on his thoughts, footsteps racing down the adjoining corridor, fading with time and distance. Vlada and the girl.

He gathered himself abruptly and shook off the lethargy that had prevented him from reacting before now. Burian raised an angry fist and pointed toward the doorway the pair had fled through. "After them!" he bellowed, his shout reverberating across the cavernous chamber. "Seize them and bring them back to me! They have killed the king!"

Vlada would die for what he had done, but now the girl would surely die as well, as swiftly as possible, for she carried Adrik's heir within her belly. It was unfortunate that he hadn't simply choked the life from her body the week before, when Vlada brought her to his chamber and the girl had the gall to mention Adrik's hated name. Now Burian would be forced to find another fair-haired woman to replace her in his bed.

Guards pounded after the fleeing pair in response to Burian's shouted orders. Nearby, several courtiers fell to one knee by Hedeon's body to pay homage to their fallen king. A servant burst into sudden tears, her sobs soon spreading to other throats. The time of official mourning had already begun for Hedeon Kiryl.

Melina stared indifferently at the puddle of blood spreading beneath her husband's body, then lifted her gaze back to Burian, the man she would make her future husband. A look of triumph flashed in her dark eyes. "You are king now, my beloved!" she told him in a hushed voice.

She turned then to the assemblage. "All hail King Burian!" she called out to them, finding it difficult to mask her glee.

Others took up the cry, shouting the new king's name.

Burian lifted his head high in response, and something that might have been a darkly victorious smile passed over his lips, curling the outer edges briefly, then vanishing from sight.

"I *am* king now," he said to Melina, repeating her announcement. Of course he would have to make doubly certain that his half brother soon joined their father in the Shadow Realm. The Arizanti girl had to die immediately as well. Neither could be allowed to live, especially with the girl breeding. No bastard child of his brother's would ever sit upon the Median throne.

Burian found that he wanted to laugh aloud. "That fool Vlada has made me king!" This time he did laugh, loud and long and joyfully.

* * *

At a signal from Adrik, scores of Median archers lifted their bows high. Almost at once a strange whining sound filled the air as the bowstrings were released in unison, a sound much like the noise fabric makes when being torn asunder. A storm of bronze-headed shafts rent the afternoon sky, the lethal lengths of wood daggering up and over the stone barriers to stab into anything their metal tips could penetrate.

Soldiers toppled from the palace walls, while others struggled to reclose the heavy carved gates to keep the attacking Magians out.

A Busae trying to pull one of the gates shut screamed as an arrow dug into his neck. Blood erupted in a small geyser, drenching his face and helmet with red. The man fell abruptly, and his body wedged itself in the opening between the gates. Another guard tripped over his body and tumbled to the ground. Two Magian arrows soon sprouted from his back.

More Busae fell as they frantically tried to close the gates, but their belated efforts proved futile. The gates should have been shut and barred as soon as the grim-faced Shadow Prince had galloped out atop his masked horse. Instead, the palace guard had foolishly allowed the gates to remain open and vulnerable to attack as they awaited the return of their missing commander, Vlada Sura, and any new orders issued by their king.

Adrik didn't hesitate to seize the opportunity afforded by the guards' mistake. "Burn the gates!" he shouted to his men. "Destroy them, and the walls will be ours!"

Another barrage of arrows was loosed, thinning the ranks of defenders even more. The Magian lancers then hurled the first of their spears. A Busae soldier cried out sharply as an iron point pierced through his leather overvest and into his gut, then partially exited his back, the long shaft pointing toward the sky. The man tumbled end over end from the battlement, felling a hapless Magian lancer who happened to be standing in formation directly below.

Pottery vessels filled with lamp oil had already been readied and were soon hurled against the arched gates, the clay shattering on impact and spraying the wood with the ignitable liquid. A single flaming arrow was sent flying, and the gates exploded in a burst of flame. The body of the man wedged in the opening caught fire, as did a Busae unfortunate enough to be standing on the other side of a gate when the flames erupted.

A thick, acrid haze of smoke plumed above the wall, enveloping the defenders on the battlement in a choking cloud. As the flames licked higher, some of the soldiers leapt from their positions atop the wall, tumbling to the earth below to escape the fury of the flames.

A moment later, one of the tall gates toppled with a groaning crash, and then the other came down as well. Soon all that was left was a fog of smoke and a few timbers of charred and glowing wood.

Despite the smoke and flames, the palace guards tried in vain to muster their ranks to defend the walls, but mounted Magians were already pushing through the newly opened gateway and forming a skirmish line that would capture the defenders within a deadly vise from both within and without.

Busae soldiers were pouring from barracks and the palace doors now, shouting frantic orders and racing to form up in ranks to defend against the mounted Magians who'd penetrated the palace's defenses and now threatened them from inside the walls.

Adrik ordered a rank each of bowmen and lancers into the palace grounds to protect the flanks of his mounted soldiers. Others made short work of disposing of the remaining defenders still clinging to their smoky, sooty posts atop the walls.

His expression cold and unforgiving, Adrik sat

grimly atop his horse and watched through the yawning hole where the gates had been as his soldiers calmly readied themselves for battle with the skill of blooded warriors.

His face and eyes turned even colder than before. He would destroy Hedeon's palace one block of stone at a time if necessary in order to free Lorienne from their clutches, and to ensure that his father was finally brought to justice for the wrongs he had inflicted.

In the distance, he could now see Burian, a blustering figure standing atop the steps leading into the sprawling palace. He was holding a sword aloft and screaming out orders to his troops, exhorting them to prepare to die in his name.

Adrik's eyes were bleak, his face stone-hard. The battle between him and Burian would soon be joined in earnest, one filled with death and gore, for the hatred between brothers was the most violent and vicious of all.

"My lord!" a soldier called from behind him, and the others whose task it was to guard their rear were turning about and staring at a patch of trees and brush rimming the outside of the long palace wall.

Adrik swung around in his saddle to see.

A man clad in the armor of a Busae officer broke from the cover of the trees and hurried down the narrow roadway, though his steps weren't nearly as swift as they would have been if he were alone. The soldier appeared dirtied and disheveled, as if he had just climbed from a hole in the ground. He held a slender-formed formed woman close at his side, one arm wrapped protectively about her shoulders.

Adrik's heart beat hard against the wall of his chest. He couldn't believe the sight before his eyes. The soldier was Vlada Sura, and the woman close at his side was Lorienne. Though she was just as begrimed as

Vlada, he could never mistake that pale hair and slender form.

"Lorienne!" Adrik shouted, and leapt from his horse, rushing down the dusty roadway to meet them. She was running as well, her arms outstretched, and he could see tears of joy wetting her dirtied cheeks.

He swallowed hard to try and free himself of the knot of feelings that had suddenly risen from somewhere deep inside him. The tears she shed were for him, the unrestrained joy visible on her face for him as well.

She threw herself into his waiting arms and clutched him tightly, overjoyed to feel his body beneath her fingertips, but terrified that she might lose him again. "Adrik!" She sobbed against the tunic of mail covering his chest and arms, and then rained a storm of eager kisses upon his jaw and neck. "I thought never to see you again! I feared you might not come for me!"

He wrapped her within his arms, cradling her body as tightly as she did him, and breathed in her heady scent, allowing it to fill his lungs, to become a part of him. The part of himself he had been missing these past weeks. "I was afraid I would arrive too late," he whispered into her tousled hair. She felt so good in his arms, so utterly *right*. "I came just as soon as I got word you had been taken from Khorazm."

The memory of how Lorienne came to be in Urmia rose to the forefront of his thoughts, and he glanced over her shoulder to the soldier who had brought her back to him. His features clouded with bewilderment. He had never imagined that the man who had stolen her away would come to his aid and then be responsible for Lorienne's safe return.

"Why?" he asked Vlada quietly, puzzled anew by the soldier's actions.

Vlada met his probing gaze without flinching. "For the sake of your mother." A look of sadness touched his rugged features. "To avenge her death."

Lorienne tugged at his arm to gain his attention. "Adrik, the king is dead," she told him softly.

He glanced from one to the other in surprise, taken aback by the news. "Dead?" Though it was his own father Lorienne spoke of, he could dredge up no emotion for him at all. Hedeon had been only a cruel stranger to him, someone he despised from afar. Other than surprise at the news, he felt nothing, no sadness or grief for the man.

His dark gaze found the soldier's. He didn't truly need to be told the how or why of his father's death. None of that mattered in the end. He understood that now, understood many things he hadn't in the past. "I am in your debt," he told Vlada, "for more than one reason. Ask what you want of me and it will be granted."

Vlada shook his head firmly. "I seek nothing other than the opportunity to serve you, my lord." He dropped to one knee and bowed his head in formal obeisance. "Perhaps by doing so I can make amends for all the years when I did nothing to aid you in any way."

Adrik gazed at him mutely, stunned by the oath of loyalty offered by the soldier. A vow of allegiance from the commander of his father's troops was the last thing he had expected on such a day as this. From the looks of astonishment on the faces of the Magian soldiers within hearing, they had not expected such a vow from Vlada either.

He glanced to Lorienne, whose happy smile left no doubt as to her thoughts on the unexpected turn of events.

"I am honored by your offer of loyalty, Vlada Sura," Adrik finally said in a voice roughened by emotion, "and I gladly accept."

The soldier clapped a closed fist to his chest in salute of his new master. "I vow my fealty to the son of Vania."

He gave Lorienne a meaningful glance. "And to his heirs . . ." His voice trailed away, as if he had purposefully left his thought incomplete.

Adrik frowned as he saw a peculiar look pass between Lorienne and Vlada. Stranger still, the soldier's words had caused her to draw away from him slightly and cast her eyes downward, her face flushing with embarrassment and uncertainty.

"What is it, Lorienne?" he queried, worried by the strange behavior.

She refused to meet his gaze, but her hands drifted downward to wrap around her abdomen protectively, an unconscious gesture on her part that had become habit in the past weeks.

"I . . ." Lorienne swallowed. How would he react to such news as this? Would he ever acknowledge a child from her loins? "I am with child, Adrik," she blurted hoarsely and blinked back a fresh haze of tears. "It was because of me that Vlada did what he did—the king discovered I carried your child and raised a sword to me. He blamed me for your refusal to grant him a spell and planned to slay me in revenge."

Thunderstruck by the revelation, Adrik took her hand and squeezed it tightly within his own. She was carrying his seed inside her—the future of them both. Now that he knew the truth, he could see it clearly in the slight mounding of her belly, the look of sudden maturity that had laid claim to her perfect features.

"My child . . ." he whispered raggedly. Those were words he had never thought to speak, thought he would never be allowed to speak. He caressed the top of her slender hand, marveling at the changes wrought within him by those two simple words. A sense of pride swelled in his chest, and with it came the certainty that his fate truly did lay with Lorienne. Through her, he had reclaimed part of the life stolen from him all those years ago.

"Do not blame yourself for my father's fate," he reassured her. "Hedeon was mad and sought revenge for my refusal. He deserved to die. The blame fell upon you simply because he feared striking out at me directly."

She rested her fingers upon the flesh of his cheek, closing her mind against the sudden rush of desire rising inside her. The mere touch of his skin to hers was enough to make her crave him once again. "But what happens now, Adrik? Burian has declared himself the new king. What will he attempt to do?"

The frown that passed over his brow was dark and foreboding. He knew what Burian would do even if Lorienne did not. The new Median king would seek to consolidate his power by dispensing with any potential rivals for his throne. Adrik was one of those rivals, and now, by virtue of blood, so was the tiny infant growing inside Lorienne's body.

There was a flurry of new movement and sound within the grounds of the palace, armor glinting in the sunlight, the thudding of boots upon loose gravel as more Busae soldiers moved into position. The face-plates of their helmets were lowered, their shields and lances held at the ready.

Adrik watched the preparations for battle with a grim expression. If he hoped to defeat his brother, he would need to draw upon all the powers at his disposal. The sorcerer closed his eyelids and glanced up at the dimming sky, the threads of energy within the earth itself gathering around him.

A hawk appeared above, struggling to stay aloft in the freshening wind. Others soon joined it, both large and small, gulls and carrion birds, as well as the small feathered creatures of the deep forest, their swirling numbers growing with each moment that passed.

He opened his eyes and watched the birds swirling and wheeling above. Burian had to be stopped somehow. If he failed, the man would kill them all in order to protect his throne.

Chapter Seventeen

Melina lifted the base of her robe and rushed up a winding staircase leading to the palace's upper levels. She swept inside an empty chamber and threw back the silken curtains from a window opening onto the front of the palace, one that gave her an unobstructed view of all that occurred below. From her vantage point she could see and observe the opposing forces gathering around the palace to do battle against each other beneath the waning sun.

Directly below, the new king was pacing back and forth along the wide steps that formed the entryway into the palace, watching worriedly as his troops marshaled on the open stretch of land before him. In the distance, she could see the Magian soldiers waiting in patient ranks for their master to give the order for an attack to begin.

And above . . . She shivered slightly and glanced up at the birds gathering in the late afternoon sky. The sorcerer's doings, she knew.

Brother would soon fight brother, and in this battle, Melina wasn't sure who would ultimately win.

Her gaze fell upon the new Median king. Clad in heavy leather armor and mail, Burian gave the appearance of a mighty warrior, a blustering, imposing figure who could slice off heads with a single blow of a sword or battle-ax. The ranks of Busae lancers and bowmen massing for the attack against the Magii were just as intimidating to behold.

But Melina knew that beneath Burian and his soldiers' imposing facade dwelled an empty, vacant husk— an army without its true leader, for Vlada Sura, who had trained and commanded the palace guard for so long, had killed the king in front of a score of witnesses then fled with the sorcerer's whore.

By now word had spread of what Vlada had done, and those very same soldiers marshaling for battle below would be wondering why their commander would do such a thing. And then they would begin to doubt their new king, the man who planned to lead them into battle against his own half brother. A half brother they feared.

Melina clenched her fists at her sides, and her mouth set itself in a fiercely determined line. All she had ever wished for was now within her grasp. But if the tide of battle turned against them this day, she would lose everything she had strived a lifetime to achieve.

"Malkaval!" she hissed into the empty chamber. "Where are you, Malkaval!" she called out, far more loudly this time. "I demand that you come to me immediately! You *must* help us!"

She turned in a slow circle, searching the shadowy chamber for signs that he was there. "If you do not help me, all will be lost. . . . the Arizanti carries the sorcerer's heir!"

The air near her shimmered, and a thin sliver began

to coalesce, to form the shape of a creature that seemed to refract light like the sun slanting across a still pool of water.

The demon's skull-like face glittered with malice, and its eyes glowed a hot, angry red. "You disturb me *now?*" Malkaval bellowed, his thunderous voice like a grating against stone.

Melina stood before the undead creature, unafraid, her dark eyes filled with as much anger as the demon's. "Obviously you are not the all-knowing creature I thought you to be! Do you not know what is taking place outside these walls?"

The red eyes glowed like scarlet coals. "You risk much by speaking to me thusly, mortal." Sparks of light crackled in his eyes. "After all, it was you who failed to carry out the task I set before you. The Arizanti would carry no bastard seed inside her if she were dead as you promised she would be!"

Melina winced but held her ground, her chin angling higher. "You did not tell me that she had found a champion in Vlada Sura. How could I succeed in having her killed when he was guarding her at every turn? He even assigned her a food taster!" She snorted loudly. "He managed to foil every plot I devised, and now he has spirited her away! Returned her to the Shadow Prince, no doubt."

Malkaval stared out the open window, at an afternoon sky now ridged with a thin veil of clouds and countless wheeling birds, all moving swiftly on a rising wind.

The time was fast approaching. He could sense it, feel it building in the air. A thousand years of planning. How had it all gone so wrong? A mere girl, a mortal, was on the verge of destroying everything he had schemed to achieve, and that he would never abide.

"Hedeon is dead," Melina snapped, angry that the demon didn't seem to be paying her any mind. "He was slain by Vlada Sura before he took the whore and escaped. And now when I am finally free to become Burian's consort, the fool may fall in battle against your cherished sorcerer! What if Adrik kills him, or a Magian arrow finds his back? What's to become of me then?" Her voice turned even more petulant than usual. "You promised that I would be queen! You *promised* me!"

The demon's orblike eyes sizzled with red fire, twin flames that seemed to swallow and hold the very air inside the chamber.

Melina gasped, suddenly short of breath. She took a swift step away from the demon but still found it hard to breathe. Her heart pounded in her breast, and a glint of fear shone in the depths of her eyes. For the first time, she grew afraid that she might have truly roused the demon's rage.

"Yes . . . you have good reason to be afraid, my sweet," Malkaval said in a whisper that seemed to slither around her like the coils of a serpent. "Remember what I promised you? I vowed that if you failed me, I would make you suffer in ways you never imagined."

He watched in amusement as Melina's eyes widened with comprehension, and she took several stumbling steps toward the doorway, as if she thought to flee from him. His thin features grew pinched with mock pity. "Poor, poor Melina. The Arizanti still lives; therefore you have indeed failed me."

Melina let out a little screech and bolted, but the demon's shimmering form appeared in the doorway long before she reached it. She tried to scream to rouse a guard, but the sound died in her throat half-born, her cry smothered into silence by the flick of a single finger from Malkaval.

She then ran in the opposite direction, toward the open window where she could cry out for aid from Burian. Again, the demon blocked her path, a malicious grin creasing his cadaverous face, as if he relished the game he played. She darted about the chamber frantically, searching for a means of escape, but each time she raced in another direction, he was there again, taunting her with his very presence.

Exhausted, she finally came to a frantic halt, her dark eyes wide and frightened, and her chest rising in sharp little gasps as she fought to pull in needed air.

Malkaval smiled again, a vicious lifting of his lips that sent a shiver through her flesh.

He raised a bony finger and slashed it through the air. "Suffer as I have suffered . . . for all eternity."

Skin that had been flawless and smooth just a moment before turned slack and wrinkled. Melina could feel it, feel her skin loosening and sliding. She gasped in horror and grabbed at her face and throat with fingers that had suddenly grown old and decrepit, the joints swollen and deformed.

"No!" She stared at her swollen fingers in horror, a sob rising in her throat. "Please, not this!" she begged the demon. "I'll do anything you want! Anything!"

The flesh on her throat bagged and slid downward, webbed by a maze of age lines. Her perfect chin sagged, and she felt the teeth loosen within her mouth. Long tufts of hair began falling around her, drifting toward the tiled floor, her silken tresses now thin and worn and threaded with whitish gray.

She didn't need to see her image reflected in the surface of the tray to know what the demon had done to her.

Melina tried to scream but the only sound that climbed from her throat was a feeble little croak.

The Busae soldiers could see the Shadow Prince clearly, a dark figure astride an equally dark horse, man and beast directly beneath the charred arch of the palace's burned gates, watching silently as they prepared to wage battle against him.

Birds soared in the sky above them, all types and colors and sizes, an unnatural gathering that chilled them to the bone. A pack of wolves was visible as well, the creatures prowling and shifting around the Shadow Prince's horse, predators of the night who had followed their master into the light of day.

They were sights that dredged fear in the breasts of all the Busae who saw them.

And then they spotted an officer ride up beside the darkling prince and take his place at his master's side.

Their fear grew like weeds sprouting in a fallow field. A frightened, querulous muttering soon traveled through the Busae ranks, spilling from one throat to another. Commander Vlada had cast his lot with the Shadow Prince, and now rode proudly beside his new lord and master.

Several lancers on the far left flank exchanged worried glances, then lowered their spears and ran, their fear of Vlada Sura and the Shadow Prince greater than that of the new king.

Burian saw them flee and chopped a hand through the air, ordering a line of bowmen to let their arrows fly. Two of the cowards fell, but one made good his escape.

The Median king's heavy features contorted with rage as he paced back and forth in front of his men. "Any coward who tries to flee as they did shall suffer the same fate!"

The muttering faded, but others within the Busae ranks shifted about restlessly, as if they too were considering the merits of flight.

A look of grim fury settled about Burian's mouth and eyes. His soldiers feared the combination of the sorcerer's magic and Vlada's skill, and the only enticement capable of overcoming such dread was the promise of a sizable reward.

"A chest of gold to the man who brings me the head of Vlada Sura!" Avarice always won out over fear, and this time would be no different. "And two chests of gold and a whore to the one who presents me with the head of the Magian prince!"

A thin cheer went up in the ranks, but to Burian's ears the cries were feeble and few, pathetically so.

He glared ominously at the man sitting so calmly astride that masked horse, a pack of wolves creeping about nearby. "It is time for you to die, brother," Burian whispered quietly, more to himself than anyone.

It was time for Lorienne to die as well. Though he had yet to glimpse her among the Magii, he knew she was there, somewhere to the rear of the ranks most likely, guarded by a contingent of Magian soldiers assigned to protect their tribe's future heir.

Burian raised an arm, then lowered it abruptly, signaling for the attack to begin.

Arrows rained down upon the fore ranks of Magians, felling several where they stood. A great cry went up among the Magii and their own bowmen let loose a storm of bronze-heads in return. The wooden shafts sang in the rising wind as they flew toward the front ranks of Burian's defenders. A man screamed and collapsed, an arrow protruding from his chest. Others dropped to the ground, blood spouting from holes torn in their limbs and torsos.

Birds suddenly began daggering down from the sky, squalling and cawing as they fell upon the frightened soldiers, pecking and clawing at any exposed flesh. But only the Busae were targets of the feathered attackers; the Magii appeared immune.

Burian shouted in frustration and swung the flat of his sword around, swatting at any birds unfortunate enough to fly in his direction. One managed to land upon his shoulder and peck at the back of his neck, its beak stabbing into the strip of exposed skin between the bottom of his helmet and his tunic of mail.

He roared his fury and grabbed the thing from his shoulder, crushing its body within his palm, and then screamed at his men to begin their advance.

As the birds arced back into the sky, Burian's lancers began to move forward slowly, climbing over their fallen comrades in their march toward the Magii. Soon the battle would be shield to sword, and he would finally have the opportunity to best his brother personally. One way or another, Adrik would die this day.

The wind rose even more, gusting and blowing in from the lake, then swirling about in a vortex as if it knew no one direction. Birds squalled and fluttered about, struggling to break free of the twisting currents of air. The sound of the wind was strange as well, like the pain-filled moans of a thousand voices wailing their woe at once, as if the earth itself were crying out in despair.

Burian glanced upward in trepidation, as did most of those there, both Magii and Busae alike. The birds were spinning in frantic circles, caught in the whirling winds. A queer grayish green cast had shaded the sky, the hue turning darker and darker as time went by. Other than the moaning of the wind, the earth had fallen ominously silent. Even the birds caught in the maelstrom made no sound.

Burian clutched his sword tighter and waited anxiously to see what new plague his sorcerer brother was about to unleash against them. Soldiers began making warding signs and covering eyes to protect themselves from the sorcerer's spell.

But the Magian prince was gazing up at the sky as well, his harsh features turning pale with dread, for the swirling winds and eerie darkness had not been wrought from his hand.

Adrik closed his lids against the sight and tried to swallow the sudden tightness in his throat and chest. The time had come, far more swiftly than he had ever imagined. Soon the battle he waged would be twofold, against both Burian and Malkaval.

The sorcerer pulled in a great breath to steady himself and stiffened the line of his shoulders. Soon now.

White-faced, Vlada shielded his eyes against the sting of blowing dust and bits of gravel and fought to control his horse. "What is it?" he called to Adrik anxiously. He squinted and looked toward the fast-darkening sky. "What does this mean, my lord?"

"The demon comes," Adrik answered over the onrush of wind. "The time of prophecy is now at hand."

Around them, the wolves suddenly lifted their heads and ears and began howling into the wind. Adrik's horse shied, dancing sideways, and pawed nervously at the gravel with a hoof.

"*Adrik!*" the demon suddenly shouted, his angry bellow a crash of thunder amidst the moaning of the wind. "Do you see what I have found for myself?"

That darkly chilling voice had reverberated from behind them, not the fore. Adrik spun his horse in a half circle as a startled Vlada did the same. The wolves turned about as well, growling and snarling when they saw the specter that had appeared behind them.

Adrik didn't move, didn't speak. He simply stared in utter silence, his face as still as a mask of death. The cadre of guards assigned to protect Lorienne lay dead upon the ground, their broken bodies limp and lifeless, scattered like sticks of discarded wood.

"By the gods!" Vlada whispered in horror when he saw the carnage.

The thing that had killed the soldiers drifted casually in the air above the soldiers' bodies, suspended high enough to injure any mortal who might fall from that height.

Adrik's eyes darkened dangerously. The demon had Lorienne. She was staring back at him mutely, her eyes fever-bright with fear and dawning horror, her face bleached of any trace of color.

"So pretty . . ." Malkaval pulled the girl's back and hips hard against his shimmering torso, imprisoning her body within his nonexistent embrace. He allowed one hand to drift downward, spreading against the fullness of her belly. Though he couldn't feel the swollen flesh beneath his fingertips, he knew that she could feel his touch and would cringe in disgust. "And breeding too, I am told."

At the demon's slithery touch, Lorienne whimpered in fear but the sound of it was lost in his malevolent laughter.

"Release her!" Adrik demanded. His voice was as cold as the ice that still capped the mountains in the north.

"You are in no position to make demands of me, Adrik!" the demon bellowed in return.

Vlada pulled his sword and lifted it toward the demon.

"No!" Adrik called to him. "He'll kill you as he did the guards!"

The sword glinting in Vlada's hand rose a fraction higher. A moment later, the soldier found himself lying in a heap upon the ground. His horse screamed in fear and bolted away.

Adrik glanced down at the fallen soldier and was grateful when he saw him move. At least the man still lived, unlike the others. "Leave him to me, Vlada," he ordered the old soldier. "You cannot hope to kill or maim Malkaval. . . . He's not even alive."

Vlada blinked to focus his eyes and stared up at the thing still hovering in the air. And then he heard a noise, a snuffling, sniffing sound, and felt a cold touch against his cheek. He glanced in that direction and frowned. The wolf again. The large gray beast was touching his face with its nose, as if seeking reassurance that he still lived.

Suddenly there were startled screams among the soldiers battling behind them, shouts of fear and shock.

"Look!" someone shouted. "An evil omen!"

The battle ceased abruptly, and both Busae and Magii alike lowered upraised weapons and lifted their faces skyward, staring in fear as the sun began to disappear. The black sliver on the surface of the sun soon grew to an ever-widening crescent.

"An eclipse!" a Busae cried out in terror.

Some fell to their knees and began to sob. Others turned their faces away, shielding their eyes from the burning glare still visible in the remnants of the sun.

Burian watched as well, falling prey to superstition like the rest. A niggle of uncertainty came to life inside him. First he had been forced to contend with Adrik and his vile creatures, and now this strange portent.

Malkaval laughed again and glanced up at the sky in glee. The sun now hung in the green-tinged sky like a glowing half-moon. "You see, Adrik? After all these years, it is finally time—time for you to fulfill your destiny!"

The sorcerer's hands clenched into fists held tight to his sides. He glanced at Lorienne with a calmness he didn't feel, and then he forced himself to look away lest the sight of her fear-blanched features weakened his resolve in some way.

"No," he told the demon flatly. The sharp planes of his face settled into resolute lines. "My destiny lies elsewhere now. I will *not* submit to your will ever again."

In the growing darkness, the demon's eyes burned hot and red like funeral pyres, the heat from them spilling outward to char those within their path. For one brief moment, his shimmering form turned red as well, then faded to a cold, cold gray that glittered like faceted ice.

"Your only destiny lies with me!" Malkaval's rage sparked and sizzled like currents of dark lightning. And then the bloody hue of his eyes deepened and narrowed with the slyness of an adder. Adrik would do what he was told. He had no choice.

The unnatural lightning crackled again, and Lorienne cried out sharply in pain.

At her cry, a tremor ran through Adrik's fists but he allowed himself no other outward reaction. "Release her, Malkaval!" he repeated, though he knew the demon would refuse to do so.

In answer, a bolt of black lightning sizzled through the air. Lorienne's face and body spasmed from the terrible pain. Gasping, she sagged limply against her captor.

"I'll destroy her!" Malkaval shouted bitterly, his grating voice echoing across the landscape. "Submit to the change or I vow I will kill her and the bastard seed she carries within her!"

Lorienne managed to shake her head feebly and fought to draw breath into her pain-wracked lungs. "No, Adrik, don't give in to him," she said raggedly, "not for me." And then the demon tightened his hold on her and she fell silent again, unable to speak.

"Submit and I'll allow her to go free," the demon hissed to him. "She and the child. Deny me and they die!"

As Adrik watched helplessly, Lorienne's slender body again contorted with agonizing pain. Her mouth opened as if to scream but no sound emerged, and he could see the bright glitter of unshed tears shining within her pale eyes.

He closed his eyelids for a moment, then reopened them, his own eyes now despondent and dark with resignation. He gazed at Lorienne morosely. He'd been a fool to believe that his fate could be altered on his whim. "Do you vow not to harm her or the child in any way?" he demanded of Malkaval.

Lorienne squirmed to free herself from the demon's insidious embrace, but the pain shot through her body again and she could do nothing but sag uselessly against him.

A look of glee flashed across the demon's liquid features. "Yes!" He knew he'd won now. To save her and the child, Adrik would crawl to him and submit on bended knee. He'd submit to the change. "I vow it!" he lied, but the sorcerer would never know his promise for a lie. When the transformation was complete, he would be the mortal and Adrik undead—and Lorienne would belong to him instead.

Adrik climbed from his horse and stood before the creature hovering in the air. "Then I shall willingly make the exchange," he told the demon bleakly.

An eerie darkness descended as the shadow of the moon fell across the land in earnest. The sun was only a thin sliver burning low in the afternoon sky, a thin circle of light surrounding a hole of blackness so total it turned day to night.

Adrik's eyes, dark with sadness and grim resolve, sought and found Lorienne's. They would never see each other again, not as they were now. Even if they did so, she would be mortal and he undead. "Live well, Lorienne," he told her, "both you and the child." A look of uncertainty touched his features, and then he drew a sharp breath and allowed all the feelings he had held inside to shine through in his face and eyes. "Know that I have grown to love you more than life itself."

Vlada heard those ominous words and fought to pull himself upright. The Shadow Prince sought to trade his life for Lorienne's. "My lord! You cannot do this!"

Adrik ignored the soldier's admonition and turned

toward him slowly. "I am trusting you to protect them, Vlada, both Lorienne and the child. When he frees her, hold her from me and keep her from interfering in any way."

"But, my lord, what of you?" Vlada asked desperately.

"I am beyond the aid of anyone. All I ask of you is to keep them safe both now and in the future. . . . Promise me."

Vlada met his eyes for a long moment, then nodded slowly. "I swear it."

Adrik's solemn gaze then moved to Sandor, who whined and rubbed against his legs in response. He caressed the wolf's head tenderly. *Good-bye, old friend,* he told the creature silently. Words had never been necessary between them, and wouldn't be now.

He glanced up finally and met those glowing red eyes. "Fulfill your part of the bargain, Malkaval!" Adrik demanded.

The demon drifted toward the ground, Lorienne with him. She staggered slightly as her feet touched earth again, and Vlada grabbed her and held her close, both to steady her and keep her from the demon's reach.

The sun was in full shadow now, the daytime sky as black as the darkest of moonless nights. The wind rose even more, sighing across the landscape. And then a circle of white light appeared before the demon, a crackling vortex of pure energy that formed the fleeting gateway between the living world and the Shadow Realm.

The demon shouted in joy as the gateway grew larger, brighter. The legends were true. All his centuries of waiting and planning had finally come to an end. "I have waited for this moment for a thousand years!"

He pushed a single arm through the sizzling vortex, saw his hand take shape and substance before his eyes.

He gasped as a breath of wind blew across the newly mortal flesh, prickling the skin. "I can feel it!" he cried. He had no words to describe the sensation, nothing he had ever known to compare the feeling to. "I can feel it!"

He flexed his mortal fingers, relishing the feel of bone and sinew and muscled flesh. "Take my hand in yours, Adrik!" he demanded, "only then will the gateway allow us to make the exchange!"

Adrik reached out to grasp the demon's hand.

"No!" Lorienne screamed. "Adrik!" She struggled to run to him, prevent him from reaching out, but Vlada held her tightly and refused to set her free.

A huge gray shape suddenly hurtled through the air, throwing its body between the sorcerer and the waiting demon. The collision knocked Adrik aside, and he fell to the ground in stunned surprise as the wolf leapt past him, its muscled shoulder and flank slamming hard into the demon's now mortal hand.

Malkaval screamed in fury as the vortex arced and crackled, then swelled around him, glowing larger and larger until the bloom of white suddenly exploded in a brilliant flash of preternatural energy. The gateway vanished as quickly as it had come, thinning to a tiny sliver and disappearing from sight. The demon's rage-filled screams faded with it, thinning until they were only distant echoes that ceased entirely when the gateway vanished.

And then the sky began to lighten as the shadow of the moon slowly lifted from the face of the sun. The queer wind died away, and the greenish cast faded from the sky, replaced by the normal shades of day.

Birds called in the distance, and soldiers muttered among themselves, uncertain whether to believe they had survived unscathed the evils wrought by the unexpected eclipse.

For a moment, Adrik simply lay where he had fallen

and stared up at the afternoon sky, shocked that he remained alive. The brightness of the explosion still burned behind his eyelids, a stark reminder of what had occurred. His mortal flesh should be dead now, not a part of the living world.

He lifted a hand and stared at his flesh to reassure himself that he truly lived. The gateway was gone, and with it, Malkaval.

Lorienne pulled free of Vlada's grip and rushed to his side. She threw herself to the ground beside him, her body shivering as if from a violent chill. "Adrik?" she said anxiously, his name carrying with it a profusion of emotions and unvoiced questions.

He gazed at her in stunned confusion. "I still live," he said in a wondering voice and reached to take her slender hand in his. The demon was gone, and he was free.

He was free.

Then he remembered all that had happened and sat up abruptly. But what price had been paid for his freedom? His friend had thrown herself into the vortex, sacrificing herself in his place.

"Sandor!" he called, and his worried gaze found the creature lying on the ground nearby, the furred body deathly still.

He scrambled to her side, knowing instinctively that she would soon die. Her golden eyes were glazed and her flanks were rising and falling in a ragged rhythm, as if she struggled to draw each breath.

Adrik blinked away the moisture building in his eyes and lifted the wolf's head into his arms, cradling her gently. Throughout his life, she had been the only constant he had ever known, the only companion who had ever cared for him, and been cared for in return. Now she lay near death. "Sandor . . ."

The wolf drew several panting breaths, her great yellow eyes stilling on the sorcerer's face. But those eyes soon grew more faded with the approach of death.

As he watched and waited, grieving for his dying friend, the wolf's gray-furred body suddenly began to change, shifting and reshaping itself. He stared in amazement as human limbs and flesh appeared where animal fur and bone had been only a moment before. The familiar golden eyes turned as dark as night, and black silky hair now framed a feminine face—a human face.

Vlada gasped and fell to his knees beside the Shadow Prince. "I should have known!" he whispered in disbelief. "I should have known." But he now understood why the wolf had seemed to possess such eerily intelligent eyes, understood why he had felt such a special affinity for the beast.

The old soldier gazed into a face he hadn't seen in so many, many years, a beloved face he thought never to view again. "Vania . . ." he said in a choked voice. She appeared older, less innocent, and far wearier of the world than before, but there was no doubt in his mind that this was the woman he had loved so desperately. "You've come back to us."

She smiled up at him sadly. "I never left, Vlada." Her voice was thin and breathy, hoarse with disuse. "You forget that I was a Magian sorceress in my own right. I have been here all along, just in a different form, watching over Adrik and waiting for this one moment in time, when I would finally have the chance to protect my son and free him from the demon that Hedeon sold him to."

An angry shadow passed through her eyes. "I am glad you killed Hedeon, Vlada. Remember that always. I can die in peace now, knowing you claimed vengeance for me, and will be here to help protect my son in my stead."

Adrik stared at her in silence, too stunned to speak. The wolf that had nurtured and protected him for so many years had in truth been the mother he thought dead. Only a Magian sorceress of immense power and skill could have been able to maintain the shape of a wolf for so long. "Mother?" he finally said, the word sounding strange on his tongue.

She smiled up at him. "Yes, my son, I have always been near, but, oh, how I have longed to speak aloud with you! To tell you how much I love and cherish you. But I didn't dare before now lest the demon or Hedeon discover I had escaped death at their hands and fled into the forest in the guise of a wolf."

Vania winced, her features growing pinched with pain. "I could not allow them to discover my true form before the day of prophecy. If they had, the demon would have prevented me from sending him back to the Shadow Realm where he belongs."

She touched Adrik's cheek tenderly. "But now all the wrongs done to us have finally been righted, and I can die knowing you are free to make of your fate what you will."

Her dark gaze, so like her son's, moved to Lorienne's face. "I am glad that my son has found you, Lorienne. Take care of him for me, keep him and the child safe and happy."

Before Lorienne had a chance to answer, Vania's dark eyes drifted closed, and she was gone.

Adrik stared quietly into his mother's face and gently stroked her silken hair. For one brief moment, he had been given that which had been stolen from him all those years ago, and now he had lost it again.

Tears slid down Lorienne's cheeks, and she clasped Adrik's hand within her own, holding it tightly.

Vlada wept openly, grieving anew for the woman he had loved.

Adrik gently laid her head upon the ground and rose to his feet, helping Lorienne to rise with him. Magian

299

soldiers had clustered around them, their swords still drawn, waiting for their prince's orders.

"Signal a withdrawal," Adrik ordered. "There will be no more fighting." His eyes were somber, dark with grief. "We return to Khorazm immediately. Prepare our dead for the journey. . . . Princess Vania as well." He glanced down to view one final time the stranger who'd been his mother. He wanted to remember how she looked. Soon she would be shrouded in linen, and he would never see that face again. "We will return them to our own lands."

An officer clapped a fist to his chest and bowed his head in respect. "Yes, my prince," he told Adrik gravely before rushing off to relay his orders.

As the Busae stared in amazement, the Magian forces began an orderly withdrawal from inside the palace grounds. Silently, they collected their dead, their discarded shields and weapons, and marshaled into disciplined ranks to withdraw.

A glowering Burian watched in disbelief the Magians' preparations for departure. After all that had passed between them, all that had been said and done, his sorcerer brother would simply gather his troops and depart?

The new Median king strode boldly toward the palace gates that the Magii had burned, directly through the midst of Adrik's forces. How could his brother even think to leave now? Despite Hedeon's death and the eclipse's evil portents, nothing had changed between them. The outcome of the battle remained unresolved, and Adrik still posed a considerable threat to his new throne. So did his seed.

"Adrik!" Burian called out to him, increasing his gait until he was nearly running. His brother had helped Lorienne to climb atop a waiting horse, and he was now mounting his own horse in preparation to depart.

Vlada sat astride a horse nearby, as if he, too, planned to leave with the Shadow Prince.

The new king clutched the grip of his sword more tightly. "I will not allow you to ride away and leave things unresolved between us! Our father is dead, and I am your new king!"

Doubled ranks of Magian archers and bowmen passed beneath the charred gates and began moving down the dusty roadway toward the city's outer gates, beginning the slow journey eastward, toward distant Khorazm and the Caspian Sea.

Adrik gazed at his brother dispassionately. "Do not press me, Burian. I have decided to let you and your soldiers live this day because you are indeed the empire's rightful king."

Burian lifted his heavy chin proudly. At least Adrik acknowledged his right to sit upon the throne. But there were others who might not think so highly of that right. "What of the Lydians, Adrik? I may be king now, but we are still at war, and you rode away from Amida and left the tribes' combined armies without a leader upon the field of battle. By now those thousands are probably dead and rotting. Do you not take responsibility for what you have done to them?"

Adrik stared back at him coldly. "All I have done is to take it upon myself to end Hedeon's war for him. By now my second in command and Prince Pantaleon have struck a bargain for peace—with you as the ultimate prize."

Burian scowled, and his mouth fell in surprise. "What is this you say?"

"The Lydians only came to me because our father had refused their pleas for peace, even going so far as to reject their offer for you to wed their princess. He threatened to send any further couriers back without their heads."

The revelation rendered Burian speechless. Hedeon

Jan Zimlich

had refused a proposal for a royal match for him, without even bothering to mention the very possibility? Such a pairing would be imminently suitable, one that would bring him much power and Lydian wealth.

The glint of greed that appeared in Burian's eyes told Adrik all he needed to know. His brother would soon agree. "The bargain is made, Burian. The only difference now is that the princess will marry a Median king, not a mere crown prince. But I am certain King Alyattes will not be averse to that change."

Burian's frown gradually faded. He was a king now. He needed a suitable consort, a woman who could provide him with heirs. The fact that he might soon take an enemy princess to his bed was of no consequence, for her father and brothers possessed wealth and lands and treasures beyond his wildest imaginings.

The Median king regarded his half brother keenly. Adrik was far shrewder than he had thought. "So tell me, brother, what do you know of this Lydian princess? Is she fair of face and limb? And if I agree, how is this marriage bargain to be carried out?"

"Your future consort is to journey here for the wedding in late summer," Adrik told him. "Her name is Aryenis, and she is said to be a ripe maiden and quite pleasing to the eye. You will not be dissatisfied, brother. I predict that you will soon have your own heirs . . . and our people will be able to inherit a true peace that will last as long as the empire itself."

Burian pursed his lips as he considered his brother's words. "Yes . . ." he said finally. "I see the merits of what you propose." Such a marriage was a far more tantalizing prospect than one to his father's former consort, a lowly outcast from a minor tribe. She couldn't be trusted anyway. He would simply have Melina banished from the palace and sent back to her tribe. "I think I shall agree to marry this Lydian princess."

A self-satisfied smile crossed Burian's mouth as he

considered the pleasant possibilities. But there was still the matter of Adrik to contend with. "But what of you, little brother?" he asked guardedly, his thick brows lowering in speculation.

Adrik was quiet for a moment. "We return to Khorazm and the lands of the Magii." His expression then turned harsh and glacial cold. "Do not broach my borders, or send your soldiers and minions against my people or my lands ever again." His features darkened, turned even more deadly then before. "If you refuse to heed my words in this, I vow to use all of the powers at my disposal to crush both you and your throne, and then I shall turn the Median Empire into dust."

Burian stared back at him for a long moment and nodded slowly. If Adrik truly remained within his own lands, there would be no need for further bloodshed between them. "Go then." With that, the new king spun on his heel and strode back toward the palace doors.

Twilight was descending as Adrik kneed his horse into motion, Lorienne safely at his side where she had always belonged. A low cloud of dust rose around the ranks of mounted Magian soldiers, kicked into the air by scores of horses.

He ignored the dust and curious gazes of the people of Urmia, who were peering at the departing Shadow Prince through cracks in doorways or from behind the safety of mud walls. Adrik knew they would likely breathe a collective sigh of relief once he and the Magii had passed from the city's walls.

Adrik knew he, too, would breathe a great sigh of relief. He was finally free, free to live his own life, to decide his own fate.

He reached across the small space between his horse and Lorienne's and joined her hand to his, riding through the gathering darkness side by side as they were meant.

He felt her fingers tighten around his and glanced

at her face. She was smiling at him contentedly, tears of happiness streaking her dust-stained cheeks.

"I love you, Adrik," she whispered so low only he could hear. "The gods truly smiled upon me when they left me in your path." Her pale eyes were filled with the heated promise of what the night would bring. "My mother's prophecy was right after all. You were indeed my fate."

He squeezed her hand more tightly, relishing the sweet prospect of taking her into his arms again. "And you are my life," he whispered back to her.

Soon they would be gone from Urmia and would reach the sheer landscape of the open steppes. And then the endless mountain ridges huddled near the Caspian Sea would beckon them onward to Khorazm.

He glanced at Lorienne again, and a gentle smile touched the edges of his lips. In the warmth of her eyes he had found all that had ever been lost to him.

THE BLACK ROSE

JAN ZIMLICH

Though Lucien Charbonneau was born a noble, he's implemented plans to bring about galactic revolution. He wears two faces, that of an effete aristocrat and that of someone darker, more mysterious. He has subtle yet potent charms, and he plays at deception with the same skill that he might caress a lover. And though Lucien is betrothed, he swears not even his beautiful fiancée will ever learn his heart's secret, that of the Black Rose.

Alexandra Fallon has of course heard of that infamous spy, but her own interests are far less political. When interplanetary concerns force her to marry, the man who comes to her bed is in for a rude awakening. But the shadowy hunk who appears lights a passion hotter than a thousand suns—and in its fiery glow, both she and Lucien will learn that between lovers no secrets can remain in darkness.

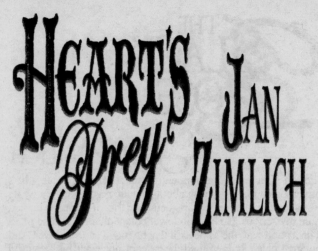

HEART'S Prey JAN ZIMLICH

She is a wild woman with flowing coppery tresses and luminous emerald eyes. Yet Rayna Syn is so much more to Dax Vahnti: She is his assassin. The savage beauty's attempt on his life fails, but the Warlord cannot let his guard down for a moment, not even when the lovely creature with wild russet hair enchants his very being. His need to possess the wondrous beauty is overpowering, yet the danger she presents cannot be denied.

___52277-2 $4.99 US/$5.99 CAN

Dorchester Publishing Co., Inc.
P.O. Box 6640
Wayne, PA 19087-8640

Please add $1.75 for shipping and handling for the first book and $.50 for each book thereafter. NY, NYC, and PA residents, please add appropriate sales tax. No cash, stamps, or C.O.D.s. All orders shipped within 6 weeks via postal service book rate. Canadian orders require $2.00 extra postage and must be paid in U.S. dollars through a U.S. banking facility.

Name_____

Address_____

City_____State_____Zip_____

I have enclosed $_____ in payment for the checked book(s).

Payment <u>must</u> accompany all orders. ☐ Please send a free catalog.

    CHECK OUT OUR WEBSITE! www.dorchesterpub.com

SPIRIT OF THE MIST
JANEEN O'KERRY

An early summer storm rages off the coast of western Ireland, and Muriel watches. From inside the protective walls of Dun Farraige, she can see nothing, yet her water mirror shows all. The moonlight reveals the face of a man—one struggling to overcome the sea.

He is an exile, of course. By clan law, exiles are to be made slaves. Yet something ennobles this man. The stranger's face makes Muriel yearn for both his safety and his freedom. She, who was raised as the daughter of a nobleman, has a terrible secret. And she can't help but believe that this handsome visitor—swaddled in mist and delivered to the rain-swept shores beneath her Dun—will be her salvation.

JANEEN O'KERRY

SISTER OF THE MOON

In the sylvan glens of Eire, the Sidhe reign supreme. The fair folk they are: fairies, thieves, changeling-bearers, tricksters. Their feet make no sound as they traipse through ancient forests, their mouths no noise as they weave their moonlight spells. And so Men have learned to fear them. But the Folk are dying. Their hunting grounds are overrun, their bronze swords no match for Man's cold iron. Scahta, their queen, is helpless to act. Her people need a king. And on Samhain Eve, she finds one. Though he is raw and untrained, she sees in Anlon the soul of nobility. Yet he is a Man. He will have to pass many tests to win her love. At the fires of Beltane he must prove himself her husband—and for the salvation of the Sidhe he must make himself a king.

_52466-X $5.50 US/$6.50 CAN

MISTRESS OF THE WATERS
JANEEN O'KERRY

Planning to relocate to Ireland, the home of her forebears, after college, Shannon Rose Gray immerses herself in her studies. But when an old book reveals a mysterious scrap of vellum with musical notes and her name, she finds herself whistling a different tune in a different time. Suddenly in pagan Eire, Shannon finds the sexiest man she's ever encountered: Lasairian. Her senses ablaze with the beauty of the Beltane feast, Shannon finds herself enflamed by the virile Celt's touch. But there are things about Lasairian that Shannon doesn't know. Is her handsome husband everything he claims—everything she wants? And the Beltane ritual—has it made her the prince's mistress, or the queen of his heart?

___52309-4 $4.99 US/$5.99 CAN